BEN BOVA

"ONE OF OUR BEST
HARD SCIENCE FICTION WRITERS."
Library Journal

MOONWAR

"BOVA IS ONE OF SCIENCE FICTION'S BEST
AT THIS SORT OF NEAR-FUTURE THRILLER
AND *MOONWAR* DOESN'T DISAPPOINT...
He begins tightening the screws from page one, with personal
vendettas and international intrigue combining for a rousing
read at a blinding pace...Bova's characters are always as real
as next year's headlines, and his clear vision of the future as
tangible as today's scientific breakthroughs."

St. Petersburg Times

"A VERY GOOD READ...
ACTION-PACKED, FAST-PACED...
A story of revenge—personal, political and corporate—
and so much more, containing a complex subset of characters
as rich as any novel could boast...
[A] worthy successor to the equally enjoyable *Moonrise*.
For engaging and engrossing reading,
I wholeheartedly recommend both."

SFRevu.com

"PACKS AS MUCH SUSPENSE
AS THE BEST PAGE-TURNERS.
Murder, lust and political intrigue fuel a novel that rekindles
the kind of excitement for the moon
Neil Armstrong generated when he made those first
dusty footprints on the lunar surface."

Naples Daily News

"AN EXCITING HIGH-TECH ADVENTURE."
Publishers Weekly

Fiction Books by Ben Bova

*collection

MOONWAR

BEN BOVA

AVON • EOS

AVON BOOKS, INC.
1350 Avenue of the Americas
New York, New York 10019

Copyright © 1998 by Ben Bova
Published by arrangement with the author
Visit our website at http://www.AvonBooks.com/Eos
Library of Congress Catalog Card Number: 97-18177
ISBN: 0-380-78698-2

First Avon Eos Paperback Printing: November 1998
First Avon Eos International Printing: March 1998
First Avon Eos Hardcover Printing: March 1998

AVON EOS TRADEMARK REG. U.S. PAT. OFF. AND IN OTHER COUNTRIES, MARCA
REGISTRADA, HECHO EN U.S.A.

Printed in the U.S.A.

WCD 10 9 8 7 6 5 4 3 2 1

To Janet and Bill Cuthbert

And to Barbara, with thanks for the vacuum cleaner

War is an evil thing, but to submit to the dictation of other states is worse. . . . Freedom, if we hold fast to it, will ultimately restore our losses, but submission will mean permanent loss of all that we value. . . . To you who call yourselves men of peace, I say: You are not safe unless you have men of action on your side.

—THUCYDIDES

Once we have lived through the rapid changes that are now marking our transition from the third to the fourth phase of history, from a period of diversification to one of unification, we shall be squarely faced with a number of serious problems. . . .

It has been shown by many social experiments that man cannot control every facet of life. All we can do is to try to isolate the factors that are the keys to the entire structure, and to work on them. These are basically: the conservation of natural resources; power-production; population-control; the full utilization of brain-power; and education. The details of the social structure will fall into place automatically as the end product of all these forces, as they always have done. . . .

Political unification of the world is not the first necessary step. By the time it has become possible without turmoil, it will also have become unnecessary.

—CARLETON S. COON

PROLOGUE

In those days, if you stood on Earth and looked up into the night sky at the whitely glowing Moon smiling its enigmatic lopsided smile as it sailed cool and aloof beyond the clouds, you would not be able to see Moonbase.

Even as you approached the Moon, hurtling toward its weary, battered face at more than five thousand miles per hour, the base would be hidden, invisible.

For Moonbase was almost entirely underground. More than two thousand people lived and worked there, in tunnels carved out of the tallest mountain in the ring that circled the giant crater Alphonsus, yet only a handful of them ever went out on the surface.

Masterson Corporation owned and operated Moonbase through a wholly-owned subsidiary headquartered in the island nation of Kiribati. Despite opposition from government and their own corporate board of directors, a dedicated, driven faction of Masterson's people had doggedly maintained the base, slowly enlarging it from a cluster of half-buried temporary shelters to its current size, an underground village on the frontier of human existence.

Only as your spacecraft fired its retro rockets to slow itself for landing would you begin to see hints that a populated settlement lay nestled into the smooth, rounded mountains of Alphonsus' ringwall: the deep open pit that would one day become Moonbase's grand plaza; the scoured-smooth landing pads of the rocket port; the glittering expanse of the solar energy farms; the long metal finger of the mass driver, out toward the middle of Alphonsus' pitted, dusty floor.

You would see one thing more: slick, smooth stretches of ground around the edges of the solar cells that made up the energy farms, looking almost like thin films of dark oily water on the barren regolith. They would puzzle you, because nothing like them existed on Earth. Nanomachines, virus-sized devices that could build new solar cells atom by atom out of the lunar regolith's silicon and aluminum, were silently expanding the solar farms, quietly, patiently enlarging Moonbase's energy supply.

Nanomachines, of course, were strictly outlawed on Earth.

PART I
SKIRMISH

Let us not deceive ourselves, sir.
These are the implements of war and
subjection; the last arguments to
which kings resort.

—PATRICK HENRY

MOONBASE CONTROL CENTER

"L-1's out."

The chief comm tech looked up sharply from her keyboard. "Try the backup."

"Already did," said the man at the console beside her. "No joy. Every frequency's dead."

The third communications technician, seated at the console on the chief's other side, tapped one keypad after another. His display screen showed nothing but streaks of meaningless hash.

"They did it," he confirmed. "They pulled the plug."

The other controllers and technicians left their own stations and drifted tensely, expectantly toward the communications consoles. Their consoles flickered and glowed, untended. The big electronic wallscreen that displayed all of Moonbase's systems hung above them as if nothing unusual was happening.

The chief pushed back her little wheeled chair slightly. "They did it right when they said they would, didn't they?"

"That's it, then," said the male comm tech. "We're at war."

No one replied. No one knew what to say. The knot of men and women stood there in uneasy silence. The only sounds were the low humming of the electronics consoles and the soft whisper of the air-circulation fans.

"I'd better pipe the word up to the boss," the chief technician muttered, reaching toward her keyboard. She started to peck at the keys.

"Shit!" she snapped. "I broke a fingernail."

TOUCHDOWN MINUS 116 HOURS
30 MINUTES

Douglas Stavenger stood at the crest of Wodjohowitcz
Pass, listening to the silence. Inside the base there were
always voices, human or synthesized, and the constant
background hum of electrical machinery. Out here, up
on the mountains that ringed the giant crater Alphonsus,
he heard nothing but his own breathing—and the faint,
comforting whir of the spacesuit's air-circulation fans.

Good noise, he thought, smiling to himself. When that
noise stops, so does your breathing.

He had climbed down from the tractor near the spot
where the plaque was, a small square of gold riveted
onto the rock face, dedicated to his father:

> *On this spot Paul Stavenger chose to
> die, in order to save the men and
> women of Moonbase.*

Doug had not driven up to the pass for the sake of
nostalgia, however. He wanted to take a long, hard look
at Moonbase. Not the schematic diagrams or electronic
charts, but the real thing, the actual base as it stood
beneath the uncompromising stars.

Everyone in the base thought they were safe and snug,
dug into the side of the ringwall mountain they had
named Yeager. Sheltered by solid rock, they had little
fear of the dangers up on the airless surface, where the

crater floor was bathed in hard radiation and the temperature could swing four hundred degrees between daylight and night, between sunshine and shadow.

But Doug saw how terribly vulnerable they all were. They had protected themselves against the forces of nature, true enough. But now they were threatened with destruction by the hand of war.

Doug looked out at the solar farm, thousands of acres of dark solar cells that greedily drank in sunlight and converted it noiselessly into the electricity the base needed the way a man needs blood. They could be blown to dust by conventional explosives, or blasted into uselessness by the radiation pulse from a nuclear warhead.

Even easier, he realized, an enemy could knock out the radiators and we'd all stew underground in our own waste heat until we either surrendered or collapsed from heat exhaustion.

His eyes travelled to the rocket pads. They were empty now that the morning's lunar transfer vehicle had loaded up and departed. Beyond, he saw the geodesic dome that sheltered the construction pad; inside it, a half-built Clippership was being assembled by virus-sized nanomachines that converted meteoric carbon dust into hard, strong structure of pure diamond. How could we protect spacecraft sitting out on the pads? We can't shelter them and we don't have the facilities to bring them underground. That dome is no protection against missiles or even bullets.

He looked farther out across the crater floor, to where the mass launcher stretched its lean dark metallic finger to the horizon. A single warhead could wreck it forever, Doug knew.

Well, we can't beat them in a shooting war, he told himself. That's certain.

Turning his gaze back to the edge of the solar farm, Doug saw the dark slick-looking film on the ground where the nanomachines were busily converting the silicon and metals of the lunar regolith into more solar cells.

That's what this war is all about, he knew. Nanomachines. And he thought he could feel the trillions of nanos inside his own body.

If I go back to Earth I'll be a marked man. Some crackpot nanoluddite will murder me, just the way they've killed so many others. But if the only way to avert this war is to close Moonbase, where else can I go?

His mind churning, he turned again and looked down at the deep pit that would one day be Moonbase's grand plaza. If we ever get to finish it.

All construction jobs begin by digging a hole in the ground, he said to himself. It doesn't make any difference if you're on the Moon or the Earth.

Under the brilliant illumination of powerful lamps spaced around the edge of the pit, front-loaders were working soundlessly in the lunar vacuum, scooping up dirt and dumping their loads onto the waiting trucks. Clouds of fine lunar dust hung over the machines, scattering the lamplight like fog. The first time I've seen mist on the Moon, Doug mused. Not a molecule of water in that haze, though.

All of the machinery was controlled by operators sitting safely inside their stations at the control center. Only a handful of construction workers were actually out on the floor of the crater Alphonsus.

I should be inside, too, Doug told himself. The deadline comes up right about now. I ought to be inside facing the music instead of out here, trying to avoid it all.

In the seven years of his exile on the Moon, Doug had always come out to the lunar surface when he had a problem that ached in him. The Moon's harsh, airless otherworldliness concentrated his mind on the essentials: life or death, survival or extinction. He never failed to be thrilled by the stark grandeur of the lunar landscape. But now he felt fear, instead. Fear that Moonbase would be closed, its potential for opening the space frontier forever lost. Fear that he would have to return to the Earth, where fanatic assassins awaited him.

And anger, deep smoldering anger that men would threaten war and destruction in their ignorant, blind zeal to eradicate Moonbase.

Simmering inside, Doug turned back to the tractor and climbed up to its bare metal driver's seat. The ground here along the pass was rutted by years of tractors' cleats clawing through the dusty lunar regolith. He himself had driven all the way around these softly rounded mountains, circumnavigating the crater; not an easy trek, even in a tractor. Alphonsus was so big its ringwall mountains disappeared beyond the short lunar horizon. The jaunt had taken almost a week, all of it spent inside a spacesuit that smelled very ripe by the time he came home again. But Doug had found the peace and inner tranquility he had sought, all alone up on the mountaintops.

Not today. Even out here there was no peace or tranquility for him.

Once he reached the crater floor he looked beyond the uncompromising slash of the horizon and saw the Earth hanging in the dark sky, glowing blue and decked with streams of pure white clouds. He felt no yearning, no sense of loss, not even curiosity. Only deep resentment, anger. Burning rage. The Moon was his true home, not that distant deceitful world where violence and treachery lurked behind every smile.

And he realized that the anger was at himself, not the distant faceless people of Earth. *I should have known it would come to this. For seven years they've been putting the pressure on us. I should have seen this coming. I should have figured out a way to avoid an outright conflict.*

He parked the tractor and walked along the side of the construction pit, gliding in the dreamlike, floating strides of the Moon's low gravity. Turning his attention back to the work at hand, Doug saw that the digging was almost finished. They were nearly ready to start the next phase of the job. The tractors were best for the heavy work, moving large masses of dirt and rock. Now the finer tasks would begin, and for that the labs were producing specialized nanomachines.

He wondered if they would ever reach that stage. Or would the entire base be abandoned and left suspended in time, frozen in the airless emptiness of infinity? Worse yet, the base might be blasted, bombed into rubble, destroyed for all time.

It can't come to that! I won't let that happen. No matter what, I won't give them an excuse to use force against us.

"Greetings and felicitations!" Lev Brudnoy's voice boomed through Doug's helmet earphones.

Startled out of his thoughts, Doug looked up and saw Brudnoy's tall figure approaching, his spacesuit a brilliant cardinal red. The bulky suits smothered individual recognition, so long-time Lunatics tended to personalize their suits for easy identification. Even inside his suit, though, Brudnoy seemed to stride along in the same gangly, loose-jointed manner he did in shirtsleeves.

"Lev—what are you doing here?"

"A heartwarming greeting for your stepfather."

"I mean . . . oh, you know what I mean!"

"Your mother and I decided to come up now, in case there's trouble later on."

Nodding inside his helmet, Doug agreed, "Good thinking. They might shut down flights here for a while."

"How is the suit?" Brudnoy asked.

Doug had forgotten that he was wearing the new design. "Fine," he said absently, his attention still on the digging.

"Do the gloves work as well as my engineers promised me they would?" Brudnoy asked, coming up beside Doug.

Holding out a hand for the Russian to see, Doug slowly closed his fingers. He could feel the vibration of the tiny servomotors as they moved the alloy "bones" of the exoskeleton on the back of his hand.

"I haven't tried to crush any rocks with them," Doug said, half in jest.

"But the pressure is not uncomfortable?" Brudnoy asked. "You can flex your fingers easily?"

Nodding again, Doug replied, "About as easily as you can in regular gloves."

"Ahh," Brudnoy sighed. "I had hoped for much better."

"This is just the first shot, Lev. You can improve it, I'm sure."

"Yes, there is always room for improvement."

The suit Doug wore was a cermet hard shell from boots to helmet; even the joints at the ankles, knees, hips, shoulders, elbows and wrists were overlapping circles of cermet. The ceramic-metal material was strong enough to hold normal shirtsleeve-pressure air inside the suit, even though the pressure outside was nothing but hard vacuum. Thus the suit operated at normal air pressure, instead of the low-pressure mix of oxygen and nitrogen that the standard spacesuits required. No prebreathing was needed with the new design; you could climb into it and button up immediately.

The gloves were always a problem. They tended to balloon even in the low-pressure suits. Doug's gloves were fitted with spidery exoskeleton struts and tiny servomotors that amplified his natural strength, so he could grasp and work even though the gloves would have been too stiff for him to use without their aid.

"Maybe we could lower the pressure in the gloves," Doug suggested.

"We would have to put a cuff around your wrist to seal—"

"Priority message." The words crackled in their earphones. "Priority message for Douglas Stavenger."

Tapping at the keypad built into the wrist of his spacesuit, Doug said, "This is Stavenger." He was surprised at how dry his throat suddenly felt. He knew what the message would be.

"All frequencies from the L-1 commsat have been cut off," said the chief communications technician. "Communications directly from Earth have also been stopped."

Doug's heart began hammering inside him. He looked at Brudnoy, but all he could see was the reflection of his own faceless helmet in the gold tint of the Russian's visor.

Swallowing hard, Doug said, "Okay. Message received. Thank you."

He waited a beat, then added, "Please find Jinny Anson for me."

"Will do."

An instant later the former base director's voice chirped in his earphones, "Anson here."

"Jinny, it's Doug. I need to talk with you, right away."

"I know," she said, her voice sobering.

"Where are you?"

"In the university office."

"Please meet me in my place in fifteen minutes."

"Right."

Doug turned and started along the edge of the construction pit, heading for the airlock in swift, gliding strides. Brudnoy kept pace beside him.

"It's started," he said.

"I'll inform your mother," said the Russian.

With a bitter smile, Doug replied, "She already knows, I'm sure. They couldn't declare war on us without her knowing about it."

TOUCHDOWN MINUS 115 HOURS 55 MINUTES

"So they've done it," said Jinny Anson, with a challenging grin. "Damn flatheads."

Anson, Brudnoy and Doug's mother Joanna were sitting before Doug's desk. Anson was leaning back in her webbed chair almost casually. Wearing comfortable faded denim jeans and an open-collar velour blouse, she looked vigorous and feisty, her short-cropped hair still golden blond, her steel-gray eyes snapping with barely suppressed anger.

Joanna seemed calm, but Doug knew that her composed expression masked an inner tension. She had let her shoulder-length hair go from ash blond to silver gray, but otherwise she looked no more than forty. She was dressed elegantly, as usual: a patterned coral skirt, its hem slightly weighted to make it drape properly in the soft lunar gravity, and a crisply tailored white blouse buttoned at the throat and wrists, where jewelry sparkled.

Seated between the two women was Brudnoy, his long face with its untidy gray beard looking somber, his baggy eyes on Doug. Brudnoy's dark turtleneck and unpressed denims seemed almost shabby next to his wife's impeccable ensemble. His gray lunar softboots were faded and shiny from long use.

Although Doug's office was little larger than a cubbyhole carved out of the ringwall mountain's flank, its walls were smart screens from padded tile floor to smoothed rock ceiling, flat high-definition digital display screens that could be activated by voice or by the pencil-sized laser pointer resting on Doug's desk.

Doug kept one eye on the screen covering the wall to the left of his desk; it was scrolling a complete checkout of Moonbase's entire systems. He needed to reassure himself that everything was operating normally. The other two walls could have been showing videos of any scenery he wanted, but Doug had them displaying the security camera views of the base, switching every ten seconds from one tunnel to another and then to the outside, where the teleoperated tractors were still working in the pit as if nothing had happened. The wall behind him was blank.

Feeling uneasy as he sat behind his desk, Doug said, "Now I don't want people getting twitchy about this. The base should run as normally as possible."

"Even though Faure's declared war on us?" Anson cracked.

"It's not that kind of a war," Doug snapped back. "There's not going to be any shooting."

"Not from our side, anyway," said Anson. "The best we could do is throw rocks at 'em."

"At who?" Doug's mother asked testily.

"Peacekeeper troops," said Doug.

Everyone in the office looked startled at the thought.

"You don't think they'd really go that far, do you?" Anson asked, looking worried for the first time.

Doug picked up his laser pointer and aimed its red spot at one of the icons lining the top of the wallscreen on his left. The wall became a schematic display of the Earth-Moon system, with clouds of satellites orbiting the Earth. A dozen navigational satellites clung to low orbits around the Moon, and the big crewed station at the L-1 position still showed as a single green dot.

"No traffic," Doug said. "This morning's LTVs stopped at L-1. Nothing at all moving between LEO and here."

"Not yet," muttered Brudnoy.

"They wouldn't invade us," Joanna said firmly. "That little Quebecer hasn't got the guts."

Brudnoy ran a bony finger across his short gray beard. No matter how carefully he trimmed it, the beard somehow looked shaggy all the time.

"That little Quebecer," he reminded his wife, "has fought his way to the top of the United Nations. And now he's gotten the U.N. to declare us in violation of the nanotech treaty."

Joanna frowned impatiently. "We've been violating that treaty since it was written."

"But now your little Quebecer has obtained the authority to send Peacekeeper troops here to *enforce* the treaty on us," Brudnoy continued.

"You really think it'll come to that?" Anson asked again, edging forward slightly in her chair.

"Sooner or later," Doug said.

"They know we can't stop using nanomachines," Joanna said bitterly. "They know they'll be destroying Moonbase if they prevent us from using them."

"That's what they're going to do, though," said Brudnoy, growing more gloomy with each word.

"Then we'll have to resist them," Doug said.

"Fight the Peacekeepers?" Anson seemed startled at the thought. "But—"

"I didn't say fight," Doug corrected. "I said resist."

"How?"

"I've been studying the legal situation," Doug said. "We could declare our independence."

His mother looked more irked than puzzled. "What good would that do?"

"As an independent nation, we wouldn't sign the nanotech treaty, so it wouldn't apply to us."

Brudnoy raised his brows. "But would the U.N. recognize us an independent nation? Would they admit us to membership?"

"Faure would never allow it," Joanna said. "The little Quebecer's got the whole U.N. wrapped around his manicured finger."

"How would the corporation react if we declared independence?" Jinny Anson asked.

"Kiribati couldn't do anything about it," said Doug.

Brudnoy sighed painfully. "If they hadn't knuckled under to Faure and signed the treaty—"

"They didn't have much choice, really," said Doug. Looking straight at his mother, he went on, "But what about Masterson? How's your board going to react to our independence?"

"I'll handle the board of directors," Joanna replied flatly.

"And Rashid?"

She smiled slightly. "He'll go up in a cloud of purple smoke. But don't worry; even though he's the board chairman now, I can keep him in his place."

"Independence," Anson murmured.

Doug said, "We're pretty much self-sufficient, as far as energy and food are concerned."

"How long is 'pretty much'?" Joanna asked.

"We can go for months without importing anything from Earth, I betcha," Anson replied.

"Really?" Doug asked.

She shrugged. "Condiments might be a problem. Ketchup, seasonings, salt."

"We can manufacture salt with nanomachines," Doug said. "Ought to be simple enough."

"Where can you get the sodium and chlorine?" Anson retorted. "Not out of the regolith."

Doug smiled a little. "Out of the reprocessors. Recycle the garbage."

Anson made a sour face.

"Could we really get along for months without importing anything from Earth?" Joanna asked.

"Maybe a year," Anson said. "If you don't mind eating your soyburgers without mustard."

Brudnoy flexed his gnarled fingers. "Aren't you glad that I insisted on planting onions and garlic, along with my flowers?"

"Do you have any jalapeño peppers out at the farm?" Anson asked.

Brudnoy shook his head.

"A year," Joanna mused. "This ought to be settled long before that."

"One way or another," said Brudnoy morosely.

"Pharmaceuticals might be a problem," Doug said, turning to the wallscreen on his right. With the laser he changed the display from a camera view of the empty rocket launching pads to an inventory of the base's pharmaceutical supplies. "We've been bringing them up on a monthly schedule. Got a . . ." he studied the display screen briefly, ". . . three-month supply on hand."

"Maybe we can use nanomachines instead," Joanna suggested. It was an open secret that her youthful appearance was due to nanotherapy that tightened sagging muscles and kept her skin tone smooth.

"I can talk to Cardenas about that," Anson replied.

"And Professor Zimmerman," Doug said.

"*You* talk to Zimmerman," she snapped. "He always tries to bully me."

Brudnoy volunteered, "I'll see Zimmerman."

"You?"

With a guilty smile, the Russian said, "He and I have been working on a little project together: using nano-machines to make beer."

"Lev!" Joanna glared at her husband.

Brudnoy raised a placating hand. "Don't worry. So far, we've accomplished less than nothing. The stuff is so bad not even Zimmerman will drink it."

Doug chuckled at his stepfather's self-deprecating manner. Then he said, "Okay. Our first move is to declare independence and—"

"How can we let anyone on Earth know we're applying for U.N. membership if all the communications links are cut off?" Joanna asked.

"We can talk to Earth," Anson assured her. "Radio, TV, even laser beams if we need 'em. We don't need the commsats; just squirt our messages straight to the ground antennas."

"The question is," said Brudnoy, "will anyone on Earth respond to us?"

"They will," Doug said. "Once they learn what we're doing. And there's always the news media."

"Ugh!" said Joanna.

"Don't knock them," Doug insisted. "They might turn out to be our best ally in this."

"Our only ally," said Brudnoy.

"Okay, okay, so we declare independence," Anson cut in. "Then what?"

"If Faure refuses to recognize us, we appeal to the World Court," said Doug.

Joanna agreed. "Tie him up legally and wait for world opinion to come over to our side."

"Lots of luck," Brudnoy mumbled.

"Do you think it'll work?" Anson wondered.

"It's got to," said Joanna.

"Jinny," said Doug, pointing a finger in her direction, "I want you to take over as base director."

"Me? Why? I haven't been behind that desk in almost eight years!"

Grinning at her, Doug said, "You know more about

what's going on in these tunnels than I do. Don't try to deny it."

"But I've got the university to run," she protested. "And what're you going to be doing?"

"The university's going to be in hibernation as long as Earthside isn't allowed to communicate with us. Your students won't be able to talk to you."

"But you . . . ?"

"I've been studying military history ever since Faure was elected secretary-general," Doug said. "One thing I've learned is that we're going to need somebody to give his undivided attention to this crisis. I can't be running the day-to-day operation of Moonbase and handle the war at the same time."

"You said it's not a war," Joanna said sharply.

"Not a shooting war," Doug admitted. "Not yet. But we've got to be prepared for that possibility."

"You can't—"

"He's right," Brudnoy said, interrupting his wife. "Doug should devote his full attention to this situation."

"And I'm gonna be base director again," Anson said. She did not seem displeased with the idea.

"So you will be our generalissimo," said Brudnoy, pointing at Doug. "Jinny becomes base director once again. And you, dear wife," he turned to face Joanna, "must serve as our foreign secretary, in charge of diplomatic relations with Masterson and the other corporations."

"And what will you be doing, Lev?" Joanna asked her husband.

"Me?" Brudnoy's shaggy brows climbed halfway to his scalp. "I will remain as usual: nothing but a peasant."

"Yeah, sure," Anson chirped.

Brudnoy shrugged. "I have no delusions of grandeur. But I think it will be important to keep the major corporations on our side."

"I'll handle relations with Masterson Corporation," Joanna agreed. "We'll try to put some pressure on the government in Washington to oppose this U.N. takeover."

"If you can keep the board on our side," Doug said.

His mother raised an imperious brow. "I told you, don't worry about the board."

"Or Rashid?"

"Or Rashid either," Joanna riposted. Turning slightly toward her husband, she added, "Rashid's a man with real delusions of grandeur."

"Okay," said Jinny Anson. "Then I'll run the base and you, Doug, you can run the war."

"Thanks a lot."

"Somebody's got to—"

"Hold it!" Doug snapped. The message icon on his left screen was blinking. Urgent message. And he saw that a cardinal red dot had cleared the swarm of low-orbit satellites around the Earth and was heading outward.

"Message," Doug called out in the tone that the computer recognized. His voice trembled only slightly.

"A crewed spacecraft just lifted from the military base on Corsica," a comm tech's voice said. "It's on a direct lunar trajectory."

"Peacekeeper troops," Doug said.

"Must be."

They all turned toward Doug.

"So what do we do now, boss?" Jinny Anson asked.

TOUCHDOWN MINUS 114 HOURS 35 MINUTES

"Five days," Doug said to the woman's image on his screen. "They'll be here in a little less than five days."

Tamara Bonai frowned slightly, nothing more than a faint pair of lines between her brows. But on her ethereally beautiful face it seemed a gross disfigurement. Her face was a sculptor's dream, high cheekbones and almond eyes; her skin a light clear teak; her long hair a tumbling cascade as lustrous and black as the infinity of space.

Like Doug, she was seated behind a desk. Her life-sized image on the wall in front of him made it look as if Doug's office opened onto her office on Tarawa: lunar rock and smart walls suddenly giving way to Micronesian ironwood and bamboo.

"When I visited Moonbase," she said, "the trip took only one day."

"We brought you up on a high-energy burn," said Doug. "The Peacekeepers are coming on a minimum-energy trajectory."

It took almost three seconds for his words to reach Earth and her reply to get back to his office at Moonbase. Usually Doug relaxed during the interval, but now he sat tensely in his padded swivel chair.

Bonai smiled slightly. "The Peacekeepers are trying to save money by taking the low-energy route?"

Doug forced a laugh. "I doubt it. I think they want to give us as much time as possible to think things over and then surrender."

Her lips still curved deliciously, Bonai asked, "Is that what you will do: surrender?"

"No," said Doug. "We're just about self-sufficient now. We can get along without Earth for a long while."

If she was surprised by Doug's answer, it did not show on her face. Doug wondered if anyone was eavesdropping on their conversation. It was being carried by a tight laser beam, but still, the tightest beam spread a few kilometers across over the four-hundred-thousand-kilometer distance between the Earth and the Moon. The island of Tarawa was tiny, but still big enough for Rashid or someone else to pick up the beamed signal.

"You are prepared to fight Peacekeeper troops?" she asked.

"We're not going to surrender Moonbase to them."

She seemed genuinely worried. "But they will have guns . . . other weapons. What weapons do you have?"

"There isn't even a target pistol in all of Moonbase," Doug admitted. "But we've got some pretty good brains here."

Once she heard his words, she shook her head slightly. "You can't stop bullets with words."

"Maybe we can," Doug said. Not waiting for a response from her, he went on, "We're going to declare our independence and apply to the General Assembly for admission to the U.N."

Her delay in responding to him was longer than three seconds. At last Bonai said, "It's my fault, isn't it? You're in this trouble because I bowed to the U.N.'s pressure and signed the nanotech treaty."

"You did what was best for your people," Doug replied. "You did what you had to do."

Masterson Corporation had owned and operated Moonbase from its beginning as a set of half-buried shelters huddled near the mountain ringwall of the giant crater Alphonsus. Nanotechnology made it possible for the base to grow and begin to prosper.

Virus-sized nanomachines scoured the regolith of Alphonsus' crater floor, extracting oxygen and the scant atoms of hydrogen that blew in on the solar wind. Once ice fields were discovered in the south polar region, nanomachines built and maintained the pipeline that fed water across more than a thousand kilometers of mountains and craters. Nanomachines built solar cells out of the regolith's silicon, to supply the growing base with constantly increasing electrical power. Nanomachines had built the mass driver that launched payloads of lunar ores to factories in Earth orbit.

And nanomachines took carbon atoms from near-Earth asteroids and built Clipperships of pure diamond, Moonbase's newest export and already its principal source of cash flow. Diamond Clipperships were not only the world's best spacecraft; they were starting to take over the market for long-range commercial air flight on Earth.

The United Nations' nanotechnology treaty banned all nanotech operations, research and teaching in the nations that signed the treaty. Seven years earlier, when it became clear that the United States would sign the treaty—indeed, American nanoluddites had *drafted* the treaty—Masterson Corporation had set up a dummy company on the island nation of Kiribati and transferred Moonbase to the straw-man corporation. As long as Kiribati did not sign the treaty, Moonbase could legally continue using nanomachines, which were as vital to Moonbase as air.

But the day after Tamara Bonai, chief of the Kiribati council, reluctantly signed the nanotech treaty, the U.N.'s secretary-general—Georges Faure—personally called Joanna Stavenger and told her that Moonbase had two weeks to shut down all nanotech operations, research and teaching.

Exactly two weeks later, to the very minute, all communications links from Earth to Moonbase were cut. And now a spacecraft carrying U.N. Peacekeeper troops had lifted from Corsica on a leisurely five-day course for Moonbase.

"You have no idea of how much pressure they put on us," Bonai said, her lovely face downcast. "They even stopped tourist flights from coming to our resorts. It was an economic blockade. They would have strangled us."

"I'm not blaming you for this," Doug said. "I only called to let you know that we're declaring our independence. As an independent nation that hasn't signed the nanotech treaty, we'll be able to keep on as we have been, despite Faure and his Peacekeepers."

She almost smiled. "Does that mean that you will continue to honor your contracts with Kiribati Corporation?"

Moonbase marketed its diamond Clipperships and other exports to transportation companies on Earth through Kiribati Corporation.

"Yes, certainly," Doug said. Then he added, "As soon as this situation is cleared up."

"I understand," she said. "We will certainly not object to your independence."

Doug smiled back at her. "Thanks, Tamara. I knew I could count on you."

The three seconds ticked. "Good luck, Doug," she said at last.

"Thanks again. I think we're going to need all the luck we can get."

TOUCHDOWN MINUS 114 HOURS

The word spread through Moonbase's corridors with the speed of sound. In workshops and offices, in living quarters and laboratories, out at the spaceport, at the mass driver, even among the handful of spacesuited men and women working on the surface, the word flashed: We're at war. U.N. troops are on their way here.

It's about time, said the mercenary to himself. Years of diplomats in their fancy suits and their evasive language, farting around, trying to talk the problem to death, and now at last they're taking action.

He looked up from the work he was doing; he took pride in his work. No one suspected that he was a deep agent, a trained killer who had been inserted into Moonbase more than a year earlier to work his way into the community and wait for the right moment. He had been without contact from his superiors ever since he first set foot in Moonbase. He would operate now without orders.

Cripple Moonbase. That was his mission. For a year he had studied all of Moonbase's systems and personnel. The underground base was pathetically vulnerable to sabotage. Every breath of air, every molecule of water, depended on complex machinery, all of it run by sophisticated computer programs. Sophisticated meant fragile, the mercenary knew. A computer virus could bring Moonbase to its knees in a matter of hours, maybe less.

There was another part of his mission. Decapitate the leadership. His superiors used words such as *incapacitate* and *immobilize*. What they meant was *kill*.

Kind of a shame, the mercenary thought. They're pretty nice people, these guys I work with. The women, too. But I won't be hurting them. It's the leaders I'm after. The Brudnoys and Jinny Anson and the Stavenger kid.

Nodding as if reaffirming his mission, he went back to his work. Got to finish this job, he told himself. Can't leave anything undone. No loose ends; no mistakes.

TOUCHDOWN MINUS 113 HOURS 22 MINUTES

Doug sat alone in his quarters, staring at his blank wallscreen. Declare our independence, he thought. Just like that. Tell the flatlanders down there that we no longer belong to Kiribati Corporation or any company or government on Earth. What words do I use to get that across?

His quarters were larger than his office, one of the new "suites" big enough to partition into a sitting room and a separate bedroom. It even had its own bathroom.

Leaning back in his comfortable chair of yielding plastic foam, Doug asked the computer to call up the American Declaration of Independence from his history program. Jefferson's powerful, eloquent words filled the wallscreen. Doug reduced the display to a less imposing size, then spent several minutes studying it. Finally he shook his head. That was fine for 1776, he told himself, but this is nearly three hundred years later. They'd sound pretty stilted now.

Besides, he thought, everybody'd recognize the source. I'd be accused of plagiarism. That's no way to start a new nation.

He thought back to his studies of military history. The American general who had commanded the Allied armies in Europe during World War II—what was his name? Ike something.

A few touches of his laser pointer and he had Dwight Eisenhower's multimedia biography on the screen. He muted the sound and scrolled slowly through it, searching for the terse statement that Eisenhower had written back to Washington when the Nazis surrendered. His aides had wanted a long, flowery announcement filled with stirring phrases and fulsome praise for the various generals. Eisenhower had tossed their suggestions aside and written—ah! There it is: "The mission of this Allied force was fulfilled at 0241 local time, May 7, 1945."

That's what I want, Doug said to himself. Short, strong, direct.

He cleared his throat and called to the computer, "Dictation." Then, after a moment's thought, he said slowly and clearly:

"Moonbase hereby declares its independence from Earth and asks for admission to the United Nations."

He stared at the words for a long moment, then decided they said what he intended to say. Briefly he thought of running them past his mother and Lev Brudnoy, but he shook his head at the idea. They'd want to tinker with the statement, maybe hedge it or decorate it with reasons and arguments. Ear candy. I'm in command, we've all agreed to that, and we've all agreed to declaring our independence. This is the message we send to Faure and the rest of Earth.

Doug called up the communications desk at the command center.

"Beam this message to U.N. headquarters in New York," he said, "and spray it to every antenna on Earth. All the commsats, too. Send it by laser to Kiribati and to Masterson Corporation's headquarters in Savannah."

The chief comm tech on duty was a young man that Doug had played against in Moonbase's annual low-gravity olympic games. He grinned as he scanned Doug's message.

"Right away, boss," he said.

Doug blanked his screen and leaned back in his foam chair. Okay, it's done. Now to see if it has any effect.

TOUCHDOWN MINUS 112 HOURS 17 MINUTES

Although Lunar University had no real campus, its heart was the plushly equipped studio where teaching was done through electronic links to Earth and virtual reality programs.

Wilhelm Zimmerman liked his creature comforts. He demanded them. He had come to Moonbase because the "*verdammt* treaty" had closed his university department in Basel. He had given up cigars and strudel and even beer, but he still managed to overeat, underexercise, and drive Moonbase's supply and maintenance staffs into frenzies with his demands for couches and padded chairs big enough to take his girth comfortably.

He still dressed in the gray, old-fashioned three-piece suits he had brought to Moonbase with him seven years earlier. He had personally designed a set of nanomachines to keep the suits in perfect repair, renewing fraying cuffs and worn spots—atom by atom. The nanomachines even kept his clothes clean.

Still, as he sat sprawled in his favorite sofa, he looked like a rumpled mess, his jacket unbuttoned and flapping loose, his vest stretched tight across his ample stomach, tie loose from shirt collar, the halo of stringy gray hair surrounding his bald pate as dishevelled as King Lear in the storm scene.

"A direct trajectory here?" he was asking Doug. "It is customary first to go to a space station, yah?"

"I think they might be worried that most of the people in the space stations are on our side," Doug said.

Doug was sitting in one of the oversized, overpadded armchairs facing the sofa. Built by nanomachines that Zimmerman himself had programmed, the furniture looked ludicrously out of place in this vast, echoing electronics studio carved out of the lunar rock. No one else was in the studio. The lights had been turned off, except for the lamps on the end tables that flanked the sofa: slender graceful stalks of lunar aluminum; the tables were built of lightweight but sturdy honeycomb "sandwich" metal, also produced by nanomachines.

Zimmerman nodded as if Doug's answer satisfied him. "And you have notified the U.N. that we are now an independent nation?"

Nodding, Doug replied, "The U.N., and as much of the news media as we could reach."

"Still the troopship has not turned around?" Zimmerman's accent seemed to get thicker each year.

"Not yet."

"And there is no reaction from the U.N. to your declaration of independence?"

"Not yet," Doug repeated.

"So," the professor stretched out his short arms, "now we have nothing to do except wait, yah?"

"And prepare."

Zimmerman's shaggy brows shot up. "Prepare for what? Either they accept our independence or the Peacekeepers come in here and close everything."

"I don't intend to allow them to close Moonbase," Doug said evenly.

Zimmerman snorted. "And how do you intend to stop them? With prayer, maybe?"

"That's why I've come here to you, Professor," said Doug. "We need your help."

"To do what? Make a magic wand for you out of nanomachines? A death ray, maybe you want?"

Doug was accustomed to the old man's blustering. "I was thinking more along the lines of medical help," he said. "We may need—"

"I thought I'd find you here, Willi."

Kris Cardenas came striding out of the shadows. Despite her years on the Moon she still kept a deep tan, thanks to ultraviolet lamps. To Doug she looked like a California surfer: broad shoulders, trim build, sparkling blue eyes. She kept her sandy hair clipped short and wore a loose, comfortable jumpsuit of pastel yellow. No jewelry, no decorations of any kind. From the easygoing, no-fuss look of her, you would never suspect she was a Nobel laureate nanotech researcher.

"Our young friend here wants me to make everyone bulletproof," Zimmerman said, grudgingly dragging his bulk to one side of the sofa so Cardenas could sit beside him. Even on the Moon, Zimmerman did not move fast.

"No," Doug protested. "All I'm asking—"

"You think perhaps that the nanomachines you carry inside you will protect you against machine guns? They saved your life twice before, but they don't make you a superman."

"Willi," said Cardenas, with a charmer's smile, "why don't you let Doug tell you what he wants?"

"Medical supplies," Doug blurted before Zimmerman could say another word. "If we're cut off from Earth for more than a couple of months we're going to run short of medical supplies. I was wondering if nanomachines could be developed to replace or augment some of the pharmaceuticals we use."

"How can I do that? Your own silly rules prevent me from using nanomachines anywhere inside Moonbase, except in my laboratory," Zimmerman grumbled.

"The safety rules, yes, I know," said Doug.

"Even my furniture I had to make in my lab and then get a crew to *schlep* into here."

"We can't take the chance of having nanomachines propagate inside the base."

"Nonsense," Zimmerman muttered. "Superstition."

Cardenas stepped in again. "So you're ready to bend the safety rules, Doug?"

"We'll have to, at least a little."

"And you need help with medical supplies, right?"

"Right."

"Aspirin maybe?" Zimmerman grumbled suspiciously.

"More than aspirin," said Doug.

"Specifically?"

"I don't know, specifically. You'll have to talk to the medical staff."

"I will *have to*? These are your orders? You are the field marshal now and I am under your command?"

"That's exactly right," said Cardenas, still smiling sweetly. "That's the situation we're in, Willi, and we've all got to do everything we can to help."

Zimmerman mumbled something in German.

"Otherwise," Cardenas warned, "we'll all be sent back to Earth—and never allowed to work on nanotechnology again."

For a long moment the old man said nothing. Then, with an enormous groaning sigh, he nodded unhappily. It made his cheeks wobble.

"Yah," he said at last. "I will speak with your medical staff. I might as well. There is nothing else for me to do, now that Kiribati no longer takes our transmissions."

Lunar University's courses had been beamed to Kiribati for distribution to students around the world. That had worked well enough for the engineering and humanities curricula. But since most nations forbade teaching nanotechnology openly, the nanotech courses had to be packaged separately and delivered in clandestine ways. Cardenas often complained that she felt as if she were dealing in pornographic videos, "shipping them out in plain brown wrappers."

"When this is over you can start teaching again," Doug said.

"You think we will win?" Zimmerman's tone made it clear that he had no such illusions.

"We'll try," said Doug, getting to his feet.

"And we'll do everything we can to help," Cardenas said. "Won't we, Willi?"

"Yah." Without enthusiasm.

"Thanks," Doug said. "I appreciate whatever you can do."

He started off toward the door, threading his way through the equipment standing idle in the shadows of the unlit studio. Behind his retreating back, Cardenas leaned toward Zimmerman and whispered a suggestion to him. The old man frowned, then shrugged.

"Maybe we can make you invisible," Zimmerman called after Doug, his voice echoing through the darkened studio.

Doug looked back over his shoulder and suppressed the urge to laugh. "That'd be great," he said, thinking that bulletproof would be a lot better.

Back in his quarters, Doug lit up his wallscreen, scanning the computer's personnel files for anyone who had military experience. It was a fruitless search. Moonbase's employees were scientists and engineers, technicians and medical doctors, computer analysts, nurses, construction specialists, agrotechnicians, managers and administrators. They had all been hired through Masterson Corporation's personnel office, back Earthside. The only military veterans were a handful among the astronauts who piloted the transfer spacecraft from Earth, and none of them were at Moonbase at the present time.

Faure picked his timing very carefully, Doug realized. Halfway through the first phase of building the main plaza, with dozens of extra construction workers on hand and not a single spacecraft at the rocket port. We've even got that dance troupe from Canada visiting; another thirty-five mouths to feed.

He sat up straight and raised his arms over his head,

stretching until he felt his vertebrae pop. Well, he said to himself, at least the dancers don't eat much. I guess.

Of all the two thousand, four hundred and seventy-seven men and women at Moonbase, only one had the slightest military experience. One of the construction technicians working on the new aquaculture tanks, a man named Leroy Gordette. His file showed that he had spent four years in the U.S. Army, enlisting when he had been seventeen, nearly ten years earlier.

His photo on the wallscreen showed a serious, almost grim Afro-American with red-rimmed eyes and a military buzz cut almost down to his scalp. He looks fierce enough, Doug thought, staring at the picture.

"It's better than nothing," Doug muttered. "Phone," he called.

"Call please?" asked the computer's androgynous synthesized voice.

"Leroy Gordette," he said to the phone system.

"No response," said the computer a moment later. "Do you wish to search for him or leave a message?"

"Leave a message."

"Recording."

"Mr. Gordette, this is Douglas Stavenger. Please call me as soon as you can. It's about the military situation we're in."

With twenty-twenty hindsight, Doug could see that this confrontation had been inevitable from the day Faure had won his campaign to be elected secretary-general of the United Nations; he intended to enforce the nanotech treaty with every weapon at his disposal. None of the others—not even Doug's mother—had foreseen that it would come down to military force. But Doug had studied enough history to understand that force was the ultimate tool of political leaders. He had no illusions about it, despite his assurances that this "war" was not going to be a shooting match.

Faure was no military genius, but he was a tyrant. He fully intended to make the U.N. into a true global government. With himself at its head.

Moonbase stood in his way. The nanotech treaty was

just an excuse. As long as Moonbase ignored the U.N.'s authority, nations on Earth could justifiably resist U.N. encroachments on their sovereignty. So Moonbase had to be brought into line. Or destroyed.

The trouble was, the more Doug studied history, the more he delved into the bloody, murderous track that led to the present day, the more he found himself reluctantly agreeing with Faure's professed aims.

Ten billion people on Earth. And that was only the official count. There were probably a billion more, at least, that the various national censuses missed. Ten or eleven billion mouths to feed, ten or eleven billion people to house and clothe and educate. Most of them were poor, hungry, ignorant. And their numbers were growing faster than anyone could cope with. Three hundred thousand babies born *every day*. All the wealth in the world could barely maintain a minimum level of existence for them.

The rich refused to help the poor, of course. Not unless the poor reduced their birth rate, lowered their numbers. Starvation swept whole continents; plagues killed millions. Still the numbers grew. The poor of the world increased and multiplied and became poorer, hungrier, sicker.

Only a world government could hope to deal with the global problem of population. Only a true world government had the faintest chance of redistributing the world's wealth more equitably. That was Faure's proclaimed goal, his aim.

Doug agreed that the goal was worthy, vital, crucial to the survival of the human species. He also knew that it would never be achieved; not the way Faure was going about it.

The beep of his computer snapped Doug out of his ruminations. Its message light blinked at him.

"Answer," he commanded the phone.

It was not Gordette returning his call. Doug recognized the face of one of the communications technicians, calling from the control center.

"Doug, we're getting a transmission from L-1. Single

frequency. The secretary-general of the United Nations is about to give a speech and they want us to see it."

"Okay," he said, sagging back tiredly in his chair. "Pipe it through. Might as well put it on the general system, so everybody can see it."

"Will do."

Then Doug got a better idea. "Wait. Make an announcement that anyone not on essential duty should go straight to the Cave. Put Faure on the wallscreens there. I want everybody to see this."

"Will you be going to the Cave, too?"

"Right," said Doug, pushing himself out of his chair.

TOUCHDOWN MINUS 112 HOURS

Georges Henri Faure felt not the slightest twinge of nervousness as he walked slowly to the podium. The General Assembly chamber was hushed, so quiet that Faure could hear his own footsteps on the marble floor, despite the fact that the chamber was completely filled. Every delegate was in his or her proper seat. The media thronged the rear and overflowed into the side aisles, cameras focused on him. The visitor's gallery was packed.

He was a dapper little man, shaped rather like a pear but dressed so elegantly that no one noticed his figure. Nor the slight limp that marred his stride. His thinning dark hair was slicked back from his high forehead, and his face was round, pink-cheeked, almost cherubic except for his old-fashioned wire-brush mustache. On the rare occasions when his iron self-control failed and he became agitated, the points of the mustache would quiver noticeably. It sometimes made people laugh, but it was a bad mistake to laugh at Georges Faure. He neither forgot nor forgave.

His eyes were small, deep-set, dark and never still. They constantly darted here and there, watching, weighing, probing, judging. Many said, behind his back, that they were the eyes of an opportunist, a climber, a politician. Faure knew what they said of him: that he was a man consumed by ego and vaulting ambition. But no, he insisted to himself; what drove him was not personal ambition but an inner desire, a drive, a sacred mission: to save the world from itself; to bring order and stability to all of humankind; to avert the tragedy of chaos and disaster that threatened the Earth's misguided peoples.

He reached the marble podium. The floor behind it had been raised slightly, cunningly, so that no one in the audience could see that he actually stood on a platform. Smiling down on the rows of expectant faces, he leaned his weight on his arms, to ease his aching foot. He waited a moment, feeling the warmth of the undivided attention of every delegate, the glow of the media's cameras and recorders, the admiration of the public. The first line of his speech was on the electronic prompter; the tumbler on the podium held the Evian water he was partial to. Everything was in its place.

He began:

"Delegates of the General Assembly and the Security Council, members of the news media, members of the public and citizens of the world—I stand before you with a heart filled with both sadness and hope.

"Since seven years ago, all work on nanotechnology has been wisely banned by mutual accord of the member nations of this august organization. I am pleased to report to you that the last remaining nation on Earth to refuse to sign the nanotechnology treaty and accede to its terms has now at last signed that treaty. Kiribati has joined the great commonwealth of nations at last!"

A storm of applause rose from the floor of the huge auditorium. A sharp-witted observer would have noted

that it began in the section where the U.N. staff bureaucrats sat: Faure's employees.

In Moonbase, Doug sat at one of the tables in the
Cave, the old cafeteria, watching the wall-sized display
screen showing Faure. The Cave was jammed with people; everyone who was not needed on duty had packed
its cavernous confines. All the seats along the cafeteria
tables were filled and people were standing shoulder-to-
shoulder in the aisles between the tables; the only open
spaces were the squares of lovingly tended grass that
were scattered across the rock floor. It was like a flare
party, Doug thought, although no one was drinking or
dancing. Or laughing.

Faure's hugely enlarged features gazed down upon
them from the wide Windowall screen up at the front of
the Cave like an electronic deity, larger than life.

"There are those misguided souls," Faure was saying,
unconsciously touching the end of his mustache with a
fingertip, "who ask why nanotechnology must be
banned. There are those who question our policy."

He looked up and smiled mechanically, almost squeezing his tiny eyes shut. "To paraphrase the American rev-
olutionary Jefferson, in respect to the public opinion we
should declare the causes that have impelled us to this
decision."

Jinny Anson, sitting next to Doug at the long cafeteria
table, hissed, "That's a real outgassing, using Jefferson."

Doug nodded and said nothing.

Faure went on, "Nanotechnology offers enormous
medical benefits, we are told. Its enthusiasts claim that
nanomachines injected into the human body can prolong
life and promote perfect health. Yes, perhaps. But for
whom? For the starving masses of Africa or Latin
America? For those dying of plagues because they are
too poor to afford simple medical treatment?

"No! Nanotechnology would be available only to the
very rich. It would be one more method by which the
rich separate themselves from the poor. This cannot be
allowed! The gap between the rich and poor is one of
the most pernicious and dangerous causes of unrest and

instability on Earth! We must strive to narrow this gap, not widen it."

"By making everybody equally poor," Joanna muttered, seated on Doug's other side.

"Furthermore," Faure continued, "nanotechnology can be used as an insidious new form of weapon, deadlier than poisonous gas, more difficult to detect and counter than biological weapons. In a world tottering on the brink of catastrophe, the very last thing we desire is a new weapons technology. We have worked for more than ten years now to convince nations to give up their armies and allow the Peacekeepers to protect their borders. We have reduced the world's nuclear arsenals to a mere handful of missiles. We stand for disarmament and peace! How could we allow scientists in their secret laboratories to design perfidious new weapons of nanomachines?"

"So," Zimmerman grumbled, down the table from Doug, "now I am an evil Dr. Frankenstein."

Faure took a sip of Evian, replaced the glass delicately on the podium, and resumed.

"As I said, every nation on Earth has finally signed the nanotechnology treaty. At last, there is no place on Earth where nanotechnology can be practiced or taught."

Another burst of applause. But Doug knew what was coming next: the real reason for Faure's speech.

"Yet there is a place where nanotechnology is practiced every day, every hour. That place is not on Earth. It is on the Moon, at the privately owned center called Moonbase."

"Pass the bread, here comes the baloney," somebody in the cafeteria said, loudly enough to echo off the rock walls. No one laughed or even stirred to see who said it.

"The residents of Moonbase have refused to suspend their nanotechnology workings. They have refused to stop their researches into new forms and uses of nanotechnology." Faure's face had become grim. "True, they have offered to allow United Nations representatives to inspect their facilities and their laboratories, but they absolutely refuse to abide by the requirements of the nanotechnology treaty."

He looked up at his audience. "This cannot be allowed! We cannot permit them to dévelop further the nanotechnology in secret, some four hundred thousand kilometers away from our supervision!"

Faure's mustache was starting to bristle. "Who knows what kinds of new and dreadful capabilities they are developing in their secret laboratories? Who knows what their intentions are?"

People in the Cave were jeering now. "The bastard knows we need nanobugs to make the air we breathe!"

Taking a deep breath, Faure raised his hands as if motioning for attention. "Therefore, I have sent a detachment of Peacekeeper troops to Moonbase to enforce the conditions of the nanotechnology treaty on the lunar residents. They will arrive at Moonbase within slightly more than four days. Their mission is one of peace; but they are, of course, prepared to defend themselves if the Moonbase residents offer resistance."

Faure looked up again and peered directly into the camera. He seemed to loom above the people in the Cave.

"To these renegades of Moonbase I have this to say: Resistance is futile. You must obey the same laws that everyone on Earth obeys. I will employ all the power necessary to enforce the conditions of the nanotechnology treaty, whether on Earth or on the Moon. If, in your misguided attempts to defy the United Nations and the will of the peoples of Earth, you use force against our Peacekeepers, you will regret it."

The audience applauded wildly. Faure smiled and dipped his chin several times: his way of bowing. Then the screen went blank.

Doug blinked several times. The crowd in the Cave stirred and rumbled with a hundred conversations.

"He didn't mention a word about our declaration of independence," Joanna said.

"Nor our request for U.N. membership," Brudnoy added.

Doug got to his feet. "And he isn't going to have a news conference, where reporters can ask him questions, either."

"How long until the Peacekeepers land?" Anson asked.

Doug pressed the face of his wristwatch; the digital readout changed from the local time to a countdown.

"One hundred eleven hours and forty-eight minutes," he said.

"Well," Anson said, digging her hands into the pockets of her jeans, "you'd better think of *something* between now and then, boss."

TOUCHDOWN MINUS 111 HOURS 48 MINUTES

"You're right," Doug said to Anson.

He clambered up onto the cafeteria table and raised his arms over his head. "Hey!" he shouted to the murmuring, scattering crowd. "Hold on! I've got a few words to say."

The crowd stopped heading for the exit and turned toward him, some looking expectant, others puzzled.

"You Lunatics so eager to get back to work that you can't hang in here a couple minutes more?" Doug asked, grinning at them.

"Hell, boss, we'll stay all day if you want us to," hollered one of the men in the rear.

"If you serve some drinks," another voice chipped in.

Doug kept his grin in place. "No drinks. And this is only going to take a few minutes."

Someone groaned theatrically. A few people laughed at it.

"I want you to know," Doug said, scanning their faces, "that we declared Moonbase's independence a few hours ago. We had to do it, so that as an independent nation we can refuse to sign the nanotech treaty and continue to work here the way we always have."

"You mean we're citizens of Moonbase now?" a woman asked.

"I have to give up my American citizenship?" another voice from the crowd.

"That's all to be ironed out in negotiations with the U.S. government and other governments," Doug said. "We're not going to ask any of you to give up your original citizenship, not if you don't want to."

"What about those Peacekeeper troops Faure's sending here?"

"We'll tell them we're an independent nation now and they have no authority here," Doug answered.

"They gonna accept that?"

"We'll see," said Doug.

"Don't give up your day job," somebody said. Everyone laughed—nervously, Doug thought. But when he looked down at his mother, still seated at the table on which he was standing, she was not laughing at all. Not even smiling.

"We'll deal with the Peacekeepers when they get here," Doug promised. "They're not looking for a fight and neither are we."

"Yeah, but they got guns and we don't."

Doug had no rejoinder for that.

TOUCHDOWN MINUS 110 HOURS
7 MINUTES

If anyone noticed that Claire Rossi and Nick O'Malley left the Cave together, with equally somber expressions on their faces, no one made a fuss about it.

Almost everyone in Moonbase knew that Claire and Nick were lovers. She was the base personnel chief, a petite brunette with video-star looks and a figure that men wanted to howl after. He was a big, lumbering, easy-going redhead who ran a set of tractors up on the surface from the snug confines of a teleoperator's console down in the control center.

Nick was happy-go-lucky, and counted the most fortunate moment in his young life as the instant he saw Claire walking down one of Moonbase's corridors. He smiled at her and she smiled back. Electricity crackled. He stopped looking at other women and she had thoughts only for him. It was like magic.

But as they walked slowly out of the Cave, neither of them was smiling.

"We could be stuck here for months," Claire said as they shouldered their way through the dispersing crowd, heading for her quarters.

Nick was somber, deep in thought. "My work contract runs out in three weeks. What happens then?"

"I guess we won't be heading back Earthside until Doug and the politicians back home settle this thing."

"Yeah, but how do I get paid when my contract term ends? What happens then?"

She tried to smile up at him. "Well, we didn't want to be separated, did we? Maybe you'll have to stay here until *my* tour ends and we can go back home together."

Looking down at her, Nick saw that her smile was forced. "You don't seem so happy about it."

"It's not that," she said. "It's . . ." She fell silent.

"What?"

"Wait until we get to my place," Claire said, so solemnly that it worried Nick.

Once she shut the door of her one-room compartment, Nick asked almost desperately, "What is it? What's wrong?"

"It's not wrong, exactly," she said, going to the bunk and sitting on its edge.

"Well, what?"

"I'm pregnant," she said.

He blinked. "You're going to have a baby?" His voice came out half an octave higher than usual.

"Yes," she answered, almost shyly.

For a moment he didn't know what to say, what to do. Then the reality of it burst on him and he broke into an ear-to-ear grin. "A baby! That's great! That's *wonderful!*"

But Claire shook her head. "Not if we can't get off Moonbase, it isn't."

TOUCHDOWN MINUS 109 HOURS

Aboard the Clippership *Max Faget*, Captain Jagath Munasinghe stared suspiciously at the schematic displayed on his notebook screen.

"And this is the control center? Here?" He pointed with a blunt finger.

"That's it," said Jack Killifer. "Take that and you've got the whole base under your thumb."

Munasinghe wore the uniform of the U.N.'s Peacekeeping Force: sky blue, with white trim at the cuffs and along the front of his tunic, captain's bars on his collar and a slim line of ribbons on his chest below his name tag. He was of slight build, almost delicate, but his large dark eyes radiated a distrust that always bordered on rage. Born in Sri Lanka, he had seen warfare from childhood and only accepted a commission in the Peacekeepers when Sri Lanka had agreed to disarmament after its third civil war in a century had killed two million men, women and children with a man-made plague virus.

Behind him, forty specially-picked Peacekeepers sat uneasily in weightlessness as the spacecraft coasted toward the Moon. None of them had ever been in space before, not even Captain Munasinghe. Despite the full week of autogenic-feedback adaptation training they had been rushed through, and the slow-release anti-nausea patches they were required to wear behind their ears, several of the troops had vomited miserably during the first few hours of zero-gee flight. Munasinghe himself had managed to fight down the bile that burned in his throat, but just barely.

Sitting beside the captain, Killifer wore standard civilian's coveralls, slate gray and undecorated except for his name tag over his left breast pocket. He was more than twenty years older than the dark-skinned captain and almost a head taller: lean, lantern-jawed, his face hard and flinty. Once his light brown hair had been shaved down almost to his scalp, but now it was graying, and he wore it long enough to tie into a ponytail that bobbed weightlessly at the back of his neck. The sight of it made Munasinghe queasy.

"Forty men to take and hold the entire base," Munasinghe muttered unhappily.

"It's not that big a place," Killifer replied. "And like I told you, take the command center and you control their air, water, heat—everything."

Munasinghe nodded, but his eyes showed that he had his doubts.

"Look," Killifer said, "you put a couple of men in the environmental control center, here"—he tapped a fingernail on the captain's notebook screen—"and a couple more in the water factory, keep a few in the control center and the rest of 'em can patrol the tunnels or do whatever else you want."

"There are more than two thousand people there."

"So what? They got no weapons. They're civilians, they don't know how to fight even if they wanted to."

"You are absolutely sure they have no weapons of any kind?"

Killifer gave him a nasty grin. "Nothing. Shit, they don't even have steak knives; the toughest food they have to deal with is friggin' soybean burgers."

"Still . . ."

Feeling exasperated, Killifer growled, "I spent damn near twenty years there. I know what I'm talking about. It'll be a piece of cake, I tell you. A walkover. You'll be a friggin' hero inside of ten minutes."

Munasinghe's dubious expression did not change, but he turned and looked across the aisle of the passenger compartment to the reporter who was sitting next to them.

TOUCHDOWN MINUS 108 HOURS
57 MINUTES

Edith Elgin had thought she'd chat with the women soldiers among the Peacekeepers all the way to the Moon. But ever since the rocket's engines had cut off and the spacecraft had gone into zero gravity she had felt too nauseated to chat or even smile. Besides, most of the women barely spoke English; the little flags they wore as shoulder patches were from Pakistan and Zambia and places like that.

If she didn't feel so queasy it would have almost been funny. The reporter who broke the story of finding life on Mars, the woman who had parlayed a Texas cheer-leader's looks and a lot of smarts into prime-time news stardom, sitting strapped into a bucket seat, stomach churning, sinuses throbbing, feeling woozy every time she moved her head the slightest bit. And there's more than four days of this to go. Sooner or later I'll have to get up and go to the toilet. She did not look forward to the prospect.

At least nobody's upchucked for a while, Edith told herself gratefully. The sound of people vomiting had almost broken her when they had first gone into zero gee. Fortunately the Clippership's air-circulation system had been strong enough to keep most of the stench away from her row. Still, the acrid scent of vomit made the cabin smell like a New York alley.

It had been neither simple nor easy to win this assignment to accompany the Peacekeepers to the renegade base on the Moon. The network was all for it, of course, but the U.N. bureaucracy wanted nothing to do with a reporter aboard their spacecraft. Edith had to use every bit of her blond smiling charm and corporate infighter's savvy to get past whole phalanxes of administrators and directors and their petty, close-minded assistants. All the way up to Georges Faure himself she had battled.

"My dear Miss Elgin," Faure had said, with his smarmy smile, "this is a military expedition, not a camp-ing trip."

"This is *news*," Edith had countered, "and the public demands to know what's going on, firsthand."

She had been brought to Faure's presence in the Sec-retariat building. Not to his office, though. The secretary-general chose to meet her in a small quiet lounge on the building's top floor. The lounge was plush: thick beige carpeting, comfortable armchairs and curved little sofas.

Even the walls were covered with woven tapestries of muted browns and greens. The decor seemed to absorb sound; it was a room that gave no echoes, a room to share whispered secrets.

Edith had chosen to wear a clinging knee-length dress of bright red, accented with gold bracelets and necklace to complement her sunshine yellow hair. Once it had been truly that happy color; for years now she had helped it along with tint.

Faure had let her wait for almost ten minutes before he showed up, a dapper little man in a precisely-cut suit of elegant dark blue set off perfectly by a necktie of deep maroon.

He took her hand so daintily that Edith thought he was going to kiss it. Instead, Faure led her to one of the plush armchairs and sat in the one facing hers. As she sat down, Edith looked past Faure's smiling figure to the ceiling-high windows that faced uptown, northward, along the East River. She could see the Fifty-ninth Street bridge and well past it, all the way up to the Triboro and beyond.

"What a sparkling day," she said.

Faure took it as a personal compliment. "You see how the electric automobile has already improved the air quality," he said, beaming. It made his tiny eyes almost disappear.

Edith wasn't willing to let him take all the credit. "I thought the electric cars were mandated by the U.S. government. The Environmental Protection Agency, wasn't it?"

"Ah, yes," said Faure quickly. "But only after our own efforts had proven successful in reducing the pollution in Tokyo and Mexico City. Now all the major cities are following our lead." Again the smile that almost swallowed his eyes.

Edith wondered silently, Is he using the editorial "we" or the imperial?

But she smiled back at the secretary-general and said sweetly, "You know that a big chunk of the American public doesn't agree with what you're doing to Moonbase."

Faure's expression turned hard for a moment, then he shrugged and put on a sad face. "Yes, I know. It is very unfortunate. But one cannot make an omelet without breaking eggs, can one?"

Now he's saying "one" instead of "we," Edith realized.

"Most of the inhabitants of Moonbase are Americans," she said.

"They are violating the treaty that Americans themselves drafted. The very treaty that the American delegation originally proposed to the General Assembly and fought so hard to have passed."

"Still," Edith said, leaning back in the comfortable armchair and crossing her legs at the ankles, "many Americans sympathize with the people in Moonbase."

Faure made a *what-can-I-do* shrug.

"They would feel better about it," Edith continued, "if an American reporter went with the Peacekeepers and sent back on-the-spot reports."

The secretary-general began to shake his head.

"The American media would feel much better about it if a reporter were allowed to go along," Edith added.

"You mean those who control and direct the news media, no?"

"Yes. The top brass."

Faure sighed heavily. "Frankly, Miss Elgin, the American news media have not always been kind to me."

Edith kept herself from grinning. In most countries the government could muzzle the media pretty effectively. But the First Amendment was still in force in the U.S. So far.

"You see," Faure said, leaning closer to her, placing his hands on the knees of his perfectly creased trousers, "it is not I who resists your request. The Peacekeepers are military men. And women, of course. They do not want a news reporter to travel with them. They fear it might hamper them—"

"The military never wants reporters around."

"Quite so. But in this case I can fully understand their hesitation."

Edith said, "If there's a news blackout, the media will have nothing to work with except rumors."

"We will furnish news releases, as a matter of course. Each day a complete summary will be given to the media."

"But some reporters will wonder how accurate it is. There's always the tendency to put your own spin on the actual events, isn't there?"

Wearily, Faure replied, "I suppose so. But you must not impugn the integrity of the Peacekeepers. They have accomplished very difficult assignments in many parts of the globe. Take Brazil, for example—"

"Are you saying," Edith interrupted, "that it's up to the Peacekeepers themselves to decide if they take a reporter or not?"

"No, not at all. Merely—"

"Because I thought the Peacekeepers reported to you. I thought you made the final decisions."

"But I do!"

"Yet in this case you're going to let them dictate to you, is that it?"

Faure's mustache quivered slightly. "Not at all! I make the decision and they follow."

Smiling her prettiest, Edith knew she had him. "In that case, you certainly understand how important it will be to have an unbiased, trusted news reporter on the scene when they land at Moonbase."

Faure's face clearly showed that he did not like being mousetrapped. But slowly his expression changed; he smiled again, showing teeth.

"Yes, you are correct," he said slowly. "The responsibility is mine. All mine. The weight of the major decisions is upon my shoulders alone."

Edith recognized the crafty look in his eyes.

"This is not an easy decision to make, Miss Elgin," Faure went on. "Special arrangements require certain . . . ah, accommodations."

"What do you mean?" Edith asked, knowing perfectly well what he meant.

Leaning forward even more and tapping a pudgy finger on her knee, Faure said, "We have much to discuss about this. Perhaps we could have dinner this evening?"

The body tax. Edith controlled her inner anger as she told herself, Even after all these years of women's rights it still comes down to the damned body tax. He's got the power and he knows it. If I want him to do me a favor he expects me to do one for him in return. And all he sees is a good-looking blonde.

"Dinner sounds fine," she said, thinking, It won't be the first time you've opened your legs to get a good assignment. Sometimes you've got to give some head to get ahead.

TOUCHDOWN MINUS 96 HOURS

The mercenary stared at the message that was waiting for him on his wallscreen.

"The prey runs to the hunter," he muttered to himself.

Slowly he peeled off his grimy fatigues and wadded them into a ball that he tossed onto his bunk as he headed for the shower stall. His quarters were one of the old rooms in Moonbase. Most people complained that they were small and cramped, but the mercenary found the space just fine for his needs. Two of the walls were smart screens, recently installed. The shower stall was new, too.

Making sure the temperature dial was still set for dead cold, the mercenary stepped into the stall and let the reviving water sluice over his body. The prey runs to the hunter, he thought again. Doug Stavenger wants to see me.

Ever since he had first begun training as a sniper, back during his army days, he had thought of killing as a sort of religious rite. A sacred responsibility. Everybody dies, the only question about it is where and when. And how.

I give them a clean death. Not like some of those freaks.

When he was taken out of the army to serve in the covert intelligence agency, he had the time and the need to take up the study of primitive hunters who believed that the animals they killed came to them for death. The prey runs to the hunter.

If you do everything just right, make all the proper rituals and set things up just the way they should be, then the prey comes to you and asks to be allowed to die. Not in so many words, of course. But they come to me for death.

Just like Doug Stavenger's going to do. Hell, he's already started along the path.

TOUCHDOWN MINUS 95 HOURS
54 MINUTES

Zoltan Kadar was a Hungarian who prided himself on being slicker and smarter than ordinary mortals. He also happened to be one of the top astronomers in the world and an extremely clever man.

But now he felt frustrated and, worse, ignored.

He strode along the corridor toward the base director's office, hands balled into fists, arms swinging like a soldier's on parade. He was on the small side, quite slim, with a fencer's agile figure. His hair was dark and straight, and came to a pronounced widow's peak centered above his heavy dark eyebrows. People called him Count Dracula, although once they got to know him they changed his nickname to Slick Willy. Kadar revelled in the characterization.

"Hey, Slick, where you going?"

Kadar barely slowed his determined stride as he recognized Harry Clemens, head of the transportation division. Clemens was one of the older engineers, a true Lunatic who had been working at Moonbase for many years.

"Hello, Harry."

Working hard to stay with Kadar, Clemens—lanky, balding, unathletic—said, "Jeez, you look like you're going to lead the charge of the Light Brigade."

"They've cancelled my farside survey flight," Kadar said through gritted teeth. "I'm going to get it back on schedule."

"Oh, yeah, I know about that. Too bad."

"Too bad for them. They can't just stop my work like that." He snapped the fingers of his left hand.

"Everything's ground to a halt. We're at war, you know."

"Pah!"

"Nothing's going out, really. There's a Peacekeeper troopship on its way here."

"What has that got to do with building the farside observatory?"

Clemens was a practical engineer, and he recognized a stone wall when he saw one. "Well, I've got to turn off here. I'm helping the nanotech crew to shut down the bugs building the Clippership."

"Good-bye, Harry," said Kadar.

"Hope you can get what you want, but I wouldn't count on it."

"Good-bye, Harry."

Another minute's march brought Kadar to the base director's office. He rapped once on the door and opened it.

Jinny Anson was sitting behind the desk, talking on the phone to some woman. She glanced up at Kadar and waved him to a chair in front of her desk. From the expression on her face, Kadar realized that she knew she was in for trouble.

"Where is Stavenger?" Kadar asked as soon as Anson clicked off her phone screen.

"Doug's taking charge of the war. I'm the base director pro tem." Before Kadar could draw a breath she added, "And *all* work outside has been suspended, Zoltan, not just yours."

"I'm not interested in the rest of them. It's my work that is important."

"Sure," Anson said good-naturedly. "But we can't hang a surveillance satellite over farside until this business with the Peacekeepers is cleared up."

"I don't see why. It's an uncrewed satellite. I will take care of all the monitoring myself. I have the programs all in place."

With a patient sigh, Anson explained, "Look, there's a Clippership full of Peacekeepers on their way here to take over the base. We're going to try to stop them—don't ask me how, that's Doug's problem."

"But what has this to do with my work?" Kadar couldn't help putting a stress on the word *my*.

"The U.N.'s already taken over the L-1 satellite. Maybe they've got Peacekeepers there, maybe not, we don't know."

"But again, what has this—"

"They're watching us, Zoltan. They're watching every move we make. With telescopes and radar and every other kind of sensor they've got."

"So?"

"So what's their reaction gonna be if we launch a rocket? They won't just ignore it. Maybe they've already got high-power lasers at L-1 and they'll zap your rocket before they can figure out where it's heading."

"Nonsense! We'll simply tell them what the rocket's mission is."

"And they'll believe you?" Anson's earnest expression eased into a sly smile. "They'll believe a Hungarian?"

Kadar grinned back at her. "That might be a problem," he conceded.

"We don't want to do anything that'll give the U.N. a reason to start bombarding us. Your rocket stays in the shed until this crisis is over."

"Bombard us? That's idiotic. We're buried deep enough so that even nuclear bombs won't harm us."

"Really?" Anson snapped. "You really want to test that theory? And what about the solar farms and the mass driver and all your astronomical equipment out on the crater floor? What happens to them?"

Kadar slouched back in his chair like a petulant child. "I want to talk to Stavenger," he said.

"He's too damned busy for picobits like this, Zoltan. I'm the acting director and I say your rocket sits."

With a slight hike of his heavy brows, Kadar got slowly out of his chair and walked to the door.

"Thank you for your time," he said to Anson.

"Nothing to it."

Kadar stepped through the door and closed it softly, saying to himself, Now where in hell can I find Stavenger?

TOUCHDOWN MINUS 95 HOURS 20 MINUTES

"When do they land?" asked Toshiru Takai.

Doug did not have to look at his watch. "In less than four days."

Takai nodded and made a sound halfway between a sigh and a groan.

Doug was walking with him slowly across the vast floor of the crater Copernicus, where the Nippon One base was situated, more than a thousand kilometers from Moonbase. Since they were communicating through a virtual reality program, they could walk on the lunar surface without spacesuits. Doug wore his usual unadorned sky-blue coveralls; Takai a similar jumpsuit of pearl gray, decorated with a single white heron over the breast pocket, the symbol of Yamagata Corporation.

"I tried to reach your corporate headquarters in Tokyo," Doug said, "but there seemed to be some difficulty with their receiving equipment."

"I imagine your transmissions are being jammed by the Peacekeepers," Takai said, showing no emotion on his lean, bony face. He was in his early thirties; Doug thought of him as his own age, roughly, even though Takai was at least five years older.

With an understanding smile, Doug said, "Our transmissions are getting through to Savannah and Tarawa and even New York."

Takai gave him a sidelong glance. "Do you want me to tell you that my superiors in Tokyo have decided not to speak with you?" His voice was low, but filled with strength.

"I'd like to know where they stand," Doug said evenly. "Where you stand."

"Why, here I am, in the middle of the most beautiful crater on the Moon!"

Doug laughed at the joke. Although they had never met physically, he had known Takai for three years now, ever since the young engineer had been chosen to direct the Yamagata lunar base. While their virtual selves could walk in the vacuum without even kicking up a cloud of dust, each of them was safely in his office, deep underground.

Yet Doug could reach out and clasp Takai's shoulder. "Toshi, I need to know what Yamagata is going to do. It's important for us. For both of us."

"I know," Takai admitted.

Nippon One was the only other lunar base still active.

Its reason for existence, aside from scientific studies, was to extract helium-three from the Moon's regolith and ship it to the nuclear fusion power plants that were springing up throughout Japan, China, and the Pacific Rim nations. Fusion power was not welcomed in Europe or North America, where anti-nuclear fears not only persisted, but were actively fanned by the nanoluddites.

The Europeans had closed down their base at Grimaldi when the nanotech treaty had gone into effect for the Euro-Russian consortium that managed the base. They still sent occasional maintenance crews to repair and refurbish the scientific gear that ran automated at Grimaldi, but even those visitors rode on Masterson LTVs or Yamagata's.

"Are you going to shut down Nippon One?" Doug asked, half-dismayed that he had to be so direct with his Japanese friend.

"That is not in my instructions," Takai replied.

Damn! thought Doug. He's not just being roundabout; he's being actually evasive.

"Toshi, I really need to know what Yamagata plans to do." .

For several moments Takai said nothing. He simply walked along the virtual crater floor and avoided looking at Doug.

"What do you plan to do?" Takai countered. "Surely you don't expect to fight the Peacekeepers."

"We've declared our independence," Doug said. "Legally, the Peacekeepers have no right to bother us."

"Only if the U.N. accepts your independence."

Doug nodded.

"They won't," Takai predicted. "You know they won't."

"I'm not so sure. Time is on our side. If we can hold on and prevent the Peacekeepers from taking over the base, we could eventually get world opinion on our side and—"

"Time is on your side until the Peacekeepers land," Takai pointed out.

"But if we can keep them from taking Moonbase,"

Doug said earnestly, "then we can get through this. All we have to do is show the world that we can survive, that we can hang in there and take care of ourselves. Sooner or later they'll recognize the fact that we *are* independent."

Takai shook his head. "You're dreaming, Doug."

"No," Doug insisted. "It's like the situation in the American Civil War. All the Confederacy had to do was keep itself intact, not let the Union conquer it. In time, the nations of Europe would recognize it as a separate nation."

"But that didn't happen, did it?" Takai asked gently.

"We can make it happen here."

"No, Doug. That isn't going to be allowed to happen, believe me."

Doug hesitated, digesting not only Takai's words, but their tone. He knows more than he's willing to tell me, Doug realized.

"Don't you think Japan would recognize our independence if we drove off the Peacekeepers?"

"No, I don't."

"Is Yamagata against us? I need to know, Toshi. Lives depend on it."

Takai said nothing.

"Well?" Doug demanded.

The pained expression on Takai's face showed the tension he was feeling. "My instructions are to continue as usual. We will operate Nippon One as we normally do, despite your present . . . difficulties."

They both knew that Nippon One carefully refrained from using nanotechnology. Instead of using nanomachines to extract helium-three from the ground, they used cumbersome bulldozers and old-fashioned mass spectrometers to separate the isotope from the other lunar ores. It kept the cost of helium-three at least ten times higher than it would have been if nanomachines had been employed to ferret out the helium-three nuclei individually.

But Nippon One bought its water from Moonbase. Shut down Moonbase and the Japanese base dies, too.

"I don't understand how that can be," Doug said.

"Those are my instructions."

Walking beside his virtual friend in silence, Doug thought, He wants to tell me what's going on, but he can't. His loyalty to Yamagata is preventing him from telling me the whole truth.

"We've already declared our independence, you know," Doug said.

"Yes, you told me. I doubt that it'll do you any good."

"What was Tokyo's reaction to that?"

"No reaction. The first I heard of it was just now, when you told me."

"Your corporate superiors didn't tell you about it?"

"Not one word."

"We beamed the information to Yamagata headquarters and to every news agency on Earth."

"I have not received any information about that," Takai said, genuinely upset.

"That must mean that Faure intends to ignore our declaration and proceed as if it's a nonstarter."

"Yes, of course."

They took a few more paces across the crater floor, skirting a fresh-looking craterlet about the size of a beach ball's indentation.

"Toshi, how are you going to get water if Moonbase is shut down? You can't use nanomachines, and—"

"We will get our water the same way we do now."

"But Moonbase will be closed. The Peacekeeper troops are on their way to shut us down."

Takai grimaced, struggling inwardly. At last he said, "The Peacekeepers are coming to remove you and your people from the management of Moonbase. That does not mean they intend to close the base entirely."

Doug stopped in his tracks. "Not . . ." His mind started spinning. "Not close the base? Toshi, are you sure?"

"It could cost me my position if anyone learns that I told you. Yes, I am quite certain. Or I should say that Tokyo is quite certain."

"They're not going to close the base?"

"Faure spoke directly to the head of the Yamagata clan himself and assured him that Moonbase will continue to supply water to Nippon One—after the Peacekeeper troops remove you and your staff from the base."

"Faure intends to continue running Moonbase," Doug repeated, feeling hollow with surprise. "The little furball doesn't care about the nanotech treaty; he wants to control Moonbase himself!"

TOUCHDOWN MINUS 93 HOURS 45 MINUTES

"But don't you understand what this means?" Joanna demanded.

"It means that Faure wants to take over Moonbase," said Doug.

"It means we can do business with him!" his mother replied eagerly. "We can cut a deal."

Doug stared at his mother. She was sitting bolt upright in the chaise longue she had brought from her home in Savannah as part of the elaborate furnishings for her two-room suite at Moonbase. Leaning toward her from the delicate little Sheraton sofa on which he sat, Doug shook his head unhappily.

"Faure won't make any deals. He intends to use the Peacekeepers to toss us out of here and then have the U.N. itself run the base."

Joanna gave her son a pitying smile. "Doug, he'll need trained personnel to run this base. He'll have to use the people who are here."

"That doesn't include thee and me."

"Don't be so sure," Joanna said. She seemed actually happy with Doug's news, pleased that Faure wanted to take over Moonbase.

"He'll want to continue to manufacture Clipperships, of course," Joanna mused. "That's where the profits are. Every transportation line on Earth wants our Clipperships and he can pump the profits into the U.N."

"Or his own pocket."

"Maybe," Joanna agreed. "Even better. The more venal he is, the easier it'll be to deal with him."

Doug shook his head again. "That's what the German industrialists thought about Hitler."

"Faure's no Hitler. He's not a fanatic. He isn't even going to stop our nanomachines. He just wants to run them for his own profit."

Getting to his feet, Doug said, "I'm still assuming that we'll have to handle the Peacekeepers, and we've got less than four days to figure out how to do it."

"What do you intend to do?"

He shrugged. "I've asked Zimmerman and Cardenas to meet me in my quarters. Lev and Jinny Anson, too. And one of the aquaculture technicians, the only guy in the base who's had any military experience at all."

"All right," Joanna said, looking up at her son from the chaise longue. "You do that. I'm going to put in a call to Faure. He'll negotiate. I know he will."

"Don't commit us to anything until I get a chance to see what it is, okay?"

Joanna nodded absently. "Oh, I don't think Faure will agree to anything concrete until the Peacekeepers get here and take over the base."

"That's what I'm trying to prevent."

"Good," she said. "If we could somehow keep the Peacekeepers out of here it would strengthen our hand tremendously."

"I'll see what we can do," said Doug.

TOUCHDOWN MINUS 90 HOURS
11 MINUTES

Moonbase had started as a clutch of temporary shelters, little more than aluminum cans the size of house trailers, dug into the lunar regolith on the floor of the crater Alphonsus and then covered over with rubble to protect them from the radiation and temperature swings between night and day. And from the occasional meteoroid strike. Meteor showers that were spectacular light shows in the night sky of Earth were potentially dangerous volleys of celestial machine-gun fire on the airless Moon.

By the time of Doug Stavenger's first visit to the Moon, on his eighteenth birthday, Moonbase had grown into a set of four parallel tunnels dug into the flank of Mt. Yeager. Offices, labs, workshops and living quarters lined the tunnels. The water factory was at the front of one tunnel, the environmental control center—where the base's air was recycled and kept circulating properly— was at the rear.

In his seven years at Moonbase, Doug had seen those original four tunnels grow to eight, with the four new tunnels sunk a level below the original quartet. Rough rock walls were smoothed with plasma torches and painted in pastels selected by psychologists—then painted over by base personnel who demanded brighter, bolder colors. And the occasional graffitist. When the grand plaza's construction was finished, twenty more tunnels would be added beneath it.

If we ever get to finish the grand plaza, Doug thought as he walked toward his quarters. He nodded and smiled automatically to everyone he passed. Doug knew most of the long-time Lunatics by sight, but there were always hundreds of short-term workers at the base. How many of them will stay with us? he wondered. Even if we keep the Peacekeepers out and establish our independence, will we have enough people left here to run the base?

There were directional signs on the walls now, and electronic maps at intersections that showed a schematic of the tunnel system. Corridors, Doug reminded himself. We call them corridors now, not tunnels.

He turned left at an intersection and bumped into a man in olive-green coveralls who was striding purposefully down the corridor. They each muttered an apology and fell into step, side by side, as they walked down the corridor.

Out of the side of his eye, Doug looked the man over. He thought he recognized him, but couldn't quite place who he was. The man was a couple of inches shorter than Doug's own six one, but built wide and solid, like a bulldozer. Not an ounce of fat on him: he had felt iron-hard when Doug had bumped into him. His skin was the color of milk chocolate, his neatly-trimmed hair dark and wiry. Doug could not see his nametag without making it obvious he was looking at it.

So he said, "I'm Doug Stavenger," and stuck out his hand without breaking stride.

The man made a perfunctory smile. "I know."

For a moment Doug thought he was going to refuse to shake, but then the man took Doug's proffered hand and said, in a clear, distinct, deliberate baritone, "My name is Bam Gordette."

"Leroy Gordette?" Suddenly the picture from the personnel file clicked in Doug's mind.

Gordette replied, "Call me Bam. It's short for Bama, which in turn is short for Alabama."

"You're from Alabama?" Doug asked.

"Yeah, but I got no banjo on my knee." Gordette smiled, but it looked purely mechanical.

"I was born in Georgia," said Doug.

"I know."

They had reached the door to Doug's quarters, which were doubling as his office now that Jinny Anson occupied the director's post. Opening it, Doug ushered Gordette in with a gesture. "The others will be here in a few minutes."

The smart walls were all blank as they stepped in. Gordette started to sit on the couch by the door, but Doug pointed to the slingchair next to his writing desk. As he went to the desk and dropped into his swivel chair, Doug said, "We can use the few minutes to get to know each other."

Gordette nodded tightly. Doug looked into his deep brown eyes and saw that Gordette would be a tough opponent in a poker game. He gave away nothing.

"You were in the army?" Doug prompted.

"Special Forces."

"How long?"

"I did a four-year hitch."

"Why did you leave?"

"Got a better offer."

Doug tapped on his keyboard and Gordette's personnel file came up on the wallscreen to his left.

"What kind of a company is Falcon Electronics?"

"Small," said Gordette. "They did customized electro-optical rigs, stuff like that."

"You were with them almost nine years?"

"Right."

"And then you got a job with Masterson Corporation and came to Moonbase."

"Right."

Leaning back in his chair, Doug asked, "How do you like it here?"

Gordette thought for a moment. "Not bad. Most of the people here are smart, civilized."

"Civilized?"

"There's not much of a color problem here. Not like back in the States."

Doug felt shocked. "You had race problems?"

Gordette smiled again, but this time it dripped acid. "There's no black man on Earth doesn't have race problems."

"I'm part black," Doug said. "My father—"

"I know all about it. But your skin is white enough, and you got enough money, so it doesn't matter to you."

Doug felt as if he were battering against a solid steel barrier. Not that Gordette seemed hostile; he simply offered nothing. It was like talking to an automaton. And yet there was *something* going on behind those unwavering eyes. The man wasn't stupid, Doug judged. He's just sitting there, looking at me. As if he's studying me.

Lev Brudnoy stuck his head through Doug's open door and broke the tightening silence. Moments later, Jinny Anson, Professor Zimmerman and Kris Cardenas joined the conference.

As they carefully, meticulously went over every inch of Moonbase's layout, equipment and supplies, Doug watched Gordette. The man said nothing, but seemed entirely focused on their discussion. He listened intently, hands clasped in front of his face as if in prayer. Every now and then, though, Doug caught him looking directly at him. Gordette never looked away. He simply stared at Doug, face utterly impassive, eyes boring as if he were taking X-ray photographs.

"So we can button up and wait for 'em to run out of air," Anson said, waving a hand at the schematic diagram of the base that filled one whole wall of Doug's office.

"Suppose they blow out the main airlock?" Brudnoy asked. "What then?"

Anson's normally perky expression paled slightly. "Why would they do that?"

"They want to take over the base," Brudnoy replied.

"Yeah, but they wouldn't want to kill us! Not if we're just sitting tight inside."

"Blowing the main airlock wouldn't necessarily kill us, would it?" Cardenas asked.

"No," said Anson, "it'd just open up the garage. All the tunnels would still be sealed off—"

"Corridors," Doug corrected.

"Whatever."

"Still," Brudnoy said, "if they blast out the main airlock that would surely mean that they are prepared to blow their way through any of the other airlocks and hatches in the base."

"It would mean they're ready to kill us," Doug agreed.

Zimmerman, sitting alone on the couch by the door, pointed out, "If they blast open the main airlock we would have to surrender. There would be no other option."

"Not unless we can breathe vacuum," Anson admitted.

Doug turned to Gordette and again the man was staring at him. "What do you think, Bam? What does your military experience tell you?"

Without the slightest hesitation, Gordette replied, "The Peacekeepers are trained to accomplish their mission with as little bloodshed as possible. They won't blow any airlocks. Not at first, anyway."

"You mean we could sit inside and wait 'em out?" Anson asked.

Gordette shook his head.

"What would you do," Doug asked, "if you were heading up this Peacekeeper mission?"

Getting slowly to his feet, Gordette walked to the wall map and pointed to the thin lines that represented the buried power cables that led from the solar farms into the base. "I'd cut your electrical power lines, here, here, and here."

"The solar farms," murmured Brudnoy.

"Without electricity this base goes down the tubes." Gordette made a diving motion with one hand.

"We have the backup nuclear system," Anson said.

"They know that," Gordette replied flatly. "They've got as good a map of this base as you do."

Doug said, "So they'll cut the line from the nuke, too."

Gordette nodded.

"Kaput," said Zimmerman. "How long can we last without electricity? Thirty seconds, perhaps?"

"We have emergency batteries, fuel cells," said Anson.

"So? How much time do they give us?"

"A few hours."

"The Peacekeepers will have enough air to wait for us to surrender, no?"

"Yes."

From his chair in front of Doug's desk, Brudnoy looked up at Gordette with gloom in his pouchy eyes. "Is there anything we can do? Anything at all?"

Gordette seemed to think about it for a moment. "There's a maneuver that we use in martial arts when your opponent points a gun at you."

"What is it?"

Gordette slowly raised his arms over his head in the universal sign of surrender.

The room fell into a dismal silence. Doug looked at them; they seemed defeated already.

"What we've learned," he said in as firm a voice as he could, "is that we've got to keep the Peacekeepers from cutting our power lines."

"How?" Brudnoy asked.

Doug pointed toward Zimmerman. "We need something to defend those power lines."

"Something?" Zimmerman growled. "What?"

"That's what you've got to figure out, Professor. And you've got less than four days to do it."

TOUCHDOWN MINUS 63 HOURS
29 MINUTES

Joanna Masterson Stavenger was not accustomed to being snubbed, not even by the world's most powerful politicians. But Faure refused to speak to her.

At first the U.N. simply did not acknowledge her calls. The wallscreen in her quarters showed nothing but electronic hash. The comm tech who was monitoring her transmission said flatly, "They're not answering."

She reached the Masterson Corporation offices in New York and tried to pipe a call to Faure through them. After nearly twenty-four hours of delays and evasions, one of the U.N. flunkies blandly told her that the secretary-general was unavailable.

Huffing with impatient anger, Joanna called Masterson corporate headquarters in Savannah on a direct laser link.

"I want to speak with the chairman of the board," she told the young man whose face appeared on her wallscreen.

"Mr. Rashid isn't here, Mrs. Brudnoy. He's in—"

Joanna did not wait for the sentence to end. "Find him, wherever he is. I need to talk to him immediately."

It took almost three seconds for her words to reach Rashid's aide and his startled expression to show on her screen.

"Get him!" she snapped.

Nearly half an hour later, Ibrahim al-Rashid's face finally appeared on the wallscreen. He had been handsome once, but now his romantic good looks were sinking into softness. His closely-clipped beard was streaked with gray, as was his tightly-curled hair. He had a look of decadence about him, Joanna thought. She knew that Rashid did not drink; he was a faithful Moslem in that regard. But there were drugs. And women, many of them. And the responsibilities that came inescapably with great power.

"Greetings and felicitations, most illustrious one," he said, his voice reedy but melodious. "How are you enjoying your visit to the Moon?"

"I need to talk to Faure," Joanna said, unwilling to engage in the usual banter.

Three seconds later Rashid's brows rose slightly. "I very much doubt that the secretary-general would be willing to speak with you at this point in time."

"Make it happen, Omar," Joanna snapped.

If her use of his old nickname upset him, Rashid showed no trace of it. He merely smiled patiently and replied, "And how do I do that, Joanna? Rub a magic lamp?"

Holding on to her swooping temper, Joanna replied, "You get that little Quebecer on the phone and tell him that I'm going to announce to the news media that he has no intention of shutting down Moonbase. He's going to continue using *our* nanomachines for his own profit!"

Rashid seemed more sobered than surprised when her words reached him.

"Your son's declaration of Moonbase's independence has not been carried by the media," he said slowly. "There is a blackout on news about Moonbase. Even here in the States the media have acceded to Faure's request for restraint."

"This isn't about Moonbase," Joanna replied impatiently. "This is about the secretary-general of the United Nations telling the world he's going to enforce the nanotech treaty when he's really planning to use our nanomachines for his own purposes."

She watched his expression intently. Does he already know about this? Has he already cut a deal with Faure?

At last Rashid said, "That does cast a new light on the situation. Perhaps the media would be interested in such a story. Do you have any evidence to back it up? Any corroboration?"

Suddenly Joanna felt wary. "Plenty," she said, thinking to herself, Omar could be part of Faure's scheme. He's never been a supporter of Moonbase.

Almost as if thinking out loud, Rashid murmured, "There is a reporter on board the Clippership heading for Moonbase."

"I don't want a reporter," Joanna said. "I want all the networks. I want every news service on Earth!"

"But the commsats have been programmed to reject all transmissions from Moonbase."

"I don't need the commsats. How do you think we're talking? The technicians here can beam my transmissions to any spot on Earth, almost. All the news services have optical receivers on their rooftops."

Rashid was silent far longer than the three seconds it took for the round-trip transmission from Moon to Earth and back again.

"Perhaps Faure would be willing to speak with you, after all," he said at last. "Let me see if I can reach him and get him to listen to reason."

"Good," said Joanna. "We've only got a little more than two and a half days before the Peacekeepers land here."

"Yes, I know."

"Don't let Faure delay until his troops land. I won't wait that long. Tell him he's got twenty-four hours to get in touch with me. Or else I go to the media."

"Harkening and obedience," said Rashid, just as he did in the old days when Joanna was chairman of the board and he was only a rising young executive.

TOUCHDOWN MINUS 38 HOURS
30 MINUTES

Edith's nausea was almost completely gone. A tendril of unease persisted deep inside her, but she thought it was probably more psychological than physical now. She still felt slightly dizzy whenever she moved her head too fast, but the moment passed quickly.

In fact, floating free in zero gravity was fun! She had set up her two minicams in the spacecraft's cargo bay, amid bulky crates marked AMMUNITION: 9 MM: FRANGIBLE and GRENADES: CONCUSSION: MARK 17/A.

She had interviewed two ordinary troopers, a shy teen-aged boy from Bangladesh and his sergeant, a tough no-nonsense Cuban woman. It was like interviewing athletes: monosyllabic answers, platitudes, and long, perplexed silences.

Edith checked her hair in her hand mirror. It was floating nicely; not so wild that it would distract the viewer, just enough to show what weightlessness could do. The cameras were tightly tethered to a pair of tied-down crates so they wouldn't bob around; there were no girders or other projections on the smooth curving bulkhead of diamond on which to secure them.

Captain Munasinghe glided through the hatch, trying to look as if he was unaffected by zero gee. He had removed the medication patch from behind his ear, but Edith saw faint rings there, like the scars from an octopus's suckers, and wondered how comfortable the captain really felt.

He was small and slim, dark skin shining as if it had been oiled. He had put on a fresh uniform, Edith saw, crisp and clean. His eyes were his best feature, large and dark and somehow fierce looking. They'll show up great on camera, she thought. But he's so little, I'll look like a horse next to him.

Then she smiled to herself. Zero gee to the rescue. I'll just let him float higher off the deck than I do. Keep the focus tight, head and shoulders. He'll look taller than me and I'll bet he'll love it. Realistic journalism.

"I just want to ask you a few questions, Captain Munasinghe," she said, trying to put him at ease. "Just look at me and ignore the cameras."

"Yes. Fine."

"Ready?"

Munasinghe nodded, then licked his lips.

Wondering who had taught him to do that, Edith pressed the switch on her remote control wand and said, "Okay, here we go."

She arranged herself facing Munasinghe and slightly below him, so his head topped hers by a few centimeters. Camera one held the two-shot; the second camera focused on the captain's face. Edith would do her reaction close-ups afterward; they would be spliced in Earthside as cutaways.

"Here with me now is Captain Jagath Munasinghe of the United Nations Peacekeeping Force, the commander of this mission to the Moon," said Edith.

"Captain Munasinghe, how do you feel about leading forty armed troops to Moonbase?"

Munasinghe drifted closer to her as he replied, "The Peacekeepers were created by international agreement to enforce the decisions of the United Nations Secretariat. Moonbase is violating the terms of the nanotechnology treaty, therefore we have been dispatched to the Moon to put an end this violation."

"Yes, but how do you feel personally about this mission?"

"I am proud to bear the responsibility of carrying out the United Nations' decision to enforce the nanotechnology treaty," he said. It sounded like a parrot repeating a line it had been laboriously taught.

The interview teetered between a disaster and a farce. Munasinghe had canned answers for every question she asked, undoubtedly written in New York for him to memorize. Worse, he kept pushing so close to Edith that she thought he wanted to rub noses with her. She could smell the cloying, faintly acrid odor of whatever breath treatment he had gargled.

She unconsciously moved away from him, trying to maintain a proper distance for their interview, but he kept moving in on her. In the back of her mind Edith remembered that different cultures have different ideas of the proper distance for social intercourse, but this was going out on the network, for chrissakes! *It's going to look like he's coming on to me.*

The cameras tracked them automatically, but after only a few minutes Edith's back bumped against one of the cargo crates and she could retreat no farther. Munasinghe hovered before her, his breath making her want to gag, his burning eyes boring into hers as if he intended to rape her.

Edith was about to give up all pretense of trying to conduct a rational interview and wind it up as quickly as she could, but some inner determination was urging her to get something, *anything* out of Munasinghe.

In desperation, she gestured with her free hand to the crates of munitions around them. "Do you think you're really going to need all this firepower against the people of Moonbase? After all, they're unarmed, aren't they?"

"They claim that they are unarmed, yes."

"You don't believe that?"

"I am a soldier," Munasinghe said, eyes burning into her. "I must be prepared for the worst that the enemy could possibly do to us."

"But what could a gaggle of scientists and technicians do to a platoon of fully-armed Peacekeepers?"

"We don't know, but we must be prepared."

"With hand grenades and explosives?"

"With every weapon at our disposal," Munasinghe

said, without an instant's hesitation. "If the people of Moonbase offer the slightest opposition, we are prepared to use whatever level of force is required."

Edith's breath caught in her throat. "You mean you're prepared to kill them?"

"If necessary. Yes, of course."

"Even though they're unarmed?"

He jabbed a finger in her face. "You keep saying they are unarmed. How do we know this? How do we know what kinds of weapons they may have at Moonbase? I am responsible for bringing Moonbase under United Nations' jurisdiction. I am responsible for the lives of my troops. If the enemy offers the slightest resistance, the slightest provocation, I have ordered my troops to shoot."

"Shoot to kill?" Edith was surprised at how hollow her voice sounded.

"When you are in battle you don't have the luxury of attempting to merely wound your enemy. Shoot to kill, yes, of course."

"At the slightest provocation?"

For the first time, Captain Munasinghe smiled. "I have served in Eritrea, in Colombia, and against the Armenian terrorists. Believe me, you do not give an enemy a second chance to kill you. Not if you want to survive the engagement."

"Let me get this straight," Edith said. "You're saying that you've ordered your troops to shoot to kill at the slightest sign of resistance from the people of Moonbase."

"At the slightest sign of resistance," Munasinghe affirmed. "Better to destroy Moonbase and everyone in it than to return to Earth with our mission a failure."

Edith swallowed hard, then said, "Thank you, Captain Munasinghe."

She had to push herself past him, then forced a smile as she looked straight into camera one and concluded, "This is Edie Elgin, in space with the U.N. Peacekeeper force, on the way to Moonbase."

Munasinghe drifted back, then asked, "Is that all? Is it finished?"

"That's it," said Edith, hoping he would go away.

"Was it satisfactory? Can I see it?"

Wearily, Edith ran the abbreviated interview on camera one's monitor. Munasinghe watched himself, fascinated. Edith wondered if the network suits would play the interview. They had made it clear they wanted to cooperate with the U.N., and this interview could stir a lot of hostility toward the Peacekeepers if it was aired.

No, she told herself, they'll play it. They'll have to. So the U.N. bitches about it, so what? This is *news*.

TOUCHDOWN MINUS 27 HOURS 51 MINUTES

The mercenary returned to his quarters and sat on his bunk. The time to strike is nearly here.

The situation was almost ludicrous. The more he thought about the base's electrical power supplies, its life-support systems, its total lack of weaponry or military capability, the more he realized that a single man like himself could bring the entire base to its knees.

They won't need a ship full of Peacekeepers. I can do it all by myself.

But the Peacekeepers were on their way and there was almost nothing that the inhabitants of Moonbase could do to stop them.

Why assassinate the leaders when they can't offer any resistance? Just knock out their electrical power system and they're helpless. It won't make any difference if Doug Stavenger lives or dies; Moonbase will cave in as soon as the Peacekeepers arrive.

The mercenary got down onto the floor in front of his bunk and folded his legs into the lotus position. Resting the backs of his hands on his knees, he closed his eyes and murmured his mantra, seeking harmony and understanding.

He saw in his mind's eye what he always saw. His ten-year-old brother in convulsions, dying of the zip he had snorted while their mother lay sprawled on the sofa, too dazed with the same shit to phone for help. He saw his six-year-old self locked in the dark roach closet because he'd been a bad boy, watching his brother die through the closet door keyhole, listening to the screams that turned into strangled, choking sobs and finally ended in a groan that still tortured his soul.

If I had been good, I wouldn't have been locked in the roach closet. I could've helped Timmy.

He saw his mother die, too. She was the first person he ever killed. He was fifteen and a father, but she still treated him like a little kid. Took the strap to him. He grabbed it away from her and swung it hard enough to knock her down. Her head cracked on the table leg and her eyes went blank.

He saw his first sergeant die, as brutal a man as any, but fair and unwaveringly honest. And the old cowboy on the rifle range, the one who taught him how to shoot. And how to hunt.

Death was his companion always. His ancient friend. He was death's best assistant. That was his destiny, his purpose in life: to bring people to death.

He opened his eyes. Deep within him the ancient calm had returned. There were no doubts, no qualms, no divisions within him. He was one again. Whole. Death was at his side, invisible but palpable, his oldest and best companion.

After all, he told himself, Stavenger's entire life revolves around Moonbase. Take that away from him and he's as good as dead anyway. I'll merely be helping him to the place where he wants to be.

Still, he sighed.

TOUCHDOWN MINUS 20 HOURS

Joanna Stavenger actually felt nervous as she sat in her favorite armchair, waiting for Georges Faure's call. The secretary-general had at first refused to speak to her at all, but the threat of telling the media that he planned to use nanomachines despite his public denouncement of them apparently had forced his hand.

Apparently, she reminded herself. The little bastard's waited until the troopship is almost ready to land before agreeing to talk to me.

Faure had put up conditions. This was to be strictly a private conversation between the two of them. No third parties. And it was to be understood that he was speaking to her as a courtesy only, not in his capacity as secretary-general of the United Nations.

Joanna had agreed easily. She knew that Faure had no private existence; whatever he said to her was being said by the man who headed the U.N. And she conveniently forgot her pledge of privacy when she told her son that Faure was going to speak to her. Doug was not in her sitting room with her, but he was plugged into their conversation, in his own quarters.

Precisely at the appointed moment the synthesized voice of the communications system said, "Monsieur Faure is calling from New York."

"On screen, please," Joanna replied.

A window seemed to open on the wall before her and Faure's face appeared, no larger than life-size. Joanna had programmed the smart wall that way; she had no desire to see Faure looming over her like an intimidating giant.

"Madame Brudnoy," Faure said, with a polite little smile.

"Mr. Secretary-General," Joanna replied.

While she waited the three seconds for his reply, Joanna examined the room in which Faure was sitting. It didn't look like an office; more like the living room of a spacious apartment in a high-rise building. She could not see much of the background behind him, but there was a window that looked out on the skyscrapers of Manhattan.

"I am not speaking as the secretary-general, Madame. This is a personal conversation between two private citizens."

Joanna nodded an acknowledgment.

"May I say that you look radiant? And your apartment, from what I can see of it, seems quite charming. I had no idea such luxuries were to be found in Moonbase."

Joanna had put on a tailored blouse of coral pink and a dark mid-thigh skirt: comfortable without being too dressy.

"Thank you," she said. "This is my personal furniture. I had it brought up from Savannah years ago. I assure you, the other living quarters here are nowhere near as elegant."

"I see," said Faure, after the annoying lag. "The privileges of the wealthy."

Joanna bit back the temptation to comment on Faure's luxurious apartment. "I appreciate your taking the time to speak with me."

This time it took more than three seconds for him to reply. His brow furrowed, his mouth pursed. At last he said, "Madame Brudnoy, it took a struggle with my conscience to decide to answer your request. I confess that my first instinct was to ignore it, and remain aloof from you and everyone else in Moonbase until this crisis is settled."

"I think it's always best to discuss problems frankly, face-to-face."

His frown eased somewhat. "Yes, I agree. That is why I am speaking to you."

"What about our declaration of independence?"

If the question jolted him, Faure gave no indication of it. "Declaration of independence? Pah!" He snapped his fingers. "A transparent ploy to avoid complying with the nanotechnology treaty."

"A right of every nation," Joanna retorted. "Just because we're on the Moon doesn't mean we don't have the same rights as any other group of people."

"You are not a nation," Faure countered. "Moonbase is a division of a corporation."

"Moonbase is a community of more than two thousand people. We have the right to be independent."

His cheeks flushed, Faure waved both hands indignantly. "But you are not a nation! Two thousand people do not make a nation! You can't even exist by yourselves without supplies from Earth. It is as if a group of people on an ocean liner declared themselves an independent nation. It is nonsense!"

"We are self-sufficient," Joanna insisted. "We produce our own food. We can exist on our own without any help from Earth." That was stretching things, she knew, and yet a part of her mind marvelled at the realization that the stretch was not all that much. Moonbase could exist without help from Earth.

Faure made a visible effort to calm himself. "Madame Brudnoy, you know and I know that this so-called declaration of independence is nothing more than a smoke screen, the camouflage to disguise the fact that you wish to continue using nanotechnology and evade the conditions of the treaty."

"But you intend to continue using nanotechnology once you've taken over Moonbase," Joanna said.

Once he heard her words, Faure's face went from red to white, as if someone had slapped him.

He took a deep breath, then said evenly, "What makes you think that?"

Smiling, Joanna replied, "Don't you think I have contacts inside Yamagata Corporation? Several of the board members of Masterson Corporation are also on Yamagata's board."

Faure sat in silence for several moments. Then he made a little shrug and admitted, "It is entirely possible that we will allow some work on nanomachines to continue, once we have taken over operation of Moonbase."

"Moonbase will continue to supply water to Nippon One," Joanna said flatly, not making a question of it.

Reluctantly, Faure nodded.

"And Moonbase will continue to manufacture spacecraft using nanomachines," she added.

"Only temporarily," Faure replied once he heard her words. "You have contracts with various international transport companies. The United Nations will see that those contractual obligations are fulfilled."

"Of course," said Joanna graciously. "And by the time all our backlog orders have been filled, the United Nations will find that nanomanufacturing can be quite profitable. And not harmful in the slightest. Right?"

Faure leaned tensely toward the camera. "Madame Brudnoy, the nanotechnology treaty exists because of the fears that nanomachines have created. Your own husband was killed by nanomachines, was he not?"

Joanna kept herself from flinching. I should have expected that, she told herself.

Without pausing, Faure went on, "Nanotechnology can produce insidious weapons, deadly weapons. Nanomachines can kill, as you well know. A mistake, an error, and runaway nanomachines could devour everything in their path, like those armies of ants in South America that devastate entire landscapes and leave nothing alive in their wake."

His mustache bristling with fervor, Faure continued, "We cannot have nanomachines on Earth! No matter what glorious benefits they promise, we cannot take the risk that they present to us."

"But we're not on the Earth. You could allow nanomanufacturing here on the Moon," said Joanna.

He replied, "I am willing to allow it on a temporary, experimental basis—under United Nations control."

With sudden understanding, Joanna said, "Because Yamagata insisted on it. And if Yamagata didn't go along with you, then the Japanese government would oppose your takeover of Moonbase, and you can't afford to have them against you."

She realized that that was the truth of it. If Japan opposed Faure's plans, a whole bloc of opposition would arise in the U.N.

"You are very perspicacious," Faure said. He leaned back in his chair, seemed to relax. "But the facts are that Japan supports my efforts and the Peacekeepers will be landing at Moonbase in less than twenty hours. Fait accompli!"

"And who's going to run Moonbase after the Peacekeepers land?"

Once Faure heard her question, he smiled like the Chesire cat. "Why, who else but specialists from Yamagata Corporation?"

Joanna could not have been more stunned if Faure had leaped across the quarter-million miles separating them and punched her. She simply sat in her armchair, mouth hanging open, while Faure smiled his widest at her.

TOUCHDOWN MINUS 17 HOURS 38 MINUTES

Dr. Hector Montana was not known for his bedside manner. He was a brusque, no-nonsense physician who had spent most of his career dealing with factory workers, construction crews, and industrial accidents. He was a capable surgeon and, thanks to Moonbase's electronic communications systems, he could consult and even work with virtually any physician on Earth.

Until the war sprang up.

Now he scowled openly at the young couple sitting tensely before his desk. He was a slim, pinch-faced man with graying hair combed straight back off his low forehead. His skin was the color of sun-dried adobe. His profile looked as if it had been carved by an ancient Mayan: high cheekbones, prominent nose.

"Pregnant." He made the word sound like an accusation.

"Yes," said Claire Rossi. "There's no doubt about it."

"I'm not an obstetrician."

"Yes, but we thought you should know."

O'Malley spoke up, "I want to make sure she gets the best medical attention possible."

"Then you should've taken some precautions beforehand," Dr. Montana snapped. "We don't have facilities for this sort of thing here."

Nick bulled his shoulders forward slightly, matching the physician's frown with one of his own. "We don't need facilities, for god's sake. I just want to see that she gets the proper care."

"I can't even get in touch with other medical centers back on Earth," Montana grumbled. "We've been blacked out."

"Surely this emergency will be over with soon enough for me to go back Earthside," said Claire. As chief of the personnel department, she knew Moonbase's policy perfectly well. Pregnant women were shipped back Earthside before their pregnancies became so advanced that rocket flight was not recommended.

"And what if it isn't?" Montana snapped.

"Then you'll have to take care of her," O'Malley said, with more than a hint of belligerence in his voice. "You're a doctor, aren't you?"

"You want my considered medical advice? Abort it. Get rid of it now, to be on the safe side. There's no telling how long this stupid blockade is going to last."

"We can't!" O'Malley said.

"You're young enough to have a dozen babies. This one is bad timing, that's all."

"I won't," Claire said quietly.

"You're both Catholic, is that it?" Montana's voice softened slightly. "I am too. The Church won't—"

"We're not going to have an abortion," O'Malley said, his voice darkening. "And that's final."

Montana huffed at him. "Well, maybe the Peacekeepers will take over the base and send us all back home."

TOUCHDOWN MINUS 12 HOURS 22 MINUTES

Doug stood atop a house-sized boulder and watched the drivers park their tractors on the three unoccupied landing pads of the rocket port. The half-built Clippership that had been towed onto the fourth pad gleamed in the starlight.

Jinny Anson, recognizable by the bright rings of butter yellow on the arms of her bulky spacesuit, stood beside him.

"Okay," her voice said in his helmet earphones, "we clutter up the landing pads so they can't use 'em. But they can still put down on the crater floor just about anywhere they want to."

Doug nodded inside his helmet. Jinny was right. Alphonsus' floor was flat enough for a Clippership to set down. The ground was cracked with rilles, pockmarked with small craters and strewn with rocks, but there were plenty of open spaces where a good pilot could make a landing.

"All you're doing is forcing 'em to set down a kilometer or so farther away from our main airlock," Anson went on. "What good's that going to do?"

"Maybe none," Doug admitted. "But I sure as hell don't intend to let them use our landing pads."

He sensed Anson shrugging inside her suit.

"Jinny, it's just about the only chance we've got, other than just folding up and surrendering."

"That damned Quebecer wants to turn the base over to Yamagata?" Anson asked for the fortieth time.

"That's what he told my mother."

"Son of a bitch." She pronounced each word distinctly, with feeling.

"Come on, let's get inside," Doug said. "They're finished here and I want to see how far Zimmerman and Cardenas have gotten along."

The nanotech lab was a series of workshops set along one of the old Moonbase tunnels. The rooms were interconnected by airtight hatches, and that entire section of corridor could be sealed off from the rest of the base, if necessary. Each workshop room and the corridor outside had powerful ultraviolet lamps running along their bare rock ceilings, capable of disabling any of the virus-sized nanomachines that might have inadvertently been released to float in the air. The floors and walls were strung with buried wires that could generate a polarizing current that would also deactivate any stray nanomachines.

These safety systems were turned on at the end of every working day, to guarantee that no nanomachines infected the rest of the base. The containment worked. Although nanomachines were assembled constantly for tasks as diverse as ferreting oxygen atoms out of the regolith and building spacecraft structures of pure diamond out of carbon dust from asteroids, there had been no runaway "gray goo" of nanomachines devouring everything in their path, no plagues of nanobug diseases.

Over the years Professors Cardenas and Zimmerman and their assistants had developed nanomachines for medical uses. Moonbase employees regularly received nano injections to scrub plaque from their blood vessels and to augment their natural immune systems. In a closed environment such as the underground base, nanotherapy helped to prevent epidemics that might endanger the entire population. It was a standing joke that people returned from Moonbase healthier than they arrived. No one in Moonbase even had the sniffles, except for those few who were allergic to the ubiquitous lunar dust.

And the Cardenas/Zimmerman team was working on that.

Or had been, until the U.N. crisis erupted.

Doug went to Cardenas. Zimmerman would see no one; he had locked himself in his lab with orders that he could not, must not, would not be disturbed under any circumstances whatsoever.

"It's my fault," Kris Cardenas told Doug. "I teased Willi that afternoon you came to us in the university studio, told him he ought to figure out how to make a person invisible."

"That's what he's working on?"

Cardenas nodded.

"But what help is that going to be?"

She shrugged. "Leave him alone. While he's pushing down that line he'll probably come up with one or two other things that'll be really useful."

Doug started to object, but Cardenas added, "It won't do you any good to try to get him onto another track. He'll just bluster and roar and go right back to what he wants to do."

"I know," Doug admitted ruefully.

"Let me show you what we've accomplished," Cardenas said, leading Doug to the massive gray metal tubing of the high-voltage scanning probe electron microscope that stood at one end of the lab table.

The two scientists working at the table made room for them. Cardenas peered at the microscope's display screen briefly, made a small adjustment on a roller dial, then turned smiling to Doug.

"Take a look."

The display screen showed a swarm of dots surrounding a flat grayish thing. The gray material was shrinking rapidly. The dots seemed to be devouring it like a pack of scavengers tearing apart a bleeding carcass.

"We've revived an old idea," Cardenas said as he watched. "Something we were working on more than twenty years ago, back Earthside."

Slowly, Doug backed away from the screen and looked into her brilliant blue eyes. "Gobblers," he whispered.

"Right. This particular set is programmed to disassemble carbon-based molecules . . ." Her voice trailed off as she saw the expression on Doug's face and realized that it had been gobblers, from her own lab in San Jose, that had killed Doug's father up on Wodjohowitcz Pass.

"Oh!" she said, fingers flying to her lips.

Doug fought the memory. It had happened before he'd been born. He'd been eighteen when he finally discovered that his half-brother Greg had used gobbler nanomachines to murder Paul Stavenger. That's all in the past, Doug told himself. Greg's been dead for seven years and it's all over and there's nothing you or anybody else can do to change the past.

"It's all right," he said brusquely to Cardenas. "I was just . . . it just caught me unaware, that's all."

"I had forgotten," Cardenas said, her voice low, trembling slightly. "Twenty-five years ago . . ."

"It's all right," he repeated. Taking a deep breath, he tried to bury the past and concentrate on the present. "By the time the Peacekeepers land, though, the Sun will be up and the nanomachines will go into estivation, won't they?"

"We can program a batch to work at high temperature."

"What about the UV?"

Cardenas nodded and leaned her butt on the edge of the work bench. "It's pretty intense in sunlight, yeah. But I think we can work around it."

"We don't want a set of nanobugs that can't be turned off," Doug warned.

She almost smiled. "Scared of the gray goo?"

"Aren't you?"

"Uh-huh." She lowered her head a moment, thinking. "Look, when the ship lands, what actually touches the ground?"

"Four landing pads. They're about two meters in diameter and twenty, thirty centimeters thick."

"And made of diamond?"

Doug nodded. "Their surfaces and internal bracing are diamond. There're some hydraulic lines inside them."

"The hydraulics are oil-based?"

"As far as I know, yes. I could check with the manufacturing division to make sure."

"Okay," Cardenas said, walking slowly away from the electron microscope. Doug followed in step beside her.

"The ship lands, right?" she said, thinking out loud. "Its landing pads come down on top of our gobblers. Covers them up, so they're no longer in sunlight. And they're shielded from the UV."

"I get it. Then they can eat their way inside the landing pads and start taking the hydraulic system apart."

"You got it."

Doug broke into a grin, but it faded before it was truly started. "Only one problem, Kris."

"What's that?"

"What good's it going to do us to prevent their Clippership from leaving the Moon? We want to stop them from getting here."

TOUCHDOWN MINUS 11 HOURS 45 MINUTES

Zoltan Kadar sat bleary-eyed in the middle of his monitoring screens, almost in tears as he squinted at the drawing of the farside observatory. A beautiful dream, he told himself. My crowning achievement. It would be called the Kadar Observatory some day.

But it's only a dream. I can't even get an observation satellite to survey the ground.

For more than three days and three sleepless nights Kadar had hounded Doug Stavenger, to no avail. Most of his calls were intercepted by Jinny Anson, who sternly told him not to bother Stavenger.

"He's got too much to do, Zoltan, to worry about your satellite shot."

Twice he actually got to Stavenger himself, by tracking down Doug's movements through the length and breadth—and depth—of Moonbase.

The first time, he accosted Stavenger as Doug was talking with the technicians in the control center. Doug listened patiently to Kadar's complaints, then gripped the astronomer's slim shoulder.

"Dr. Kadar—"

"*Professor* Kadar!"

Doug almost laughed in his face. "Professor Kadar, I understand how upset and frustrated you must feel. But you're not the only one. All our outside activities have been shut down, except for our preparations for defending Moonbase against the Peacekeepers. I'm afraid your survey of Farside is just going to have to wait."

And with that, a solidly-built grim-faced black man took Kadar's other arm and firmly led him to the door. Kadar glared at him, and when that didn't work, he stared at the man's nametag on his shirt front.

"Mr. Gordette," Kadar said with as much dignity as he could muster, "there is no need for you to leave your fingerprints on my arm."

Gordette released him. "Sorry," he muttered. "Just wanted to make sure you leave Doug alone. He's got a lot to do, you know."

"So I've been told."

Late that night, Kadar actually got Stavenger on the phone. If I can't sleep, Kadar told himself, why should he?

But Stavenger didn't seem to be sleeping. His image came up immediately on the smart wall of Kadar's quarters. Stavenger was sitting at a desk in his own quarters, wide awake.

"Dr. Kadar," Doug said as soon as he recognized his caller's face.

"I'm sorry to call so late—"

"It doesn't matter. I was just going over our inventories of supplies."

"My satellite is ready for launch," Kadar said. "All I need is your approval and—"

"With all due respect, Professor Kadar, there's no chance in hell of your getting your satellite launched until this crisis with the Peacekeepers is resolved."

"It's only one small rocket. They'll see that it's going into a lunar orbit."

"I'm not going to debate the point, Professor. No launch."

"You're standing in the way of science!"

Wearily, Doug replied, "Maybe I am. It can't be helped. If it's any consolation, there are a lot of other frustrated people in the base right now. We've got a whole troupe of ballet dancers here who can't return Earthside until this mess is resolved."

Ballet dancers did not assuage Kadar's feelings. But as he sat amid his monitoring screens, admiring the drawings of what would someday be the Kadar Observatory on the far side of the Moon, he suddenly realized that frustrated ballet dancers might be more appreciative of his predicament than the management of Moonbase.

Ballet dancers. Kadar pulled himself up from his console chair and headed for his quarters. A shower, a shave, some clean clothes—if I must spend this crisis in frustration, perhaps there is a charming ballerina or two who can understand me and offer consolation.

TOUCHDOWN MINUS 9 HOURS 45 MINUTES

"I've never felt so frustrated in my whole life!" Joanna slapped her palm against the ornate little table that stood at the end of her couch.

Startled, Lev Brudnoy looked across the room at her.

"No one answers my calls," Joanna complained. "No one even acknowledges that they've received my calls! It's like shouting into a deep, dark mine shaft!"

Brudnoy turned off the wall display he had been studying, got up from his chair and went to sit beside his wife.

"Faure's people are in control of the commsats," he said gently. "Most probably they are not letting your messages get through to Earth."

"But I've beamed calls directly to the World Court in The Hague. I've even had our own people in Savannah relay my messages to Holland. No response. Not even a flicker."

Brudnoy shrugged his bony shoulders. "Faure isn't going to let the World Court consider our claim of independence until his Peacekeepers have taken control of Moonbase."

"And turned it over to Yamagata to operate," Joanna growled.

"Yes, I suppose so."

Fists clenched, Joanna jumped to her feet and started striding across the furniture-crowded living room. "That little turd! He's in with Yamagata. It's been a Yamagata operation all along, from the very beginning. They'll end up operating Moonbase under a U.N. contract and we'll be out in the cold."

"Expropriated," muttered Brudnoy.

"It's illegal! It's illegal as hell! But he's going to get away with it."

"How is your board of directors taking this?"

She glared at him. "I've asked for an emergency meeting of the board, but they're taking their sweet time getting everybody together."

"Perhaps—"

"They *know* Doug can't live on Earth!" Joanna blurted. "He'll be a marked man."

"We'll be able to protect him," Brudnoy assured her.

But Joanna shook her head. "No, they'll get to him. Fanatics. Assassins. Just because he's got nanomachines in his body, they'll kill him, sooner or later."

"Zimmerman won't be safe from the nanoluddites, either," Brudnoy pointed out. With a sigh, he added, "None of us will."

"We *can't* let them send us back to Earth, Lev! It'd be a death sentence for Doug, for Zimmerman, for all of us!"

"If only—"

The phone chime interrupted Brudnoy.

"Answer," Joanna snapped.

The phone's computer voice said, "Call from Mr. Rashid, in Savannah."

"Put him on!"

Ibrahim al-Rashid's swarthy face with its trim little

beard appeared on the wallscreen. To Brudnoy, the man looked like the crafty pirate chieftain of his childhood tapes.

He smiled at Joanna. "You'll be pleased to know that the emergency board meeting is scheduled to start in ten minutes."

Joanna sank back onto the couch beside her husband. "Good," she breathed. "Good."

TOUCHDOWN MINUS 8 HOURS 57 MINUTES

Rashid hated these electronic meetings. He sat at the head of the nearly-empty board table while the walls around him displayed the images of directors who were in their homes or offices in California, London, Buenos Aires, the middle of the Pacific Ocean—and one, of course, on the Moon.

Only three of Masterson Corporation's directors lived close enough to Savannah to come to this emergency meeting in person, and one of them had to be ferried by a special medevac tiltrotor plane because he was on life support, awaiting a heart transplant.

"We have got to get the World Court to issue an injunction to stop the Peacekeepers from invading Moonbase!" Joanna was saying, her voice urgent, somewhere between cajoling and pleading.

McGruder, the old man on life support, wheezing through his clear plastic oxygen mask, said testily, "The World Court doesn't work that way. They have no power to issue injunctions or control the Peacekeepers."

"Only Faure can direct the Peacekeepers," said the

director from London, a well-preserved matron whom Rashid had pursued amorously from time to time.

"With the oversight of the General Assembly," the man from California added. "If they don't like the way he's handling things, they can override him or even replace him."

Fat chance, Rashid thought.

Tamara Bonai, sitting on her patio on Tarawa with palm trees behind her swaying in the trade wind, asked, "But what about the news media? Couldn't we put some pressure on the U.N. by exposing this plot to the media?"

Rashid said, "Most of the world's media has been effectively muzzled by Faure. Here in the United States the media executives I've talked to tend to see this as a struggle between a giant corporation—which is bad by definition—against the poor people of the world, represented by Faure and the U.N."

Joanna's anguished face almost filled the far wall of the board room, like a giant portrait or a hovering djinn.

"Do you mean that they're ignoring our declaration of independence?" Joanna demanded.

"Yes," said Rashid, dipping his chin slightly. "They see it as a transparent ploy of Masterson Corporation to maintain control of Moonbase and continue using nanotechnology."

The meeting room fell silent. What Rashid had told his board was not entirely true, he knew. Yes, the media executives he had spoken with knew that Masterson still controlled Moonbase, despite the legal fiction that the base was owned by the Kiribati Corporation. Tamara Bonai's beauty and earnestness were not enough to disguise the maneuver that the Moonbase people had pulled to evade the nanotech treaty. But when Rashid had met with his friends among the news media in New York to brief them on the Moonbase situation, he had conveniently overlooked the independence angle.

And from all the communications beamed from Moonbase to Masterson corporate headquarters in Savannah, Rashid had carefully excised all mention of independence before sending them on to the news outlets.

Of all the members of Masterson's board of directors, Rashid was the least surprised to learn that Yamagata was behind Faure's grab of Moonbase. Let them have Moonbase, he thought. We still have the patents on the Clipperships. Let Yamagata manufacture them with nanomachines on the Moon; we will still get the patent royalties and our costs will drop to zero. Nothing but profit for us.

And, of course, sooner or later Yamagata will want to initiate a merger with Masterson Corporation. That's when I will become wealthy enough to retire in true style.

Joanna's insistent voice snapped him out of his pleasant reverie.

"Once the Peacekeeper troops land here and take over the base we won't have a chance of stopping Faure from turning Moonbase over to Yamagata."

"We will be compensated for the takeover," Rashid pointed out.

And now we have to wait three infernal seconds for her reply, he grumbled to himself.

Joanna stared down the length of conference table at him, her eyes ablaze. "Compensated? You mean it's all right with you if Faure screws us as long as he pays for the pleasure?"

Rashid's own temper rose, but he maintained his composure. "I believe it is an ancient piece of oriental wisdom, Joanna: When rape is unavoidable, you might as well relax and enjoy it."

Joanna stared into Rashid's beady eyes and battled with every ounce of self-control she possessed to keep from screaming at him.

All across the walls of her living room, the images of the board members were watching her, some sympathetic, some apathetic, a few looking tense with apprehension.

"Omar," she said, deliberately using Rashid's belittling nickname, "you might enjoy getting raped, but I don't, and I don't think the other members of this board do, either."

Raising her voice slightly, she said, "I move we take a vote of confidence in our chairman."

For three tense seconds she waited for a response. None came. No one seconded her motion. Brudnoy, sitting off in a corner of the room where the camera could not pick him up, looked at her with growing pain in his expression.

That's it, Joanna told herself. Rashid's in control of the board and I'm not. He's been using this crisis to solidify his position and undercut mine.

"Very well," Joanna said at last. "It's clear that this board is not going to support Moonbase. We'll have to defend ourselves in spite of you."

When Rashid heard her words he smiled thinly. "And how to you propose to defend Moonbase, may I ask?"

"We'll fight with everything we've got!"

Rashid's smile widened. "You sound like Churchill after Dunkirk, Joanna. 'We shall fight them on the beaches and the landing fields. We shall fight them in the cities and the streets.' Do you intend to turn Moonbase into a battlefield?"

"If I have to," she snapped.

Before Rashid could respond she added, "Churchill won his war. I intend to win mine."

And she banged the manual switch that cut off the transmission. The smart walls went dark.

Brudnoy got up from his chair and walked across the small room to sit beside his wife. "At the end of that famous speech that Churchill gave," he said, "he supposedly added, under his breath, that the British would have to throw beer bottles at the Nazis, because that's all they had left to fight with."

Joanna looked into his sad eyes.

"We don't even have beer bottles, I'm afraid," Brudnoy said softly.

"I know," said Joanna, fighting back the tears that wanted to fill her eyes. "I know."

TOUCHDOWN MINUS 6 HOURS 11 MINUTES

Captain Munasinghe pushed the plastic plug deeper into his ear and waited impatiently for his laptop to finish decoding the message from New York.

At last the computer's synthesized voice said, "Commander-in-Chief, United Nations Peacekeeping Forces to Commander, Lunar Expeditionary Force: Urgent and Top Secret. Message begins. Latest intelligence on enemy intentions. Sources indicate Moonbase will resist your force with all means available to them. You are advised to take every precaution and to be prepared for armed resistance. Message ends."

Munasinghe nodded to himself and glanced at the American newswoman sitting across the aisle from him. She seemed deep in earnest conversation over her own comm link back to Earth.

He floated out of his chair, fighting back the queasiness that still assailed him whenever he moved. Hovering in the aisle next to his second-in-command, he said, "Start them checking their weapons."

"Now?" The Norwegian lieutenant blinked his ice-blue eyes at Munasinghe. "We still have six hours before touchdown."

"Now," Munasinghe said firmly. "I want the grenades and other explosives checked out and parcelled among the troops. All guns checked. Then start them getting into their spacesuits. We must be prepared for hostile

action the instant we land. Fully armed and fully
prepared."

Edith Elgin was furious.

"What do you mean you can't run the interview?" she
hissed into the pin mike that almost touched her lips.

The spacecraft was so far from Earth that it took seconds for her boss' answer to come back to her.

"The decision was made on the twentieth floor, Edie.
Nothing I can do about it."

"But the captain as much as admitted that they're
going in shooting!" Edith wanted to shout, but she had
to whisper. It made the whole situation doubly frustrating. "He'd just as soon blast Moonbase with a nuke, if
he had one."

Again the agonizing wait. "Don't you think I want to
run the piece, Edie? It's great stuff. But my hands are
tied! The suits upstairs want to play ball with Faure and
the Peacekeepers. At least for now."

Yeah, Edie said to herself. And after this bloodthirsty
captain wipes out Moonbase, the suits will want the interview burned because it'll show what shitheads they
are.

"They're coming right down the pipe," said the landing controller.

Doug leaned over her shoulder and looked at her
radar screen. Only one blip, the Peacekeepers' Clippership. It was precisely aligned on the grid of thin glowing lines that represented Moonbase's landing corridor.
The spaceport control complex was dark and empty except for this one console. Still, Doug felt the tension that
the solitary blip generated.

"You've told them that all four pads are occupied?"
Doug asked.

"Yep," the controller replied without turning from
her screen.

"No response from them?"

"Not a peep. They're not gonna turn around just because we haven't laid out the welcome mat for them."

"No," Doug admitted. "I guess not."

"Six hours, four minutes," the controller said, pointing to the digital time display on her console.

"Keep sending them the message. I don't want them to crash on landing."

The controller turned in her little chair and looked up at him for the first time. "Why the hell not?" she asked.

The mercenary was sweating as he slipped the fingernail-sized chip into the computer on the desk in his quarters. Electronic germ warfare, he thought: a computer virus.

He was far from being a computer expert, but the chip he had carried in the heel of a shoe was supposed to be totally self-sufficient. Just get access to the right program and stick the chip's virus into it. Easy, they had told him. Still, the mercenary sweated as he worked his way into the guarded programs that ran Moonbase's vital systems.

It had been no big deal to ferret out the necessary passwords and coded instructions. Security at Moonbase was a joke. A couple of rounds of expensive real beer, hauled up from Earthside, and a guy was your buddy for life, even if you were black.

The computer program that ran Moonbase's electrical distribution system was an expert system, with built-in fault diagnosis. The virus was designed to infiltrate the fault diagnosis subprogram and indicate that a dangerous overvoltage had suddenly appeared in the main trunk that connected the solar farms with the base transformers. That would cause the computer to lower the voltage throughout Moonbase: a brown-out. When the virus insisted that the voltage was still too high, the computer would be forced to shut down the main distribution system altogether and throw Moonbase onto its backup fuel cell systems, which were good for only twelve hours, maximum.

By the time they debugged the computer, the Peacekeepers would be running the base.

The only light in the mercenary's quarters was the glow from the display screen, projecting onto his face the multicolored lines and nodes of the distribution system's schematic diagram like the warpaint of a Sioux brave.

SYSTEM ANOMALY DETECTED

The mercenary nodded to himself. You bet you got a system anomaly, he said silently to the computer.

CHECKING SYSTEM ANOMALY

Go right ahead and check your ass off, he told the machine. Check yourself into a nervous breakdown.

SYSTEM ANOMALY REJECTED

"What?" he yelped aloud. He jabbed at the keyboard, expanding the message.

Goddamn, he said to himself. The display screen showed that the program had automatically checked the overvoltage message against independent sensors built into the electrical lines and decided that the message was false.

VIRUS LOCATED, the display screen announced, with no emotion whatever.

VIRUS ELIMINATED

The mercenary banged his fist on the console hard enough to make the screen blink. Damn! he said to himself. Goddamn virus they gave me isn't worth shit. Fuckin' expert system is smarter than the fuckin' virus.

He tried to insert the virus twice more, and both times the fault diagnosis subprogram identified the virus and erased it. Wondering if the program kept a record of attempts to bug it, and if so, whether it automatically notified the security department, the mercenary angrily yanked the chip from the computer slot and decided to toss it into the garbage reprocessor.

That's all it's good for, he thought. Garbage.

He slumped down on his bunk and turned on the wall-screen. Stavenger was piping the radar plot from the landing control complex onto the base's general information channel. Less than six hours until the Peacekeepers landed.

He's a strange one, thought the mercenary. He's a couple years younger than me, but he's old beyond his years. Or maybe it's just that most guys his age haven't faced any real responsibilities, so they still act like kids.

Stavenger knows what responsibility is. Got to respect him for that. Like me, a little. We both know what it feels like to have a load on your shoulders.

Over the past several days there had been four times when he had been alone with Stavenger, when he could have snapped Stavenger's neck or driven the cartilage of his nose into his brain with a single sharp blow from the heel of his hand. Stavenger would be dead before he hit the floor.

Yet the mercenary had stayed his hand. Not yet, he had told himself. Don't kill him yet. Let the virus do the job. He's not ready to die.

But the virus has failed. Now it's up to me.

Stavenger did not act like a man seeking death. The young man brimmed with life, with energy and purpose. Wait, the mercenary advised himself, wait until the precise moment.

They were so unprepared to fight, these men and women of Moonbase, so totally lacking in weapons and skills and even the will to resist, that the mercenary found it almost laughable. Why kill Stavenger or any of the rest of them when the Peacekeepers will be able to walk in here and take over without firing a shot?

Wait. Watch and wait. If it actually comes down to a fight, then that will be the time to take out Stavenger and as many of the others as he could reach.

It would be a shame, though. He was getting to like Stavenger. Almost.

TOUCHDOWN MINUS 4 HOURS 4 MINUTES

Loosely restrained by her seat harness, so that she floated lightly in her seat, hardly touching its plastic surface, Edith looked across the Clippership's aisle at the man sitting beside Captain Munasinghe. He was a civilian, and a few hours after they had lifted off from Corsica he had made a point of introducing himself: Jack Killifer.

He was coming on to her, but Edith frosted him off with a polite smile and buried her nose in her notebook computer. I'm not spending the next four days getting groped by some stranger in front of forty soldiers, she decided.

There was something grim about him. He didn't seem fazed in the slightest by the zero gee of spaceflight, the way Munasinghe and the other troopers were. Instead he looked as if he were impatient to get to Moonbase and get the job over with. A lean, lantern-jawed, intense man, Edith thought. A man with a personal agenda.

The personnel list in her notebook gave only his name and place of residence: Boston, Massachusetts. Well, that's a starting point, Edith thought. She went hunting through the background database that she had put together before leaving Atlanta. And soon she found his history, in the material that her source in the Masterson Corporation had given her.

Killifer had been a Masterson employee, she saw. Worked for eighteen years at Moonbase, coming back to Earth only long enough for the mandatory health checks and then shipping back to the Moon immediately. Then, seven years ago, he had abruptly taken early retirement and never went back to Moonbase again. Until now.

Digging deeper, Edith found that Killifer had become an executive in the New Morality movement, one of the key pressure groups that pushed the nanotech treaty through the U.N. and got the U.S. Senate to ratify it.

He's anti-nanotechnology, Edith realized. But, glancing at him across the aisle, she thought he looked as if he had personal demons driving him. There's more to it than a religious conviction, she thought. I wonder what's really itching him?

It was boring as hell sitting in the damned Clippership with nothing to do but listen to Munasinghe's nitpicking worries. Killifer had spent as much time as he could roaming through the ship, but it only took ten minutes to see everything there was to see. The passenger cabin, filled with a mongrel lot of Peacekeeper troops, most of whom couldn't even speak English. The galley, where their tasteless prepacked meals were microwaved. The cargo bays, stuffed with enough weapons to blow Moonbase into orbit. The head, with the seatbelt and stirrups on the unisex toilet.

He thought about popping into the cockpit, but he figured that the astronauts up there weren't looking for company, and there wouldn't be all that much to see, anyway. It's crowded enough here in the passenger cabin, Killifer told himself, friggin' cockpit's about the size of a shoe box.

There was only one bright spot in the whole mess, and that was the good-looking blond reporter sitting across the aisle from him. Killifer had tried to strike up a conversation with her, but she didn't seem interested.

Yet now, as he sat wedged in beside the ever-whining Munasinghe, she seemed to be giving him the once-over. Killifer laughed to himself. After four days in this sardine can she must be getting horny.

*   *   *

Only about four hours to go, Edith thought. I can handle Killifer for that long. So she smiled the next time he looked her way and, sure enough, as soon as Munasinghe left his seat to see to some problem, Jack Killifer unstrapped and floated out into the aisle beside her.

"Boring trip, isn't it?" he said, grinning down at her wolfishly.

Edith turned up the wattage on her smile a little. "I'd rather be bored than scared to death."

Without asking, Killifer pulled himself into the empty seat beside her. "It won't be long now," he said.

"You've been to Moonbase before, haven't you?" Edith prompted, as she quietly clicked on the audio recorder built into her electronic notebook.

Killifer huffed. "Spent the better part of eighteen years there."

"Eighteen years?" she said, wide-eyed. "Wow! You must have been there right at the very beginning."

"I sure was. Lemme tell you . . ."

That was all it took to get Killifer talking about himself and Moonbase. But as he talked, the dark brooding anger that simmered inside him started to rise to the surface.

"Joanna Stavenger," he growled. "She's the bitch that runs the whole thing up there."

"I thought Douglas Stavenger was in charge of Moonbase," Edith said innocently.

"Hah! Maybe he thinks he's in charge, but it's his mama who's the real boss. The spider woman."

"Isn't her name Brudnoy now?"

"Sure," Killifer answered. "He's her third husband, you know. The first two died on her."

"Really?"

He chuckled unpleasantly. "I wonder how long this one'll last."

Edith asked, "Douglas Stavenger . . . isn't he the one who has the nanomachines in his body? He was nearly killed on the Brennart expedition to the south lunar pole, wasn't he?"

"I was on that expedition," Killifer said. "I was Brennart's right-hand man."

"Really? Wow!"

For nearly four hours Killifer gabbled away and Edith realized that his nanoluddite leanings were merely the surface manifestation of a deep hatred for Joanna Brudnoy and her son, Doug Stavenger.

TOUCHDOWN MINUS 2 HOURS 38 MINUTES

Sitting alone in his office, Doug watched the smart wall's view of the crater floor, where teams of spacesuited men and women were desperately setting up microwave transmission equipment to back up the hard-wire system that carried electrical power from the solar farms to the base's electrical distribution center.

The microwave transmitters were dark, flat plates, innocuous looking. They were aimed at relay transceivers being set up atop the ringwall mountains, a circuitous route that Doug and his cohorts hoped would fool the Peacekeepers. They can blow the wires, he told himself, but they won't recognize the backup equipment for what it is.

For maybe half an hour, a sardonic voice in his head sneered. They're not dummies. They'll figure it out soon enough.

It's the best we can do, Doug admitted silently. It's the best we can do.

Nervously, a feeling of dread gripping him like the freezing hand of death itself, Doug programmed the smart walls to show him every square centimeter of

Moonbase. He inspected each of the corridors, the water factory, the environmental control center, the rocket port, the solar farms and the mass driver out on the crater floor, the labs, the workshops, the Cave, where a handful of people were taking a meal in desultory silence, the control center, where tense men and women monitored every part of the base.

"Hold there," he said.

The walls froze on a panoramic view of the garage. It had been a natural cave in the mountainside, enlarged and smoothed over by Moonbase construction crews. Now it served as a shelter for the tractors that worked out on the surface, a storage area, even a playing arena for the annual low-gee basketball matches. It also served as a buffer between the corridors that housed the living and working areas and the airless lunar surface, outside.

Doug leaned back in his swivel chair and stared at the main airlock. Big enough to let tractors through, its heavy metal surface was dulled and scratched from years of constant use. On the other side of the airlock was the open crater floor. On the opposite side of the garage were the smaller airlocks that led to the individual corridors of Moonbase.

A buffer zone.

"Phone!" Doug called out. "Find Jinny Anson, Professor Cardenas, Lev Brudnoy and Leroy Gordette. Urgent priority. Tell them to report to my office *immediately*."

TOUCHDOWN MINUS 1 HOUR 57 MINUTES

"But it's crazy," Anson snapped.

Doug sat straight up in his chair and stared across his desk into her steel-gray eyes. "Jinny, a very smart man once said, 'Just because an idea is crazy doesn't mean it's wrong.'"

"Doesn't mean it's right, either."

"Do you have something better in mind?"

"If we're going to do anything," Brudnoy said, "it should be done out on the crater floor, as far away from us as possible."

"What can we do out there, Lev?"

The Russian thought a moment, then shrugged his shoulders.

Doug looked at Cardenas for support, but she merely sat silently in the slingchair in front of his desk, looking thoughtful. I'm putting a lot on her shoulders, he thought. She doesn't want to commit herself, one way or the other.

He turned to Gordette, sitting off to the side of his desk, slightly separated from the others. "Bam, you're the only one here with any military experience. What do you think?"

Gordette's dark face looked utterly serious. "What do I think? I think you're blowing smoke. All of you. There's no way in hell you can keep those Peacekeeper troops out of here."

Doug broke into a grin, his automatic reaction to a challenge. "We'll see," he said.

"You're going to do it?" Anson asked.

"Yep," said Doug. "We've got less than two hours and we've got to do *something*."

"But it won't work! It'll backfire and—"

"Jinny," Doug interrupted, "I understand that the four of you are against it. But like Lincoln said when his whole cabinet voted against the Emancipation Proclamation and he was the only one in favor: The ayes have it."

TOUCHDOWN MINUS 32 MINUTES

In his cermet spacesuit Doug stood on the rock floor of the garage as the last of the tractors trundled through the open hatch of the main airlock.

"Only thirty-two minutes left," Brudnoy said.

Doug had to turn his whole body to see his stepfather's cardinal-red spacesuit standing beside him.

"We'll make it," he said. "Cardenas is ready to start laying down the bugs."

"For what it's worth, commander, I wish you wouldn't do this. It's too risky." Brudnoy's voice sounded more morose than usual in Doug's earphones.

"I wish I didn't have to do this," Doug admitted, "but I can't see what else gives us a chance to get the Peacekeepers off our backs."

"It won't work."

"Come on, Lev! It's worked for Mother Russia all through history."

Brudnoy was silent for a moment, then he replied, "May I point out that Mother Russia had thousands of kilometers of territory to absorb the invader's armies. We have—what? ten thousand square meters?"

"Forty-three thousand and sixteen," Doug answered promptly. "I checked it in the base plans."

"I should have known you would."

Encased in his bulky spacesuit, Captain Munasinghe had to squeeze through the hatch to get into the cockpit. His eyes widened with sudden terror as he looked past the two astronauts through the narrow forward window. The rugged, bare rock surface of the Moon was hurtling up to meet him.

He swallowed hard, not wanting to show the two astronauts that he was afraid.

Before he could speak, the pilot—in the left seat—told him, "We're programmed to rotate in twelve minutes, so take a good look at the view while you've got the chance."

Munasinghe would rather not. It looked as if they were going to crash and kill everyone aboard.

Forcing his voice to remain even, he asked, "Are you still receiving transmissions from Moonbase?"

"Yeah," said the copilot. "They say all four of their landing pads are occupied and there's no place for us to put down."

"Is that believable?"

"Sure," the pilot said. "Why the hell not?"

The astronauts were both civilians from the transport line that had provided the Clippership to the U.N. For a fat fee, of course. Munasinghe resented their informality with him. True military personnel would have been preferable. And properly respectful.

"Then how will you land?" Munasinghe asked.

"We're coming down on a trajectory that'll put us on their landing pad number three. At T minus fifteen we'll start scanning the Alphonsus crater floor. If all of their pads really are occupied, we'll pick out a smooth area to set down."

"You can do this in fifteen minutes' time?" Munasinghe demanded.

The copilot chuckled. "Don't you fret none. We can do it in fifteen seconds if we have to."

"Fifteen seconds!" Munasinghe's knees went weak at the thought.

The pilot explained, "What he means is, we can hover over the crater floor and pick out our landing site, then jink over to it and sit her down. Nothing to it."

"Piece of cake," said the copilot.

"Ten minutes to rotation," said a synthesized voice from the speaker overhead.

"Enjoy the view while you can," the pilot said to Munasinghe.

"I must get my troops ready," he replied. He thought he heard the astronauts laughing at him as he closed the cockpit hatch behind him.

Edith Elgin felt as if she'd been swallowed by some weird creature made of plastic and metal. The spacesuit helmet smelled kind of like a new car, and she could hear the tiny buzz of air fans from inside the suit, as if there were some gnats droning in there with her.

She had been relieved when Munasinghe's order for everyone to suit up had finally interrupted Killifer's nonstop monologue of hate. With a smirking grin, Killifer had offered to help Edith get into her spacesuit, but she declined as politely as she could manage, unwilling to give the man a chance to play grab-ass with her. Instead, Edith asked two of the women troopers to help her worm into the spacesuit and check out all the seals and connections.

Killifer did not suit up, she saw. He was going to remain aboard the Clippership with the two astronauts in the cockpit.

Looking through the open visor of her helmet, she saw what appeared to be a collection of fat, bulbous snow monsters, all in white, with human faces peeping out at their tops. Funny, she thought: all the times I've been to space stations I've never had to get into a spacesuit. Good thing, too. I must look like a roly-poly eskimo in this outfit.

She knew from her Earthside briefings that the backpack she now wore massed fifty-two kilos. One hundred

and fourteen point four pounds. In zero gravity it
weighed nothing, but Edith was surprised at how difficult
it was to move, once the backpack was loaded onto her.

She saw that she was one of the last people still hovering weightlessly in the cabin's central aisle. Most of
the troopers were back in their seats, spacesuits and
backpacks and all. And weapons. Each trooper carried
a rifle and a bandolier of various types of grenades
strung around their shoulders. One of the women had
explained the different types: concussion, fragmentation,
smoke, and—what was the other one? Oh, yes: flare. It
made a brilliant light that blinded people temporarily.

Slowly, feeling as if she were pregnant with an ele-
phant, Edith pushed herself back into her seat. The
backpack forced her to sit on the front few centimeters
of the chair.

Munasinghe came through the hatch up forward, from
the cockpit. He looked at the watch set into the left cuff
of his suit.

"Touchdown in twenty-three minutes," he announced.

TOUCHDOWN MINUS 15 MINUTES

"All buttoned up," said the chief of the monitoring crew.

Standing behind him, Doug turned his glance from the
chief's set of display screens to the giant electronic wall
schematic of the entire base. Every system was functioning within normal limits, every section of the base was
secure, almost all the personnel were in their quarters
instead of at work, every airtight hatch along each corridor was closed, all the airlocks sealed shut.

Except the main airlock in the now-empty garage.

"They've rotated," said the controller's voice, from the rocket port. "Coming down the pipe."

Doug stared at the radar plot that was displayed on the chief's center screen. Eight smaller screens were arrayed around it, like the compound eye of some strange electronic insect. Each showed a different view.

Leaning over the seated chief's shoulder, Doug said as calmly as he could, "I want to talk to the controller, please."

Wordlessly, the chief touched a keypad on the board of his console and the controller's face suddenly appeared in the upper leftmost of his set of display screens, replacing a view of the crater floor outside.

"I want you to get out of there as soon as they touch down," Doug reminded the controller. "Shut down all your equipment and get back here as fast as you can."

"Don't worry, boss," she said, with a nervous grin, "I'm not gonna hang out here until they barge in, believe it."

The rocket port was more than a kilometer away from the base proper. Its underground chambers were connected to the base by a long, straight tunnel. The plan was for the lone controller to drive the old tractor that was used as a taxi to the base, after shutting down all her systems and sealing the two airlocks that opened onto the crater floor. Once she was safely through the airtight hatch at the Moonbase end of the tunnel, the technicians in the control center would pump the air out of the rocket port facility and the connecting tunnel.

"There they are," said the chief, pointing to a screen on the upper right corner of his complex.

Doug saw a speck of light against the darkness of space, a glint of sunshine reflecting off the curved diamond surface of the Clippership. That ship was built here at Moonbase, he realized. It's returning home.

Swiftly the glimmer took shape. Doug could see the spacecraft was coming down tail-first.

"Still heading for pad three," the controller's voice said, a hint of nervous excitement in her normally laconic tone.

Doug glanced at the screen that showed pad three. A pair of empty tractors sat on it. No way a ship could land there.

"Hovering."

The spacecraft's rocket exhaust glittered bright and hot. The ship hung in emptiness, as if thinking over the whole business.

"Translating."

It moved sideways in a quick series of jerky little bursts. Then it slowly descended on tongues of silent flame, blowing a fair-sized blizzard of dust and grit from the crater floor as it settled.

"Show me the map of their landing site," Doug said to the chief monitor.

"Checking the coordinates . . . there you are."

The geological map of the area where the spacecraft was landing came up on the chief's center screen. It was half a kilometer from the quartet of landing pads. A sinuous rille ran off to the left, like a dry streambed. The ground looked strong enough to hold the spacecraft's weight; no problem there. A few minor craterlets scattered around the area, and the ubiquitous rocks strewn across the ground.

"They're down," came the controller's voice. "I'm splitting."

"Right," said the chief into his lip mike. "Give me a positive call when you close the tunnel airlock behind you."

"Will do."

Doug took a deep breath. Okay, he said to himself. They're down. They're here. Now the fight starts.

TOUCHDOWN

The descent was so smooth that Captain Munasinghe could not tell the precise instant when the ship's landing pads actually touched the ground. He realized that he could feel weight again; after nearly five days in zero gravity it felt almost odd.

As he slowly got up from his seat, awkward in the cumbersome spacesuit, he realized that it *was* odd. He felt weight, yes, but it was very slight. Almost negligible.

The Moon's gravity is only one-sixth that of Earth, he reminded himself. That is why our boots are studded with weights, to keep us from jumping and stumbling when we try to walk.

"Good luck," Killifer said, still sitting in his chair. Munasinghe barely heard his words, muffled by the space-suit helmet. He nodded at Killifer, who had a strange, tight smile on his face. Was he pleased that the troops were going out to take Moonbase? Or pleased that he didn't have to go with them? Probably both, Munasinghe thought.

Sergeants barked commands and his platoon got to their feet and lined up in the central aisle. The news-woman got up, too, and stood beside Munasinghe. He glanced at her. She seemed calm enough.

"You must stay by me at all times," Munasinghe reminded her.

"You bet I will," Edith promised. No smile. No glamour now, inside the spacesuit. She was entirely serious.

His two lieutenants stood at the head of the aisle and

saluted. "The troops are ready for debarkation, sir," said the senior of them, the Norwegian. The other was a short, squat, dour-faced mestizo woman from Peru.

"Visors down," Munasinghe said. "Check the suits for leaks."

"What're they *doing* in there?" Jinny Anson demanded.

A small cluster of people had gathered around Doug and the chief controller: Anson, Lev Brudnoy, Professor Cardenas, even Zimmerman had come out of his lair and found his way to the control center. Doug also saw Gordette hanging on the fringe of the little crowd, watching everything the way an eagle glares out at the world from its aerie.

The controller's central screen showed a telescopic view of the Clippership standing out on the crater floor. The other screens showed interior views of the base: corridors, labs, workshops, the rocket port's underground chambers, the garage—all empty, silent, still.

Brudnoy answered, "I doubt that many of those Peacekeepers have been in space before. They must be checking out their suits very carefully."

"They don't seem very scared of us," Doug muttered.

"Yeah," Anson agreed. "They're not worried we're going to zap their ship."

"Is anything happening?"

They all turned to see Joanna striding into the control center, looking radiant in a clinging metallic gold dress and silk scarf decorated with colorful butterflies.

Zimmerman grunted. He was wearing his usual baggy gray suit; the others were in coveralls or jeans and pullovers.

"You look as if you are going to a party," Zimmerman grumbled.

Joanna gave him a frosty look. "If I'm going to be taken prisoner by Faure's troops, I at least want to look presentable."

Doug almost laughed.

"Hey!" Anson snapped. "Lookit! Both hatches are opening!"

*   *   *

Edith had covered enough military operations to know that all armies operated in the same way: hurry up and wait. Munasinghe's platoon was in the hurry-up mode now.

"Go! Go!" she heard a sergeant's grating yell in her helmet earphones.

The troopers were clumping into the twin airlocks down at the end of the passenger cabin. They could go through the airlocks only one at a time, no matter how loudly their sergeants screamed at them. They moved awkwardly in the spacesuits, and once through the outer airlock hatch they had to negotiate their way down the ladders that led to the ground. Not easy to do, encased in the cumbersome suits and carrying rifle, grenades and ammunition belts.

She and Munasinghe were at the end of the line, the last to go outside. Edith's nose twitched at the metallic tang of the air she was now breathing. It was supposed to be the same mix of oxygen and nitrogen that the ship had been using for the past five days, but somehow it felt drier and colder. It made her nostrils feel raw.

She clumped down the aisle behind Munasinghe in her weighted boots, reaching up to check the minicam she had attached to her helmet. It would show whatever she looked at. If it worked right.

When at last the outer airlock hatch opened, Edith could see that it was brilliant daylight out there. Harsh unfiltered sunshine glared off the rocks and Alphonsus' dusty floor. The Peacekeeper troops were spreading out across the pockmarked floor of the huge crater, moving slowly, cautiously toward the tractors that seemed to be scattered haphazardly across the ground. She noticed a partially-built Clippership sitting out there, too.

"They thought that they would prevent us from landing by placing their machines on the landing pads," Munasinghe said, his voice sounding higher-pitched in her earphones than it had previously. "All they have done is to give us cover from any fire they might aim at us."

Indeed, the farthest troopers had stopped at the

parked tractors, huddling behind them as if expecting to be shot at.

"Your troops are afraid of being fired on?" Edith asked, flicking on the backup recorder at her waist. It was patched in to her suit radio's circuitry.

"We are taking all the necessary precautions," Munasinghe said. "There is no sense taking chances when we face an enemy of unknown capabilities."

"But I thought there weren't any weapons in Moonbase," she prodded.

"That is what our intelligence reports have indicated," Munasinghe admitted. "But nevertheless, it is better to be cautious than surprised."

"What on earth are they doing?" Brudnoy asked, genuine puzzlement in his voice.

Doug turned to Gordette and motioned the black man to his side.

"They're acting as if they expect us to shoot at them, aren't they?" Doug said, half-questioningly.

Gordette nodded solemnly. "They're also setting up fields of fire so they can sweep the area if they have to."

"Absolute nonsense," Joanna huffed.

"They know we don't even have spitballs to throw at 'em," said Anson.

With a tight smile, Gordette replied, "They *think* you don't have anything to throw at them. But they're not taking any chances. Standard operating procedure."

"Their guns can fire in vacuum?" Zimmerman asked.

"No problem. Cartridges' powder is like a solid rocket propellant. They'll fire in vacuum, all right."

"And their impact velocity will be higher than on Earth," Doug added, "because there's no air resistance to slow down the bullet."

"H'mph," Zimmerman grumped.

"Well, are they gonna come in here or just stand outside and have a cookout?" Anson asked.

"They'll be here," Gordette said. "Don't think they won't be."

TOUCHDOWN PLUS 23 MINUTES

Munasinghe saw that his troops were well positioned. Better still, there had been no sign of opposition from Moonbase. The base might just as well be abandoned and empty, for all the resistance they had offered so far.

Good, he thought. The troops had been most vulnerable when they were coming out of the spacecraft. If Moonbase could do us any real harm, that was the moment for it. Now we are on the ground, deployed well, and ready to advance.

He was standing behind a massive bulldozer, its heavy metal body a comforting shield between him and the unknown. The machine had been anodized a brilliant Day-Glo orange, but years of use had dulled its finish and spattered it with gray lunar dust. Munasinghe had been warned about the dust; it clung to everything and got into the hinges of spacesuits. It even clouded spacesuit visors, if you weren't careful. But he estimated that they wouldn't be out in the open long enough for the dust to be a problem.

Off to one side there was an enormous hole in the ground, a deliberate excavation. Some kind of a trap the Moonbasers were trying to build? he wondered. It looked empty, abandoned, whatever it was supposed to be. He decided it could be ignored—and avoided.

His two lieutenants crouched behind him, although they could only bend partway down in their suits. The newswoman had stayed at his elbow all the way from the spacecraft hatch to their present position.

"Very well," he said into his helmet microphone, "our forward command post is established. Now we start the advance to their main airlock."

Peering over the back of the bulldozer, he fumbled for the binoculars clipped to his equipment belt. Even the simplest tasks were troublesome in the bulky gloves. Finally he got the binoculars free, only to bump them jarringly against his visor when he tried to put them up to his eyes.

Hoping that neither his lieutenants nor the newswoman noticed his clumsiness, he held the binoculars steady while their rangefinder automatically focused the optics. Munasinghe made the fine adjustment with a gloved finger and . . .

The airlock hatch was open!

Munasinghe blinked and stared, not quite believing his eyes. The massive metal outer hatch had been swung open. And the inner hatch, as well. He could see the area inside: it was brightly lit. It looked entirely empty.

Of course, he thought. They took all their equipment out of the garage area to place it on the landing pads, hoping to prevent us from landing.

But why would they leave the airlock hatch open? That means the entire garage area must be in vacuum. Is this some sort of trap?

With the press of a thumb he activated the binoculars' rangefinder. Its readout appeared in the lower left of his view in red alphanumerics: one point six-six kilometers.

Munasinghe put the binoculars down and studied the ground between him and the open airlock hatch. Not much cover in the area, only a few small rocks, not enough to shelter a man from enemy fire. But there was no other way to reach the main airlock.

The open hatch bothered Munasinghe.

He pressed the stud on his forearm that opened the comm channel back to the ship and asked for Killifer.

"Killifer here."

"Can you see the main airlock?" Munasinghe asked.

"Yeah. I'm in the cockpit; I can see it on the panel display screen."

"The hatch is open!"

"Yeah. It is."

"What does this mean?" Munasinghe demanded.

"Damned if I know."

"Is it a trap?"

Killifer's voice sounded exasperated. "How the hell should I know? It sure ain't normal operating procedure, I can tell you that much."

Munasinghe thought over the situation for a few moments, wishing he had more information, more options, more time to make a decision. At last he turned to the Norwegian, obviously the taller of his two lieutenants, even in the impersonal spacesuits.

"Move your squad up to the airlock hatch," Munasinghe commanded. "Second squad will cover you."

The lieutenant hesitated only the slightest fraction of a second, then replied, "Yessir."

It looked to Edith as if the airlock hatch was open. She hadn't thought to bring binoculars with her, and she knew Munasinghe wouldn't loan his even if she asked. It was a little hard to see in the glare of the lunar daylight, but she could make out the brightly-lit interior of the base against the dark rock face of the mountainside.

Some of the troops were moving up, hip-hopping in the low gravity when they tried to run, despite their weighted boots.

"Is the airlock open?" she asked Munasinghe.

No answer. He was probably on a different frequency, talking to his troops.

Edith thought it over for half a second, then moved away from Munasinghe, around the corner of the bull-dozer, and headed across the crater floor, following the advancing troops to the airlock hatch.

It *was* open. She could see it clearly now. The first of the troopers had reached the open hatch and stopped, dodging around to its sides where they had some protection if anyone inside the big empty chamber tried to shoot at them.

"Where are you going?" she heard Munasinghe's

voice yelling in her earphones. "Stop! I command you to stop!"

Edith grinned and kept on going toward the open airlock hatch.

TOUCHDOWN PLUS 38 MINUTES

The control center felt hot and stuffy to Doug. Everyone was watching the chief controller's main screen, which showed the spacesuited Peacekeeper troops lumbering warily from the tractors scattered across the crater floor to the edge of the open main airlock.

"They won't go in until their commanding officer comes up and looks around for himself," said Gordette.

Doug licked his lips. "Are you ready?" he asked Kris Cardenas.

Sitting at one of the control center's consoles, she nodded slowly.

"Okay then," Doug told her. "Start the bugs."

"This had better work," Jinny Anson muttered.

"It'll work," Cardenas said as her fingers moved carefully across the console keyboard. But to Doug she sounded a trifle defensive, as if she weren't entirely certain.

Brudnoy quipped, "If it doesn't work we can always surrender."

Joanna gave her husband a disapproving frown.

It was a big empty chamber carved into the mountain, Edith saw. Glareless strip lights ran across the rough rock ceiling. The floor was stained here and there; probably some sort of garage, she figured. But now it's empty and all their vehicles are parked outside.

Not a soul in sight.

And painted on the floor in bright blood-red letters she saw:

WELCOME TO MOONBASE
PLEASE DO NOT ENTER
ROUTINE CLEAN-UP PROCEDURE IN PROGRESS
DANGER! NANOMACHINES IN OPERATION

She stared at the words, neatly stencilled on the smooth rock floor.

Munasinghe's angry voice grated in her earphones. "You were to stay behind me! You had no right to run up here on your own!"

Turning, she saw the captain galumphing awkwardly toward her. Edith grinned inside her helmet: the leader of the troop has to run hard to stay abreast of his troopers.

Ignoring his pique, Edith pointed to the lettering on the garage floor. "Look," she said.

She could not see the captain's face behind his gold-tinted visor, but she imagined his red-rimmed eyes bugging out.

"What does this mean?" Munasinghe was panting from the exertion of running.

"They don't want us to go in."

"Of course! But—nanomachines? What nanomachines? Where is the danger?"

His voice sounded frightened to Edith. Nanomachines had such a bad reputation virtually everywhere on Earth that the mere mention of them was enough to worry almost anyone.

The tall Norwegian, recognizable by the lieutenant's insignia on his nametag, pointed a gloved finger.

"Look!" he said, his voice shaking slightly.

A big grease stain on the garage floor was noticeably shrinking.

And then the stencilled letters of the warning sign started to get ragged around the edges, as if something was chewing on them.

"My god," Munasinghe breathed.

*   *   *

"They're not going into the garage," Brudnoy said.

"Not yet," Gordette replied.

"Do you think they will?" Doug asked him.

Gordette nodded. "They'll fuss around a bit, but they're not going to be stopped by some paint and a few grease stains."

"You don't think so?"

"They'll come in. And once they're past the garage, we've got nothing to stop them."

Munasinghe had to make a decision. Instead of a trap, this was starting to look like a ruse to him. Yes, nanomachines had killed people, he knew, but what danger could nanomachines pose to armed troops encased in spacesuits? This is nothing but a trick, a desperate attempt to keep us from entering Moonbase.

Still, he switched from the suit-to-suit frequency to call Killifer, back at the ship.

"Nanobugs, huh," Killifer said.

"Can they truly be dangerous to us?" Munasinghe demanded.

No answer for several heartbeats. Then, "Well, yeah, if they're programmed to gobble organic molecules."

"What do you mean?"

"If they've spread nanobugs across the garage floor to eat up oil stains and paint and stuff like that, the same bugs might be able to eat up the rubber and plastic materials in your spacesuits."

"Nothing but the soles of our boots will touch the garage floor," Munasinghe said.

"Uh-huh. And what're the soles of your boots made of? Plastics, aren't they? Organic molecules."

"But there is a layer of metal mesh inside the plastic sole."

"Sure. That mesh'll look like a gang of wide-open doorways to the nanobugs. They're the size of viruses, y'know."

"They can rupture our suits, then?"

"Right. And then start chewing on the organic molecules of your bodies."

Munasinghe shuddered involuntarily.

TOUCHDOWN PLUS 51 MINUTES

"They're not coming in!" said Jinny Anson, almost exultant.

"They'll come in," Gordette assured her. "Soon's they work up the nerve."

Doug agreed with him. Sooner or later they would try to get past the garage. He pulled up a wheeled chair and sat beside the chief tech.

"Have you figured out their suit frequency?"

"Yep. Wanna listen to 'em?"

"No. I want to talk to them. Patch me in."

Munasinghe was in an agony of indecision. To come all this way, nearly half a million kilometers, and be stopped by what may be a clever trick—it was intolerable. Worse still, his superiors back at headquarters would never stand for it. Munasinghe saw himself broken, perhaps even cashiered from the Peacekeepers altogether and sent home to rot in shame the rest of his life.

On the other hand, nanomachines could kill. Wasn't that why the U.N. banned them? Wasn't that why they had been sent here to Moonbase in the first place, to stop these renegades from developing deadly nanomachines? How could he order his troopers into such danger?

Munasinghe had been in firefights. He had been shelled by rocket artillery and bombed by smart missiles. He was not a coward. But nanomachines! The thought made him shudder. Invisible, insidious. If they got inside his suit and started eating his flesh . . .

120

"What are your orders, sir?" the Norwegian lieutenant asked, his voice low and earnest. "We can't stand out here forever," he added, needlessly.

Suppressing a reflex to snap at his arrogant criticism, Munasinghe made up his mind. After all, he had sent men into battle before. Soldiers took risks, deadly risks. It was part of the profession.

"Take your squad through the open area to those airlock hatches on the far wall. Get those hatches open as quickly as you can. Don't waste time; use the grenades."

"I wouldn't do that if I were you." A strange voice sounded in Munasinghe's earphones. From the way the lieutenant's spacesuited form twitched, he must have heard it too.

"Who said that?" Munasinghe demanded.

"This is Douglas Stavenger, of Moonbase. The floor of our garage is covered with nanomachines that will devour the materials of your spacesuits. The airlock hatches are coated with them, too."

"You are bluffing," Munasinghe said.

"No, I'm not. We use the nanobugs routinely to clean up grease and oil stains that accumulate on the garage floor. You happened to pick a time when our semiannual cleanup is just starting."

"I don't believe you!" Munasinghe snapped.

"Don't send your troops to their deaths. The nanomachines will destroy them before you can get our airlock hatches open."

Hot boiling anger replaced Munasinghe's indecision. Hatred welled up inside him. This smug upstart is trying to bluff me into ruining my career!

"Surrender your base!" he raged. "Now! You have fifteen seconds to surrender!"

More than ten seconds passed before the voice in his earphones said, "You're sending your troops to their deaths needlessly. We have no quarrel with you. Return to Earth and leave us in peace."

Practically quivering with fury, Munasinghe jabbed the Norwegian lieutenant's shoulder with a gloved finger.

"Get your squad moving! If you go fast enough the nanomachines won't have a chance to harm you."

"That's not true," Doug said.

"Go!" Munasinghe screamed. "That's an order!"

The Norwegian scuttled away, gathered his squad, and
started them into the garage. The warning sign was almost completely gone, Munasinghe saw; nothing left but
a few streaks of red.

"You're making a serious mistake," Doug said in the
captain's earphones.

"No," Munasinghe snapped. "You are. I will destroy
Moonbase and everyone in it before I leave here."

TOUCHDOWN PLUS 59 MINUTES

Edith was getting it all on her digital recorder and minicams. In addition to the camera fastened to the top of
her helmet, which saw whatever she looked at, she held
another in her gloved hands, almost forgotten in the excitement of the moment.

She watched, wide-eyed, as the squad of troopers
thumped in their heavy boots and spacesuits across the
wide expanse of the empty garage.

It would have been funny if it weren't so scary. The
Moonbase guy who spoke to them was Douglas
Stavenger, the one who carried swarms of nanomachines
inside his body. Was he telling the truth? Were the bugs
on the garage floor capable of ruining spacesuits? Killing people?

She remembered that Stavenger's father had died on
the Moon a quarter-century ago, killed by runaway
nanobugs.

This could get hairy, she thought.

Two troopers had outraced the others and reached one of the dulled metal hatches of the airlocks that led into the base proper. They rested their rifles against the wall and started to unpack the grenades they carried on their equipment vests.

"Look at your boots," Doug Stavenger's voice said, with just a touch of urgency in it. "Your boots are being digested by nanomachines."

One of the troopers awkwardly lifted one foot and tried to bend over far enough in his spacesuit to see the sole. His buddy looked down, and dropped the set of grenades she'd been handling.

Edith heard a panicky jabbering in a language she didn't understand.

"Speak English!" Munasinghe's voice demanded.

"The boots . . . they're coming apart!"

"My glove!"

The other troopers in the garage stopped in their tracks. For an idiotic moment, each of them tried to inspect his or her boots.

"The nanomachines!"

"They'll kill us all!"

Stavenger's voice came through again, strong and calm. "Get out of the garage. Ultraviolet light deactivates the nanobugs. Get out in the sunlight where the solar UV can save your lives."

Munasinghe screamed, "No! No!"

"If you don't get out *now*," Stavenger's voice urged, "the nanobugs will eat through your boots and start digesting your flesh. Once that begins there's no way to stop them."

"I *order* you to blow those hatches!" Munasinghe screeched.

Military discipline is often a fragile thing. For several seconds the troopers stood immobile, torn between the ingrained reflexes of their training and the hard-wired drive for self-protection. One trooper, in the middle of the garage, threw down his rifle and ran out into the sunshine.

That was all it took.

The entire squad bolted like green soldiers facing enemy fire for the first time. The troopers stomped and stumbled back across the garage floor, streamed past their raging captain, and flung themselves down on the dusty regolith, raising their legs high so the sunlight could get to the soles of their boots.

"I'll have you court-martialled for this!" Munasinghe raged. "Cowardice in the face of the enemy! You'll be shot! Each and every one of you!"

"Why don't you go in?" Stavenger's voice asked calmly.

Edith turned to face the captain squarely, so that her helmet-mounted camera would capture this moment in its entirety. Munasinghe was shaking, visibly shaking even with the cumbersome spacesuit enveloping him. Whether he quaked with fear or fury, Edith could not tell.

"I'll show you!" Munasinghe screeched, fumbling on his equipment vest for one of his grenades. "I'll show you all!"

The Norwegian lieutenant, last to leave the garage, reached a hand toward him. "Captain, wait—"

Edith watched, wide-eyed, as the lieutenant tried to calm Munasinghe. But the captain struggled free of the taller man's grasp and ran a staggering few steps to the entrance of the garage, the grenade in his gloved hand.

"I'll destroy you all!" Munasinghe screamed, tugging at the grenade's firing pin.

"Don't!" the lieutenant was saying. "You can't reach the hatches from here. It's too far—"

But Munasinghe stumbled on, into the garage, and tried to throw the grenade. Encumbered by his spacesuit and the clumsy gloves, his throw went only a few yards. The grenade bumped on the garage floor, rolled once, then exploded.

The lieutenant had thrown himself down on the ground, a curiously slow, dreamlike fall. Edith involuntarily ducked behind the rock face at the side of the airlock hatch. She saw a flash but heard nothing.

She looked out into the garage again. Munasinghe was

still standing, turning slowly to face her. The lieutenant was clambering to his feet.

Edith saw that the front of Munasinghe's spacesuit was shredded. The man took a faltering step, then another, and pitched face-forward, slowly, slowly falling to the smooth rock floor of the garage.

The lieutenant did not hesitate for an instant. He raced into the garage, grabbed his captain's inert form under the shoulders, and dragged him outside into the sunlight.

TOUCHDOWN PLUS 1 HOUR 11 MINUTES

Doug stared at the display screen. "He killed himself," he whispered.

No one in the control center moved or said a word.

"He went crazy and killed himself," Doug said, his voice still hollow with shock.

"He was trying to blow one of the hatches," Joanna said.

"And fragged himself instead," Anson added.

Doug shook his head. "I don't know if he meant to, but he committed suicide."

"That tall guy did a gutsy thing," Gordette said, "dragging him out of the garage like that."

"But I never meant for anybody to get killed," Doug said.

"It's not your fault," said Joanna firmly. "The idiot went berserk."

"He was trying to kill us," Brudnoy pointed out.

"But I never meant for anybody to get killed," Doug repeated.

*   *   *

The Norwegian lieutenant assumed command of the mission and sent a radio report Earthside.

"What happens now?" Edith asked him.

"We wait for orders from Peacekeeper headquarters," said the Norwegian, his voice low but even.

"I didn't get your name," Edith said.

His spacesuited shoulders moved slightly in what might have been an attempt at a shrug. "What difference does that make?"

Edith hefted her minicam. "I'll have to know."

"Hansen," he said bleakly. "Lieutenant Frederik Hansen, from Kristiansand."

"Thank you," she said.

Lieutenant Hansen looked down at the body of Captain Munasinghe, lying stiffly in his torn spacesuit on the dusty lunar ground. "What a waste," he muttered. "What a waste."

TOUCHDOWN PLUS 1 HOUR 24 MINUTES

"Mexican standoff," Jinny Anson said. "They're not coming in, but they're not going away, either."

"We can sit tight inside the base longer than they can stay out on the crater floor," said Brudnoy, the slightest hint of optimism in his low voice.

"This won't do us any good," Joanna said. "We've got to get them to leave, go back to Earth."

Still sitting on the wheeled chair, Doug turned it around to face them.

"They're waiting for instructions from Earthside," he said. "This might take some time."

"How much oxygen can they be carrying with them?" Anson wondered.

Doug said, "They've suffered a casualty. That changes everything. We've got to give them an honorable way out, something that they can take back Earthside with them to show that their mission hasn't been a complete failure."

"Why bother?" Joanna scoffed.

"Because otherwise, even if this troop leaves, Faure will just send another force, bigger and better prepared. Or maybe he'll drop a few missiles on the solar farm, just to get our attention."

"They'll be out for blood next time." Gordette agreed.

"Like they weren't this time?" Anson shot back.

"What do you suggest, Doug?" Kris Cardenas asked.

Doug took a deep breath. He had been thinking about this for more than four days now. The first part of his plan had been accomplished: the Peacekeeper troops had been kept out of Moonbase. But it had cost the life of their captain. That raised the risks for all of them.

"When I read about the Cuban Missile Crisis of 1962, I saw that the American president was willing to make some concessions, as long as he achieved his major objective, getting the Soviet missiles out of Cuba."

"Ancient history!" Anson complained. "What's that got to do with anything?"

Doug looked up at her and refrained from quoting Santayana. He saw that Brudnoy understood.

"We should be willing to give up something that we can do without, if the Peacekeepers agree to leave," Doug said.

"But what do we have that we can give up?" Cardenas asked. "We can't give up the nanomachines, and that's what Faure's after, isn't it?"

"No," said Doug. "From what he told you, Mom, he wants Moonbase to continue using nanomachines—under Yamagata's control."

Joanna scowled with the memory. "That's right. Faure may think he's running the U.N., but Yamagata's running him."

Leaning back in the chair far enough to make it

squeak, Doug said, "So we need someone who can negotiate with Faure—and with Yamagata, behind Faure."

"And who might that person be?" Brudnoy asked,
needlessly.

Everyone in the little group turned to Joanna.

TOUCHDOWN PLUS 1 HOUR 45 MINUTES

"We can't stay out here forever." Edith heard the Norwegian's words in her helmet earphones. He sounded
uptight, tense.

It had been nearly a half hour since he'd sent his report Earthside. No orders had come up from
Peacekeeper headquarters.

They were standing off to one side of the open airlock
hatch, in the shadow of the mountain's glassy-smooth
flank. The troopers were spread around the crater floor,
silent, waiting like obedient oxen, ashamed of their pan-
icked flight from the garage. Edith wondered if they
blamed themselves for Munasinghe's death. Apparently
the harsh sunlight bathing the crater floor actually did
stop the nanomachines from damaging their suits
further.

"If we had missile launchers with us, we could blow
those inside hatches from here," Lieutenant Hansen
said, "and then run through the garage and inside the
base before the nanomachines could do any real
damage."

"But we don't have missile launchers," Edith said.
"Do you?"

Edith could sense the Norwegian shaking his head inside his helmet. "Well, we can't remain out here forever.
We must do something."

Then Edith heard Stavenger's calm, almost pleasant voice again. "I'd like to speak to whoever's in charge of your operation, please."

For some seconds no one replied. Finally, "I am Lieutenant Hansen."

"I want you to know," Stavenger said, "that we regret very deeply the death of your captain."

Hansen replied, "That's good of you."

"We seem to have an awkward situation on our hands," Stavenger said evenly. "I suggest we try to negotiate some way to solve it."

"You could surrender to us," Hansen suggested mildly.

But Stavenger merely responded, "That isn't negotiating, sir. That is demanding."

"I'm awaiting orders from Peacekeeper headquarters."

"I'm afraid those orders won't reflect the actual situation here. The real question is, what can you accomplish? We don't want you to have to retreat back Earthside with nothing at all to show for your mission."

"Except a dead captain," Hansen said.

For a long moment there was no response. Then Stavenger answered, "Yes, except for that."

Hansen seemed to draw himself up straighter. "What do you suggest?"

Edith listened, fascinated, as Stavenger slowly, gently led Hansen to the possibilities of salvaging something from his captain's failure to capture Moonbase.

He wants to get the Peacekeepers to go on back to Earth, Edith realized, before they do any real damage to Moonbase. He's smooth, this Stavenger guy, Edith told herself.

For nearly an hour Stavenger talked with Lieutenant Hansen, soothingly, sanely, trying to move from confrontation to compromise.

Then a new thought struck Edith. If Stavenger's successful, we'll all pack up and go back to Earth. I'll never see the inside of Moonbase! I'll never get to interview any of their people. All I'll have is a story about the

Peacekeepers being humiliated, and the suits upstairs might not even want to run it!

The hell with that, she told herself. I've got to get inside the base. I've got to see this Stavenger guy and the other rebels.

But how?

There was only one way that she could think of. Hansen was still talking with Stavenger, the other lieutenant standing glumly by him, the rest of the troopers out on the crater floor, standing, sitting, pacing restlessly.

Slowly, without calling attention to herself, Edith sidled away from the Peacekeeper officers, toward the lip of the open airlock hatch. It was much bigger than anything she had expected to see at Moonbase, big enough to allow two tractors through, side by side.

They wouldn't let me die from their nanobugs, Edith reassured herself. They didn't want any of the troopers to get killed, after all. They'll come and get me. If they don't, I'll just run back out here again.

If I have time, she added.

Okay, Edith asked herself. How big a risk are you willing to take for an exclusive interview with the Moonbase rebels?

She hesitated one moment more. Hansen and Stavenger were still talking: something about Mrs. Brudnoy coming back Earthside with the Peacekeepers to negotiate face-to-face with Faure.

Edith took a deep breath of canned air, then started to run as hard as she could in the cumbersome spacesuit across the smooth rock floor of the Moonbase garage. The floor that still teemed with deadly nanobugs.

TOUCHDOWN PLUS 2 HOURS 6 MINUTES

Doug tried to keep the tension out of his voice. It was weird, trying to negotiate with someone you can't see. Why did the lieutenant decide to stay off to one side of the hatch, where our outside cameras can't pick him up? Is there a reason for that, or is it just a fluke?

His throat was getting dry from so much steady talking. Somebody handed him a tumbler of water and he sipped at it gratefully.

No one had left the control center. They were still gathered around him. Doug could feel the heat of their bodies, the sweat of their anxiety.

On the screens before him Doug saw the empty garage and a good swath of the floor of the crater, where most of the Peacekeeper troops seemed to be milling about aimlessly. We should count them, he thought as he talked with Hansen, make certain they're all accounted for.

"Mrs. Brudnoy is willing to accompany you back Earthside," he was saying as he reached for the keyboard and began typing. "She's a member of the board of directors of Masterson Corporation, and its former chairperson. She could negotiate this problem directly with the secretary-general."

On the screen to his right appeared his message: COUNT THE TROOPERS. MAKE SURE NONE ARE MISSING. THEY COULD BE TRYING TO FIND THE EMERGENCY AIRLOCKS.

Hansen was saying, "I will have to communicate with

my superiors. I don't have the authority to make such a decision."

"Of course," Doug said. Anything, so long as they don't get the notion to cut the power lines from the solar farms, or damage the farms themselves.

The mercenary watched Doug's performance with grudging respect. He just might pull it off, he told himself. He just might get the Peacekeepers to haul ass out of here and leave us alone.

The mercenary looked at the faces of the people gathered around Doug. Anxiety, plenty of it. But there was hope in their perspiration-sheened faces, too. And more than hope: admiration. Unadulterated admiration for this young man who was shouldering the burdens of leadership for them, and succeeding at it.

Deep within himself, the mercenary felt a tangled skein of conflicting emotions. He admired Doug Stavenger, too. But he knew that the more successful Doug was, the closer he was moving to death. If he really does drive the Peacekeepers off, then I'll have to kill him, like it or not.

It was strange. For the first time in his life he approached an assassination reluctantly.

But then he realized that it was Stavenger himself who would force the issue. Like all prey, Stavenger was moving willingly toward his final moment. The mercenary wasn't stalking him; Stavenger was coming to him, seeking death. If the kid would just let the Peacekeepers come in and take over, I wouldn't have to touch him, the mercenary told himself.

But no, he's going to outsmart the Peacekeepers and make himself a hero. A dead hero.

"Hey, what's that?"

Doug caught the flicker of movement in the upper right screen and jerked his attention away from his dialogue with Lieutenant Hansen.

A spacesuited figure was running into the garage. A kamikaze? Doug's heart lurched in his chest. A suicide trooper clutching explosives to blow the hatch to one of the corridors?

"I'm Edie Elgin from Global Network News!" the figure shouted as she ran clumsily toward the hatch to corridor one. "I'm not a soldier, I'm a news reporter and you've got to let me in!"

"Get out of there!" Doug yelled. "The nanobugs will eat out your suit and kill you!"

"No!" Edith shouted back. "I'm a reporter and I want to talk with you people face-to-face!"

She reached the hatch and skidded to a stop.

"The nanobugs are already chewing on your boots," Doug said. "Get back outside while you still have a chance!"

"No! You come and let me inside the base."

"Flathead," Jinny Anson growled.

"It's a trick," said Joanna.

"But she'll die!" Brudnoy said.

"Let her! It's her own damned fault."

Doug stared at the display screen showing the space-suited figure standing defiantly at the hatch. If she were nervous or frightened, it didn't show. She just stood there, arms folded across her chest.

"Jesus Christ," someone muttered.

Kris Cardenas leaned over Doug's shoulder. "The bugs will work their way through her boots in a couple of minutes, Doug."

"You can't let her kill herself."

"Why not?" Anson snapped.

"Bad publicity," Joanna answered.

While they argued above his head, Doug flicked to the Peacekeepers' suit-to-suit frequency. Hansen and several others were bellowing to the reporter to get back into the sunlight before the nanobugs killed her. She did not reply to them. Probably not even tuned in to the suit-to-suit freak, Doug thought.

He looked up at Brudnoy. "Lev, get a team of people down to that airlock. Bring a UV lamp to deactivate the bugs."

Brudnoy nodded once and started off.

Doug called after him, "Do not let any part of her suit inside the base! Understand? Her suit stays in the airlock chamber until we can make absolutely certain it's been fully decontaminated."

Zimmerman lumbered off, too.

"Where are you going, Professor?" Doug asked.

"To meet this foolish woman, where else?"

Doug turned back to the display screens on the console. Hansen and the others were still jabbering on their suit-to-suit frequency.

"Lieutenant Hansen!" Doug broke in. "Lieutenant, this is Douglas Stavenger."

"She's going to kill herself," Hansen said grimly.

"We're going to take her inside," Doug said. "Don't try to take advantage of the situation."

"I assure you," Hansen said, "that this insanity is entirely her own doing. I want no part of it."

"Fine," said Doug. Yet in his mind's eye he saw this as a ploy by the Peacekeeper lieutenant. Get us to open the hatch to save the life of a nutty reporter and they rush a squad of troopers to get to the hatch before we can close it again.

"Just to be on the safe side," Doug said, "I would appreciate it if you and your troopers began filing back toward your Clippership."

"You don't trust me?" Hansen's voice sounded surprised.

"It's easier to trust," said Doug, "when I can see that you're not going to rush that hatch."

"And if I refuse?"

"Then you'll bear the responsibility for the reporter's death."

That was a stretch, Doug knew. We can't let a reporter die, he told himself. Bad enough their captain killed himself. Everybody on Earth would be turned totally against us. Reporter killed by Moonbase nanobugs. They'd nuke us and feel justified about it.

"I will order my troopers to stand clear of your airlock," Hansen said. "That will have to do."

Nodding wearily, Doug said, "Okay. I can accept that."

TOUCHDOWN PLUS 2 HOURS 11 MINUTES

Lev Brudnoy tapped Gordette's shoulder as he started out of the control center.

"I'll need your help," he said to the black man.

Gordette looked startled, but quickly recovered and followed Brudnoy as the old ex-cosmonaut hurried along the corridor toward the cross-tunnel that led to corridor one.

Brudnoy stopped at one of the wall phones only long enough to call security and ask for an emergency team with a pair of UV lamps to meet them at airlock one.

"Why two lamps?" Gordette asked as they started trotting down the corridor toward the airlock.

"In case one fails," Brudnoy said, puffing.

"Redundancy." Gordette understood. An astronaut's way of thinking.

The emergency team was not there yet when they got to the end of the corridor. Brudnoy muttered under his breath in Russian.

"Here they come," Gordette said, pointing up the corridor.

With a tight glance, Brudnoy reached out his long fingers and touched the MANUAL OVERRIDE stud on the airlock control panel set into the wall.

"Tell Doug that I am cycling the airlock manually," he said to Gordette as he pressed the stud that opened the outer hatch.

Gordette picked up the wall phone and spoke into it

with a hushed urgency. "He's telling her to step inside the airlock," he said to Brudnoy.

The emergency team came up. Its leader, a roundish dark-haired woman, was panting. "We were in the Cave with everybody else when the call came through. Hadda run all the way down to the storage lockers to find a second ultraviolet lamp. Why the hell you need two?"

Brudnoy ignored her. "Is she inside?" he asked Gordette.

"Yeah, you can close the outer hatch now."

Edith never doubted for a moment that they would let her inside. Stavenger sounded too level-headed, too *organized* to do something stupid.

"We're going to open the outer hatch," his voice said in her helmet earphones. "Get inside quickly, because we'll need to shut it before any of your Peacekeeper buddies can make a charge for it."

The hatch slid open before she could reply. She stepped into what looked like an empty telephone booth with walls of smooth blank metal, lit by a single lamp set into the metal ceiling.

Soundlessly, the hatch slid shut again.

Nothing happened. It was like being in a spacious metal coffin. Room enough for two; maybe three, if you really squeezed it.

Edith heard a throbbing sound. She didn't really hear it so much as feel it through the soles of her boots. *I wonder if the nanobugs really are chewing up my boots, or is the whole thing just an elaborate trick?*

She could really hear a pump chugging away now, and the hiss of air.

"In a minute or so the inner hatch will open," Stavenger's voice told her. "Don't move. Do not step through the hatch. Understand me? Do not step through."

"I understand," Edith said. *He sure sounds uptight all of a sudden.*

"Good," Stavenger said. "One or two men will come

into the airlock with you and help you out of your suit. Do exactly what they tell you."

"Okay, sure."

"We're risking the safety of this entire base and everybody in it," Stavenger said. "If the nanobugs infesting your suit get inside we'll all be dead."

Edith blinked with surprise. *He really means it! He's putting the whole base in jeopardy to save my neck.*

The hissing and chugging noises stopped, and for a long moment she stood alone and still in the metal sarcophagus.

Then the inner door slid open and a lanky, grave-faced old man with a ratty gray beard stepped inside. Behind him was a shorter African-American, solidly built. He looked somber, too.

"Welcome to Moonbase," said the old man, breaking into a boyish smile. "It is my pleasant duty to help you take off your clothes."

TOUCHDOWN PLUS 3 HOURS 25 MINUTES

Wilhelm Zimmerman scowled at the woman. She was pretty, in an All-American, blond, coltish way. And completely stupid.

"You came this close to killing yourself," he growled at Edith, holding his thumb and forefinger a bare millimeter apart.

Sitting on the examination table, wrapped in nothing but a thin sheet, Edith nodded somberly. "I didn't realize I'd be putting the whole base at risk."

"You think perhaps all this is a game?"

"Not hardly."

Zimmerman locked his hands behind his back and

stared at the readouts on the display screens lined above the exam table. Everything looked normal. The UV lamps had deactivated the nanomachines infesting her boots. None of them had penetrated to the inner soles. This woman was clean of nanobugs. Her boots and the rest of her spacesuit were in the nanolab, down in the old section of Moonbase. Zimmerman wanted to inspect those boots personally, to see how much damage the gobblers had done to them. He intended to play back the video of the reporter's dash through the garage and establish a timeline to determine the rate at which the nanobugs ate through the plastic of the boots.

"When can I get my clothes back?" Edith asked, clutching the sheet under her chin.

Startled out of his thoughts, Zimmerman waved a pudgy hand in the air. "Now. They were not contaminated."

With a shy smile, she asked, "Then where are they?"

Zimmerman scowled again. "Am I your valet? How should I know where they are?"

Hansen had returned to the Clippership and spent a weary hour discussing the situation with his superiors. He started with his commanding officer at the Peacekeeper base in Corsica, then was bucked up to Peacekeeper headquarters in Ottawa and finally to the U.N. secretary-general, Georges Faure himself.

Patiently he explained how Captain Munasinghe had been killed. Faure listened, a strange little smile playing about his lips.

"The captain died in battle against the rebels, then." Faure made it a statement, not a question.

"He killed himself accidentally," Hansen corrected.

Faure's expression hardened once he heard the lieutenant's words. "No, no, no. He died in battle. How it happened is of little consequence. If the Moonbase rebels had not resisted, he would not have been killed."

Hansen let the point pass. More than one soldier had become a hero after the fact, he knew.

"Tell me then," Faure said, "what do you propose to do now?"

"Our only alternatives," he reported, "are to return to Earth with our mission unfulfilled, or to destroy Moonbase's electrical power equipment, which will force them to surrender within a few hours."

Faure's face, on the cockpit's small screen, looked perfectly composed. Only the slightest tremble in his voice hinted at the seething rage boiling within him.

"And if you destroy the electrical equipment," Faure asked, with exaggerated patience, "what happens to the people of Moonbase?"

Hansen said, "They will be forced to surrender."

Three seconds passed. Faure asked, "Why will they be forced to surrender?"

"Because without electricity their air-recycling system will shut down and they will soon have no air to breathe."

Another three seconds. "And once they surrender, do you have air for them to breathe? Do you have space aboard your ship to carry two thousand men and women back to Earth?" Faure's voice rose to a snarl. "Or do you propose to let them all die, choking to death while you watch?"

Hansen stared back evenly at the secretary-general's image. "I was merely stating what our options are, sir. I was not recommending a course of action."

While waiting for Faure's response, Hansen glanced at Killifer, who seemed grimly amused. "Friggin' politicians want to have their cake and eat it too," Killifer whispered. "And when they can't, they blame it on you."

"Attend to me, Lieutenant," Faure snapped. "You were sent to Moonbase to take over its operation and remove its leaders from control. It now seems that you cannot accomplish that task."

"Not without destroying the base, sir," Hansen replied. "And killing everyone in it."

Faure seemed to mull the situation over. "You say that Mrs. Brudnoy is willing to accompany you back to Earth?"

"To negotiate directly with you, yes, sir."

The secretary-general toyed with his mustache. Then he asked, "And this news reporter, this Edie Elgin, she is still in Moonbase?"

"Apparently she intends to stay there. She says she does not wish to return with us."

Hansen thought he might be mistaken, it was hard to tell on this small screen, but Faure's face seemed to be getting quite red. As if he might explode into fury at any instant.

But instead, the secretary-general said mildly, "Very well. Bring Mrs. Brudnoy back with you. Leave the news reporter. The mission is a failure, Lieutenant. A complete and utter failure."

Then he added, "Except, of course, for the martyrdom of Captain Munasinghe."

TOUCHDOWN PLUS 4 HOURS 48 MINUTES

"At least we don't have to pack anything," Joanna said as she sat at her delicate curved writing desk of light walnut and booted up her personal computer.

"Are you sure?" Lev Brudnoy asked, from the doorway to their bedroom.

"Of course," she answered, without even glancing up at him. "We'll go to the house in Savannah. My god, I'll be able to go shopping again!"

Brudnoy ambled into the living room and sat on one of the little Sheraton sofas. "Are you sure we'll get to Savannah?"

Joanna looked up from her computer. "What do you mean?"

"We're being carried Earthside on a military transport. It will land at the Peacekeeper base in Corsica. Has it occurred to you that we might be held there, incommunicado?"

"Incom—what makes you think Faure would do that?"

Brudnoy shrugged. "It's easier to negotiate with someone when you have him in prison."

"Are you serious?"

"Very."

"Lev, I'm not some nobody Faure can hide from public view. I'm Joanna Brudnoy! There'd be an uproar if he tried anything like that."

"Maybe. Maybe I'm just a worried old man. But," Brudnoy ticked off on his fingers, "one: Faure has controlled the news media very effectively. Two: As far as everyone Earthside is concerned, you are at Moonbase. Faure isn't telling anyone that you're returning with the Peacekeepers. Three: You would make a very good hostage."

"I'm sending word to Savannah right now," Joanna said. "The board of directors will know that I'm coming back with the Peacekeepers."

"Can you trust Rashid to inform the board?"

Joanna stared at her husband for a long, silent moment. Then she nodded. "I don't think he'd have the guts to keep this information from the board, but just in case, I'll send the word to each individual board member."

"Good," said Brudnoy.

"And the news media, too."

Brudnoy gave her a sad smile. "Don't expect a brass band when we arrive on Corsica. Or reporters, either."

"You really are a reporter for Global News," Doug said, feeling foolish even as the words left his lips.

"I really am," said Edith Elgin, sitting in front of his desk.

She was back in the coveralls that the Peacekeepers had given her: sky blue with white trim. The color showed off her thick blond hair very nicely, Doug thought. Her eyes were her best feature: big, lustrous, emerald-green eyes. Startling eyes. Eyes that made you want to believe whatever she told you. Long legs. She must be almost as tall as I am.

Edith was studying Doug, too. She saw an earnest-looking six-footer in his mid-twenties (which she knew from checking his bio before coming to the Moon). Olive skin, nice smile, dark hair, gray-blue eyes. Broad shoulders. His coveralls were a couple of shades darker than her own.

"I'm glad you decided to come into Moonbase," Doug said, "although your presence here is a little awkward for us."

"Awkward?"

He made a gesture with both hands. "You don't have any clothes except what you're wearing. And I'm not quite certain what to do with you, now that you're here."

"Do with me? I want to interview you and the others here. I want to beam your story back to the news media on Earth."

"The media haven't paid any attention to us," Doug said. "They even ignored our declaration of independence."

"Declaration . . . ? You've declared independence?"

"Five days ago, when Faure told us he was sending Peacekeepers here to take over the base."

"I didn't hear a word about it!" Edith seemed genuinely shocked.

"You see what I mean?" he said. "The media have smothered us."

"Well, they won't now," she said. "Not with Global News' top personality on the scene."

Doug almost laughed. She seemed serious, and not at all embarrassed at describing herself that way.

"There's more to it, though," he said, sobering at the thought.

"More? What?"

"Well . . ." He hesitated, then decided he might as well let her know. "You might be a spy."

"A spy?" Edith's emerald eyes went wide. Then she burst into full-throated laughter.

"You find that funny?" Doug asked, feeling a little disconcerted.

"Man, I've never kept a secret in my life! Some spy."

Doug found himself grinning back at her. But he heard himself saying, "Look at it from my point of view. The Peacekeepers just happen to bring a news reporter along with them. Once it becomes obvious that they can't muscle their way into Moonbase, this reporter talks her way into the base—"

"By risking her neck," Edith pointed out.

"By depending on the good graces of the Moonbase people," Doug countered.

"And now this reporter is in your midst, and she's going to stay with you while the Peacekeepers are leaving."

Doug nodded.

"That doesn't make me a spy."

"Probably not, but the thought has crossed my mind."

Edith stared at him. He was pleasant and charming and very careful. He took his responsibilities seriously.

"For one thing," Edith said, "how would I get information back to Earth, if I'm a spy?"

"In your news broadcasts."

"Really?"

"In code, I guess."

She could feel her brows knitting. "Are you serious, or are you just pulling my leg?"

"I'm serious," Doug said, "although I've got to admit that the more I think about it, the less likely it all seems."

"Good. I'm not a spy."

"I hope not."

"In fact, I can do you some good. I can get your story out. The media can't ignore me."

Doug nodded and decided that, whether she was a spy or not, she might be useful after all. And it's going to be fun showing her around Moonbase, he thought.

TOUCHDOWN PLUS 8 HOURS 3 MINUTES

Georges Faure took Rashid's call in his office atop the U.N. secretariat building because his comfortable, luxurious apartment was a wreck.

The secretary-general had spent long, agonized hours speaking with the timid lieutenant who had taken command of the Moonbase mission. Faure had felt his blood pressure rising, his innards burning with rage and frustration as the Peacekeeper officer reluctantly admitted his failure to capture the base.

Struggling to keep his temper under control, Faure had left his office and had his chauffeur drive him the three blocks through Manhattan's noise and filth to his penthouse apartment on the East River. He gave the driver the rest of the evening off, smiled his usual condescending smile at the heavily-armed doorman, and went straight to the private elevator that rose directly to his penthouse apartment.

Once safely inside, with the door locked and the phone's answering machine on, Faure took off his pearl-gray homburg and flung it across the room. He stripped off his suit jacket and slammed it to the carpet, then stamped on it. He grabbed the vase by the doorway and smashed it against the wall. He went through the apartment like a one-man band of vandals, smashing, tearing, breaking everything he could lay his hands on.

He spoke not a word, made no sound except for the gasping of his labored breath. Paintings came down from the walls and were torn to shreds. Chairs were overturned, kicked, pummelled. The coffee table was splintered, the bedclothes ripped.

Only his clothes closets were spared his ravages. And the bathroom. When at last he was too weak to continue, sweating and gasping for breath, Faure tore off his sodden clothes, showered, then slowly dressed in an immaculate suit of dove gray. Dressing always soothed him. He found his homburg in the litter of the living room, picked it up, dusted it off, and set it carefully on his head. Feeling almost relaxed, he rode the elevator down to the lobby and asked the concierge to call another limo for him. He had a dinner engagement with six delegates from Latin America.

"By the way," he told the concierge, "please send a team of people to clean up my apartment. It has been wrecked."

And he left the astounded young man sitting at his little desk in the marble-floored lobby, open-mouthed.

After dinner, he went to the Secretariat building instead of the apartment. He would sleep in the suite adjoining his office, and give the cleaning team the whole night to put his apartment back in order.

A telephone message from Ibrahim al-Rashid, chairman of the board of Masterson Aerospace Corporation, awaited him. Faure toyed with the idea of waiting until the morning to return Rashid's call. Then he decided not to; *I will interrupt his evening, instead.*

Now he looked across his office at the image of Rashid's somber, darkly bearded face on the flat screen wall display. It certainly looked as if Rashid were in a house or apartment, not an office. Faure smiled inwardly, pleased with himself.

"I am sure that I don't have to remind you," Rashid was saying, "that Mrs. Brudnoy is not only a leading citizen of the United States, but a very important member of the board of directors of Masterson Aerospace Corporation."

"If you do not have to remind me," Faure said testily, "then why are you reminding me?"

"Believe me," Rashid replied, "I don't enjoy this any

more than you do. But it is my duty to make certain you understand that Mrs. Brudnoy is be treated with every respect."

Faure felt his blood pressure rising again. He opened his right-hand desk drawer slightly and reached for the weighted silver balls that he kept there. They were supposed to help calm him. Fondling them in his hand, he felt no relief from the frustrated anger building inside him all over again.

"I assure you, Monsieur Rashid, that Madame Brudnoy is not being brought back to Earth as a prisoner. She will be brought to New York to discuss the Moonbase situation with me, personally. She will be accorded every courtesy."

Rashid nodded once, barely. His eyes looked bleak. "My board of directors has instructed me to tell you that we expect Mrs. Brudnoy to have full freedom of movement and association. She will want to go to her home in Savannah, of course—"

"Of course," said Faure, trying to smile.

"And she will *not* want to have Peacekeeper or United Nations personnel escorting her."

Faure did not reply.

"Mrs. Brudnoy is quite capable of getting herself to New York for her meeting with you. She is in no way a prisoner or a hostage."

Studying Rashid's face as the man spoke, Faure realized that the chairman of Masterson Corporation's board was no more pleased with this situation than he was himself.

"Monsieur Rashid," Faure said, relaxing slightly as he jiggled the silver spheres in his right hand, "let us be candid with one another."

"By all means."

"Madame Brudnoy represents the illegal and immoral rebels of Moonbase who are defying international law. A Peacekeeper officer has been killed by them, you know."

"I was told he was killed in an accident he himself caused," Rashid replied warily.

"I am sure that is what you were told," said Faure.

"However, the inescapable fact is that he was killed because Moonbase is resisting international law."

Rashid nodded gravely.

Faure resumed, "I am perfectly willing to treat Madame Brudnoy as an ambassador plenipotentiary, and accord her diplomatic immunity."

"Good," said Rashid, tonelessly.

"But technically, she is a criminal. Just as all the leaders of Moonbase are."

Rashid hesitated, passed a hand across his neatly-trimmed beard. Then he asked, "If that is your attitude, then to what avail are the negotiations going to be?"

"None," Faure said, feeling cheerful for the first time since Lieutenant Hansen had reported the failure of the Peacekeepers' mission. "None whatsoever."

"I see," said Rashid slowly. It seemed to Faure that he did not look displeased at all.

TOUCHDOWN PLUS 12 HOURS 26 MINUTES

In the old days, when he'd been just a teenager, Doug had liked to come out to the rocket port and watch the ships arriving or departing in the eerie silence of the Moon. He would climb up the narrow ladder to the observation bubble, a tiny dome of clear plastic, and get a worm's eye view of landings and liftoffs.

The old rocket port was a set of storage chambers now. The new port was not much bigger, and had been dug into the floor of Alphonsus more than a kilometer from the flank of Mt. Yeager, where the main plaza was going to be built.

Doug drove the spring-wheeled crawler down the long

tunnel to the port, his mother and Lev Brudnoy seated behind him, the reporter at his side.

"Does the head of the base work as a taxi driver very often?" Edith asked, grinning at him.

The tunnel was long and straight and bare. Strips of fluorescent lamps lined its unfinished rock ceiling, their light making everyone's skin look sickly, almost green.

"I'm not the head of the base anymore," Doug answered lightly. "And around Moonbase, everybody pitches in and does what needs doing."

"I thought you were Moonbase's director," Edith said, her grin replaced by a puzzled frown.

"I was, but I gave it up for the duration of this crisis."

"Then what's your title? How do I identify you for your interview?"

Doug lifted his shoulders in a shrug. "Damned if I know. Titles don't mean all that much around here."

"Call him the chief administrator of Moonbase," Joanna said, leaning forward slightly in her seat.

"Generalissimo," Brudnoy joked.

Edith was serious. "Chief administrator. That sounds good. And who's the director of the base? Or is there one now?"

"Jinny Anson," Doug said. "You'll want to interview her, too."

"And my wife's title is ambassador plenipotentiary," Brudnoy said, "while my own title is luggage handler."

Edith fingered the minicam in her lap. "I want to squeeze in an interview with you before you take off, Mrs. Brudnoy."

"It'll have to be a quick one," Doug said, glancing at his wristwatch. "Liftoff's scheduled for twenty-six minutes from now."

With a laugh, Edith said, "Twenty-six minutes is an *eternity* in video news, Doug."

She got down to business immediately and began questioning Joanna about what she hoped to accomplish in negotiations with Faure.

"It's very simple," Joanna said. "I'm going to New

York to get the U.N. to recognize Moonbase's independence."

"And if they refuse to recognize it?" Edith prompted.

Joanna shook her head. "We *are* independent. Physically, we are self-sustaining. All we're asking is for the United Nations to recognize reality."

"And if they don't?"

For a heartbeat, Joanna did not reply. Then she said, "Then we'll have to prove to Faure and the rest of the U.N. that we won't be intimidated."

"Do you think the U.N. will send more Peacekeeper troops to try to take over Moonbase?"

"I hope it doesn't come to that," Joanna said.

"But it will," Doug added, realizing the truth of it as he spoke the words. "We've won the opening skirmish, but this war won't be over for a long time."

TOUCHDOWN PLUS 12 HOURS 52 MINUTES

Jack Killifer stood in the open hatch to the cockpit, trying not to sound as if he were pleading with the two pilots.

"You gotta let me ride up here with you," he said. "On the jumpseat."

The copilot's eyes were fixed on the control panel's gauges. He and the command pilot had lifted the Clippership from its landing spot on the regolith to one of Moonbase's rocket port pads, where the spacecraft was being refueled for the flight back to Earth.

The command pilot looked up at Killifer. "We're not supposed to take passengers up here. We got work to do."

Killifer wheedled, "Come on, guys. You're making a

high-energy burn, aren't you? Friggin' flight's only gonna take nineteen hours, right?"

"Why d'you want to ride up here, instead of in a nice comfy seat with the rest of the passengers?"

"You're bringing two extra people along, right? Mr. and Mrs. Brudnoy, right?"

"That's Lev Brudnoy, isn't it?" asked the copilot, without taking his eyes off the control panel. "He used to be a cosmonaut back in the old days, didn't he?"

It was Brudnoy's wife that bothered Killifer. Joanna. *She'll recognize me*, he knew. *Haven't seen her in damned near eight years, but she'll recognize me if she sees me. Especially if we're locked up in this sardine can for nineteen hours. She'll see me. She'll remember who I am.*

"And you got the captain's body, too," Killifer said.

"He goes in the cargo bay."

"Yeah, but you need two extra seats for the Brudnoys. Mine and the reporter's. Makes it all come out even."

The pilot glanced at his copilot, then looked up again at Killifer. "Okay, I guess it'll be all right. Just don't chatter at us while we're taking off."

"Okay!" said Killifer, a surge of gratitude gusting through him.

"Or reentry," said the copilot.

"Or landing," the pilot added.

"Okay, okay." Killifer laughed shakily. *I can sit here for nineteen hours and never go out into the passenger compartment*, he told himself. *They got a relief tube here in the cockpit. I can go nineteen hours without taking a crap.*

He had never acknowledged it before, but he was deeply afraid of Joanna Brudnoy. It was irrational, but he feared her. That realization made him feel shame. And a burning, relentless hate.

The mercenary lay slouched in his bunk and watched his wallscreen display of the Peacekeeper ship taking off. He was startled by the suddenness of it. One instant the big Clippership was sitting out on the floor of the crater, sunlight glinting off its curved diamond body. The next, it was gone in a puff of hot exhaust gases and blown dust and pebbles. When the dust cleared the crater floor was empty. The ship was on its way.

Got to hand it to the kid, the mercenary thought. He faked them out and got them to turn tail. Peacekeeper troops ought to be tougher than that; letting the threat of nanobugs panic them.

He lifted his feet off the floor and wormed off his softboots, then swung his legs onto the bunk. Get some rest, he told himself. The next few days are going to be tough.

He considered his options. There was no way out of it: Doug Stavenger was going to die. The only questions were when and how. Can I do it without getting caught? Maybe make it look like an accident. Or will it be more effective if they all know that he's been assassinated?

Even if they catch me at it, about all they'll do is ship me back Earthside. Or will they? That Jinny Anson's a pretty feisty broad. Would she have guts enough to execute me? Yeah, maybe so, if she's pissed enough at my killing Stavenger.

Maybe I ought to get her first, he thought. But then he shook his head. No way. Knock off Stavenger first. He's the key, especially with his mother back Earthside. Knock him off, and then afterward get Anson and anybody else you can reach.

So they kill me, he told himself. I've been running toward death all my life. I'll take a lot of them with me.

PART II
SIEGE

These are the times that try men's souls. . . .
Tyranny, like hell, is not easily conquered . . .

—THOMAS PAINE

DAY FIVE

It was hot, unbearably hot. Georges Faure hated to wear black, but for this occasion it was necessary. The steaming tropical heat was boiling the vast crowd standing in the sunshine like patient cattle, yet inside his suit of mourning Faure felt comfortable, almost cool. He wore an astronaut's undergarment, threaded with plastic capillaries that circulated cooling water over his body.

As he sat on the dais listening to the interminable eulogies, Faure's only worry was that perspiration was beginning to gather on his forehead. The Sri Lankan government had put up an awning of colorful silk to shade the VIPs from the blazing sun, of course, yet even with the cooling undergarment, the broiling heat was making his unprotected head perspire.

As surreptitiously as possible, he mopped his sweating brow, hoping he would not look like a sodden mess when he got up to speak.

He kept his face an impassive mask, although he could feel rivulets of sweat running down his cheeks. It will appear ridiculous if I drip perspiration from my nose while I am speaking, he told himself. Again he pulled out his capacious handkerchief and wiped his face.

At last he heard the Sri Lankan prime minister say, "I present to you the secretary-general of the United Nations, Monsieur Georges Faure."

As he walked slowly to the teak podium, carefully hiding his limp as much as possible, Faure realized that it was the rebels at Moonbase who had inflicted this indignity on him. If not for them, he would be comfortably ensconced in his air-conditioned office in New York instead of attending the funeral services of an obscure Peacekeeper captain who was so inept that he killed himself with his own grenade.

He focused his mind on the hateful Moonbase renegades even as his eyes looked out on a sea of dark, solemn-eyed faces. The Sri Lankan government had made a media extravaganza of Captain Munasinghe's funeral. After decades of civil war, they desperately needed a hero, a martyr, whom every citizen could admire. Jagath Munasinghe, at best a mediocre officer in life, was being built into an international hero in death.

Thousands of solemn faces stared up at Faure. He kept his own face blank, suppressing the smile that wanted to break out at the thought of having the world's media focused on him. By his express order, this funeral service was being beamed to Moonbase, too.

Leaning on the teak podium, he began, "The cause of peace has seen many heroes, many men and women who have given their lives. Captain Jagath Munasinghe has joined their illustrious ranks . . . "

Before long, Faure was virtually snarling, "And why has this brilliant young officer met such an untimely death? Because a handful of renegades at Moonbase refuse to accept international law. Scientists and corporation billionaires want to live beyond the law in their secret base on the Moon. Captain Munasinghe was killed trying to enforce the law which they resist. They killed him."

Doug watched Faure's performance from the bunk in his quarters, where his digital clock read 6:28 AM. Even before Faure had completed his diatribe, Doug pressed the keypad at his bedside that activated the phone.

He started to ask for Jinny Anson, but heard himself say instead, "Edith Elgin, please."

He muted Faure's image on the smart wall. Edith's voice came through, but no picture.

"This is Edith Elgin," she said, as clearly as if she

were signing off on a news report. At least I didn't wake her up, Doug thought.

"Doug Stavenger," said Doug. "Are you watching the funeral services?"

"Sure am. Faure's working himself to a stroke, looks like."

"He's blaming us for that Peacekeeper's death."

"What'd you expect? Munasinghe's handed him a great public relations club and Faure's going to beat you with it as hard as he can."

Feeling frustrated that he couldn't see her, Doug asked, "Well, what can we do about it?"

Edith immediately replied, "I've got the whole thing on a pair of chips."

"What?"

"I've checked both my cameras. They show what really happened."

Doug's surge of hope dampened quickly. "But the media have been ignoring us. Would they play your chips?"

Edith laughed. "Does a chimp eat bananas?"

"No, really," he said, "the media all seem to be on Faure's side."

Her voice grew more serious. "I'll take care of *that*."

"Can you?"

"If I can't, nobody can."

Despite himself, Doug had to smile at her self-confidence. Or was it just plain ego?

"Are you really a billionaire?" Edith asked.

"Me?"

"Faure said you're a billionaire. Is that true?"

With a puzzled blink, Doug replied, "I don't know. Maybe. I guess my mother is, certainly."

"Say, have you heard anything from her? Your mother, I mean?"

"No."

"Doesn't that worry you?"

Doug leaned back against his pillows. Suddenly he felt very tired of it all. "You know," he said to Edith, "I haven't even had the time to worry about her. But now that you mention it, yeah, I had thought she would've called by now."

For several heartbeats Edith did not reply. Then she said, her voice low, "I'm sorry I brought it up, Doug. You've got enough on your shoulders without me adding to it."

He felt himself smiling at her. "That's okay. I guess if you hang out with reporters you've got to expect troubles."

She laughed. "That's it. Blame the media."

DAY SIX

Edith was surprised at how difficult it was to make contact with her boss at Global News in Atlanta. She had beamed the contents of her camera chips to headquarters, then spent the whole day trying to get through to the programming department to make certain they had received it okay.

Now it was past midnight, and still the smart wall display read: YOUR CALL HAS NOT BEEN ACCEPTED.

"Shee-it," she muttered in her childhood Texas accent, sitting tensely on the spindly desk chair in the one-room apartment the Moonbase people had given her.

Doug had told her that the commsats were blacked out, but Global should be able to take a message directed straight at their rooftop antennas. Yet her call did not go through.

"Did they take my broadcast chip?" she asked herself, wondering for the first time if Global would accept anything she sent from Moonbase.

She sank back in her chair, thinking hard. It was well past midnight at Moonbase. A few stabs at the keyboard on her desk brought up the information that it was 7:23 PM in Atlanta.

Manny'll be home, knocking back his first cocktail of the evening, she thought. Good!

But how to get him, if neither the commsats nor Global's private antennas were taking calls from the Moon?

She hated to call Doug and admit she couldn't get through on her own, especially since the guy was probably asleep at this time of night. Yet she couldn't think of anything else to do.

Doug's face popped up on her smart wall immediately. He was wide awake, still dressed, at his desk.

He listened to her problem, then showed her how to route calls through Kiribati. Edith thanked him, keeping her face serious, strictly business. Yet she found herself feeling glad that he wasn't in bed with someone else.

It took a few minutes more, but the wait was worth it once she saw Manny's look of shock when he recognized who was calling him.

"Edie! You're in Kiribati?"

"No, I'm still at Moonbase. How come y'all aren't taking calls from here?"

In the three seconds it took for his reply to reach her, Manny's surprised expression knitted into a frown. "That's not my doing, kiddo. If it were up to me I'd keep a special link open to you twenty-four hours a day."

"Well, put your drink down and get on it, then," Edith said sternly.

"We're getting everything you send," he said, looking worried, guilty. "We're just not allowed to acknowledge receiving your transmissions."

"Not allowed? By who?"

For three seconds she waited, and got, "Whom."

"Don't smart-ass me, Manny. Who's not allowing what?"

Manny took a long pull from the old-fashioned glass he was holding before replying. "Orders from the very top," he said.

"McGrath himself?"

"That's right. He wants us to cooperate in every way we can with the U.N."

"You mean he won't run the stuff I sent? Eyewitness report of the Peacekeeper's death?"

Manny shrugged. "I'm trying to get it past the suits upstairs, Edith. Honest I am."

"Honestly," she muttered.

"Honestly," he said, three seconds later.

"This is a weird situation," Edith said.

"Tell me about it."

For more than twenty-four tense hours, Joanna feared that the Peacekeepers were going to keep her and Lev in Corsica. When their Clippership landed at the Peacekeeper base, the two of them were shuffled through several layers of bureaucracy, including the most thorough medical examinations they had undergone in years.

"You will need a few days to adjust to terrestrial gravity," the chief doctor told her and her husband, from behind his metal desk.

In truth, Joanna did feel the sullen weight of Earth more than she had expected. She had spent more time on the Moon than on Earth for a quarter-century now, but she always exercised every day while in Moonbase and never considered her returns to Earth as health-threatening.

"I'll be fully adjusted in another few hours," Joanna said. She glanced at Lev, who seemed blithely unaffected by the six-fold increase in gravity.

The doctor shook his head good-naturedly. "No, I am afraid it will take several days, at least."

He was a smiling, plump, golden-skinned Chinese with many chins and rolls of fat showing at the open-necked collar of his short-sleeved Peacekeeper tunic. Joanna thought he might have been the model for statues of the happy Buddha that she had seen in gift shops. He spoke with a cultivated British accent, which sounded very strange coming from his round, almond-eyed Chinese face.

Joanna smiled back at him coldly. "Doctor, have you found anything in the examinations your people have given us to indicate a health problem?"

"No," he said, drawing the word out. "But still the effects of increased gravity must be taken into account."

Sweetening her smile, Joanna asked, "You're waiting for the results of our blood tests, aren't you? You're stalling for time until you learn whether or not there are nanomachines in our bloodstreams."

The doctor's fat-enfolded eyes widened for just a heartbeat. Then he folded his hands across his ample belly and admitted, "Just so. We must be extremely careful about allowing nanomachines into the terrestrial environment."

Satisfied, Joanna replied, "We're not harboring nanomachines."

"We are not Trojan horses," Brudnoy chipped in.

"But you have both undergone nanotherapy on the Moon, haven't you?" the doctor asked.

"No," Brudnoy replied simply. "I've never had to, although I admit as I get older the temptation grows stronger."

"It does?"

Scratching at his beard, the Russian explained, "Each morning brings a new ache. My eyesight isn't what it used to be. My prostate is growing."

"That is natural," said the doctor.

"Yes, but my nanotech friends tell me that they could bring my eyesight back to twenty-twenty and shrink my prostate back to normal and strengthen my poor old muscles, with nanomachines."

Joanna looked at her husband with new eyes. Lev had never complained; she had never had an inkling that he felt his years. In bed he was as vigorous as men half his age. But if he feels old and creaky on the Moon, he must be in agony now, here. Yet he won't show it, not even to me.

She reached out and grasped his hand. He looked surprised, then grinned sheepishly at her.

The doctor was oblivious to their byplay. He said to

Joanna, "But you, Mrs. Brudnoy, you have used nano-machines, haven't you?"

Joanna nodded easily. "Many times. For cosmetic reasons, mainly, although I've had them scrub plaque from my arteries more than once."

"You see?" the doctor said, as if she had just confessed to a crime. "We cannot take the risk of having nanomachines infect our terrestrial environment."

"Doctor, I'm surprised to hear such nonsense from an educated man," Joanna said.

"Nonsense?"

"Of course it's nonsense. To begin with, there are no nanomachines in me. I underwent therapy and then the machines were flushed out, quite naturally."

"How can you be sure—"

"They know the number of machines they put in," Brudnoy explained, "and they count the number that come out. It's quite simple."

"But they could multiply inside the body, couldn't they?"

"Only if they're programmed to do so," said Brudnoy.

Before the doctor could reply, Joanna went on, "Second, and more important, is that nanomachines are *machines*. They are not alive. They cannot mutate and change. What if there were a few nanomachines left in my bloodstream? What harm could they do, even if they got loose into your environment?"

"That depends on what they were designed to do, I should think."

"Yes." Joanna's smile returned. "If a few got into you, for example, they might remove some of the fat you've accumulated."

For an instant she did not know how the doctor would respond. He stared at her as he digested her words. Then his round pudgy face opened into a hearty laughter.

"Nanomachines could make me slim!" he gasped. "I could eat whatever I like and still become thin!"

Joanna leaned back in the stiff metal chair, thinking that she had won the man over.

But his laughter died away. "All this may be very

true, but suppose you are carrying nanomachines that are harmful?"

"Harmful?"

Leaning his heavy forearms on his desk, the doctor said, "You are assuming that the specialists who treated you with nanomachines are benign people. Suppose they are not? Suppose they put into you nanomachines that can . . ." He fished for an appropriate subject.

"Gobble up plastics?" Brudnoy suggested.

Joanna scowled at her husband.

"Destroy plastics," the doctor agreed. "Or invade computers and eat up their memory drives. Or destroy red blood cells in humans. Or attack the human immune system. Or—"

"Aren't you being melodramatic?" Joanna said, almost sneering at the man.

"This is what we fear," said the doctor. "You may think it is not important, but we cannot take such a risk."

"I told you before," Brudnoy said, "we are not Trojan horses. Nor Frankenstein monsters."

"How do you know?" the doctor shot back. "You may have been infected without your knowledge."

"Nonsense!" Joanna spat.

"That is a risk we will not take," the doctor repeated firmly.

"Do you honestly believe *anyone* at Moonbase would inject us with nanobugs that would be dangerous to Earth? Why would they do something like that? What possible reason could there be?"

The doctor folded his hands over his middle again. "Mrs. Brudnoy, the chances of such an event are minuscule, I admit. But the consequences of such an event— no matter how unlikely it may be—would be catastrophic."

Joanna looked at Brudnoy, who shrugged helplessly.

"Those are my orders," the doctor said. "You are to be held here until the results of your blood tests come in."

"Where are the tests being done?" Joanna asked.

"There are very few facilities with the necessary equipment and personnel who are capable of performing such tests."

"Of course," said Brudnoy. "You've closed all the nanotechnology facilities."

"Where are the tests being done?" Joanna insisted.

"It is very difficult to analyze blood samples for nanomachines."

"Where?"

The doctor hesitated, then said, "At the University of Tokyo."

"At a lab funded by Yamagata Corporation, I imagine," Brudnoy said.

Joanna was too furious to speak.

DAY SEVEN

"This is Edie Elgin, speaking to you from Moonbase."

Edith smiled into the minicam being held by one of the technicians from the defunct Lunar University. Doug Stavenger stood beside the camerawoman, smiling encouragement to Edith.

She looked bright and beautiful in a close-fitting sheath of cardinal red. Doug had appropriated his mother's wardrobe, the most extensive in Moonbase, hoping that she would understand and not be too angry when she found out. Edith had to do some fast alterations, and now she prayed that the dress would hold together without popping one of her hastily-sewn seams.

"Behind me you can see Moonbase's extensive farm," she went on, thinking that maybe a popped seam would improve her ratings. If the shitfaced suits back in Atlanta put her report on the network at all.

"More than five hundred acres have been carved out of the lunar rock," she said, reading the script she and Doug Stavenger had put together. The words appeared on the flat display screen attached to the minicam just above its lens.

"Here, deep underground, the agricultural specialists of Moonbase grow the food that feeds the two thousand, four hundred and seventy-six men and women who live at Moonbase. This corner of the farm," she started walking toward a row of dwarf trees, "is the citrus arbor, where fresh oranges, grapefruit, lemons and limes are growing . . ."

Edith described the hydroponics trays, bending down to show how the plant roots reached down not into soil but into liquid nutrients that were carefully matched to each plant's needs. She walked down one of the long rows, pointing out soybeans, legumes, grains and leafy vegetables.

"Over in that enclosed area," she pointed, "biologists are experimenting with growing plants in an atmosphere that is higher in carbon dioxide than normal. The scientists need to wear breathing masks to work in there."

Edith explained the full-spectrum lighting strips that ran along the farm's high ceiling. "This artificial sunlight is on twenty-four hours a day. Moonbase's farm never knows night, and its crop yield is more than five times the yield from a similar acreage on Earth."

She showed the flower bed that Lev Brudnoy had started years ago in lunar soil. And the pens of rabbits and chickens that provided Moonbase's meat. She did not mention the need for nitrogen, which had been imported from Earth, but now would have to be mined from asteroids orbiting near the Earth-Moon system, just as the carbon for building the diamond Clipperships was mined.

"Before the current crisis erupted," Edith went on, walking smoothly to an area where two large titanium tanks stood empty, with holes where piping should be attached, "this area was going to be used for an experimental aquaculture section. The idea was to use some of Moonbase's precious water to grow fish, frogs and algae. Aquaculture can yield more protein per input of energy than even Moonbase's advanced hydroponic farming, and the water can be recycled almost completely."

Her smile faded, her face grew serious. "Unfortunately, the aquaculture project has been put on hold while Moonbase's leaders and the political leadership of the United Nations discuss independence for Moonbase."

The camera panned slowly across the farm's rows of hydroponics tanks as Edith continued:

"Moonbase can feed itself. Even though no spacecraft has been allowed to land here for a week—except for the Peacekeeper troops who attempted to seize Moonbase—the men and women of this community on the Moon are self-sufficient. The question before the world's leaders now is: Will Moonbase's determination to be free be allowed to flower into true independence?"

The camera stopped on Brudnoy's little flower bed.

"This is Edie Elgin, at Moonbase."

"We're out," said the camerawoman, lowering the minicam and its awkward prompter screen.

"Good work," Doug said, reaching out to shake Edith's hand.

"And I didn't mention nanomachines once, did I?" Edith said, grinning back at him.

"You did a great job," Doug said.

Edith's grin faded. "Now I've got to get the suits to run the damned thing."

Still clutching her hand, Doug started toward the airtight hatch that led out of the farm. "I've got an idea about that."

"Oh?"

"You talk to Atlanta, I'm going to talk to Kiribati."

Tamara Bonai was on the rooftop of the Tarawa Kiribati Hotel and Casino when Doug's call came through. As chairwoman of the board of the Kiribati Corporation, her responsibilities to her people were many and weighty. She knew that the Americans and Europeans regarded her people as childish islanders and regarded her as little more than a figurehead, an attractive front for the real power behind the corporation: Masterson Aerospace and its board chairman, Ibrahim al-Rashid.

Until the Moonbase crisis rose up like a sudden typhoon, Bonai had been content to be regarded as a figurehead. Kiribati Corporation was making good profits from its ownership of Moonbase, where the diamond Clipperships were manufactured for sale all over the world, and from its hotels and casinos, scattered across a dozen islands in the broad Pacific. A strange combination, nanomanufacturing on the Moon and resort hotels on tropical islands, but no stranger than other corporations that took their profits wherever they could find them.

Her father had bequeathed the corporate responsibilities to her. The old man had spent as many years as he could stand behind a desk; finally he had declared his early retirement and gone off to fish and play with his grandchildren. Tamara, the youngest of his five daughters and the only one still unmarried, inherited his desk.

With it came gradually building pressure from the United Nations to force Kiribati to sign the nanotech treaty. Knowing that it would mean the death of Moonbase, Bonai resisted as long as she could, looking to Masterson and the other international corporations for help. They gave none. She was especially surprised, even hurt, that Rashid stayed aloof from the struggle with the U.N. There were raging arguments in the Masterson Corporation board of directors. Joanna Brudnoy fought for Moonbase's survival. But Rashid insisted that the nanotech treaty was unavoidable; sooner or later they would have to obey it.

Now Moonbase had defied Faure and the Peacekeepers. They had declared their independence, a move that Bonai supported with all her heart.

Is it because of Doug that I want Moonbase to win? she asked herself. She had never seen Douglas Stavenger in the flesh; they had never been closer than the Moon's distance since they'd first met. Their only contact had been through videophones or virtual reality links. Yet she felt that Doug was important to her; she could fall in love with him someday.

She sat at a table near the railing that edged the roof and looked out at the sparkling ocean and the surf breaking on the reef beyond the island's white sand beach. One of the hotel's small army of assistant managers brought a phone to her and placed it softly on the table.

"Mr. Stavenger is calling from Moonbase," the young man said.

Bonai thanked him and activated the phone with the touch of a manicured finger. Doug's earnest, handsome face filled the tiny screen as she worked the receiver plug into her right ear.

"Tamara, did you look at the video we beamed down to you a couple of hours ago?" Doug asked immediately.

"Yes. The Peacekeeper officer killed himself, didn't he?"

She glanced out at the ocean again as she waited for his response, thinking that he never called except on business. We have no personal relationship, she told herself. It's never even entered his mind.

"Global News Network is having difficulty deciding whether they want to air it not," Doug said.

"I understand that they are leaning over backwards to support Faure," Bonai replied, "although I don't see what good it will do them."

A boy was spearfishing for octopus out in the shallows by the reef, she saw. He lunged and pulled a pulpy tangle of tentacles out of the water on the end of his spear. It writhed helplessly, no larger than his hand. He bit its head and the writhing immediately stopped. She wished she could be out there too, having fun. With Doug.

"We're talking to the head of the network and trying to make a case for fairness, balanced reporting and all that," Doug said. Without waiting for her to reply, he added, "In the meantime, it occurred to me that Kiribati might broadcast the video in your hotels—maybe even bounce it off your commsats so the rest of the Pacific nations can see it."

She frowned slightly. "But isn't the video the property of Global News? Wouldn't our airing it cause copyright problems? To say nothing of the U.N.'s reaction."

This time she watched Doug's face as she waited. He looked so earnest, so determined. "Yes, it probably would cause a flap. But we've *got* to show the world what really happened here!"

"Ah," she said, understanding.

Doug was continuing, "We need airtime, Tamara! We need to tell the world that we've declared independence and we're serious about it and we didn't kill that Peacekeeper captain. Especially in the United States, we need to get our side of the story to the people."

"And this will force the issue. I see."

For nearly three seconds she waited. Then Doug asked, "Will you do it for us, Tamara? Will you help us?"

"On one condition," she replied.

She enjoyed watching his face turn perplexed.

"One condition? What is it?"

"That after all this is over you come here to Tarawa and go fishing with me."

He smiled at her once he heard her words. "You've got a deal!" Doug said fervently.

DAY EIGHT

"This is intolerable!" Joanna was raging. "We've been kept in quarantine for three days now!"

The image of the U.N. flunky on her phone screen seemed serenely unperturbed, as bland and inflexible as a wax dummy.

"I'm terribly sorry, Mrs. Brudnoy," he said in an infuriatingly soft voice, "but the quarantine is for your own safety. You have no idea how strongly public opinion feels about the killing of Captain Munasinghe. If you were allowed out without our protection, it could be quite dangerous for you."

Joanna glanced up from the screen to her husband, stretched out on the couch across the room. Lev knows how to accept imprisonment, she thought. It must be in his Russian genes.

But to the image in the phone screen she said, "Now look. I'm perfectly capable of arranging my own security. I could have a small army of bodyguards here in Corsica in a few hours if you'd allow me to make a phone call back to my corporate headquarters in Savannah."

"Aren't you comfortable in your quarters?" the bureaucrat asked. "Our instructions were to see that you had the very best suite—"

"The best suite in your jail!" Joanna spat.

"Really, Mrs. Brudnoy . . . "

"Your damned medical tests have shown we're not infested with nanobugs. I don't care what your so-called security risks are. I want to get out of here!"

"I'm afraid—" The bureaucrat's vapid expression suddenly changed. He blinked several times and a small knot of anxiety appeared between his brows. "One moment, please."

The phone screen went blank.

Joanna wanted to scream. She looked over at her husband. "Lev, how can you just lie there?"

"I am planning our escape," he said, quite seriously. "All we need is a tunneling machine."

Before Joanna could reply the screen chimed and Georges Faure's face appeared, scowling like a miniature thundercloud.

The newscast from Kiribati came through while Faure was in his office discussing economic controls over international air traffic. He did not have the luxury, then, of demolishing the furniture or any other way of venting his fury.

He dismissed his underlings and watched the newscast alone, his anger and blood pressure rising with each second. There was Captain Munasinghe, screaming uselessly at his troops as they ingloriously ran away from Moonbase's garage. There was Munasinghe, obviously in a fit of hysteria, fumbling with a grenade and charging through the wide-open airlock. And there was Munasinghe, killed by his own grenade.

Idiots! Faure fumed silently. Who allowed this to happen?

He banged a chubby fist on his phone console and demanded to be put through to Edan McGrath, owner of Global News. But even before the electronics could make the connection he cancelled the call.

It will do no good, Faure told himself. The cat has escaped the sack. Whether or not McGrath has gone back on his promise to me no longer matters. Neither of us can put the cat back inside now.

Yet he made a mental note to work more closely with the New Morality zealots in Washington who wanted to put more limits on the news media.

Breathing deeply in a vain attempt to calm himself, Faure put through a call to Corsica, instead of Atlanta.

By the time Joanna Brudnoy's surprised face appeared on his desktop phone screen, Faure had almost regained his self-composure.

"Madame Brudnoy," he said as pleasantly as he could manage.

"Mr. Faure," she snapped back. Obviously she was not happy at being detained in Corsica.

"It has come to my attention that you wish to return to your home," Faure said.

Joanna cocked a brow at him. "I didn't come back to Earth to sit in a Corsican jail cell, no matter how nicely furnished it may be."

"I quite understand," said Faure, "and I agree. Your detention has been a sad error on the part of certain over-anxious members of my staff. I apologize most humbly."

Joanna looked totally unconvinced.

Faure went on, "I am giving orders this instant that you are to be released and provided transportation for whatever destination you wish."

Warily, Joanna replied, "We've been given to understand that we'll need some hefty security because of public resentment over the Peacekeeper's death."

Faure made himself nod reluctantly. "Alas, that may be true, Madame."

"If you don't mind," said Joanna, "I'd rather provide my own security. And my own transport, too."

"Of course! Whatever you wish."

The woman looked suspicious. Faure made himself smile at her as he thought, With a bit of luck, some fanatic will assassinate her.

Joanna mumbled her thanks to Faure and broke the phone link. Looking up from the screen, she saw that Lev was already on his feet.

"We're free to leave," she said, not quite believing it.

Lev scratched at his beard. "Something's changed Faure's mind. I wonder what it was?"

Joanna had no answer.

"Do you think Rashid got to him, at last?"

With an angry shake of her head, Joanna replied, "No. I think Rashid was very happy to keep us bottled up here. I think he's going to be badly shook up when we arrive in Savannah. At least, I intend to shake the little rat as hard as I can."

DAY TEN

He hasn't been alone for more than five minutes, the mercenary grumbled to himself. I don't mind taking him out in front of witnesses if I have to, but it'd be better to get him alone, make it look like an accident or something natural, like a heart attack.

He almost laughed to himself. Heart attack. The kid's twenty-five years old and healthy as a horse. It's going to have to be an accident.

Plenty of places for an accident to happen, he reasoned. Might have to take out a whole lot of people, though. Knock out the air pumps or rig an explosion in one of the labs.

He hasn't gone out on the surface since this thing started. It'd be easy to get him when he's in a spacesuit. Or maybe in the airlock. Christ, I'm starting to grasp at straws! Why's it so fucking tough, knocking off one guy?

Because you don't want to do it, he answered himself. Because you really admire the kid. He's everything you could've been if you'd been born different.

Yeah, sure. And I could fly if I had wings. The facts of the matter are that you've been assigned to decapitate the leadership here and this Stavenger kid *is* the leadership. Sooner or later the Peacekeepers are going to come back in force and either take this base or flatten it. If you haven't done your job by then you're dead. Either you get killed in the battle or they drag you back to headquarters, a failure. And you know what that means. Better to get yourself killed trying to do your job.

He tried to calm himself and think his problem through. *The only time Stavenger's alone inside the base here is when he sleeps. And he hasn't been doing much sleeping, the past ten days. Conferences all the time. He's always got a gaggle of people around him.*

Maybe tonight, though. He's got to sleep sometime. Maybe I'll walk him to his quarters and do him there and get it the hell over with.

"All right," Doug said, standing on a table in the Cave. "This is your meeting. Let's hear what you have to say."

Almost the entire population of Moonbase was jammed into the Cave. Only a skeleton crew was left on duty at the monitoring center, and they were piped into this meeting through the base intercom. The dinner shifts were finished. The other tables and chairs had been pushed against the far wall so everyone could gather into the space. From his vantage atop the table, Doug saw their faces focused squarely on him. They were standing shoulder to shoulder; the only empty spots on the floor of the big cafeteria were the little squares of grass.

Edith Elgin, now in a Moonbase-issue white coverall, stood off to one side, where she had set up both her minicams on tripods to record the meeting.

Jinny Anson was standing in the front row at Doug's feet. She asked, "Well, are we independent or not?"

The acoustics in the Cave were good enough so that she didn't need amplification.

Doug answered, "There's been no confirmation of our declaration of independence from the U.N., or any recognition by any country on Earth."

"Great," someone sneered.

"Physically, though," Doug went on, "we're showing that we can exist independently of supplies from Earth. The U.N. hasn't allowed a flight here since the Peacekeeper mission took off. We're under siege."

"Big deal."

"Wait a minute," one of the women asked. "You mean we can't go back Earthside if we want to?"

"I don't know," Doug said. "I'm sure we could arrange with Faure for transport to take people back Earthside, if there're enough who want to leave to make a flight necessary."

"What about us?" asked the manager of the Canadian dance troupe.

Doug lifted his hands in a gesture of helplessness. "Until we can negotiate your return Earthside, you'll have to remain here as our guests, I'm afraid."

"But we have contractual obligations! Dates in a dozen cities!"

"I can let you call Faure yourself, or your government in Ottawa," Doug suggested. "Unfortunately, no one is returning our calls."

"I don't want to be stuck here forever!" another voice called out.

"It won't be forever," Doug said with a grin. "It'll just seem that long."

"My son's birthday is next week."

Doug made a *can't be helped* shrug.

"How soon can I launch my survey satellite to the Farside?" asked Zoltan Kadar. He had pushed his way to the front row, Doug noticed.

"That's a good question," Doug replied, stalling for time to think. "We'll have to work it out with the logistics program, to see if your launch will use any supplies that we might want to hold onto, in case this siege goes on for a while."

"All I need is rocket propellant and some electricity," Kadar shot back.

His rocket would be propelled by powdered aluminum and liquid oxygen, both extracted from the regolith and both in plentiful supply, Doug knew.

"We'll see," he said to Kadar.

"What're Lev and Joanna doing?" a man's voice asked from the crowd.

"They went Earthside to negotiate face-to-face with Faure and the rest of the U.N. leadership," Doug said.

"Have they met with Faure yet?"

"Not yet. They were detained at the Peacekeeper base in Corsica for a couple of days, but they're back in Savannah now. She should be meeting with Faure in a few days, at most, I guess."

"How is this thing going to be settled? Are we going to be an independent nation, or will the U.N. take us over?"

"It won't be the U.N.," Doug said. "It's starting to look as if Yamagata is really behind this whole business. If we lose, then it'll be Yamagata Corporation that takes over Moonbase."

"You mean this whole thing is a fight between corporations?"

"No," Doug snapped. "That is *not* what I mean. This crisis is a fight between our right to live and work the way we want to, and a power grab by the U.N. and/or Yamagata Corporation. The question is: Do you want to keep on living and working the way you have been, or do you want to be shipped back Earthside without a job?"

Someone said, "But if Yamagata's going to take over the base—"

"They'll staff it with their own people," another voice countered. "Yamagata's not going to keep us, that's for sure."

"What the hell can we do?"

Jinny Anson turned her back to Doug, to face the crowd. "I'll tell you what we can do. Fuck 'em! We don't have to *ask* the U.N. for independence. We *are* independent! We can live here indefinitely. And if we have to expand the farm, or build more solar cells outside, we can do that! We don't need those fuckers! We're free!"

The crowd roared, but from Doug's vantage atop the table it seemed that almost half the people in the Cave were roaring in protest against Anson's outburst.

"Okay, okay," Doug said, waving his hands to quiet them down. "I've got to admit it, Jinny, I agree with you about ninety-five percent."

"Only ninety-five?" She planted her fists on her hips defiantly.

"Hey, I wanna get back home!" a man hollered. "I don't intend to spend the rest of my life here."

"Me neither."

"Listen," Doug said. "For the time being, nobody's leaving. We're in a state of siege, looks like."

"For how long?"

"Until this thing gets settled, one way or the other," Doug answered.

"Or until the Peacekeepers come back with more troops," came a voice from the rear.

Doug conceded the point with a nod, thinking that if he were pushed far enough, Faure might destroy Moonbase rather than admit defeat.

"Okay," Doug said, loud enough to bounce his voice off the Cave's back wall. "We're going to have to act as if we really are independent. Jinny's right about that. As long as we're under siege, nobody can leave, so we might as well go about our work and show Faure and the rest of those flatlanders that we can get along without them."

"Then I can launch my rocket?" Kadar asked.

"We'll look into it."

"But I still wanna get home!" a voice wailed.

"Once this matter is settled," Doug told them, "anyone who wants to leave Moonbase will be free to do so. And anyone who wants to stay here permanently and become a *real* Lunatic, you'll be free to do that, too."

They asked questions and gave opinions and griped and argued among themselves for more than another hour. As Doug watched and listened, he realized that very few of these men and women had ever thought about remaining at Moonbase indefinitely. They were all contract workers, even Jinny Anson, accustomed to working on the Moon for a fixed period of time, then returning to Earth, to home.

Of all the people here, he realized, only Zimmerman and Kris Cardenas and her husband have consciously decided to live in Moonbase permanently. Maybe Jinny, he conceded. Her marriage had broken up because she spent so much time at Moonbase while her husband stayed Earthside.

And me. If I have to go back Earthside with these nanobugs in me, some crackpot nanoluddite will kill me, sooner or later. That's the sweet part of religion, Doug thought, you can be as fanatical as you want in the name of God.

The mercenary hung at the rear of the crowd, wondering how long these people could go around the same mulberry bush. Then Kadar climbed up on the table beside Doug and began telling them all, in elaborate detail, how wonderful the Farside astronomical observatory was going to be and how important it was to the future of the human race.

People started to drift out of the Cave, most of them still talking among themselves as Kadar droned on, unperturbed. As if talk's going to do any good, the mercenary thought. They've been talking for damned near four hours with nothing to show for it but a bunch of sore throats.

He watched Doug climb down stiffly from his perch on the table. Okay, he told himself, Doug's going to go back to his quarters now. Christ, it's after midnight. Okay, just tail along behind him and when he gets to his quarters, invite yourself in and get the job done.

DAY ELEVEN

"It's past midnight," Claire Rossi said tiredly as she trudged along the corridor that led from the Cave to her quarters. Nick O'Malley, at her side, towered over her like a redheaded bodyguard.

He nodded. "I've got the early shift tomorrow. Gotta be up and moving by six AM."

She smiled up at him. "You can sleep in my place. It's closer."

He smiled back. "How could I refuse?"

But once they were snuggled in her bunk together, Claire whispered in the darkness, "Maybe I should get an abortion."

She felt the shock that went through him. "Abortion? Why? You can't! I don't want you to."

Feeling more miserable with each word, Claire said, "With all this going on, all this uncertainty . . . and if there should be any complications . . ."

He touched her bare shoulder tenderly. "You feel okay, don't you? There's nothing wrong, is there?"

"No," she said, "I feel fine."

"Then what's this talk about abortion? I don't like it."

"It's just . . ." She couldn't put the words together.

"Just what? This siege thing? Don't let that frighten you. Even if we have to go back Earthside we still have employment contracts. Masterson Corporation'll have to honor our contracts. We'll have our jobs."

"Suppose there's fighting?"

"How could there be?" he said. "We don't have anything to fight with."

"But Doug said Yamagata wants to take over the base."

He propped himself on one elbow and looked down at her. "And what's that got to do with it? We'd have to go back Earthside anyway, now that you're pregnant."

"*I'd* have to go back," Claire said. "I'm the one who's pregnant."

"Well, I'd have to go back with you, wouldn't I?"

"Why? We're not married. You're not under any obligation."

For a moment he was silent, then Nick chuckled softly in the darkness. "So that's it, then. You're worried that I won't make an honest woman of you."

"I never tried to—"

He smothered her lips with a kiss. "Listen to me,

Claire darling. I love you. I love our baby, too. I'm going
to marry you . . . if you'll have me."

She wrapped her bare arms around his neck and
pulled him down to her. "I love you, Nick. I'm mad
about you."

After a few moments he caught his breath and said,
"So there'll be no more talk of abortion, right?"

"Right."

He fell silent for several heartbeats. Then he murmured, "I wonder if there's anybody here in Moonbase
who can perform a wedding?"

Doug sat on the table's edge up at the front of the
cafeteria until even Kadar ran out of steam. Only a
handful of people were still in the Cave. Most had left
long ago.

Edith was still by her minicams, recording every word
of Kadar's monologue. Doug walked slowly over to her
as the astronomer at last climbed down from the table
and headed for the double doors to the corridor.

"You're a glutton for punishment," Doug said as she
clicked off the two cameras.

Edith grinned. "He seemed to enjoy being recorded.
He played to the camera for the last half hour or so."

"Is any of that stuff useful to you?"

She started to dismount the minicams. "Maybe," she
answered over her shoulder. "A couple sound bites, add
a few clips of the artist's renderings of what the farside
base will look like."

"Artist's renderings?"

"You do have drawings of the facility, don't you? Ar-
chitect's sketches?"

"Computer graphics."

"Fine," said Edith. "Perfect."

Doug helped her to collapse the tripods, then hefted
them both in one hand.

"I borrowed those from your photo lab," Edith said.

"Oh. I thought you smuggled them into the base beneath your Peacekeeper's uniform."

She gave him a searching look. "For a guy who's staring disaster in the face, you're pretty chipper."

"Must be the company," Doug said.

He walked with her, still gripping the folded tripods, toward the double doors. The Cave was empty now, except for them and Bam Gordette lingering by the doors.

"Now which way is the photo lab?" Edith asked. "I still get a little lost in these tunnels."

"Corridors," Doug corrected. "We call them corridors. And I'll take these back to the photo lab. No need for you to walk all the way there; it's way past your own quarters."

"You mean that teeny little monk's cell you gave me?"

"It's as spacious and luxurious as any compartment in Moonbase, almost."

"I'll bet your quarters are bigger."

Doug felt his cheeks coloring. "Well, yeah, but I'm a permanent resident—"

"And the big cheese."

"Your quarters are just as good as any part-timer's. Better than most, in fact."

"Really?"

She's teasing me, Doug realized. And I'm enjoying it.

Gordette held one of the doors open for them and they passed out into the corridor.

"Thanks, Bam," Doug said.

Gordette nodded without saying a word. Doug walked along the corridor with Edith, toward her room, and forgot about him and everyone else.

"Tell me about the nanobugs," Edith said. The corridor lights were turned down to their overnight level. It made the bare stone walls seem somehow softer, less austere.

"The ones we used to scare off the Peacekeepers?"

"No. The ones in your body."

Doug looked into her bright green eyes. She's a news reporter, he reminded himself. Her interest is in a story, not in you as a person.

"I took a really bad radiation dose, about eight years

ago. Got caught out in the open during a solar flare. My mother brought Professor Zimmerman up here, and Kris Cardenas, too. But Zimmerman was the one who pumped me full of nanobugs."

"They saved your life."

"More than once," Doug said.

"And they're still in your body?"

He nodded. "Zimmerman turned me into a walking experiment. The bugs he put in me are programmed to protect my cells against infection or any other kind of damage."

"And they just stay inside you? Do they reproduce?"

"According to Zimmerman, they rebuild one another when they wear down or become damaged themselves."

"Can you *feel* them inside you?" Edith asked, grimacing at the thought.

Doug laughed. "No more than you can feel your white blood corpuscles or your alveoli."

"My what?"

"The air sacs in your lungs," Doug said. "Here's your door."

"The Moonbase Hilton," Edith said.

"Is it really that bad?"

She tapped out her combination on the electronic lock. "See for yourself," she said, sliding the door back and motioning him into the room with a sweeping gesture.

Doug propped the tripods on the wall outside the door and stepped into Edith's quarters. It was a standard compartment, roughly ten square meters, maybe a little more. A bunk with built-in dresser drawers, a desk and chair, a slingchair made of lunar plastic, a table that folded into the wall with two stools beneath it, an empty built-in bookcase.

"You've got your own bathroom," Doug said, pointing to the half-open door. "You've got nothing to complain about."

"The shower turns off just when I'm getting relaxed," Edith said.

He shrugged slightly. "That's automatic. Water's not scarce, exactly, but we don't play around with it."

"And then those air blowers come on."

"Electricity's cheap. And the heat is recycled."

"It ain't the Ritz."

"You'd feel better if you had some of your personal things with you."

She agreed with a rueful nod. "I did come kind of light, didn't I?"

Doug went to the wall panel at the head of the bunk and turned on the display. The far wall showed a camera view of the crater floor.

Edith gaped. "Hot spit!"

"Didn't anybody tell you about the smart walls?"

"Well, sure, but I didn't know you could see outside. It's kinda like a window, isn't it?"

Doug pulled one of the stools over to the bunk and began to show Edith how to work the electronic display.

She sat on the edge of the bunk and watched views of the bleak, harsh lunar landscape. Then he started showing videos from Moonbase's library: educational stuff, mostly, although he rippled through a menu of entertainment vids.

"And we have all the university courses available. Some of the lectures are fascinating; they're all illustrated of course, multimedia."

Gradually Edith's attention wandered from the wall-screen to Doug. She saw an intense young man, so strong within himself that he didn't even realize the aura he radiated. He's only twenty-five, she told herself. You're damned near ten years older. Well, seven, at least. So what's age got to do with it? another part of her mind answered. You've bedded enough old farts. Maybe robbing the cradle would be fun.

But not tonight, Edith decided firmly. You'd be giving him totally the wrong impression if you flopped in the sack with him tonight.

Doug let his hand drop from the wall panel and turned to face her. "Well, there's a couple of hundred choices available. And that's even with Earthside communications blacked out."

"You can't get anything from Earth?" Edith asked.

"They're not transmitting to us. Even the commercial commsats have gone dark."

"That's pretty damned rotten."

"All's fair in war."

"Still . . . what harm would it do to let you see commercial TV?"

Doug smiled. "It might do us all some good to be without commercial TV for a while. Improve our minds maybe."

"Thanks a lot!"

"I didn't mean news broadcasts," he apologized quickly.

"No, you're right. News is just as bad, almost."

"I'm sure you're a top-flight serious journalist," he said.

He was sitting inches away from her. She could touch his knee merely by moving her leg slightly. Don't do it! she warned herself.

Doug could smell her perfume: like the flowers Lev grows in the farm. She certainly is beautiful, with those big green eyes. But she's an important news reporter back Earthside. She probably thinks I'm just a kid. Or worse, a freak stuffed with nanobugs.

Yet Doug saw her strange half smile, as if she were waiting for him to say something, do something.

"I'm not contagious, you know," he heard himself say, surprised at his own words.

She blinked, as if stirring from a dream. "What?"

"The nanobugs. They won't contaminate you if we touch, or . . . er, kiss. You can't catch anything from me."

Edith laughed, softly, gently. "Shee-it, back Earthside you've got to be worried about catching all kinds of diseases from the guys you date."

Doug raised both hands. "I'm disease-free, believe me."

"You look pretty healthy."

"And you look very lovely," he said.

"I'm a lot older fhan you."

"Does that bother you?"

She hesitated only a moment. "No, I don't think it really does."

Doug moved next to her on the bunk and put his arms around her. Her lips felt soft and warm on his.

That voice in Edith's head was still warning her not to do this, but she almost giggled in the middle of a kiss as she answered, What's the matter, you scared he won't respect me in the morning?

What the hell, Edith said to her voice. And then she stopped thinking altogether.

Out in the corridor, almost exactly thirty meters from Edith's door, the mercenary let his back slide down the stone wall and hunkered down on the floor.

God*damn*, he said to himself. Looks like the kid's going to spend the night with her.

He draped his arms across his upraised knees and rested his head on his arms. Get some sleep. Maybe he'll come out before the morning shift starts to come through the corridor.

But he felt pretty certain that Doug was the kind who would spend the whole night.

DAY TWELVE

Edan McGrath, president of Global News Network, was sometimes called Edan McWrath. This was one of those mornings.

Unexpected because he was on vacation, he had stormed into his Atlanta office and demanded that his vice presidents for programming, news and legal meet him in his office *immediately*.

He was a big man who radiated power even though his once hard and muscular body was now weighed down with the fat of overindulgence. Bald, he kept the same trim mustache he had sported when he'd been a Georgia Tech football lineman. Even though his grandfather had handed him Global News as an inheritance, McGrath told anyone and everyone that being born with a platinum spoon in your mouth wasn't easy. "I've had to *work* to keep Global on top of the international competition," he would say. "I *earn* my keep!"

For an industry that rewarded egomania, his office was comparatively modest. No bigger than a minor airfield, its decor was muted Persian carpets and quiet little marble busts and statuettes from ancient Greece and Rome. No desk, but a large round table dominated the room. The walls were display screens, naturally. One of them perpetually showed the Global News feed from its Atlanta studios. The other at present displayed a trio of sleek yachts slicing through New Zealand waters in a trial heat of the Americas Cup race.

The head of the round table was wherever McGrath chose to sit. At the moment he was standing, big hands gripping the back of one of the padded chairs, a stern overweight father figure in a white open-necked sports shirt and whipcord navy blue slacks. He was deeply tanned and obviously boiling mad.

His three (out of dozens) vice presidents dutifully arrived in his office and took chairs around the table. McGrath thought of them as Larry, Moe and Curly, although his evaluation of which was which changed constantly.

"McWrath" did not sit down. He pointed the fingers of one hand like a pistol at the vice president for news.

"This Edie Elgin works for you, doesn't she?"

The man swallowed obviously before answering with a timid, "Yes." He was lean and sallow; he looked as if he hadn't been out of doors since puberty.

McGrath pointed the finger-gun at programming.

"How come her report from Moonbase was aired from freakin' Kiribati instead of from Atlanta?"

Programming was made of sterner stuff. He too had been a football player and was still young enough to have retained his muscular physique.

"We agreed with the U.N. people on a blackout from Moonbase, chief. Remember? You talked to Faure yourself, weeks ago."

"But the freakin' broadcast aired out of Kiribati! We look like idiots! Every independent station on Earth is picking it up. Even our own subscribers are using it. They think it originated here!"

"We were just following your orders, chief," the news VP found the strength to say. "You told us not to air anything from Moonbase until further notice."

"Live footage of that shithead Peacekeeper blowing his own ass off and you keep it in the can?" McGrath roared.

"But you made this agreement with Faure . . ."

"That two-faced little frog let me think the Moonbase people had killed the Peacekeeper! He *lied* to me!"

"You didn't tell us—"

"And they've declared independence! This is the biggest story of the year! Of the decade! Don't you have any freaking sense?"

"You mean you'd've *wanted* us to air it?"

McGrath walked around the table to loom over the news VP. Leaning over until his nose almost touched the younger man's, McGrath pointed to the elaborate corporate logo engraved on the wall above the doorway.

"What's our middle name?" he asked sweetly. Before the anguished vice president could open his mouth, McGrath bellowed, "*NEWS*, goddammit! Global *NEWS* Network. A colony on the Moon declares independence and chases off a regiment of Peacekeeper troops—that's freakin' *NEWS*!"

The vice president was perspiring, his face white with fear and shock.

Straightening, McGrath whirled on the head of the legal department, a distinguished-looking man with the chiselled features of a video star, carefully coiffed silver-gray hair, and a tan almost as deep as McGrath's own.

"How can Kiribati pick up a report from one of our employees and broadcast it around the world?"

The lawyer arched an eyebrow. "They can't. Not legally. We can sue them for billions."

McGrath stared at the man for several silent seconds. "It would make a great news story, wouldn't it?" he asked rhetorically. "Global News Network sues the nation of Kiribati in the World Court because a bunch of half-naked islanders have the brains to broadcast news from one of Global's own reporters while Global's news department *DECIDED NOT TO AIR THEIR OWN REPORTER'S STORY*!"

"He *was* following your own orders," the lawyer said mildly.

"That's right, chief," said programming. "You can't blame the news department for doing what you told them to do."

McGrath stood silently for a moment, then crossed his beefy arms across his chest.

"We look like freakin' assholes," he muttered.

"As I understand it," the head of the legal department tried to explain, "Edie Elgin beamed her report here from Moonbase. We were under your orders not to reply to any messages coming from Moonbase—we expected her to return with the Peacekeepers, after all."

"Okay, okay," McGrath grumbled, "so I told you not to carry anything coming from Moonbase. But our own reporter, for chrissake! Shows the world that Faure's a lying little sneak. And they've declared independence. Doesn't anybody think for themselves around here?"

An uncomfortable silence greeted his question.

The lawyer resumed, placatingly, "Apparently Elgin, or the Moonbase people, repeated her report to several locations around the world. Maybe she was trying to get one of our offices to acknowledge receiving it."

"We don't have an office in Kiribati," McGrath mumbled.

"That's true. But those islands are spread out over a

considerable portion of the Pacific. Somebody out there must have picked up Elgin's report and decided to pirate it."

"So what can we do, legally?"

"Sue them, of course."

McGrath shook his head. "I'm not going to give the competition a chance to show the world what buffoons we've been."

"We've got to do *something*," the lawyer insisted, "even if it's just a suit to protect our copyright."

McGrath fumed for a few moments. "I'll talk to whoever's in charge there. I want to keep this as quiet as possible."

Programming piped up, "So what do we do about Moonbase now?"

"Edie Elgin's still up there?"

The news VP nodded.

"Then we run her reports, goddammit. We've got the only reporter on the scene at Moonbase. We play it for all it's worth!"

"But your agreement with Faure . . . ?"

"Fuck him! You think the United Nations is more important than Global News Network?"

Ibrahim al-Rashid was not happy when his executive assistant—a lissome sloe-eyed Jamaican woman with a delightful lilt in her voice—informed him that another news broadcast was coming from Moonbase. Rashid watched Edie Elgin's report from Moonbase's farm in glum silence. His heart sank when she told the world that Moonbase could sustain itself indefinitely and did not need supplies from Earth.

Even before her report ended, Rashid's intercom chimed softly. He glanced at the phone screen: GEORGES FAURE, UNITED NATIONS, NEW YORK.

With a sigh, Rashid muted the news report from Moonbase's farm and activated the phone. Faure's face, even on the small screen, looked bleak.

"You have seen this latest news broadcast from Moonbase?" Faure asked, without preamble.

"I was just watching it now."

"The situation deteriorates with each moment," Faure said. "Now the entire world knows that Moonbase has asked for independence."

"I thought Global News had agreed to the blackout," said Rashid.

"They did. But once Kiribati broke the blackout, Global and the other networks broke their agreements with me."

Rashid sank back in his chair. Kiribati. That means Tamara Bonai has betrayed me. And Joanna's out there whipping up the other directors against me.

"It was my belief," Faure almost snarled, "that the Kiribati Corporation was under your control."

"It was my belief, too. Apparently we were both wrong."

"Then something must be done to correct them!"

"What do you have in mind?"

Faure's image glowered out of the screen, like a little imp trying to look threatening. "I might ask of you the same question," he retorted.

"I'll call the person responsible for this. I'll see to it that it doesn't happen again."

"Too late for that," Faure snapped. "Now that the cat is out of the sack, we will not be able to stuff it back inside again. All the news networks are besieging my public information office for permission to send reporters to Moonbase."

"You don't have to grant such permission," said Rashid.

"Certainly not! But this means that the news networks will carry any propaganda that Moonbase beams to Earth!"

Rashid thought about that for a moment, and reluctantly decided that Faure was right.

"In that case," he said to the fuming image, "all we can do is counter their propaganda with information of our own."

"Yes, and in the meantime the World Court will meet to decide whether or not Moonbase can be considered as a nation of its own."

"Surely you can delay the World Court."

"Only to a certain extent."

"Long enough to send a stronger contingent of troops to seize Moonbase?"

Faure nodded tightly. "Yes, long enough for that, I should think."

For some time after Faure's call, Rashid sat in his desk chair, fingers steepled before his face, swivelling back and forth slightly. He was wondering what he could do about Tamara Bonai. This broadcast from Moonbase had to be her doing. She was defying everything that Rashid had worked so patiently to achieve.

There would be a showdown with Joanna soon, he knew. She's trying to drum up support on the board for a special meeting. Bonai will undoubtedly be on her side, unless I can prevent her from it.

The problem was that Bonai was not merely the figurehead president of the hollow-shell Kiribati Corporation. She was also the head of the Kiribati council of chiefs; technically, legally, she was a chief of state.

I will have to deal very carefully with her, Rashid thought. But she must be dealt with, one way or another.

A slow smile worked across his face. Bonai is a very beautiful woman. It could be quite enjoyable dealing with her—one way or another.

DAY FIFTEEN

Joanna's call woke Doug. He almost told the smart wall to answer it without cancelling the video, but Edith stirred drowsily beside him and mumbled, "What's that?"

"Nothing," he whispered, bending over her and kissing her bare shoulder. "Go back to sleep."

Doug slipped out of bed and padded to his desk on the other side of the partitioned room. The phone kept on chiming softly, insistently.

The chair felt cool to his bare rump. He picked up the old-fashioned receiver and spoke softly, "Stavenger here."

From the delay he realized the call was coming from Earthside. His mother's voice asked testily, "Where are you? Why isn't there any video?"

A smile creased Doug's face. "Because it's almost four AM here, Mother, and I'm not dressed." He pressed a stud on the phone console and his mother's features appeared on the wallscreen opposite his desk, slightly larger than life.

"Are you all right?" he asked, and heard the same question from her, almost at the same instant.

"I've had a long talk with Rashid. He's as much as admitted that he's working toward a merger with Yamagata."

"A merger?" The thought alarmed Doug. He had never considered that Masterson Corporation might be taken over by another company.

"It would be a buyout, really. Lord knows how much cash Yamagata's promised him under the table."

"What can you do about it?" Doug asked.

He knew her answer before he heard it. "I'm rallying the members of the board. If Yamagata wants us, it's going to be a hostile takeover, and we intend to fight it every inch of the way."

"Do you have enough votes?"

As he waited for her response, Doug realized he didn't know the board well enough to count the votes himself.

"It'll be close," Joanna admitted. "Rashid's got a solid bloc on his side. But I think I can turn some of them around. Tamara Bonai might be the swing vote."

"Tamara?"

A slight smile turned the corners of Joanna's lips. "It

might be worthwhile for you to visit her with the VR system. She's a year or so older than you, but a little sweet talk might help us."

Doug stared at his mother. Despite the smile, she meant it.

"Mom," he said, thinking of Edith sleeping in his bed, "I'm no Romeo." He couldn't help smiling.

But Joanna was already saying, "Faure's been ducking me, as usual. His office has set up a meeting with two of his underlings, so I'm sending Lev to meet with them."

"We want to send some of the people here back Earthside," Doug said. "The dance troupe . . . and there's at least a dozen others who want to get home as soon as they can."

Joanna nodded once she heard his words. "I'll tell Lev to see what he can work out. An evacuation flight might be good publicity for us. Faure won't be able to turn down such a request. If he does—"

"Speaking of publicity," Doug interjected, "are Edith Elgin's reports doing us any good?"

Her face lit up once she heard the question. "Are they! She's going to get a Pulitzer, you mark my words."

"Great," said Doug. "But are they having any effect?"

"Everybody knows you've declared Moonbase's independence," Joanna said excitedly. "All the talk shows and newsheets are full of debates about it. I've gotten three U.S. senators to ask the White House to request a hearing in the World Court. Faure's turning blue over it!"

"Good," Doug said. "Great. How soon will the World Court take up our case?"

Joanna's reply came three seconds later. "We're pushing for an emergency session of the court. Otherwise it'll have to wait until November, when they convene again. At least they'll put it at the head of their agenda, even if it's November."

"November? That's more than six months away."

"I'm trying to get to them sooner."

Doug felt his brows knitting. "Faure could do a lot of damage in six months."

Once she heard him, Joanna nodded. "But at least the public knows what's going on now. Here in the States, especially, it's the hottest thing in the media. You tell that reporter that she's done more for Moonbase than a thousand troops could do."

Doug looked up and saw Edith standing by the partition that screened off the bedroom, quite naked.

"Okay," he said with a grin that he couldn't suppress. "I'll tell her right away."

The digital clock on Jack Killifer's desk said eleven PM. The offices of the Urban Corps' headquarters in Atlanta were nearly deserted.

The offices took up the entire top floor of the tallest tower in the Peachtree Center. Looking out through the sweeping windows, Killifer saw a city darkened, blacked out, as if fearful of an air raid. Only far down at street level were there bright anti-crime lamps blazing through the night. Otherwise all the buildings seemed totally dark and abandoned.

The sonofabitch enjoys making me stew around, waiting for him, Killifer groused to himself. Going on eight friggin' years I've been working for these people and he still treats me like some office boy.

The Urban Corps was one of the many disparate organizations loosely held together under the banner of the New Morality. They had elected presidents, won control of the House of Representatives, and had enough senators on their side to block legislation that they didn't like. The anti-nanotechnology treaty had originated in the New Morality. Nanoluddite fanatics had gunned down pro-nanotech advocates, even women suspected of having nanotherapy instead of plastic surgery, and then proclaimed at their trials with the fervor of true belief that they were doing God's work.

For years, though, Killifer had urged his superiors in the Urban Corps that Moonbase was a danger to them. As long as Moonbase exists it must use nanotechnology. As long as Moonbase exists it will continue to make its profits by building Cl;pperships out of pure diamond, using nanomachines, and selling those rocket craft to transport lines on Earth. As long as Moonbase exists, the nanotechnology treaty is a farce and everything that the Urban Corps and the New Morality has worked to achieve is in danger of crumbling away into dust.

And now it was all coming true. Moonbase was laughing at them, Stavenger and his bitch of a mother were thumbing their noses at them. The news media were all full of bullcrap about Moonbase's declaration of independence. Even some politicians were starting to say that maybe the nanotech treaty shouldn't be interpreted so strictly.

It could all fall apart, Killifer had been warning them for years. Only now, only with the humiliating rout of the Peacekeepers from Moonbase, were they beginning to take his warnings seriously.

His desk phone beeped once. Killifer didn't have to pick it up. He knew that he had been summoned at last into the presence of General O'Conner.

Killifer hurried past rows of empty, silent desks and down a corridor formed by flimsy shoulder-high plastic partitions. Through an open door he stepped, into a reception area that was tastefully carpeted and furnished with small consultation desks. The door at the far end was shut. He knocked once and opened it.

General O'Conner was sunk in his wheelchair, half dozing, a shrivelled shell of the dynamic powerful savior Killifer had met when he had joined the Urban Corps nearly eight years earlier.

They had kept the news of the general's strokes a secret, of course, known only to the innermost circle of the corps. Not even the highest leaders of the other New Morality groups knew about it. To the outside world, General O'Conner was still the vigorous, forceful, charismatic leader of the organization that was transforming American cities from crime-ridden slums into rigidly controlled urban centers.

With the staff's careful handling of the crisis, General O'Conner had become an inaccessible figure, too lofty to waste his time with meetings and rallies. And the more inaccessible he became, the greater the tales of his power and saintliness. The less he was seen, the more he was admired and sought after. Rumors abounded of his appearances in disguise among the poor. He was "seen" all across the country, sometimes in more than one place simultaneously. Thanks to clever electronic simulations that kept his image before the public, the general was becoming a figure of mythic power.

"Well, what're you waiting for?" General O'Conner said, in his cranky slurred croak of a voice.

"I thought you had fallen asleep," said Killifer, going to the armchair beside him.

The general worked the toggle on his wheelchair's control box and trundled off toward the windows. "Is the whole city blacked out, except for us?"

Killifer had to get up and follow him. "Most of the city," he replied. "When curfew strikes, the power goes down. Electricity stays on for residences, of course."

"Apartments, too? Condos?"

"Yeah. It wouldn't be smart to shut off their power."

"Then why's everything pitch-black out there?" the general demanded. "Are we the only ones showing any light?"

Killifer had explained this to the failing old man a dozen times since the blackout decision had been announced.

"That's right, we're the only one," he said. "The apartment blocks and condo buildings curtain their windows as a sign of respect."

The wizened old man glared at him. "And whose idea was that?"

"Yours, of course," he said.

"I never made such a decision. I'd remember it if I did."

"Well," said Killifer, "it was mine, really. Acting in your name, of course."

Actually, it had been the bright idea of one of the young psychologists on the staff. But Killifer had implemented it and he'd be damned if he'd let the young snot take the credit.

"Why?" O'Conner asked testily.

Killifer replied, "It gives the ordinary people the feeling that they're making a sacrifice. It makes them feel that they're contributing to the general welfare."

"You've learned well," rasped O'Conner. "Make them *want* to obey. That's the secret!"

"You've taught me well," Killifer said, feeling something almost like affection for the old man.

Wheeling his chair around to face Killifer, General O'Conner said, "Now what's happening with the Moonbase problem?"

Killifer shook his head. "It's getting worse instead of better."

"I see they're broadcasting news reports from Moonbase. I thought the media had agreed to a blackout."

"They had. But it's been busted wide open."

The general's bloodshot eyes narrowed. "How? Who did it?"

Killifer explained the series of events, tracing the break of the news blackout to Tamara Bonai in Kiribati.

"Kiribati?" General O'Conner's ravaged face glared at him. "Where's that?"

"In the Pacific. Micronesia."

The general seemed to sink in on himself, thinking. Then he started cackling.

"What's funny?" Killifer asked.

"I did missionary work out there when I was a kid."

That surprised Killifer. "You did?"

"Tonga. Fiji. I wore the black suit and tie and went out among the heathen." He wiped at his eyes with a frail hand.

"I never knew."

"They were good people. They listened to me and smiled and agreed with everything I said. Helped me build a church for them. They even attended services."

"Terrific," Killifer muttered.

"But it didn't do one bit of good. They went about living the way they always had. Dressed up for me, of course. But other times they went back to being as naked as sin. To them, sex was about as casual as taking a swim in the lagoon."

He almost sounded wistful, Killifer thought. "Well, now they have office buildings and shopping malls and major tourist centers."

"And this woman, what's her name?"

"Tamara Bonai."

"She broke the news blackout?"

"She sure as hell did."

"Then she ought to be punished," General O'Conner said. "Swiftly and obviously. People ought to know that those who oppose God's will are struck down."

Killifer's insides shuddered. "You mean kill her?"

"Yes," said the general. "See to it."

"Me?"

"You. And nobody else."

He started to say, "But why me? I'm no . . ."

O'Conner's burning red eyes silenced him. The general had made up his mind and he had chosen Killifer for the job. That was unalterable.

One thing that Killifer had learned in his eight years with the Corps: you obey, but you ask for something in return.

"If we're going to punish people, what about Joanna Stavenger . . . I mean, Brudnoy."

"She's back here, back from the Moon?"

"Yeah."

O'Conner mulled it over for ten seconds. "You're right. Strike her down, too."

Killifer nodded, satisfied. The woman who had ruined his life was going to get what she deserved, at last.

"Too bad we can't get her son."

"Douglas Stavenger?"

"Yeah. He's up at Moonbase, though. Out of reach."

General O'Conner pointed a wavering finger at Killifer. "Don't be so sure of that, my boy. No one's out of reach of the angel of death."

DAY SIXTEEN

"Hey, what're you doing there?"

The mercenary looked up. A woman in the slate-gray coveralls of the transportation division was striding down the line of spacesuits toward him. She looked to be in her thirties, a little heavyset, mousey brown hair chopped short, and an angry frown on her face.

"Doug Stavenger asked me to check out his suit," the mercenary said.

"*I* maintain the suits," she said, jabbing a thumb toward her ample chest. Her nametage said LIEBOWITZ. "Since when does Stavenger send strangers to do *my* job?"

She was almost the mercenary's own height, and now that she was almost nose-to-nose with him he saw that her size was probably muscle, not fat.

He put on a smile. "Doug's worried about sabotage," he said. The best lies are always based on the truth, he knew.

"Sabotage? Are you kidding?"

The mercenary shook his head slowly. "No, I'm not kidding, Liebowitz. We're at war, aren't we? Under siege?"

"But who the frick's gonna sabotage anything here? Everybody here's *for* Moonbase. We're all on Stavenger's side."

"Yeah? Were you at the meeting in the Cave last week?"

"Sure."

199

"How many people there wanted to go back Earthside right away?"

Liebowitz's expression turned thoughtful. "Well, a few, I guess."

"And they won't be able to go until this war is settled, right?"

"Oh, I dunno. Stavenger talked about arranging an evacuation flight for 'em."

"You seen any evacuation flight arrive? The U.N. wants to keep us bottled up here until we cave in."

"Yeah, maybe . . ."

The mercenary was enjoying sparring with her. He began to think it might be fun to share a meal with her, get to know her better. She was white, of course, but maybe . . .

He pushed those thoughts aside. "Well, don't you think that maybe some pissed-off technician or administrator might figure that a little sabotage here or there will help make us surrender and end the war? Then he can go home."

Liebowitz almost bought it. But after a few moments she said, "Naahhh. I just don't see anybody who's lived here for more'n ten minutes going around sabotaging anything. That could *kill* somebody, for chrissakes."

"Maybe so," the mercenary said. "But Stavenger's worried about it and he asked me to check out his suit."

She puffed out a breath between her teeth. "Okay. Okay. It sounds wonky to me, but if the boss wants you to check his suit, go right ahead."

She folded her arms across her chest and stood there, solidly planted, not budging. The mercenary went through the motions of checking Doug's hard suit, wishing she would go away, knowing she wouldn't, and telling himself that he'd have to come back when Liebowitz was off duty and some less dedicated technician was on the job.

"When's your shift end?" he asked as he looked over the seal ring on Doug's helmet.

"Same's yours."

"I'm working directly for Stavenger. No shifts; it's twenty-four hours a day for me."

She h'mphed. "Well, I'm on the day shift, as you can see. I finish at four, just like everybody else."

The mercenary returned the helmet to its rack, above the suit. "How about having dinner with me? Seven o'clock, in the Cave?"

She gave him a quizzical look. The mercenary knew exactly what was going through her mind. Would she want to be seen having dinner with a black man?

"Okay," she said guardedly. "Seven o'clock at the Cave."

It took him a couple of heartbeats to realize she had accepted. "See you there," he said, with a genuine smile.

And as he walked away, down the long line of empty spacesuits hanging like medieval arrays of armor with their helmets racked above them, he thought that after dinner with her he'd return and finish the job here.

Stavenger's going to go outside sooner or later, and when he does, a malfunction in his suit is going to kill him.

Later that day Doug was in Jinny Anson's office, meeting with the base director and the heads of the mining, transportation and research divisions.

Anson had rearranged the furniture so that the oblong conference table now butted against the desk like the vertical leg of a letter T.

Kris Cardenas was also sitting at the table, across from Zoltan Kadar, the astronomer. No one had invited the Hungarian to this strategy meeting; he had shown up with the others and grabbed a chair before anyone could shoo him away. His precious survey satellite to farside had been launched the day before, so Doug wondered what he wanted now.

And sitting silently on the couch along the far wall of the office was Bam Gordette, silently watching, listening. He's become like my shadow, Doug thought. Everywhere I go, he goes. He doesn't say anything, but he takes in everything with those dark brown eyes, like a detective looking over a crime scene. Then a new thought struck Doug: Maybe Bam thinks he's my bodyguard. He sure acts like one. The thought made him smile to himself. I don't need a bodyguard here, not in Moonbase. But it made him feel almost grateful to Gordette for caring enough to act as one.

Doug took the chair at the foot of the table, facing Anson, who sat behind her desk.

"I've asked you here—most of you, anyway," he added, with a wry grin in Kadar's direction, "to talk over the chances of developing defenses against the next Peacekeeper assault."

"You think they'll be back, then," said Deborah Paine. Head of the research division, she had a frizzy blond hairdo and an hourglass figure that had driven many men to distraction. She happened to be a very serious biologist, a topflight science administrator, and a cheerful lesbian.

"They'll be back," Doug said. "Faure's delaying any negotiations as much as he can. He's going to try to take us by force before agreeing to any compromise."

"We don't want any compromise, either," Anson snapped. "It's independence or bust."

Harry Clemens clasped both hands behind his bald head and tilted his chair so far back Doug was afraid it would fall over. "So we've got to be prepared to defend ourselves, then?"

"That's right," said Doug.

"Against what?"

"More Peacekeeper troops," said Vince Falcone, head of the mining division.

"Worse than that," Clemens said in his mild, soft way.

"Like what?" Falcone asked.

"One modest nuclear warhead exploded a few hundred meters above the crater floor could knock out all our solar farms."

Doug countered, "But we've still got the nuclear backup. It's buried—"

"Nuclear warhead number two will be a ground blast, to knock out our generator."

Falcone nodded solemnly. "The second one doesn't even have to be a nuclear warhead. Conventional warhead will do, if they've got the generator pinpointed."

"Okay," said Doug, looking at each of them in turn. "The first thing we've got to do is figure out what they can throw at us. Then we've got to look for ways to defend ourselves against each possible threat."

"Lotsa luck," Falcone grumbled. He was built like a fireplug, with short thick arms and a nearly perpetual scowl on his dark face. Instead of the usual coveralls, he preferred to wear dark turtlenecks and comfortable, loose-fitting jeans that he jammed into scuffed old cowboy boots.

"There may be a way to defend against a nuclear warhead," said Deborah Paine.

Doug felt his eyebrows hike halfway to his scalp.

"The physicists have been using the mass driver's magnets to power a particle accelerator," Paine said. "If we could focus the beam on an incoming warhead, it could destroy the nuclear device's switching and fusing mechanisms."

"Are you sure?" Doug asked.

"It's actually pretty old stuff," she replied, "from the anti-missile defenses that the Peacekeepers maintain in Earth orbit."

"So it turns the nuke into a dud, huh?" Falcone asked.

"Yes. The warhead will crash onto the crater floor, but the bomb won't go off."

"That'd still do some damage to the solar panels," Clemens pointed out.

"Yeah, but not that many of 'em," said Falcone.

Doug asked, "Could we actually focus the particle beam that way?"

Paine shrugged. It looked delicious to all the men around the table, even though they knew she didn't do it for their benefit.

"I'll have to ask the physicists about it," she said. "We should have plenty of time to aim the beam, if they fire the missile from Earthside. Days."

"Suppose they take over L-1 and use it as a staging base. They could fire the missile from there."

Nodding, Paine said, "That would still give us a couple of hours or so, maybe more."

"Maybe less," Anson said, "if they fire it at high boost."

"Maybe."

Doug turned to Cardenas. "Kris, what are you and Zimmerman developing? Anything useful?"

She sighed. "Willi's got this bug in his ear about using nanomachines to make a person invisible. I was hoping something practical might come out of it, but so far I haven't seen a thing."

"And your own work?" Doug prompted.

"We can be a big help medically, of course. As far as weaponry is concerned, I haven't come up with anything except the gobblers. We can program them to eat metals, if you like."

"We can't strew the whole crater floor with gobblers," Doug said.

"Why not?" Anson shot back. "It'd only be for a short time."

Doug ticked off on his fingers, "One, they'll most likely land during daylight—"

"You can program gobblers to operate in sunlight, can't you?" Anson asked Cardenas.

"It's more difficult, but doable. I'd worry about deactivating them, though."

"Two," Doug went on, "what's to stop the gobblers from destroying our solar farms, the launch pads and their equipment, even the mass driver?"

Anson pursed her lips. Then she grinned. "Yeah, it *would* be like shooting ourselves in the foot, wouldn't it?"

"Shooting ourselves in the head," Clemens said, with surprising fervor. Doug realized he wanted no part of nanomachines that ate metals.

Turning in his chair to look at Gordette, Doug asked, "Bam, if you were in charge of the Peacekeepers, how would you go about taking Moonbase?"

Gordette shook his head. "I wasn't an officer, just a dogface."

"You're as close to a general as we've got here," Anson said.

"What do you think they're going to do?" Doug repeated.

Slowly, reluctantly, Gordette got to his feet. All eyes focused on him. "Well, to begin with, I agree with Mr. Clemens. They'll start with a bombardment to knock out our electrical power."

"Nuclear warheads?"

"Most likely. But they might use a conventional warhead for our nuclear generator, if they know its location precisely enough."

"They've got the same maps we use," Falcone grumbled.

"Then what?" Doug asked.

"Most likely they'd have already landed troops outside the crater, on the Mare Nubium side. They'll wait for the bombardment, then come over Wodjohowitcz Pass to get into the base."

Doug saw most of the people around the table nodding agreement.

"If our electrical power is out, all they'll have to do is knock on our door. We'll have to surrender to them."

"We have the fuel cells," Anson said.

Gordette shrugged. "How long do they give us? A few days? A few hours? The Peacekeepers will be occupying the crater floor; we'll have no chance to repair the solar farms. We'll be forced to give up."

"A nuclear blast probably'd screw up our radiators, too," Falcone pointed out. "We'd be boiling in here inside of a few hours."

The meeting became grim, depressed. No one could offer a way to counter the scenario Gordette had drawn.

Then Kadar spoke up. "It may not be necessary for the Peacekeepers to destroy so much of our generating equipment."

"Oh?"

"All they have to do is put some biological agents

in the drinking water we bring in from the south polar
ice fields."

"Poison us?" Clemens blurted, looking shocked.

Almost smiling, Kadar said, "It wouldn't have to be
fatal. A virus that causes a disabling disease. An especially nasty variation of influenza, for instance. Or viral
pneumonia. Brought in through our drinking water."

"We don't use that much new water," Anson pointed
out. "Our recycling's pretty efficient."

"Perhaps so, but over a time scale of months? They
could make us all deathly ill."

"Do we have to defend the south pole, too?" Anson
wondered aloud.

With a shake of his head, Doug replied, "We just
don't have the resources."

"But we can test the water coming in," Paine said,
"and not allow it into the base supply until we're satisfied that it's all right."

"Or," Cardenas suggested, "we could run the incoming water through a nanomachine screen, program the
nanos to pass only water molecules and divert everything else."

"That would help," Doug said.

"They won't be that subtle," Gordette said, still standing by the couch. "They won't want to wait weeks or
months for a biological agent to take effect. Besides,
they know we've got nanomachines that we could use
to cure any disease they cause."

"So it'll be a direct attack."

"That's what I think," Gordette replied. "They'll land
their troops, bomb out our electrical power equipment,
and then march in here."

Cardenas slumped in her chair. "Nanomachines aren't
going to be much help, then."

"We can knock out a nuclear warhead," Paine
insisted.

"Maybe," said Doug.

"How'll we deal with a whole regiment of
Peacekeeper troops?" Anson asked glumly.

"We'll have to think of something," said Doug, trying to show a cheerfulness he did not feel.

"If we can keep on generating electricity . . ."

Doug pushed his chair back from the table. "I want to talk to the head honcho of the physicists about this particle beam idea."

"The new guy," Anson said. "He came up here on the last flight before this mess started."

"What's his name," Doug asked, "Wickens?"

"Wicksen," Paine corrected. "Robert T. Wicksen."

DAY SEVENTEEN

After the meeting Doug went straight to the office of Robert T. Wicksen. The physicist was a small, slight man, built like a sparrow, but with large intelligent gray eyes magnified by old-fashioned rimless glasses.

"Focus the particle beam on an incoming missile warhead?" Wicksen asked. His voice was flat and calm. He was not perturbed by Doug's question, he merely repeated it to be certain he understood what Doug was asking. Physically he reminded Doug of a tarsier: little, cautious, big staring eyes. Yet he seemed composed, unruffled, perhaps unflappable.

Wicksen's office was a cubbyhole crammed with electronic gear. No desk, not even any chairs; only a pair of stools that looked as if Wicksen had crafted them himself out of lunar metals. Yet everything was as neat as a picture out of a sales catalogue. Everything in its proper place. All the equipment humming reassuringly. All the screens displayed data curves that flickered and shifted as they spoke. Wicksen himself was equally neat, in a crisp open-necked white shirt and perfectly creased dark gray trousers.

"We need to know if it's possible to convert your particle accelerator into a beam weapon," Doug said, sitting on one of the room's two stools.

Sitting on the other stool, facing Doug like an elfish wizard in modern clothes, Wicksen nodded somberly. "It's possible. Anything is possible."

"But can you do it, Dr. Wicksen?"

"Wix."

"Excuse me?"

"Wix. Everyone calls me Wix."

"All right . . . Wix. Can you do it?"

Wicksen extended one arm and tapped idly on the keyboard nearest him. "Have to increase the power output, of course," he muttered, more to himself than his visitor. "And focusing the beam isn't a trivial problem."

Doug asked his question again, silently, with his eyes.

Wicksen scratched his pointed chin a moment, then said, "Meet me at the mass driver tomorrow at ten. I'll be able to answer you then."

Doug sensed that trying to urge this man or hurry him would be a waste of breath. Wicksen understood the situation they were in. Doug had noticed him at the meeting in the Cave the previous week. Yet the physicist showed neither worry nor disappointment at being asked to break off his experiments and convert his accelerator into a weapon. He seemed more curious than upset.

"He's a strange duck," Doug said to Edith that night, in his quarters. She had moved in her meager possessions after their first three nights together.

"I've interviewed lots of scientists," Edith said, unzipping her white coveralls. "They're all pretty weird, one way or the other."

"I've got to make a call Earthside," Doug said, padding barefoot to his desk on the other side of the room partition. "Won't take long," he called to Edith.

"I'll keep the bed warm," she called back.

Grinning, Doug called Tamara Bonai at Tarawa. She

was his one sure source of news about how things were going Earthside. His mother's calls were tapped, both Doug and Joanna were certain, so she had to be careful about how much she told her son.

But Tamara, as head of both the Kiribati Corporation and the island nation itself, could speak much more freely.

"You owe me a fishing trip," her image on the wallscreen teased.

She was on the beach, obviously just after a swim in the lagoon. Her flowered *pareo* clung wetly to her graceful figure; drops of water beaded her bare shoulders; her long dark hair glistened in the high afternoon sun.

"As soon as I can get Earthside," he promised anew. Then he asked, "How's our publicity campaign?"

As he waited for her reply, Doug admired her long slim legs and the nipples that pushed against the *pareo*'s thin fabric. Since he'd started sleeping with Edith he'd been noticing a lot more about the women he saw.

"Every network is carrying your reports from Moonbase now," Bonai said, smiling brightly as she sat crosslegged before the phone camera set on the sand before her. The camera automatically moved to keep her in focus.

"And there is considerable turmoil among the board of Masterson Corporation. Now that your mother is here on Earth, she's demanding a special meeting to take up the question of Moonbase's political independence."

"How's Rashid reacting?"

Bonai turned to look out at the lagoon as she waited for Doug's words to reach her. Then she turned back to the phone and said, "It's difficult to read his reaction. I'm sure he wants to push through a merger with Yamagata, but that possibility could cause a major rift on the board, and he'd prefer to avoid a confrontation, if he can."

Within a few seconds Doug forgot how enticing Bonai looked and fell deeply into a discussion with her about the politics of Masterson Corporation, the United Nations, and world public opinion.

"Faure has not said a peep about Moonbase for more than a week now," she reported. "He's trying to ride out the waves your broadcasts have created."

Doug replied, "He's planning another attack on us. I'm certain of it."

Once she heard him, Bonai shrugged her bare shoulders. "Could be, I suppose."

"Can you try to get closer to Rashid, Tamara? I need to know what he's thinking, what he's planning to do."

When her reply came to him, it was, "Are you asking me to use my feminine wiles on him?"

"No, I—"

But Bonai hadn't waited for his response. She continued, "He has some reputation, you know. There are rumors he keeps a harem over in North Africa somewhere."

"I didn't mean—"

She kept on, "It might be fun to see what he's really like. Maybe I'll invite him here for a private get-together."

"Tamara, I didn't mean you should try to seduce him," Doug said.

She laughed. "Don't be so uptight! He won't be able to turn down a chance to win me over to his side."

"But—"

"It's nothing I won't do for you when you come here for your fishing trip," she added, mischievously.

Feeling perplexed, Doug didn't know what to say.

Still smiling, Bonai said, "Don't worry, Doug. I know what I'm doing. And I have plenty of big, strong bodyguards here to protect me—if I ask them to."

She clicked off the connection before Doug could reply.

Frowning at the empty wallscreen, Doug got to his feet. Edith was standing by the partition, wrapped in a towel, eying him.

"Should I be jealous?" she asked.

"No!" Doug blurted. "Of course not."

"She's awful purty." Edith used her Texas accent.

"She's the CEO of Kiribati Corporation," Doug said.

"She's the person who got your first news report on the air Earthside."

"She's still awful purty," said Edith, reaching for him.

Doug thought he should feel annoyed. Instead, he felt almost pleased with himself.

As Doug rode on the tractor across Alphonsus' cracked and pockmarked floor, he realized that this was the first time he'd been outside in weeks.

He took a deep breath of canned suit air and felt his spirits rise. Strange, he thought, even sealed inside a spacesuit I feel free out here, happy. He looked up at the worn old mountains of the ringwall marching off across the horizon and recognized each rounded hump as an old friend from his childhood.

It was my childhood when I climbed those mountains and rode around the whole ringwall, he realized. I don't have time for that anymore. I've got an adult's responsibilities now.

Still, he relaxed and enjoyed the passing scenery: stark, barren, full of promise.

Driving the tractor was second nature to him. The big lumbering machine would probably trundle out to the mass driver on its own, even if Doug let go of the controls, following the cleated ruts laid down by thousands of tractor journeys across the dusty regolith. But Doug held onto the T-stick. There were enough craterlets and rocks strewn across the ground to cause trouble if he got careless, he knew.

He realized that this was the first time he had been alone in weeks. Not even Bam Gordette was with him. Doug thought about the somber-faced black man. Gordette had been his constant companion wherever he went in Moonbase, his self-appointed protector. Bodyguard, chauffeur, military consultant: I've become dependent on him, Doug thought. I wonder what he thinks about all this. I'd like to think of him as a friend, but he's so quiet and reserved it's hard to tell what's going on inside his head.

He said he wanted to come outside with me, but he

gave up the idea pretty easily when I told him it wasn't necessary. Is he afraid of being out here on the surface? Doug almost laughed, inside his helmet. He couldn't imagine Gordette afraid of anything.

The mass driver came into view, a long dark finger of metal stretched across the crater floor. It had its own acreage of solar farms to provide electricity for the magnets that flung lunar ores toward the factories in orbit around the Earth. Since the U.N.'s siege had begun, the space factories had shut down their operations and the mass driver stood unused in the silence of the lunar landscape.

Unused as an ore supplier.

The physicists had been overjoyed at the shutdown. Years earlier they had built a linear particle accelerator along the three-and-a-half-kilometer length of the mass driver, using its powerful cryogenic magnets to energize subatomic particles for their experiments. But they could use the facility only when the mass driver wasn't busy flinging packets of lunar ores off to the factories in Earth orbit. With the war the factories had been taken over by the U.N. The mass driver stood idle—and the physicists went into a frenzy of activity, ecstatic to use their particle accelerator twenty-four hours each day.

It was easy to spot Wicksen among the space-suited figures milling around the hardware. His slight figure was encased in a white spacesuit that had WIX stencilled in electric blue on the front of his helmet and across his backpack.

Doug clambered down from the tractor and walked the last twenty meters to the group of people standing with Wicksen. They seemed to be huddled around him like a football team getting instructions from their quarterback.

Flicking to the suit-to-suit frequency, Doug heard the physicist saying, " . . . you'll be able to finish this series of runs while I'm putting the focusing magnets together."

"Here's Doug now," said one of the suited figures, pointing with a gloved hand.

Wicksen turned and stepped toward Doug. "You're a few minutes early."

"I made better time in the tractor than I expected," Doug said.

"That's all right." The diminutive physicist clasped the sleeve of Doug's cermet suit. "Come along here, I want to show you what's involved in this problem."

He walked Doug the length of the mass driver, explaining in minute detail every step that had to be accomplished in converting the accelerator to an anti-missile gun. Doug's head was soon whirling with numbers and terms such as "beam collimator" and "tesla limits."

Doug found his attention wandering to the solid bulk of the mass driver itself. It was a triumph of nanotechnology, the most intricate piece of machinery yet constructed by nanomachines. The project had floundered through several false starts, but once Kris Cardenas had come to Moonbase and sunk her teeth into it, the mass driver had slowly taken shape out here on the crater floor: cryogenic aluminum magnets and all.

"Are you sufficiently confused?"

Wicksen's question snapped Doug's attention back to the here and now.

"What did you say?"

He could sense Wicksen smiling gently. "I've snowed you with a pile of details. Does any of it make sense to you?"

"Not much," Doug admitted. "What I really need to know is, can you do it?"

"Turn the accelerator into an anti-missile weapon?"

"Yes."

"Yes."

"You can?"

"That's what I've been telling you."

"How soon?" Doug asked.

Wicksen hesitated a moment, then answered, "Two days."

"Two days? That's all?"

"Two lunar days," Wicksen said.

"Oh. You mean two months, then," Doug said, crestfallen.

"We might get lucky and have everything work the first time we try it. That could shave a week or so."

Two months, Doug thought. Will that be soon enough, or will Faure strike before then?

"We'll need a target satellite to test it against," Wicksen added. "I was thinking that Kadar's survey bird would make a good test target. He's got all the data from it that he needs."

Doug heard a strange guttural sound in his earphones. Wicksen was chuckling at the thought of zapping Kadar's satellite.

He thanked the physicist and climbed back onto the tractor, wondering if there was some way to delay the attack that Faure was undoubtedly planning. Maybe Mom can get the World Court to hear our case before November. Or negotiate with Faure and try to settle this without another military confrontation.

His mind was filled with possibilities, alternatives, strategies as he steered the tractor back across the twenty-kilometer distance to Moonbase's main airlock.

He had only gone a few kilometers, though, when his suit's emergency alarm shrilled in his earphones.

"What . . . ?"

Doug glanced down at the tell-tales on his wrist display. Air supply below safety minimum! Impossible, he told himself. I checked the suit out when I put it on. The air tank was full.

Must be a malfunction in the electrical circuitry, he told himself. Still, he jammed the tractor's throttle to its highest pitch. The ponderous machine lurched forward. There was no speedometer on the control panel; the tractor's electrical motors could not move the machine more than thirty klicks per hour, Doug knew.

Half an hour to the base, Doug thought. Better top off the backpack.

With his left hand on the T-stick, Doug fumbled for the tractor's oxygen hose, nested between the two front seats. He located it by feel and pulled it out of its hous-

ing. But when he tried to unscrew the cap of his backpack's emergency fill-up, it would not move.

How could it be frozen? Doug wondered, his mind
racing. He could not remember if he'd tested it when
he'd checked out the suit. I should have, he told himself.
But he doubted that he had. Too goddamned compla-
cent. Taking shortcuts in the checkout routine.

"Air level approaching redline for life support," the
suit's automatic emergency system warned. "Replenish
air supply or change to another suit."

Good advice, Doug grumbled silently, out here at least
fifteen klicks from the airlock.

I *can't* be running out of air, he insisted to himself.
But he coughed.

Desperately, he flicked to the base frequency and
called, "This is Stavenger. I'm almost out of air! Need
help!"

"Got your beacon, Doug," said the technician from
the control center. "Hang on, we'll send a team out
for you."

Won't do any good, he knew. They'll be riding tractors, too. They can't get to me any faster than I can get
to them.

His breath caught in his throat. He felt as if he were
gagging.

"No . . . air . . ."

An incredibly searing pain flamed through his chest.
Christ almighty, my lungs are collapsing!

Yet he remained conscious, acutely aware of everything happening to him.

Can't breathe! He was gasping, his right hand clawing
at the collar of his helmet. Can't breathe! The pain in
his chest was excruciating, yet he did not pass out. His
mind was still alert, still functioning.

This is what drowning must be like. You try to
breathe, but there's no air.

Deliberately, he turned off his suit radio. They've got
the tractor's beacon to track me. Don't want them to
hear me screaming.

But he could not scream. There was no air in his lungs,

no air in his throat. Nothing but pain and pain and more pain.

And he could not collapse into oblivion. His legs, his gut, even his hands and arms were flaming with agony now, but the mercy of unconsciousness was not allowed him. Doggedly, tears blurring his vision, pain racking his body, he slumped over the tractor's controls, too weak to sit upright. But still conscious.

Time lost all meaning. Doug knew he was in hell: endless, eternal suffering. Damned, damned, damned to torment forever. The silent, stark lunar landscape trundled past slowly, maddeningly slowly. Doug felt as if he were mired in quicksand, already sucked down into it, unable to catch a breath, impossible to breathe, to move, to do anything but suffer.

He wanted to faint, he wanted to die and get it over with. He thought deliriously that he must already be dead. Why, this is hell.

He could not breathe. He could not cough or gasp or cry or beg for mercy. Yet he could not end the pain. It went on and on, endlessly, while his mind shrieked and gibbered with horrified terror.

Something banged into his helmet. He felt himself jerked back against the seat.

Slowly the pain eased away. His last touch with the world drifted away from him, leaving him floating in darkness, alone, silent, free of pain and desire and fear.

I'm dead, he thought. At last it's over. I'm dead.

He was breathing. He opened his eyes, but saw nothing but mist, a gray fog.

". . . had his suit radio off."

"Visor's fogged over. Turn up his fans, for chrissake."

"How the hell did he get into this fix?"

"Never mind that! Is he coming around?"

The voices were urgent, frightened; to Doug they sounded like a chorus of angels.

"Can't tell—"

"I can hear you," Doug said, coughing. "I can hear you."

"He's alive!"

"Barely."

Their frightened, urgent voices faded and Doug sank into blessed black oblivion.

DAY EIGHTEEN

"You are awake now, yes?"

Doug opened his eyes to see Zimmerman looming over him like a rumpled mountain, his fleshy face deathly serious, his eyes burning with inner fire.

The infirmary, Doug realized. I'm in the infirmary. He could smell the antiseptic, feel the crisp sheets on his skin. The little cubicle was clean and cool, walls and ceiling pastel. Electronic monitoring equipment hummed and beeped softly somewhere behind Doug's head.

"So," said Zimmerman quietly, "my little machines have saved your life again."

The old man's face wore an expression Doug had never seen before. Not tenderness, not from Zimmerman. But he seemed—concerned. He was standing over Doug's infirmary bed like a worried uncle or grandfather, looking faintly ridiculous in his disheveled, wrinkled, old-fashioned three-piece gray suit.

"When are you . . ." Doug asked, his voice little more than a faint whisper, "When are you going to program nanobugs to keep your clothes pressed?"

"Jokes?" Zimmerman's shaggy brows shot up. "You almost die and now you make jokes at me?"

"What happened?"

The old man ran a hand across his bald pate. "You had no oxygen for breathing. My nanomachines extracted oxygen from the cells of your body and fed it to your brain, to keep you alive."

"The pain . . ."

"Both your lungs collapsed, of course. My nanomachines kept your circulatory system going, however."

"Oxygen from my cells?"

Nodding vigorously, as if glad to get onto an impersonal topic, Zimmerman launched into a minor lecture about the amount of residual oxygen stored in the body's major organs.

"And the nanobugs extracted the residual oxygen?" Doug asked.

"Yah. And fed it into your bloodstream. That way your brain was kept alive even though your lungs collapsed."

"How did the bugs know to do that?"

Zimmerman scowled down at him. "You think they are stupid? They sensed your lungs collapsing and acted to keep you alive."

"You programmed them to do that? All those years ago when you put the bugs in me, you foresaw such a possibility?"

"I programmed the nano*machines*," Zimmerman emphasized the word slightly, "to maintain homeostasis and attack foreign invaders of your body. They sense any deviation from your normal condition and take immediate steps to counter it."

"They must work pretty fast."

"They react in the millisecond range, usually."

Doug looked into the old man's intense eyes. "That's the third time you've saved my life, Professor."

Zimmerman shrugged as if it didn't matter. "It gives me the chance to write a new research paper—although who will publish it is a question, with this *verdammt* war going on."

"I don't know what I can do to thank you," Doug said.

For just an instant, the professor's expression softened. Then he took in a breath and said sternly, "Try to stay out of mischief."

With that he turned on his heel and headed out of the cubicle.

"Wait!" Doug called, his voice a painful croak.

Zimmerman looked back over his shoulder, one hand on the sliding partition.

"What're you doing in your lab? I haven't seen you in so long—"

"We discuss that later, when you are stronger."

"But what are you working on?"

With an impatient gesture, Zimmerman said, "This and that. You will see."

He slid the partition back and left the cubicle. Doug thought that perhaps Zimmerman didn't want him to see that he actually cared about him. But then he realized:

He hasn't come up with anything yet. All these weeks tinkering in his lab and he hasn't accomplished a mother-loving thing.

Before a full minute passed, Edith rushed into the cubicle, up to Doug's bedside, her green eyes staring at him.

"Are you okay?"

"I'm fine," he said, reaching out to her.

She leaned into his arms and kissed him hard. "You really okay?"

"A little weak, but I'll be back to normal in a couple of hours."

"Hours?"

"The nanomachines work fast," he said.

Edith sat on the edge of the bed and laid her head on his chest. "Christmas bells, I was so scared! They said your suit had malfunctioned and you might die."

Holding her tightly, Doug said, "Not yet, Edith. Not for a long time."

Hours later, after several sessions with the medics and Kris Cardenas, Doug was sitting up in bed, surrounded by Jinny Anson, Harry Clemens and Bam Gordette.

"The cermet suit failed," Doug said.

"We've gone over it," Clemens said. He was tall and lanky; it always surprised Doug that he spoke with a

Down Maine twang instead of a cowboy's drawl. "Found a rupture along the seal between the air tank and the backpack frame. Looks like a pinhole in the insulation started it, then the pressure inside the tank broke it into a major leak."

"How could a pinhole get into the insulation?"

"Search me."

Anson said, "Somebody could've put it there."

Doug turned his head toward her. "Somebody? You mean sabotage?"

She nodded silently.

"I can't believe that, Jinny."

"The suit didn't fail," she said. "Somebody tampered with it."

Doug looked back at Clemens. "Harry?"

"I can't see how it could've failed by itself. I even thought maybe a micrometeorite hit the air tank, but when I started figuring out the angle it would've had to come in, it would've had to come *up* out of the ground!"

"So it wasn't a micrometeorite."

"Somebody dug out a pinhole in the insulation," Anson insisted. "Somebody who knows enough about suits to understand that the oxygen pressure inside the tank would break through the weak spot in half an hour or so after the tank was pressurized."

"Nobody here at Moonbase would do something like that," Doug insisted.

"Oh no?" Clemens countered. "Whoever it was covered up the pinhole with a smidge of foamgel insulation, so the leak wouldn't start until you'd been out on the surface for a half hour or so."

"The kind of foamgel the construction crew uses?" Doug asked.

Clemens nodded. "For stiffening temporary walls and stuff like that, right."

"The foamgel held the pressure in your air tank until it got brittle from exposure to vacuum," said Anson.

"If your tank had been down at a regular suit's pressure you would've been okay, I think," Clemens said. "But at fourteen-point-seven psi, it blew out."

"And what about the emergency fill valve?" Anson added.

Clemens looked almost sheepish as he said, "The threads were smeared with dust. Froze the valve shut just as effectively as if they'd soldered it."

The realization made Doug's insides feel hollow. "We've got a saboteur among us?"

"A traitor," Anson snapped.

"But who? Why?"

"That's what we've got to find out. And fast."

Doug looked at Gordette, standing slightly behind Clemens, silent, taking in every word.

"Bam, I want you to look into this."

His eyes went wide. "Me?"

"Jinny and Harry have plenty of responsibilities to keep them busy. I want you to devote full time to this."

Gordette seemed startled. "But I don't know enough about spacesuits or any of that stuff. I'm not a cop. That's what your security department is for."

Doug shook his head. "Security doesn't have the personnel for this kind of investigation."

"But I'm just a glorified plumber."

"Jinny and Harry will give you all the help they can. You can call on anybody in Moonbase for technical assistance. And I'll tell security to cooperate with you fully."

Gordette's brows knit. It was clear to Doug that the man didn't want the job, but he couldn't refuse it.

"Another reason for you to do it, Bam," Doug added. "I don't want anybody outside this cubicle to know we're hunting for a saboteur. No sense stirring up everybody. And it might be easier to catch our traitor if he doesn't know he's being tracked down."

"Or she," Anson said.

Doug stared at her. Who did she have in mind? "Or she," he conceded. "Now get out of here and back to work."

"When are you going back to work?" Anson jibed.

"I'll be out of here as soon as the medics run one

more set of tests. But I can work from this bed, don't worry."

"Me worry?" She laughed. "What have I got to worry about?"

"Someone tried to kill you?"

Her son's revelation shocked Joanna to her roots. She had taken his call in the comfortable little upstairs sitting room of her home outside Savannah. It was early summer beyond her windows: trees were in leaf, birds chirping in the afternoon sunlight. And there was an assassin stalking the confines of Moonbase's underground corridors.

"That's what Jinny and the others think," Doug said. He seemed cheerful and healthy enough, although now Joanna realized that he was sitting up in an infirmary bed.

He assured her that he was all right. "And I'm not completely convinced this wasn't just a freak accident, Mom."

Joanna realized she was biting her lip. "No," she said. "It wasn't an accident. It's just the kind of thing that Faure would do, the little sneak."

Doug smiled when he heard her words. "But how could he get an assassin smuggled in here?"

"That dance troupe," Joanna replied. "Faure timed all this so that the dance troupe would be stranded up there with you."

This time Doug actually broke into laughter. "You think one of the ballet dancers tampered with my spacesuit? They don't even know how to put one on."

"What about that reporter?"

She saw his eyes go wide once he heard her words. "Edith? She—it couldn't be her. It couldn't be!"

"Why not?" Joanna persisted. "You didn't have this kind of trouble before she talked her way into the base, did you?"

"It's not her," Doug said firmly. "It can't be."

Joanna did not reply, but her suspicions did not fade an iota.

"What's happening down there?" Doug asked, changing the subject.

"Lev's in New York, talking to Faure's flunkies. I've finally gotten Rashid to convene an emergency meeting of the board in two weeks. I have an item on the agenda calling for the board to urge the White House to recognize Moonbase's independence."

Doug's brows rose when he heard her. "Do you think you can carry that?"

"I've been counting noses. Tamara will be the swing vote, I'm certain of it."

"She'll vote on our side," Doug said.

"I want you to do everything you can to make sure of that."

She watched his face closely as he listened to her and digested her meaning.

"Mom," said Doug, "there's not much I can do from this distance except talk to her."

"Use the virtual reality link," Joanna urged. "Take her for a walk on the beach. Or a swim. She likes you, I'm certain of it."

From his infirmary bed, Doug stared at his mother's intense image on the little screen he had propped up on his lap. Good thing we're not living in the days when families arranged their children's marriages, he thought.

Then he wondered when he should tell his mother about Edith. And what do I really have to tell her? How serious is our relationship?

Do I love her? The question stunned him. Is this what love is, wanting to share your life with somebody? It's all happened so quickly, like falling off the edge of a cliff.

Does she love me? Will she want to share her life with me after this war is finished and she can go back Earthside again?

Yet in the back of his mind he realized that there had never been any hint of a traitor in Moonbase before Edith Elgin had arrived.

He heard his mother's voice, *You didn't have this kind of trouble before she talked her way into the base, did you?*

Doug ignored the voice. Or tried to.

DAY TWENTY-FOUR

Jack Killifer found that he was enjoying his visit to Tarawa. Despite his orders.

Outwardly, he was an American tourist taking in the beaches and fishing excursions by day, the gambling casino and musical shows by night. There were plenty of women, especially in the casino, most of them Asian, although he saw a couple of terrific tall blondes that must have been from Sweden or Germany or maybe even the States. Funny that there were hardly any island women in the casino, he thought. But he preferred big broads, anyway, not the dark little *wahines*.

There was one particular island woman that he had to find, though: Tamara Bonai.

Killifer had balked when General O'Conner told him to take care of Bonai himself. "Why not hire a professional?" he had demanded.

The wizened old man had glared at him from his wheelchair. "God's work has to be done by God's people, Jack. It would be wrong to bring in an outsider. Wrong, and dangerous. The fewer people know about this, the better off we are."

Killifer had been forced to agree. Get a professional and you'd be blackmailed for life.

"If the woman was in the States, or Europe, or even Japan," O'Conner had added, "we could get one of our local zealots to do her. But out there on those islands, we don't have anybody we can depend on. That's why it's got to be you, Jack."

224

Reluctantly, he had bowed to the general's order.

"Besides," the old man had said, a vicious smile on his lips, "this won't be your first time. You murdered Foster Brennart, didn't you?"

Sitting at the bar closest to the roulette table, nursing a rye and ginger-ale, Killifer thought back to Brennart and the first expedition to the lunar south pole. He'd wanted to kill Doug Stavenger; Brennart's death was more of an accident than anything else. He'd tried to trap the Stavenger kid up there on the mountaintop during the radiation storm. But Brennart had to be a friggin' hero and go out there with him. So Brennart died and became a legend, while Stavenger pulled through and survived.

It was Joanna Stavenger that he had really wanted to kill. Joanna Brudnoy now. The bitch blamed him for her husband's death. Paul Stavenger had been killed by nanobugs from Killifer's lab. So his widow exiled Killifer to Moonbase. Either go to Moonbase or face trial for murder, she had told him. He picked Moonbase. It wrecked his career, ruined his life.

And she's still running other people's lives, Mrs. Rich Bitch, lording it over everybody else. I'll get her. One way or the other I'll get her.

The tall glass in his hand suddenly shattered, spraying rye and ginger-ale and ice cubes across the bar. The guy next to him jumped up from his barstool and wiped at his shirt front, his expression halfway between surprise and anger. Fuck you, Killifer told him silently.

The bartender, a burly Micronesian in a loose-fitting mesh shirt, hurried up to him.

"You okay?"

"Yeah," Killifer said, shaking his drenched hand. "I'm all right, don't worry."

"Man, that's some grip you got," said the bartender as he quickly set up another drink. "Take it easy, Iron Man, we only got a couple hundred of these glasses!"

"You didn't cut yourself, did you?"

A delicious redhead in a strapless gown took his hand

in her gentle fingers, then looked up at him with big blue innocent eyes.

"Naw," Killifer said, smiling at her. "I'm okay."

"You must have some kind of troubles, crushing the glass like that. Like, real tension, huh?"

He admired the curve of her cleavage. "Everybody's got troubles," he said.

"Boy, is *that* true."

"You too?"

"Don't even ask," she said.

"Come on up to my room," Killifer said, "and we can tell each other about our troubles."

She didn't hesitate a microsecond. "Okay. Let's."

"Well," said Lev Brudnoy to his wife, "they agreed to evacuate up to sixty people from Moonbase. They're calling it a mercy flight."

Brudnoy had just returned to Savannah from a two-day trip to United Nations headquarters. Joanna met him at the Masterson Corporation airport. Now, in the privacy of their soundproofed limousine, he told her what he'd accomplished in New York.

"A mercy flight," Joanna echoed.

With a ghostly smile, Brudnoy said, "They intend to get as much publicity out of it as possible: bringing back people from Moonbase who might have been held as hostages."

"Hostages! Why, that lying little—"

Brudnoy put a lean finger to her lips. "Publicity is very important. Faure is very much aware that public opinion must remain on his side."

Joanna nodded understanding. "That's why they tried to make a hero out of that Peacekeeper captain."

"And why Faure went berserk with anger when the news networks started playing the reports coming out of Moonbase."

"I hope he bursts a blood vessel."

"They wanted Moonbase to stop broadcasting news reports," Brudnoy said, "in return for the evacuation flight."

"What?"

"I refused, of course. That's why a half hour's conference took two days. They were adamant, but I"—Brudnoy placed a hand on the breast of his open-collar shirt—"I outsat them. They demanded that we stop the broadcasts; I simply told them that it was impossible. After ducking into Faure's office fifty times or so, they gave in at last."

Joanna grabbed him by the ears and kissed him. "Good for you, Lev!"

"It was nothing. Had I known your reaction, I would have made more demands on them."

She studied his smiling face. Behind his grin, Lev looked tired, worried.

"Faure's building up a new military force to take Moonbase," he said softly.

"You're certain?"

He nodded wearily. "All the signs point to it. The U.N. bureaucrats are merely stalling for time, nitpicking about the evacuation flight and the arrangements for a meeting between you and Faure. In the meantime, I saw plenty of Peacekeeper officers heading into Faure's office."

"Really."

"And worse," Lev said. "There were several Yamagata Corporation people there, too."

Joanna leaned her head back against the limousine's plush upholstery. "I've *got* to get the board of directors to support Moonbase. If they back me, we can start to put pressure on the White House."

"And if they don't?" Lev asked.

"They will," Joanna said firmly. "They've got to."

Ibrahim al-Rashid steepled his fingers as he gazed at Tamara Bonai's image on the wallscreen of his office. She is certainly beautiful, he thought. If only I could convince her to see things my way.

"Then you will attend the emergency board meeting in person?" he asked.

"Yes," Bonai said. "I want to be there."

She was apparently in her office, too, although it was difficult to tell, with all the rattan and bamboo decor and the wide windows looking out onto a delicious tropical beach.

"Perhaps you could come a day or so early," Rashid suggested. "I would be pleased to take you to New York City or wherever else you would like to visit."

Bonai seemed to think the matter over for a few heartbeats. "I've never been to Washington. I understand it's quite lovely in the spring."

"Washington," Rashid said, thinking quickly. "The national capital. I know a very comfortable hotel just a short walk from the White House. Perhaps I could arrange a visit with the president."

She smiled delightfully. "I'm afraid that would have to be arranged by my own foreign secretary. I am a chief of state, remember, and there is protocol involved."

Rashid smiled back at her. "Of course. But perhaps I could be of some help. I know the president personally, and a little friendly persuasion always makes the wheels turn more smoothly."

"That would be very kind of you."

"Nothing at all," he said. "I'd be happy to do it."

Bonai's face grew more serious. "You understand that I am fully in support of Moonbase's independence, don't you?"

"Of course. But you won't mind if I try to convince you otherwise?"

"You can try."

"You see, I have believed for many years that the true future of Masterson Corporation lies in the development of fusion power."

"As Yamagata is doing in Japan?"

"Yes, exactly. If we can work together with Yamagata we can open up the market for fusion power plants in North America. The market is worth trillions of dollars!"

"As long as you can import helium-three from the Moon."

Rashid kept the disappointment from showing on his

face. She knows the whole story; there's no way to fool her about this.

"Yes," he admitted. "Fusion power makes economic sense only if we can use helium-three as a fuel."

"Which is why Yamagata wants Moonbase."

"Yamagata is producing helium-three at its own base in Copernicus."

"But without nanomachines to do the work, their costs are prohibitively high."

"I wouldn't say prohibitively," Rashid argued.

Bonai smiled brightly. "Then why do they want Moonbase, if not for our nanotechnology?"

"With nanomachines extracting helium-three from the Moon's soil," Rashid said, warming to his subject, "the costs of fusion power go down dramatically. We could offer the world the ultimate energy system, the energy source the stars themselves use! It would be cheap, efficient, and clean: no radioactive wastes!"

"*No* radioactive waste?" Bonai probed.

Rashid waved a hand in the air. "Well, some, of course. But very little, and totally manageable. Not like the old-style fission reactors, with their uranium and plutonium."

"I see."

"We could be the primary producer of fusion power systems for North and South America," he said, regaining his enthusiasm. "The market will be trillions of dollars every year! Think of the profits!"

"And who would make these profits? Masterson Corporation or Yamagata?"

"Both," Rashid answered.

She said nothing for several moments. Then, rather thoughtfully, Bonai offered, "We must talk about this in more detail."

"Yes. When you visit Washington. Before the board meeting."

She nodded. "Yes. Before the board meeting, certainly."

Rashid felt delighted. I'm winning her over! he told himself.

DAY TWENTY-FIVE

"He makes a certain amount of sense, Doug," Bonai was saying. "Fusion power could be an enormous market."

Tamara and Doug were strolling along the beach, side by side, even though separated physically by nearly four hundred thousand kilometers.

Doug had gone to Moonbase's virtual reality studio and donned a full-body sensor suit. Instead of the cumbersome helmets that VR systems had once required, he wore contact lenses over his eyes. Produced by nanomachines, the contacts served as miniaturized television screens that fed visual input to his retinas. A microcamera was mounted just above his eyes on a headband. Equally tiny microphones were plugged into his ears.

As far as Doug could see, hear or touch, he was sloshing through the gentle surf on Bonai's private islet, on the far side of the Tarawa lagoon, away from Bonriki and Betio, where the airport and hotels were.

It was beautiful, Doug had to admit. Gorgeous, with the sun dipping down toward the ocean horizon and the trade wind bending the palm trees. The surf broke out on the coral reef with booming roars; here in the lagoon it lapped softly at their feet as they walked along the golden beach.

Tamara was beautiful, too, in a wraparound flowered *pareo* of blue and gold, her bronzed shoulders bare, her lustrous black hair cascading down her back. She stumbled slightly on the wet sand and Doug reached out a hand to steady her. Even with the three-second lag between Earth and Moon, her hand was still there for him to grasp. He felt her hand clutch his, and she smiled up at him as they continued down the beach, hand in hand.

She could have stayed in her office and simply programmed the VR equipment to show us this beach scene, Doug knew. But Tamara actually was strolling on one of the small islets up at the far end of the lagoon, wearing a full-body sensor suit and a set of microminiaturized cameras that ringed her head like a diadem to provide a complete picture of the island environment for the virtual reality link.

Sweeping his gaze from her lovely face to the curving length of the beach, the graceful palms, the brilliant white clouds parading across the bright blue sky, Doug realized why he had been so reluctant to meet with Tamara in virtual reality. This was the world that was denied him. This was the world that humans were meant to live on, not the harsh lifeless Moon, but this tropical island where you could stand naked in the warm breeze and breathe free.

I could live here, he thought. I'd be safe enough here; nanoluddite fanatics wouldn't even know I'm down here.

There was another world, though: stark, barren, dangerous—yet full of promise. We can make a paradise on the Moon, Doug told himself. We can build a world that's fair and free, a world where people can live and work and create a better future.

But it'll never be like this, he knew—the world I left behind me. Someday we'll have something approaching this on the Moon. Someday. But it will never be the same.

A powered outrigger was chugging along slowly in the lagoon, heading their way, its electric motor almost completely silent as it sluiced through the marvelously clear water. Doug could see its shadow undulating across the white sandy bottom of the lagoon, hardly a meter deep.

"I thought this was your private islet," Doug said to Tamara.

She followed his gaze. "Everybody knows the islands up on this end of the lagoon are off-limits. The boys who handle the boats tell tourists not to come this far."

Frowning, Doug said, "Well, there's one tourist who didn't listen."

Bonai watched intently as the outrigger hit the current flowing between islets and slewed badly. The man in the canoe worked the gimballed engine back and forth to straighten out again.

"He'll get himself in trouble," she said.

"Serves him right," said Doug.

Still watching, she said, "But he might overturn the canoe."

"An outrigger?"

He waited, then heard her reply. "It's been done before."

Doug laughed. "Then he can walk back to Bonriki. The lagoon's not deep and the water's warm."

Another electric-powered outrigger came into view, bigger, more powerful, faster. KIRIBATI CORP. was painted on its prow in bright orange letters.

"Here come my bodyguards," Bonai said.

"Bodyguards?"

She smiled at him. "The beach patrol from the hotel. They make sure none of the tourists comes up this way."

Doug watched as the beach patrol boat pulled up even with the smaller outrigger. Three men were in the bigger canoe, he saw: young, muscular, bronzed skin. One of them had an electric bullhorn in his hand.

"I'M SORRY, SIR, BUT THIS PART OF THE LAGOON IS OFF-LIMITS TO VISITORS. PLEASE TURN AROUND AND HEAD BACK TOWARD THE HOTEL."

For a moment Doug thought that the visitor would try to defy the patrol. But then he turned around and both canoes slowly headed back down the lagoon.

"You see?" Bonai said teasingly. "We can be alone together. I have my bodyguards to ensure our privacy."

"You mean that if I tried to come here in the flesh, they'd stop me?"

"No, Doug. Not you," she said, growing serious. "I would always allow you to come here whenever you wanted to."

He realized he was still holding her hand. Tamara looked up at him. "You did promise, you know. This virtual reality visit doesn't count."

"I know," he said. She gave no indication that she wanted him to release her hand, and he felt too awkward to let go.

So they walked in silence, hand in hand, for several moments.

"When do you go to Savannah?" he asked.

Again the wait. Then, "I leave Monday morning."

"Monday? But the board meeting isn't for another week."

"My foreign secretary is arranging a quick visit with your president, at the White House."

With a pang, Doug realized that the president of the United States was no longer his president.

"It's something that Rashid suggested," she said. "He's going to give me a tour of the city afterward. Then I'll go to Savannah for the board meeting."

"Rashid suggested you see the president?"

"No, he suggested escorting me wherever I'd like to go. I picked Washington, and my foreign secretary has moved heaven and earth to get me a five-minute meeting with the president. Rashid's been helping, of course."

"A photo op," Doug muttered.

Bonai agreed. "I imagine that's about all it will be: a public relations gesture toward the chief executive of the Kiribati Council."

Suddenly realizing what an opportunity her visit could be, Doug asked urgently, "Tamara, could you do us a favor?"

"Us?"

"Moonbase."

She looked up at him from beneath long eyelashes, the expression on her lovely face almost sly. "I'd be happy to do a favor for *you*, Doug."

Oblivious to her nuance, Doug went on, "When you're talking to the president, could you ask her to consider backing our independence?"

The three seconds ticked slowly. "The American president? She's as anti-nanotechnology as they come!"

"I know, I know. But if you tell her that Yamagata will take over Moonbase, and Japan will be using nanotechnology to take over the aerospace industry and god knows what else—maybe she'd have second thoughts about us."

Bonai disengaged her hand from Doug's and walked in thoughtful silence along the beach. He followed her, wondering if he was pushing her too far, but unwilling to give up the chance to make a plea to the president.

"All right," she said at last. Then she laughed. "I was wondering what I'd have to say to her. Now I know."

"Great!" said Doug.

"And then," she added, "Rashid wants to show me the city of Washington. He's already picked out the hotel we'll stay in."

"Hotel?" Alarm bells rang in Doug's mind. "You're not staying at the same hotel with him, are you?"

"Why not?" she asked innocently.

"You know his reputation. With women, that is."

"He's very romantic, apparently."

Feeling nettled, Doug said, "He'll just try to add you to his list."

"Perhaps I'll add him to my list," Bonai shot back.

Doug stood there on the beach, staring at her, dumbfounded.

"All's fair in love and war, isn't it?" Bonai teased.

"All he really wants from you is your vote at the board meeting," said Doug, frowning.

"And you think he'll try to convince me in bed?"

"Yes," he snapped.

Bonai giggled and threw her arms around Doug's neck. "You're jealous, aren't you?"

"Jealous?" Doug sputtered. "How—why . . ."

She pressed against him. "You are jealous." She seemed delighted.

"Rashid's not to be trusted," Doug mumbled.

"Would it make you feel better if I said I won't sleep with him?"

"Yes," he blurted.

"Good. Wonderful." She kissed Doug swiftly on the lips, then pulled away and almost danced along the waves lapping the beach.

Doug stood in confused silence, wondering what he was getting himself into, uncertain of what he felt about Tamara, and feeling more than slightly guilty about Edith.

Jack Killifer rammed his rented outrigger up onto the sand, not caring whether he ripped off the electric motor's propeller or not.

She was all alone out there, he thought as he trudged up the sand toward the tiki hut that sheltered the beach bar. I could have done it and gotten away with nobody seeing me. Except for that goddamned boat from the hotel. They must look out for her all the friggin' time.

He sat in moody silence on a rickety stool at the bar, sipping mai tais and wondering how he could get Tamara Bonai alone. He also wondered if he'd actually have the guts to murder her. Yes, he decided. I'll do it. I'll just pretend she's Joanna Brudnoy.

He grinned at the thought. Bonai will be a practice run for Joanna. He laughed aloud, startling the young Australian couple sitting a couple of barstools away.

DAY THIRTY-ONE

There were more news people than dignitaries or U.N. employees, Joanna saw. The meeting chamber was jammed with reporters and photographers, all focused on the little ceremony that she and Faure were prancing through.

Lev stood off to one side, in a corner where the cameras did not peer, hands clasped quietly behind his back, looking slightly uncomfortable in a dark blue business suit and a tie that refused to stay knotted tightly against his collar. Lev's done most of the real work, Joanna knew, but he'll get none of the credit.

Faure was at his haute couture best, wearing an impeccable dove-gray suit with a vest of sky blue over a crisp white shirt: the U.N.'s colors. His cravat matched the vest. Joanna, knowing she'd have to compete with Faure's fashion statement, wore a simple white mid-sleeved dress of classic lines, with a vee neckline cut low enough to arouse the cameras' interest. Her earrings were gold Incan sunbursts, her choker and one bracelet also gold.

They entered the chamber from doors on opposite sides of the room, stood together before the long baize-covered table for a few moments while photographers snapped still shots of them. Neither of them looked at the other, both stared straight ahead as if an invisible wall separated them.

As the video cameras hummed, one of Faure's aides brought a slim leather-bound document to them and laid it open on the table. Only then did Joanna and Faure sit in the high-backed chairs placed there for them.

Faure looked into the phalanx of cameras as he picked up one of the pens that had been laid on the table.

"The signing of this agreement sets in motion a mercy flight to the rebellious Moonbase, allowing the rescue of sixty-five men and women who have been trapped on the Moon by the unfortunate stubborness of the Moonbase management."

He bent his head and wrote his name at the bottom of the document. Then, with a beaming smile, he offered the pen to Joanna.

Ignoring his gesture, Joanna picked up one of the other pens waiting on the table top. She too looked into the cameras.

"This evacuation flight has been made necessary by the unprecedented actions of the United Nations against

Moonbase, a community that has declared its political independence and should be treated as an equal member nation of the U.N."

She signed in a flowing hand, making certain that her signature was larger than Faure's tiny, cramped letters.

The small band of dignitaries and U.N. workers standing behind them clapped perfunctorily. Faure scooped up the pens and started to hand them out to the onlookers.

"Mr. Faure!" yelled several dozen news reporters. "Mrs. Brudnoy!"

Faure raised both his hands, as if in surrender. But he said, "I regret that we will have no time for your questions. My schedule is much too pressing." He started to get up from his chair.

With a smile, Joanna said, "I've got lots of time. Ask away."

"What's happening at Moonbase?"

"When do you expect the World Court to take up your case?"

"Why can't Moonbase agree to shut down its nano-tech operations?"

"How does it feel to be in rebellion against the whole world?"

"One at a time!" Joanna pleaded. "One at a time, please."

His face darkening, Faure plopped back onto his chair.

"How long can Moonbase hold out against the Peacekeepers?"

Joanna glanced sideways at Faure, then turned her attention back to the reporters. "Moonbase is physically self-sufficient. They grow enough food to feed themselves, and generate all the electrical power they need from solar cells built out of elements from the lunar regolith—"

"By nanomachines?"

"Yes. Nanomachines are essential to Moonbase. They produce the air we breathe and purify the water we drink. We use them to expand and maintain our solar-energy farms, and—of course—nanomachines build the

Clipperships that we sell to the world's commercial aerospace lines."

"Are you saying that Moonbase can hold out indefinitely?"

"Yes, of course. Unless the base is attacked by overwhelming military force, which would probably kill most of the people in the base."

"Mr. Faure, will the U.N. attack Moonbase with overwhelming military force?"

Obviously struggling to maintain his self-control, Faure replied, "The United Nations has a responsibility to see that international law is enforced. The nanotechnology treaty forbids all work in nanomachines, yet as you have just heard from the mouth of Mrs. Brudnoy, Moonbase insists on continuing its insidious use of nanotechnology."

"There's nothing insidious about it," Joanna said to him. "We've been quite open about it."

"The nanotechnology treaty is quite clear!" Faure snapped. "And it applies to all the nations of the world!"

Coolly, Joanna pointed out, "Moonbase is not on Earth, and the nanomachines we use there never leave the Moon. They are no threat whatsoever to anyone on Earth."

"The law is the law!" Faure insisted, his mustache twitching slightly.

"And the law states that any nation that does not sign the nanotech treaty is not bound by its restrictions."

"But Kiribati has signed the treaty."

"And Moonbase has declared its political independence."

One of the reporters jumped in: "Could Moonbase survive without using nanomachines?"

"No," said Joanna flatly.

"You see?" Faure made a dismissive gesture. "They refuse to abide by the law."

"We are no threat to anyone on Earth," Joanna repeated.

"How do we know that for certain?" Faure demanded. "How do we know what your scientists are doing, four hundred thousand kilometers away?"

"Send inspectors to Moonbase," said Joanna. "We've offered to show U.N. inspection teams everything and anything they want to see. The offer still stands."

A reporter called out from the rear, "You mean you'd allow U.N. inspectors to look over your nanotech operations?"

"Of course," Joanna replied. "We made that offer at the very beginning. It still stands, if Mr. Faure is willing to take us up on it."

"What about it, sir?"

Faure brushed a fingertip across his mustache before answering. "Of course we have planned to send inspectors to Moonbase. Several of them will fly there on the mercy mission we have just agreed upon. But that does not change the fundamental situation. Moonbase must accede to the law!"

Joanna quickly added, "But if—or, rather, when—the World Court agrees that Moonbase is an independent nation, then the law allows Moonbase to continue using nanotechnology."

The reporters weren't interested in the legal fine points anymore. They had something new to deal with.

"You're sending inspectors to Moonbase?"

"Does this mean some sort of compromise can be worked out?"

"Who will the inspectors be?"

"What are their names? What nations do they come from?"

Faure raised his hands to silence their questions. With a little smile of satisfaction that their attention was once more focused on him, he said, "Please! Please! I cannot divulge all the details at this moment."

Joanna said to herself, Of course you can't divulge all the details, you lying little fart. You just made up your mind to send inspectors on the evacuation flight, right here on the spur of the moment.

But she decided not to embarrass him further. Inspectors could be a step toward gaining Moonbase's independence, and she did not want to do anything that would interfere with that.

You've won a small victory, Joanna told herself. Be content with that. For now.

"That's good news," Jinny Anson said. "Isn't it?"

Doug had asked Anson and Kris Cardenas to meet him in the Cave to discuss the latest news from Earthside over dinner. Edith sat at Doug's side, the two other women across the table from them.

Leaning over his dinner tray, Doug said, "It's good from the political aspect, I suppose."

"It's the first break in the deadlock," said Edith, as she spooned up some chicken soup. It was almost a stew, it was so thick, but it tasted flat and bland to her. She longed for just one little jalapeño.

"I'll be happy to show the U.N. inspectors our entire nanotech operation," Cardenas said eagerly. "Of course, if they want to get into Willi's lab they'll be on their own."

Doug almost grinned at the idea of strangers trying to talk Zimmerman into allowing them to inspect his laboratory. Then he thought, On the other hand, Zimmerman might be pleased to have other scientists see what he's accomplished here.

"But will they be scientists?" he wondered aloud.

"What?" Cardenas asked.

"Will the U.N. inspectors really be scientists, or will they be spies for Faure?" he said.

"Both," Edith replied immediately.

"Then how much do we really want to show them?"

Anson said, "Everything—except whatever you guys are doing to help defend the base."

With a rueful smile, Cardenas admitted, "We can show them everything, then. We haven't come up with anything that's specifically military in nature."

"Okay," said Doug, "then the inspectors will be no trouble."

"Not unless they rub Willi the wrong way."

"Does he have a right way?" Anson jabbed.

Doug looked past his table companions. The Cave was almost filled with diners selecting meals at the dispensers, carrying trays to tables, meeting friends. The big rock chamber buzzed with dozens of conversations.

He forced his attention back to the problems at hand. "Jinny, how are you deciding who goes back Earthside on the evac flight?"

Anson shifted mental gears smoothly. "The ballet troupe, of course."

"Their manager told me he's going to sue the U.N. for all the dates they've missed," Edith said.

"Lotsa luck," said Anson.

"That leaves thirty seats on the evacuation ship," Doug said.

Nodding, Anson replied, "We're going by contract dates. People whose employment contracts ended the longest time ago get first priority on the evac."

"Sounds reasonable," said Doug.

"Plus, we've got one pregnant woman," Anson said.

"Really?" Edith's interest was immediate. "Who is she? How far along?"

"A couple of months, from what the medical report says."

"I'd like to interview her before she leaves."

"I'll set it up," Anson said.

"What about the father?" Doug asked.

Anson shook her head. "His contract's up, but there are too many people ahead of him. He'll have to stay here."

"Won't somebody give up his seat so he can go with his wife?" Edith asked.

"They're not married. Not yet, anyway. And if somebody gave up a seat I'd have to put the next guy in line in it, not the daddy."

"How far down on the list is he?" Doug asked.

"Eighteenth."

"You think they'll get married Earthside?" Cardenas asked.

"They want to get married right here and now,"

Anson said, "but there's nobody here to perform a legal ceremony."

Doug leaned back in his chair and stared at the rough rock ceiling for a few moments. "I don't see why we can't get a man of the cloth from Earthside to marry them by video."

"They're both Catholic," Anson said.

"How about the Pope?" Edith quipped. "Or at least a cardinal. Make a great news feature."

Doug grinned at her. "Let's see what we can do. At least they'll be married, even if they have to separate for a while."

Suddenly Anson looked uncomfortable, and Doug realized that her husband was still on Tarawa. They had separated several years earlier; Jinny was at home in Moonbase, her husband had not been. Not at all.

To get off the subject, Doug said, "I wonder just who Faure's going to send here to check out our nanotech work."

Anson snorted. "At least one of 'em'll be Japanese, from Yamagata Industries, I betcha."

DAY THIRTY-SIX

"It's too bad you missed the cherry blossoms," Rashid said to Tamara Bonai. "They were magnificent this year."

The city of Washington was in bloom: Bonai saw the roses and magnolias that flowered brightly on the White House's lawn as their limousine glided past the heavily-guarded gate and out onto Pennsylvania Avenue.

Her five minutes with the president had not gone well. True to her word, Tamara had urged the president to support Moonbase's bid for independence. True to her expectations, the president had politely but firmly answered that she could not do that as long as Moonbase used nanotechnology.

"But without nanotechnology, Moonbase will have to shut down," Bonai had said.

The president shrugged it off. "My record is quite clear," she said. "The potential threat from nanotechnology is so severe that it's worth the loss of Moonbase to be safe from it."

For a long moment the two women sat facing each other in plush armchairs set before the Oval Office's dark and empty fireplace. Bonai wore a sleeveless sheath of pink, with pearls at her throat, earlobes and wrist. The president was in a navy blue suit with a modest mid-calf skirt and jewelry of silver and turquoise from her native Arizona.

"Are you aware," Bonai asked slowly, "that the United Nations intends to turn over the operation of Moonbase to Yamagata Industries, once they have taken the base?"

The president glanced at her aide, sitting quietly across the room behind Bonai's back with a cyberbook-sized computer in the palm of one hand. The young man had a miniaturized microphone clipped to the inside of his shirt collar, so that he could subvocalize information to the all but invisible receiver in the president's left ear.

"Yamagata Industries?" she said, stalling for time. "They already have a base on the Moon, don't they?"

"Yes," said Bonai. "And they intend to take over Moonbase and continue using nanomachines for many purposes—including manufacturing Clipperships."

"Are you certain?" The president was now glaring at her aide, who had given up all pretense of secrecy and was scrolling madly through his computer files.

"That would give Yamagata—Japan, really—the world leadership in aerospace transportation," Bonai said.

The aide shook his head and whispered. The president put on a smile and parroted, "I have had no indication from Mr. Faure that the U.N. intends to turn Moonbase over to Yamagata."

"Then may I suggest," Bonai said, "with all respect, that you ask Mr. Faure directly if he plans to do this?"

The president's brows knit slightly. "May I ask what your interest is in all of this? After all, Moonbase is trying to break away from Kiribati's ownership, aren't they?"

"Kiribati supports Moonbase's independence. It will have no effect on our business relationship with Moonbase. We intend to formally recognize Moonbase's independence."

"Is that so?" The president leaned slightly toward Bonai and made a motherly smile. "Let me give you a bit of friendly advice, young lady. Kiribati's recognition of Moonbase won't affect the political situation one iota. So don't stick your neck out; you might regret it later on."

Bonai smiled back thinly. "I appreciate your frankness, Madam President. But I do think that America's recognition of Moonbase's independence would be in keeping with the finest traditions of your nation."

The president sighed, her signal to her aide to end the meeting. He immediately got to his feet and walked across the Oval Office to bend over her and say:

"I'm afraid the ambassador from Uganda has been kept waiting for more than three minutes now."

Bonai took the hint, got to her feet, and left the Oval Office.

Now she leaned back on the limousine's fine leather seat, resting her head on the backrest as the car inched through the traffic on its way to her hotel.

Rashid was either too polite or too crafty to ask her how the meeting had gone.

"I've arranged for dinner in the hotel's restaurant," he said, rubbing his hands together. "It's quite a lovely place, very quiet and private. The food is excellent."

Bonai said, "That's fine." And she realized that Rashid hadn't expected anything of significance to come out of her five minutes in the Oval Office. His whole attention was focused on their evening together.

Jack Killifer had just enough time to down a premixed martini on the commercial flight between Washington and Boston. He had followed Bonai to Washington and immediately given up any hope of killing her there. Too many guards, too many police, too many people on the streets and in the hotels.

I'm no professional hit man, he grumbled to himself on the brief flight home. Why'd O'Conner pick me for the job?

He knew perfectly well. Killifer had brought Bonai's intransigence to General O'Conner's attention. And O'Conner had always been a firm believer in the idea that the man with the problem should be the man to produce the solution.

But murder? Maybe when she's all alone out on that little island of hers. Or even in the town on Tarawa atoll; the only real security those islanders have is guards for the casino.

As the plane lowered its landing gear and lined up for landing at Boston's ancient Logan Aerospace Port, Killifer toyed with the idea of calling O'Conner in Atlanta and asking for a professional to do the work. Or even one of the faithful Urban Corps fanatics.

But it'd be a waste of breath, he knew. O'Conner had made it clear: he wanted Killifer to do this job personally. "The fewer people know about this," the general had said, "the better off we are."

Yeah, Killifer told himself as the plane's tires screeched on the runway. And knocking off Bonai'll give him an absolute grip on me.

Yet he was almost smiling as he got out of his seat and followed the other passengers to the plane's exit hatch. Okay, he told himself. When Bonai goes back to Tarawa I go back, too. I'll hit her there. Now that I know the layout of the islands, it oughtta be fairly easy.

And he began to lay his plans.

DAY THIRTY-EIGHT

They watched the Clippership settle down gracefully on landing pad one from the snug confines of her quarters.

"Well," said Nick O'Malley, "there she is."

Claire Rossi nodded.

"Aren't you excited?" he asked, forcing a grin.

Sitting on the edge of the bed, Claire said, "About the wedding, yes. About leaving, no."

"Well, you've got to go," Nick said. "It's for your own good. And the baby's."

Claire nodded again. But she said, "It's not an illness, you know. Pregnancy is just as normal as breathing, really."

"The rules are the rules," Nick insisted. "Besides, you'll get better medical care back Earthside. And your mother'll be there with you."

"But you won't."

"I'll come down on the next flight."

"Nick, there might not *be* a next flight!"

"Now look—"

The phone chimed and Claire immediately called out, "Answer."

Jinny Anson's chipper face appeared on the wall. "Okay, you two, we're down to two hours and counting."

Claire said, "We'll be there."

"With bells on," Nick added.

They forgot their argument and began dressing for the wedding. Claire had borrowed liberally from her friends and put together a beige long-skirted dress (the closest she could find at Moonbase to a wedding gown) and various accessories that almost looked right. Nick could find nothing that fit his big frame except a fresh pair of white coveralls from the medical stores.

The wedding was held in Jinny Anson's office, with half a dozen of their friends in attendance and Claire's arms filled with a bouquet of flowers freshly plucked from Lev Brudnoy's little garden.

The archbishop of Kiribati, brown skin and flashing white teeth, looked out at them from the wallscreen. Dressed in the full regalia of purple stole and skullcap, he appeared to be in a chapel made of stuccoed walls and a timbered roof.

Anson, Doug, and Harry Clemens stood off to one side while Edith, camera glued to one eye, panned across the office. Joanna and Lev Brudnoy watched from the wallscreen on the other side of the room.

The ceremony was brief, a little awkward with the transmission delay, yet somehow touching. Doug heard Anson sniffle slightly, beside him. Looking over to the far wall, he thought that his mother looked just a bit teary-eyed, too. Why do women cry at weddings? he wondered.

When he finished, the archbishop grinned at them and said in a strong voice, "There will be no collection."

The Catholics in the small crowd laughed.

The married couple and their friends trooped out of Anson's office, on their way to a reception in the Cave.

"Some honeymoon they're going to have," Anson said, sounding a little wistful. "The Clippership lifts off tomorrow at ten hundred hours."

"Well, at least they were able to get married," Clemens said. "I hope that makes them happy."

Doug had already turned his attention to his mother's image on the wallscreen.

"Any progress with Faure?" he asked.

After three seconds she shook her head gravely. "He's making the maximum media noise about this so-called mercy flight. Otherwise, he's stonewalling me."

"Any indications of preparations by the Peacekeepers?" Doug asked, standing before his mother's larger-than-life image.

Brudnoy, standing slightly behind her, answered, "No indications at all. They seem to be doing nothing at present. Of course, they could be getting ready for another assault in secrecy."

"That's what I'd do, I suppose," Doug agreed. "No sense letting your enemy see you coming."

"The board meeting is tomorrow," Joanna said. "I've got to turn Rashid around and get him to support you."

"Tamara Bonai got nowhere with the president," Doug muttered.

Once she heard his words, Joanna raised a finger. "Don't be too sure of that. The ambassador to Japan just flew back unexpectedly to Washington on a Clippership. Something's stirring, I think."

Doug thought about that for a moment, then said, "Mom, this may be off the wall—but have you considered talking directly to Yamagata?"

The delay was much more than three seconds this time. "You mean the old man himself? Seigo Yamagata?"

"If he'll see you."

Her expression hardened. "He'll see me. I'll make certain of that!"

It took an effort of will for Nick to pull his gummy eyelids open. The party had been glorious, but now it was morning and the fun was over. Claire had to pack her few belongings and get aboard the Clippership.

She was curled next to him in the bunk, sleeping soundly with a beatific smile on her lips.

Nick struggled up on one elbow and squinted at the digital clock.

"It's nine-twenty!" he yelped. "Good lord, Claire, you've gotta dash!"

She opened one eye and snaked a bare arm around his neck. "Married hardly more than eighteen hours and you're already giving me orders."

"But the time—"

"Relax," Claire said dreamily. "I'm not going anyplace."

"Not going? What do you mean not going?"

"I'm staying right here with you," she said, opening both eyes at last.

"But you can't do that!"

"I gave my boarding papers to Ellen Berson," Claire said. "Last night, while the rest of you were getting blotto on rocket juice."

"You what?"

"Ellen's got a boyfriend in Philadelphia. My boyfriend is right here."

"You can't do that," he repeated, his voice high, panicky. "They'll stop her at the rocket port."

"No they won't. And even if they do, I decided I'm staying right here with you."

"But they'll force you—"

"Nobody's going to force anybody," Claire said quite firmly. "And if they send some goons from security, I'll put up such a battle they'll be afraid of harming the baby."

"You're crazy!"

"Over you, sweet-face."

"But you can't have the baby here. It's not allowed."

She smiled knowingly. "Nick, there's a first time for everything."

"But . . ." He ran out of steam and sank back on the pillow, defeated. Yet delighted.

"It was during the wedding," Claire said, "when the archbishop said that bit about cleaving together. I made up my mind then that I'm not going Earthside until you can go with me."

Staring up at the low ceiling, Nick said, "There's going to be hell to pay over this."

But he was grinning from ear to ear.

DAY THIRTY-NINE

Joanna deliberately took the seat at the end of the long conference table, where she could look directly at Rashid, up at the head. Every member of the board was present in person, even old McGruder in his powered wheelchair and its bulky life-support system. The old man was still waiting for a heart donor; he was more heavily wired up than an astronaut, Joanna thought.

Rashid and Tamara Bonai came in together, not exactly holding hands, but obviously happy to be in each other's company. Joanna seethed. If that little tramp has gone over to Rashid's side, I'll . . .

She stopped, not knowing what she'd do. Or what she *could* do. She had told Doug to woo Bonai and win her over. It looked as if Rashid had done it, instead, and there was nothing Joanna could do to counter that.

The conference table was buzzing with whispered conversations, board members catching up with the latest news and gossip among themselves. No one spoke to Joanna. She sat as if in an isolation ward down at the foot of the table.

The murmurs died away as Rashid sat down and smiled brightly at the board members.

"I'm delighted that all of you could manage to make it here in person to this special meeting," Rashid said in his slightly reedy tenor voice. "Including you, Mac."

From behind his oxygen mask McGruder rasped, "Couldn't keep me away from this one if you tried, my boy. When all this nonsense with the U.N. is over, I'm

250

going to Moonbase and get some of those nanomachines
to fix my heart."

He broke into a cackling laughter; the other board
members joined with him, politely. All except Rashid,
Joanna noticed, who sat with his original smile frozen
on his face. *Mac's on our side,* Joanna knew. *She had
been feeding him information on nanotherapy for
months now.*

"There's only one item on the agenda," Rashid said,
"and we should be able to take care of it fairly quickly."

All the heads along the table swivelled to Joanna.

"Since you called for this meeting," Rashid said to
her, "and it's your resolution that we're here to discuss,
why don't you give us the formal reading, for the minutes, Joanna?"

She didn't bother even glancing at the display screen
set into the table before her. Joanna said in a clear,
strong voice:

"Resolved: That Masterson Corporation exert its best
efforts to support the political independence of
Moonbase."

A dead silence fell upon the boardroom.

Finally, one of the white-haired men halfway up the
table asked, "You mean we *don't* support Moonbase's
independence?"

"Why should we?" a woman board member asked.

"Because if we don't," Joanna answered before anyone else could reply, "we stand to lose the Clippership
manufacturing to Japan."

"Japan?"

"That's not entirely fair, Joanna," said Rashid.

"The Clippership product line belongs to our Kiribati
subsidiary, doesn't it?"

"How's Japan going to get it? I assume you mean
Yamagata Industries, not the Japanese government."

"They're pretty close to being the same thing," Joanna said.

"I don't understand how Yamagata can take the Clippership manufacturing away from us."

"But we don't manufacture them; Kiribati does."

"We get the profits, don't we?"

"Wait, wait," Rashid called out, motioning them to silence with both hands. "Let's go through this calmly and logically."

Joanna immediately said, "We set up Kiribati Corporation to get out from under the nanotechnology treaty."

"Yes, and then the damned islanders signed the treaty anyway," said one of the men. Suddenly he realized that Tamara Bonai was sitting across the table from him, and his face reddened. "Ah, sorry," he mumbled. "No offense intended."

Bonai looked directly at him as she said, "Kiribati was forced to sign the nanotech treaty by unbearable pressure from the United Nations. We never expected the U.N. to try to extend the treaty to Moonbase, however."

"Where do you stand on Moonbase's independence?" asked the woman sitting next to Bonai.

"We have been assured that Moonbase's political independence will not interfere in any way with their contractual agreements with Kiribati Corporation. Therefore, we support their independence."

Several people along the table nodded.

Bonai added, "What we fear is that the U.N. will turn over all Clippership manufacturing to Yamagata once they have thrown us out of Moonbase."

Rashid's face clouded. "There's more to it than that," he said. "Much more."

"The core of this issue," said Joanna, "is that the U.N.'s fervor to force the nanotech treaty on Moonbase is a sham—a coverup for turning the base and all its operations over to Yamagata."

"And that includes manufacturing Clipperships with nanomachines?"

"Yes. Certainly."

McGruder swivelled his wheelchair slightly toward Rashid. "You knew about this?"

"I found out about it," Rashid answered.

"And what are you doing about it?"

Rashid took a deep breath. "I am trying to lead this corporation to a new level of profitability. And to a new product line, while we make a greater profit than ever from the Clipperships."

He had their full attention now, Joanna saw.

Leaning forward intently, Rashid said, "I want to negotiate a partnership between us and Yamagata to produce nuclear fusion power plants—"

"We went over this ten years ago," McGruder rasped.

"It was eight years ago and we made a mistake then," Rashid said hotly. "Let's not repeat the same mistake. Fusion power will be a multitrillion dollar business. This corporation has a chance to get in on it; one chance, take it or leave it."

Forcing her voice to remain cool, Joanna said, "So you're offering Yamagata the Clippership product line in exchange for a partnership in their fusion program."

"Fusion can be profitable if it can be fueled by helium-three, which can be mined on the Moon," Rashid said.

"Then why don't we mine it ourselves?" Joanna asked. "With nanomachines we can produce helium-three at a fraction of Yamagata's costs."

"Joanna, it's time you stopped clinging to Moonbase as if it's your personal nursery!" Rashid snapped.

She felt his words like a slap across her face. "You've been carrying a grudge for eight years now, Omar; ever since this board voted to back Moonbase in preference to your ideas about fusion."

"That was a mistake and we have a chance to correct it."

"By giving up Moonbase and allowing Yamagata to take the Clippership line away from us."

"We own the patents," Rashid countered. "Yamagata will pay us royalties while our costs go down to zero."

One of the women muttered, "Yamagata will pay us royalties until they figure out how to reverse engineer the Clipperships and come up with a manufacturing system that's different enough from ours to break our patents."

"Which will take a year or two, at most," another board member said.

"Not if we merge with Yamagata," Rashid said.

Silence again. They all looked stunned, Joanna thought.

"A merger makes perfect sense," Rashid went on, more calmly. "Our combined corporation will be the world's leader in aerospace transportation and fusion power. Your stock will be worth ten times what it's going for now. Even more."

"I will never vote to merge with Yamagata Industries," Joanna said, her voice venomously low.

"And why not?" Rashid taunted. "Are you afraid that your son will have to come back to Earth and live with the rest of us?"

"That is unforgivable," Joanna said.

"It *is* out of line, Mr. Chairman," said the bald, portly man sitting at her right. Others muttered and nodded.

Rashid closed his eyes briefly, then said softly, "You're right. I went too far. Joanna, I apologize. The heat of the moment . . ."

She glared directly into his eyes. The silence around the table stretched painfully.

Tamara Bonai broke the spell. "I move that we vote on the resolution presented by Mrs. Brudnoy."

"Second," said the man across the table from her.

The resolution passed by one vote: Bonai's. Joanna sighed with relief. She's not in his camp, she realized. Maybe in his bed, but not in his camp.

Then she thought, But the resolution doesn't mean much, not compared to this issue of merging with Yamagata.

Rashid was saying, ". . . each board member should express our support for Moonbase with his or her senators, I imagine. And I will appoint a committee to meet with the president in support of this resolution. Joanna, I suppose you should chair that committee."

He seemed to be taking his defeat graciously enough. Why not? Joanna asked herself. He's got every member of the board dreaming of a tenfold increase in the worth of their stock.

"I think we should set up another committee, as well," Joanna heard herself saying, not realizing where she was going until the words formed in her mouth, "to work with our board chairman in his negotiations with Yamagata."

"That's not on our agenda," Rashid snapped.

"Call it new business," said Joanna.

"Yes, I want to be on the Yamagata committee," said the oldest member of the board.

"And so do I," Joanna added sweetly.

DAY FORTY

Tamara Bonai cancelled her plans to return to Kiribati and extended her stay in Savannah for twenty-four hours—at Rashid's request.

As the board meeting had broken up, he had asked her to remain an extra day. "Now that the pressure is off, I'd like to take you sailing."

She saw something in his eyes that surprised her: not anger or worry over Joanna Brudnoy's intransigence, but relief, almost satisfaction. So she thought it over for a few moments, then smiled and agreed. There is something going on in his mind that he didn't tell us at the board meeting, she thought. It could be simple lust, she realized. Alone together on a boat, it would be difficult to evade his ardor. But what she saw in his eyes was more than that. Tamara saw triumph in Rashid's pleased expression.

He was happy, carefree, as he guided the power cruiser down the river, past Fort Pulaski and the Clippership port on Tybee Island, and out onto the deep swells of the blue-gray Atlantic.

"It's going to be a beautiful day," Rashid said cheerfully as he sat in the pilot's chair, one bare leg hooked over its armrest. "And a lovely, starry night," he added.

He was barefoot, wearing nothing but blue swim trunks and a tee shirt with a Masterson Corporation logo on its breast. Bonai wore a sunshine yellow bikini with a gauzy see-through hip-length robe over it.

"Not a cloud in sight," Rashid enthused.

Bonai was not worried about the weather. She was disappointed that Rashid hadn't taken out a sailboat, which would have been more fun than chugging along on power. At least the boat's electric motor was quiet and clean; no diesel fumes to assault her sense of smell.

The day passed uneventfully. By lunchtime they were out of sight of land. The sun set and the stars came out, as promised, different from the constellations she knew in Kiribati's skies, but just as beautiful.

There was no Moon in the night sky.

All day long Rashid's conversation had been innocuous, as if the last thing he wanted to talk about was the board meeting and Moonbase. Over dinner, though, he spoke of his long struggle to reach the top of Masterson Corporation.

"It hasn't been easy for a Moslem to move forward in corporate America, even a Moslem born and raised in Baltimore," he said, with growing bitterness. "But I've worked harder than any of the others. When they called me Omar I let it pass. And they've called me worse, behind my back, I know. Towel-head. Camel humper."

Tamara offered sympathetic noises as they made their way through the prepackaged veal and salad.

Dessert was figs and dates, and champagne. Tamara knew what was coming next, and almost welcomed it. Soon enough they were together in the bunk up at the boat's prow, heaving in rhythm to the ocean waves. Rashid was a well-versed lover, Bonai discovered; he made pleasure pleasurable for her as well as himself.

It was afterward, as they lay sweaty and spent with the curved overhead less than an arm's length above them, that Tamara gently, slowly got Rashid to tell her more about himself. Of his rise to Masterson's board of directors. Of his victory in the battle to be chairman. Of his ambition to bring efficient, clean, economical fusion power to an energy-hungry Earth.

"That's what I'll be known for, after I'm gone," he said quietly in the darkness. "Future generations will remember that I made fusion power practical."

For long moments Bonai said nothing. She listened to the creaking groan of the boat as it rose and fell in the endless ocean waves, thinking that it was Yamagata's researchers who had doggedly worked to make fusion practical.

"That's a magnificent achievement," she said at last.

"Yes," he agreed. "Magnificent."

"But if Mrs. Brudnoy prevents the merger with Yamagata . . . what then?"

He chuckled softly and turned toward her. "There's nothing she can do to prevent it. You saw how the board members reacted when I showed them how much their stock will increase in value."

"Mrs. Brudnoy is a very determined woman. Very powerful."

"Not for much longer. In a month or so Moonbase will belong to Yamagata Industries, and her power base will be gone."

"In a month or so?"

Rashid ran a hand along her bare thigh. "Yes. For weeks now Yamagata's been ferrying Peacekeeper troops up to their base at Copernicus. Together with a special team of Yamagata's own security forces, they'll hit Moonbase and take it over so swiftly that neither Joanna nor her pup will know what hit them."

She realized he was aroused again. Is it me, she wondered, or the thought of beating Joanna in their corporate power struggle?

She giggled at her own question. Rashid thought it was his doing and began stroking her more fervently.

She sighed and caressed his bearded face, then whispered into his ear, "You've been building up an army on the Moon and the Moonbase people don't even know it."

"Not quite an army," Rashid replied, pleased at her reaction. "Only a few hundred troops. But they'll have missiles and tracked vehicles and everything they need to surround Moonbase and force it to surrender. Or demolish it."

"When? How soon?"

But he stopped talking and pressed his body atop hers. Tamara closed her eyes and thought of Doug Stavenger.

"General O'Conner is in conference and cannot be disturbed, sir," said the woman.

Jack Killifer stared angrily at her image on his phone screen. Typical Urban Corps flunky, he thought: gray dress buttoned up to her goddamned chin, not a speck of makeup, hair tied up in some kind of knot on the top of her head. She could be attractive if she'd unwind a little.

"Did you tell him it's Jack Killifer calling?" he asked, through gritted teeth. "From Savannah?"

"The general is not to be disturbed," she repeated, like a brain-dead robot.

Killifer thought it over swiftly. The general's probably sleeping, or maybe in another coma. He kept getting these ministrokes that knocked him out for days at a time. I can't tell this receptionist that Tamara Bonai's off on a friggin' boat ride and I can't get to her. Nobody's supposed to know about Bonai except me and the general.

"Okay," he said to the unblinking image. "Tell General O'Conner that I called from Savannah, will you?"

"Certainly, sir."

"And I'm leaving tomorrow for a little vacation in Kiribati."

"Have a pleasant vacation, sir."

He killed the connection and the screen went dark. I'll get her there, Killifer told himself. Back in the islands. I'll do her there and that'll be the end of it. All I need is a boat.

*   *   *

Tamara dared not call Doug Stavenger until she was safely back in Kiribati. Rashid brought the boat back to Savannah the next morning and she hurried to her hotel, where she showered for half an hour, then headed for the rocket port on Tybee Island. Her aides had packed her bags and accompanied her in the limousine that Masterson Corporation had provided.

All through the half-hour ballistic flight Bonai struggled against the temptation to call her office in Tarawa and have them patch her through to Moonbase. Too dangerous, she warned herself. Wait until you can make a tight-beam laser link to Moonbase.

The Clippership lifted off from the Savannah area at noon, local time. It was 7:42 AM in Kiribati when she arrived at her office. With a quick flick of her computer keyboard, she saw it was 5:42 PM at Moonbase. Perfect.

In less than ten minutes she was talking to Doug's intently serious image on her display screen.

"In a month?" Doug looked startled.

Bonai nodded. "Several hundred troops. They've been gathering at the Yamagata base in Copernicus."

Doug seemed to stare off into space. "Coming in on the regular LTVs," he muttered.

She started to ask what LTVs were, then remembered: lunar transfer vehicles, the ungainly, unstreamlined carriers that plied regular schedules between the space stations orbiting Earth and the lunar outposts. All such traffic had been cut off from Moonbase by the U.N., but Yamagata's base had not been affected at all. Trojan horses, Bonai thought, carrying soldiers to the Moon a few at a time.

Doug could see that Tamara was terribly worried, frightened. She really cares about us, he told himself. Maybe Mom's right and she really cares about me.

"And they're armed with missiles?" he asked.

Three seconds later Bonai replied, "He said they'll have tractors and missiles and everything they need to surround Moonbase and force you to surrender."

Doug muttered, "So that's why we haven't seen any

Peacekeeper buildup. They've been building their forces a little at a time over at Nippon One."

"Yes."

"And training. Getting acclimatized to lunar conditions."

"What are you going to do, Doug? They'll be ready to strike in a month!"

"I don't know," he replied honestly. "I don't know if there's anything we *can* do in that short a time."

Tamara's face looked anguished once she heard his response. "Doug, don't let them destroy you! Surrender to them. Don't let them kill you."

He said nothing. There was nothing he could say. Yamagata and the Peacekeepers were going to come in and overwhelm them. Doug realized that his efforts to build some sort of defense for Moonbase had been nothing but a child's game. He'd been pretending to be a military leader when he didn't have the knowledge, the experience, the resources—like a kid with a plastic raygun playing soldier.

"Doug?" Tamara called again. "You can surrender now, you know. I can send a Clippership up there to get you and as many others as you want. You can live here in Kiribati. You'll be safe here."

"Thanks," he muttered, his mind still reeling. It's all been for nothing, he told himself. We never had a chance, not from the very beginning.

"I'll call you back in a little while," he said to Tamara absently. "I have to—I need some time to think this through."

"I'll be here, Doug. I'll be waiting for your call."

He sagged back in his desk chair as the wallscreen went blank, his thoughts spinning.

Edith came in from the corridor, all smiles. "Just sent another Pulitzer-quality report to the network," she said, bending to kiss his cheek swiftly. Then she breezed past the partition into the bedroom.

Before Doug could reply to her, someone rapped at the doorframe and slid the accordion-pleat door back enough to stick her head into the room. Jinny Anson.

"I need to talk to you, boss," she said crisply. "Got a minute?"

With that, she slid the door all the way back and stepped into the living room. Behind her, Nick O'Malley and Claire Rossi trooped in.

The little cubicle was suddenly crowded, especially with O'Malley's bulky form. The redhead looked shame-faced, like a guilty little boy. Claire Rossi looked stubborn, defiant.

Doug struggled to his feet. "What's this all about?"

"This mother-to-be," Anson said sharply, "was supposed to be on the evacuation flight."

"You're the couple who got married," Doug said, feeling thick-headed, stupid.

"I decided to stay here with my husband," Claire said, clasping O'Malley's arm.

"But you're pregnant."

"She's fractured her employment contract," Anson said. "The rules are specific—"

"I don't care about the rules," Rossi insisted. "I want to stay with my husband."

Doug looked up at O'Malley, whose wiry red hair almost brushed the ceiling. "Don't you have enough sense to know what a risk she's taking?"

Looking miserable, O'Malley replied, "I told her. I wanted her to go. But she wouldn't listen to me."

Out of the corner of his eye, Doug saw Edith step from behind the partition to watch the proceedings. She thinks this'll make a good news story, Doug thought. Great human interest.

But he felt anger welling up inside him. "She wouldn't listen to you?" Doug said to O'Malley. Turning to Rossi, he almost snarled, "And you, how idiotic can you be? Haven't you given any thought to your baby? Don't you care at all?"

"I care—"

"Then why aren't you on your way back Earthside, where you can get proper medical attention?" Doug yelled at her.

O'Malley stepped between them. "Now wait just a minute here . . ."

"Wait for what?" Doug hollered. "Wait until the next attack on this base, so both of you can get killed? And the baby, too?"

He turned on Anson. "How in the whole dimwitted congregation of blockheads that passes for your cracker-jack staff could she get away with this, Jinny? Didn't you have anybody checking on who went aboard the evac flight? Are they all blind or stupid or just plain corrupt? What the blazes happened?"

"I don't know," Anson said, her voice suddenly small and hushed.

Rossi started, "I gave my paperwork to—"

Doug silenced her with a fearsome glance. "Do you think this is all a game? We're facing a life-and-death situation here and you put your unborn child at risk! What kind of irresponsible, unfeeling people are you? I don't need this! Haven't I got enough on my shoulders without worrying about an idiot pregnant woman and her baby?"

Edith put a hand on Doug's shoulder and Anson grabbed at Rossi's arm.

"Come on, let's get out of here," Anson said. "Doug, I'm sorry I laid this one on you. There's nothing any of us can do about it now." And she tugged at Rossi, urging her toward the door.

O'Malley glared angrily at Doug and for a moment he looked as if he'd like to throw a punch or two. But he snorted and turned to follow Anson and his wife.

Doug stood in the middle of the little room, realizing how small it was, how the low ceiling pressed down on him, how many people were going to die if he kept up this charade of trying to defend Moonbase.

Edith whispered, "I was wondering when you'd blow off some steam. I'm just glad I wasn't in your line of fire."

DAY FORTY-ONE

It was well past midnight. Doug lay wide awake in the darkness, Edith beside him. They had not even tried to make love; Doug was too wired, too angry to either give or receive tenderness.

I'm scared, he realized. I'm really frightened. And there's nothing I can do to help. Not a blasted thing.

"Are you sleeping?" Edith whispered so low he barely heard it.

"No."

"Me neither."

Doug stayed flat on his back, staring at the dark ceiling. "I shouldn't have yelled at those kids."

"They broke the rules, didn't they?"

"Yelling at them didn't help anything. I've just made them sore at me."

"You've got to let off steam somehow," Edith said. "If you don't you'll bust."

"I still shouldn't have done it to them."

Edith was silent for several heartbeats. Then she whispered, "If you want to curse, go right ahead."

"What?"

"Don't hold it in. Sometimes a good string of cussing can be real satisfying. Go ahead, turn the air blue. I won't mind."

For long moments he didn't know what to reply. Then he confessed, "I don't know any."

"Any what?"

"Any curses. I never learned to swear. My mother didn't like it, and I never heard it when I was a kid."

"Nothing at all?" Edith was incredulous.

"Hell and damn. Sonofabitch bastard. Fuck, shit, asshole."

"Lord, you make it sound like you're reciting a list."

He shrugged. "They don't mean much to me. Not emotionally."

Edith turned to face him. In the darkness she could barely make out the outline of his head against the pillow.

"What do you do when you get real mad? When you want to spit and kick your faithful ol' hound dog?"

He knew she was trying to cheer him, trying to lighten his foul mood. "I never had a dog."

"Didn't you ever want to kick anybody?"

"I go outside," he said.

"Huh?"

"When I'm really ticked off, when it gets too heavy, I suit up and go outside. That usually makes me feel better."

"Then let's go outside," Edith said, propping herself up on one elbow.

"Not now," Doug said. "It won't help."

"But you said—"

"Get some sleep, Edith. The problems I'm facing aren't going to be solved by a walk outside."

"Come on," she urged. "You've never taken me outside. We could—"

"Not now," he repeated. "Go to sleep."

She gave up with a reluctant sigh and curled next to him. Neither of them closed their eyes.

When he tried to reach Tamara Bonai in the morning, her phone relayed a message that she had gone to her private island and was waiting for him to make VR contact with her.

Tiredly, Doug trudged down to the virtual reality studio, pulled on a full-body sensor suit and let a technician help him insert the contact TV lenses. Within minutes he was standing on the sandy beach, surprised that it was night on Tarawa atoll.

"I'm a working woman," Bonai told him, smiling brightly in the starlit night. "I have responsibilities that keep me at my desk most of the day."

Doug forced a grin. "Here I thought you had nothing to do but swim in the lagoon and go fishing."

Bonai was wearing a wraparound *pareo*, Doug was in his usual sky-blue coveralls. The night was magnificent: a warm salt breeze blew across the beach and thousands of stars sparkled in the great dome of the heavens. Doug searched the sky for the Moon but could not find it. Of course, he realized. We're in the nighttime part of our cycle; from Earth it's a new moon, invisible.

"Have you thought about my offer?" Bonai asked, almost shyly.

For a moment Doug felt puzzled. "Offer?"

"Asylum here in Kiribati," she said. "For you and as many of your people as you want to bring with you."

Doug took a deep breath. It was one place where the VR simulation failed. Instead of soft tropical sea air he tasted the flat, canned, slightly metallic mixture of Moonbase.

"I need to know more about what the Peacekeepers are planning," he said.

"I've told you as much as Rashid told me," Bonai said. "Several hundred troops, equipped with missiles, are being assembled at the Yamagata base in Copernicus. They plan to attack Moonbase within a month."

"Do you know anything about *how* they plan to attack?"

She shook her head.

Doug hesitated, then asked, "Tamara, can you find out anything more?"

In the starlit shadows he could not make out the expression on her face. But her voice sounded strained as she replied, "Doug, I don't want to see Rashid again. Once is a fling; twice . . . he'll either get suspicious or begin to think he owns me."

"Oh," he said, suddenly embarrassed. "I see. I understand."

"Do you?"

"I tried to talk with the director of Nippon One," he said, almost mumbling the words. "He won't take my calls."

Tamara touched his sleeve with her virtual hand. "Doug, I know it's terribly difficult for you, but you've got to face the fact that Moonbase is lost. You've got to start thinking about your own safety."

He nodded, feeling miserable. "I know you're right. And yet—"

He stopped. Out in the shadows beneath the palm trees that fringed the beach he saw something move.

Killifer was delighted. About time I caught a break, he said to himself.

He had bought an inflatable boat, barely big enough for himself and the box of food and drink he had brought with him, and chugged out into the lagoon at sunset. The beach boys who watched the hotel's rental outriggers paid him scant attention: a tourist going out for a little night fishing.

As soon as it got fully dark, Killifer set out for the private little islet on the far end of the atoll where Tamara Bonai sometimes went. Alone.

It wasn't easy, out on the lagoon all by himself in the dark. The lights from the hotel and casino soon sank below the watery horizon. His eyes grew accustomed to the starlight, but each of the flat, palm-fringed islets looked pretty much alike to him. Bonai's private little isle was the last one in the chain, he knew. Still, he almost missed the islet and drifted out to the reef in a sudden swirl of current between islands.

Finally he got to "her" islet, the farthest one from Betio and Bonriki. Sooner or later she'll come here, he told himself as he beached the inflatable boat. Once he had pulled the boat safely out of sight, into the bushes beneath the palms, he took a quick swig of beer from

the cooler and settled down to wait for her. Could be
days, he knew. What the hell.

And there she was! Killifer could hardly believe his
eyes. The woman steered her outrigger up onto the
beach just as pretty as you please and stepped out for a
walk under the stars. Alone.

Grinning to himself, Killifer thought that maybe General O'Conner's god was looking out for him, after all.

"Somebody's out there," Doug said, pointing toward
the palm trees and low shrubbery beneath them.

Bonai followed his gaze. "There couldn't be. Not at
this time of night. The canoe rental closes at sundown."

"He's coming toward us," Doug said.

"Yes. I see him."

Doug started to wave the man off, then realized that
he was on the Moon, and the approaching man couldn't
see him.

"Damn, we'll have to put up NO TRESPASSING signs,"
Bonai said, staring at the man striding toward her.

"Or guards," Doug muttered.

She looked up at Doug. "I wanted us to be alone."

"Me too. Why don't you tell him he's not allowed
here."

With a sigh, she said, "I suppose I'll have to."

Starting up the beach toward the intruder, Bonai
called out to him, "I'm sorry, sir, but you're not allowed
onto these islets. You'll have to go back to Bonriki."
She pointed toward the faint glow on the horizon from
the high-rise hotels.

The man showed no sign of understanding. Bonai repeated her warning in German, then Japanese.

"He doesn't look Japanese," Doug said, squinting
through the shadows at him.

"You're not allowed here," Tamara said, louder, in
English.

The man came closer and smiled maliciously at her.
With a sudden cold hand clutching his heart, Doug recognized Jack Killifer.

"Tamara, stay away from him," he said, grabbing for her arm.

"Why . . ."

"I know him," Doug said. "He almost killed me, once."

Bonai's eyes went wide. She turned from Doug to Killifer, close enough now almost to reach her, and back to Doug again.

"Keep away from him!" Doug urged. "Call for help!"

Bonai raised her arm to speak into her wristphone. But before she could, Killifer lunged at her.

She looked weird to Jack Killifer, covered from neck to feet in some kind of scuba suit. Then he realized that she was wearing a virtual reality full-body sensor suit. She's out here on this empty little island making out with somebody in VR, Killifer said to himself. Hot little tramp.

He grinned at her. No helmet, though. Probably got contact lenses instead.

He grasped her by the wrist and pulled her toward him.

"Don't give me any trouble, doll," he said.

Doug reached for Killifer, but it was useless. The man was real and solid, Doug was nothing more than an electronic ghost. He started shouting for the technicians to call the police in Kiribati.

Tamara clawed at Killifer's face with her free hand, but he blocked it, then knocked her to the sand with a backhand slap across her face.

Doug howled and leaped at Killifer but went right through him onto the sand.

"Doug!" Tamara screamed as Killifer dropped to his knees beside her.

"Doug?" he growled. "Is that who you're screwing with? Little Douggie, on the Moon? Getting laid in VR?" Killifer laughed and started ripping the sensor suit off Bonai.

She struggled and kicked, but he cuffed her hard enough to draw blood from her mouth and peeled the rubbery suit down off her shoulders.

"Nothing underneath," he said, grinning down at her. "Makes it easy."

Doug was screaming for somebody to alert the Kiribati police, but he knew there was no time to help Tamara. He pounded his fists in helpless fury on the virtual sand as Killifer stripped the suit off her struggling body. He punched her once in the midsection hard enough to double her up. Her struggles stopped.

"You killed her, you sonofabitch!" Doug raged.

Killifer did not hear him.

But Tamara wasn't dead. Not yet. Doug watched helplessly as Killifer spread her naked legs apart and raped her, his hands squeezing her windpipe as his body covered hers.

Killifer watched the light in her eyes fade. He fucked her good, pumping years of hate and fury into her as he slowly, slowly cut off her air. Then he stopped and pulled away from her limp body.

"Come on, kid, you're not finished yet," he said. "And neither am I."

He grinned as her eyelids fluttered and she coughed.

Doug was raving like a lunatic when the electronics technicians burst into the VR chamber. It took four of them to get him down on the floor and peel the sensor suit off him.

The last thing they took off were the contact lenses, so Doug was able to see Killifer sitting on Tamara's chest, pinning her arms to the sand, slapping her to full consciousness as he came erect once again.

"She's dead," Jinny Anson told Doug. "The Kiribati police found her on the island. She was pretty badly beaten up. Neck broken."

Despite the tranquilizer the medics had given him, Doug was quivering like a knife thrown into a wall.

"I couldn't do a thing to stop him," he chattered. "I couldn't do anything."

Edith was sitting on the edge of his bunk. Anson and one of the medics crowded next to them. Bam Gordette stood by the partition, watching silently with brooding eyes.

"It's not your fault," Edith said gently. "There's nothing you could've done."

"I should've killed him years ago, when he murdered Foster Brennart. When he tried to kill me. I should've killed him then. Executed him. Then this wouldn't have happened. Then Tamara would still be alive."

"It's not your fault," Edith repeated.

"It's *all* my fault," Doug snapped. "All of this mess is my doing. If I hadn't . . . if I'd just let Faure . . ." His voice sank to an exhausted moan.

Looking uncomfortable, Anson said, "Speaking of Faure—just who the hell is Killifer working for?"

"What do you mean?" Edith asked.

"You don't think he went all the way out to Kiribati and murdered their chief of state all on his own, do you? Who's pulling his strings?"

"The police will find out when they catch him," Edith said.

Anson shook her head. "He's already left Kiribati. Never went back to his hotel. Chartered a plane and took off at first light."

"Interpol will find him," Edith said confidently.

Anson was not so certain. "Interpol works for the U.N. now, doesn't it? Besides, what evidence do they have that he murdered Bonai?"

"An eyewitness," Doug said from his bunk.

"In virtual reality," Anson countered. "I wonder if Interpol or anybody else is gonna take that seriously."

Sinking back on his pillows, Doug admitted, "You're probably right. The Kiribati police certainly took their sweet time getting out to the islet to find her body."

Edith looked intrigued. "An eyewitness in VR. That's a helluva story."

"They won't accept my testimony," Doug said weakly. "I won't even be able to testify against him. It's totally useless. *I'm* totally useless."

Edith sat on the edge of the bunk. "Don't think that for a minute, Doug. We'll get him, you'll see."

Doug closed his eyes. "Let me sleep for a while. I just want . . . I need to sleep."

"The tranquilizers are hitting him," the medic said.

"About time," said Anson.

"Come on, let him get some rest," Edith said, shooing them out of the bedroom.

The others left, all except Gordette.

"I'll wait outside," he said to Edith. "If you need to go someplace, I'll stay with him."

DAY FORTY-TWO

Edith worked through the night at the computer in Doug's living room, splicing together a coherent story about the rape and murder of a national leader that was witnessed by a man from four hundred thousand kilometers away. She called down to Global News headquarters in Atlanta a dozen times, rousting researchers and fact-checkers until she had the whole thing pieced together.

Once she squirted the basic bits through to Atlanta, she looked in on Doug, who was still asleep in his bunk. Afraid of disturbing him, she took the slingchair in the living room and leaned back to catch a few winks. Her sleep was interrupted almost immediately by the phone chime.

It was Manny, her programming chief in Atlanta, bouncing in his chair with excitement.

"Edie, cheez, this is terrific! The assassination on Tarawa was witnessed by a guy on the Moon! Absolutely fantastic!"

"And it's our exclusive," Edith pointed out.

Manny hadn't stopped talking. "Legal says we can't

name the killer; can't make any accusations until the
guy's arrested and charged. But, cheez, the story's
tremendous!''

Edith smiled at the screen, but for the first time in
her career she realized that behind the story she was
filing there were human beings in pain. A dead woman.
Doug, sick with frustration and responsibilities that no
one could take off his shoulders. And a murderer somewhere on Earth who would probably never be arrested,
let alone brought to justice.

"Yeah," she said wearily to her boss. "Tremendous is
the word for it, all right."

Manny eyed her questioningly. "You don't look so
hot, kid."

"I'm kinda tired," she admitted.

"Pull yourself together. We missed the evening news
slot but the suits upstairs want your personal report in
the system in time for our affiliates' eleven o'clock."

Edith had been on the Moon long enough to make a
quick mental calculation. She had a little less than three
hours to show up at Moonbase's studio looking bright
and perky for a live broadcast.

"Okay," she said. "Let me get a little nap."

"And some makeup."

"Yeah, sure," she said, knowing that it might be a
problem. She had been borrowing makeup from the supply that Joanna Brudnoy had left behind, but she had
always scrupulously asked Doug's permission to raid his
mother's quarters. Now Doug was sleeping, tranquilized,
and she didn't want to wake him.

She stretched out again on the slingchair, this time
using the desk chair to rest her feet upon. She set her
wristwatch's alarm for one hour. Maybe Doug'll be
awake by then, she thought. She fell asleep almost at
once, a trick she had learned years ago. News reporters
had to grab their sleep when they could, like soldiers.

The wrist alarm beeped softly. Edith woke as instantly
as she had gone to sleep, alert and feeling refreshed.

She tiptoed to the partition and looked in on Doug.
He was tossing restlessly, the sheet twisted around his

legs. Edith went in and straightened the sheet, kissed him lightly on the forehead, then tiptoed out again.

I'll have to go over to Mrs. Brudnoy's place without asking him, she thought. Yet she hesitated, not wanting to leave Doug alone. If he wakes up, I ought to be here. Or somebody oughtta be here, at least.

Who to call? Then she remembered that Bam Gordette had offered to watch Doug. The man acted like a bodyguard anyway, Edith told herself. She phoned him, but there was no answer at his quarters.

It's past two in the morning, she saw, glancing at the digital clock set next to the computer screen. He couldn't be still waiting out in the corridor, could he?

She pushed the door open, and Gordette was sitting on the floor, his back against the opposite wall, his eyes wide open and focused squarely on her.

"You've been out here all night?" Edith asked, incredulous.

Getting to his feet, Gordette nodded. "I can sleep any-place," he said, by way of explanation.

Swiftly, almost whispering, Edith told him that she had to get to the studio and do a live broadcast.

Gordette nodded solemnly. "I'll take care of Doug."

"Wonderful," said Edith, suppressing an urge to kiss him on the cheek. Gordette did not seem like the kind of man to play the usual media kissy-face ritual.

Gordette watched her hurry down the corridor. Silently he slid the door shut and walked to the partition that separated the two sections of Doug Stavenger's quarters.

Doug lay on his back, his eyelids flickering, his fists clenched.

Not while he's asleep, Gordette told himself, fingering the obsidian blade in his coverall pocket. That wouldn't be right. You don't slaughter a sleeping victim.

The blade had drunk many victims' blood, centuries ago. Gordette had found it in a crumbling Mayan temple deep in the jungle during the Yucatan uprising. A cere-monial killing knife, the anthropologist attached to his unit had told him. Used for slicing open the chest and taking out the still-beating heart.

The anthropologist had been assigned to the army to help win the hearts and minds of the rebellious Yucatan villagers. Gordette had been a sniper then, sighting his victims in his telescopic sights and firing virus-soaked flechettes into their unsuspecting flesh. It felt like a mosquito bite, and the victim died of fever within two days. When all went well, the victim infected his entire village before he died.

The anthropologist never won the villagers' hearts and minds. He was killed in a vicious ambush. By the time Gordette and the survivors among his unit were flown out of the jungle, there were almost no villagers left alive.

Gordette sat calmly next to Doug's bunk and willed him to awaken. It's time, he said silently to his victim. Death has waited long enough.

Doug opened his eyes. He blinked once, twice.

"Bam," he said.

Gordette nodded solemnly. "Ms. Elgin had to go to the studio to do a live broadcast."

"Oh." Doug made a weak grin. "And you're babysitting me."

"If that's what you want to call it."

Without lifting his head from the pillow, Doug asked, "So how's it going?"

"How's what going?"

"Your investigation. The sabotage of my suit."

"Oh. That." Gordette took the obsidian blade from his pocket. Its curved side fit into the palm of his hand perfectly, as if it had been made all those centuries ago expressly for him.

"Well?" Doug asked.

"That's not important now," said Gordette.

"What do you mean, not important?"

"You're defeated, Doug. You know that, don't you?"

Doug's eyes had no fire in them, no zest. He merely stared at Gordette blankly.

"Moonbase is lost. You can't save it. You couldn't

even help Ms. Bonai. You watched her being raped and murdered and couldn't do a thing about it."

Doug opened his mouth but no words came out. He nodded dumbly.

"Everything you want has been taken away from you," Gordette said, speaking slowly, sonorously, like a priest at a sacrificial altar. "Even your life."

So swiftly that Doug could not even raise his arms, Gordette clamped his left hand over Doug's mouth and nose, yanking his chin up, and with his right hand sliced the blade deeply across Doug's throat, making certain to sever the carotid arteries behind each ear.

Blood spurted high up the wall, gushed over Gordette's green coveralls and into his face, making him blink and wince. Doug's body shivered and twitched, then went still.

His hands soaked in Doug's blood, Gordette stalked out of the room and headed down the empty corridors of Moonbase, shadowy in their nighttime lighting, toward the garage and the main airlock.

For the first time since he'd been a boy, there were tears in his eyes.

"The last time I was on the Moon ended unpleasantly," said Keiji Inoguchi.

"So?" replied Zimmerman, coolly.

Inoguchi was a full head taller than Zimmerman, and gracefully slim. He seemed to glide rather than walk, totally unperturbed by the low lunar gravity.

"I worked at Nippon One eight years ago," he told Zimmerman, "but I was sent back to Japan after being injured in an accident. Several of my ribs were broken."

Zimmerman nodded absently. Of the three U.N. inspectors sent up on the evacuation flight, Inoguchi seemed to be the only one who knew anything about nanotechnology. He claimed to be a professor of mechanical engineering at the University of Kyoto, but to Zimmerman he seemed too young for a full professorship—unless he was actually working in a new field, un-

cluttered by tenured old men, a field such as
nanotechnology.

For four days, since the evacuation flight had touched
down at Moonbase, Inoguchi and the two other U.N.
inspectors had been making their methodical way
through the nanolabs. Kris Cardenas had personally con-
ducted their inspection tour, showing them everything—
except Zimmerman's lab.

Zimmerman stayed to himself behind locked doors,
unwilling to allow U.N. *spionin* to poke through his
work. From what Cardenas told him, Inoguchi was
bright, inquisitive, polite and knowledgeable. The other
two seemed to be out-and-out intelligence agents, ham-
fisted and hard-eyed, looking for nanotech "weapons"
without understanding what they might be.

The inevitable happened late in the evening of their
fourth day at Moonbase. Cardenas phoned Zimmerman,
still barricaded in his lab, and warned him that Inoguchi
was heading his way. Alone.

Zimmerman heard a polite tap at his door almost before he clicked off the phone. Muttering to himself, he
went to the door, determined to tell the interfering Japanese upstart that he had no business bothering the great
Professor Zimmerman and he should go away and stay
away.

Inoguchi bowed deeply as soon as Zimmerman slid
the door open. "I am Keiji Inoguchi of the University
of Kyoto," he said, staring at his shoes, not daring to
look at Zimmerman. "I know it's an imposition, but I
am required to ask you to allow me to inspect your
laboratory."

Grudgingly, Zimmerman waved the younger man into
his lab.

"It is an honor beyond my greatest expectations to
actually meet you," Inoguchi said. His English was
American-accented, and Zimmerman thought the man
sounded sincere enough, even though he kept his face
almost totally expressionless and still avoided making
eye contact.

"Professor Cardenas tells me you appear quite knowledgeable," Zimmerman said gruffly. "You are engaged in nanotechnology research at Kyoto?"

Inoguchi hesitated the merest fraction of a second, then replied, "As you know, Professor, nanotechnology research is forbidden by law."

"Yah. Of course."

They stood just inside the doorway, Zimmerman blocking his visitor's further access into the lab, and spoke of many things, from the quality of students to the obtuseness of deans, without again mentioning nanotechnology. Despite their verbal sparring, or perhaps because of it, Zimmerman found that he enjoyed the younger man's company.

"How long will you remain at Moonbase?" Zimmerman asked.

"I wish I knew," Inoguchi replied wistfully. "Our mission to Moonbase was arranged very hastily, and with the blockade in effect—"

"Blockade?"

"No flights to Moonbase have been permitted for six weeks now. Surely you were aware of that."

"Oh, that. Yah. I didn't think of it as a blockade," Zimmerman said.

With a rueful gesture, Inoguchi said, "They told us back home before we left that they would try to arrange a mission from Nippon One to pick us up here and then bring us back to Copernicus. From there we can take a flight back to Earth. But I have no idea of how long that will take to negotiate, or how long I must remain here."

"I see."

"One thing is certain, however. Even if there were a hundred ships ready to take me back to Kyoto, I could not leave until I had looked through your laboratory."

Zimmerman grunted. "You think I am cooking up nanomachines to wipe out Japan, maybe?"

Inoguchi actually broke into a grin. "No, sir, I don't. But the people at the U.N. who sent me here fear that you might be brewing nanobugs that will spread deadly plagues all across Earth."

"Nonsense!"

"You know it is nonsense, and I know it is nonsense, but they do not have enough knowledge to allay their fears."

Zimmerman looked at the younger man with new-found respect.

"Let us be frank with one another," Zimmerman said. "I will show you my work, but you must tell me about your own. Fair?"

Inoguchi nodded. "Quite fair."

"Your laboratory is funded by Yamagata Industries, I trust?"

"My entire department is funded by Yamagata. Seigo Yamagata himself has taken a deep interest in my work."

"Which is?"

"Nanotechnology, of course. You must have known that."

Turning to lead him to the bench where the electron microscope and micromanipulators were, Zimmerman said over his shoulder, "I had my suspicions."

Several hours later they were sitting on stools at the back end of the lab, where Zimmerman kept his dwindling supply of imported beer. He had led his visitor through his whole lab, congratulating himself on not once letting him guess that his most recent work was all aimed at helping Moonbase to defend itself against Peacekeeper attack.

Zimmerman took a long draught of beer from the plastic beaker he used as a stein. "If the *verdammt* blockade continues much longer," he groused, "I will be reduced to drinking fruit juice."

Inoguchi said nothing.

"We've been trying to make beer with nanomachines, you know."

"Ah?"

Shaking his head, Zimmerman confessed, "It tastes like piss."

"Mr. Yamagata is most interested in the therapeutic uses of nanotechnology," Inoguchi said, holding his lab beaker of beer in both hands. "He is concerned about cancer, especially."

"So? How old is he?"

"Hardly fifty, but the family history—"

"PROFESSOR ZIMMERMAN, PLEASE REPORT TO THE INFIRMARY IMMEDIATELY," the wall speaker blared. "PROFESSOR ZIMMERMAN TO THE INFIRMARY AT ONCE. EMERGENCY."

DAY FORTY-TWO

Even nanomachines need a finite time to react.

The virus-sized machines teeming in Doug's bloodstream sensed the sudden drop in pressure and the desperate chemical changes that tried to activate the natural clotting factors before Doug bled to death. His windpipe was cruelly ruptured and blood was leaking into his lungs, choking him.

Unconscious, gasping for breath, bleeding to death as his heart spewed his life's blood out through his severed arteries, Doug's hands spasmed, his body shuddered, and then he was still.

Inside him hundreds of millions of nanomachines were working with millisecond frenzy, seizing individual atoms and locking them in place like a stubborn team of men doggedly packing sandbags onto a flood-broken levee. With mindless purposefulness other nanomachines pulled apart the droplets of blood leaking into Doug's lungs, broke up the liquid into molecules of gas. Doug coughed and retched as nanomachines seamlessly knitted together his carotid arteries and began to close the gash across his throat.

Nearly half his blood had been splashed over the

bunk, the wall, even the ceiling above the bunk before the nanomachines sealed his arteries and stopped the major bleeding. It took longer—minutes—to completely close the wound in his throat.

Still unconscious, Doug sank into a deeper coma while the nanomachines cleaned his lungs and augmented the natural chemical factors that prompted his bone marrow to start producing more red blood cells. Yet his blood supply was dangerously depleted. He needed plasma and liquids. He lay there, between life and death, unable to move, unable to open his eyes or stir himself out of the coma.

Hours later, Edith came back to the apartment, tired yet keyed up with the excitement of having pulled off a masterful broadcast. By golly, I *am* good, she told herself as she slid the door shut and started across the living room to see how Doug was doing.

She screamed when she saw all the blood. Her knees buckled and she felt as if she was going to faint.

No! she raged at herself. Get help! Quick!

She banged on the phone keyboard and shrieked for an emergency medical team. Then she ran back to take a closer look at Doug. Despite the blood she saw no wounds, nothing but a thin red line across his throat. It looked more like a paper cut than anything serious. Yet there was blood all over the bunk, soaking him, splattered on the wall, the ceiling. He was unconscious, totally out of it. He was breathing, though. Or is he? Fighting down her panic, Edith saw that Doug was breathing slowly, deeply, like a man innocently asleep.

The medical team barged into the apartment: the base's resident doctor and two paramedic aides drafted from other duties.

"What the hell happened here?" Dr. Montana scowled at the scene. Within minutes Doug was being wheeled to the infirmary by the aides while the deeply puzzled doctor again and again asked Edith questions that she could not answer as they ran behind the gurney.

*   *   *

By the time Doug opened his eyes, Zimmerman and Kris Cardenas were hovering over his infirmary bed and Jinny Anson was standing beside a pale and shaken Edith, both women peering worriedly at him through the glass partition that closed off his cubicle. A tall youngish Japanese man was out there, too; Doug remembered him as one of the U.N. inspectors.

Doug looked up at Zimmerman, who was staring intently at him, as if sheer willpower could make his patient waken. The old professor looked more dishevelled than usual, straggly hair in wild disarray, both vest and jacket unbuttoned and flapping across his paunch. Yet there was a gentleness in his gaze, like a grandfather watching over a sleeping infant.

"This is getting monotonous," Doug said, weakly. His voice was hoarse, grating.

Zimmerman's expression immediately hardened into his usual disapproving frown. "So? Even a cat has only nine lives," he said bruskly. "You are using up yours at a rapid rate."

"I'm getting a lot of help," Doug breathed. He realized there were intravenous tubes in both his arms. Monitors beeped away quietly somewhere behind his head.

"What happened?" Zimmerman asked.

Doug blinked, remembered. "Bam. Leroy Gordette. He tried to murder me." His sandpaper voice was filled with the surprise and grief that he felt at Gordette's betrayal.

"It was Gordette?" Cardenas asked, her clear blue eyes snapping. "The ex-soldier?"

"He slit my throat," Doug said, fingering his throat, finding neither wound nor pain there.

Edith pushed into the narrow cubicle, Anson right behind her. Inoguchi remained on the other side of the observation window.

Flinging herself on Doug, she burst into the tears she'd been holding back for hours. "I thought you were dead!"

Doug held her close; felt the sobs racking her body.

"I'm okay," he whispered into her golden hair. "I'm okay now."

"God, was I scared," Edith gushed. She kissed him on the lips. The others fidgeted around the bed.

Once Doug let go of Edith and she straightened up, Anson surmised, "Gordette must've been the one who malfed your suit."

"Yeah." Doug tried to push himself up on his elbows. The room spun and he dropped back onto the pillow.

"You lost much blood," Zimmerman said, glancing at the monitors over the bed. "You need time to build up your supply."

"Where's Bam now?" Doug croaked.

Anson shrugged. "I'll get security to roust him." She ducked out of the cubicle.

"Are you really all right?" Edith asked, wiping at her eyes.

"I'm okay," said Doug. "Weak, though."

"A blood transfusion would help," Cardenas suggested.

Doug thought a moment. "How much do we have on hand? If we're attacked, we might need a lot."

"No transfusion," Zimmerman said flatly. "I must see how long it takes my nanomachines to rebuild his blood supply. A transfusion would obscure the data."

Edith started to say something, but Doug gripped her hand and stopped her.

Smiling weakly at the old man, Doug said, "I'm still your walking experiment, huh?"

Zimmerman put on his scowl again. "Except you spend more time on your back than walking."

"It's not my idea of fun, believe me."

Dr. Montana came in and shooed them all out of the cubicle with the authority and impatience of a minor tyrant.

"If he's not allowed a transfusion," the doctor grumbled, glancing sideways at Zimmerman, "then he needs rest."

"I am kind of sleepy," Doug admitted. "And hungry."

"My nanomachines need energy," Zimmerman mumbled.

"We're pumping nutrients into you," Montana said, touching one of the IV tubes gently.

"He can take solid food, as well," said Zimmerman.

Montana looked skeptical, but said nothing.

Edith kissed him again and they all left, the doctor and Zimmerman in a heated, whispered conversation about who should be making the decisions about the patient. A few minutes later, an aide brought Doug a tray of food. He had to be helped up to a sitting position. He ate quickly, then fell asleep almost immediately.

When Doug awoke he saw that Edith was sitting in the little observation area on the other side of the glass partition, staring intently into the display screen of a laptop. The IV tubes had been removed. He felt strong enough to sit up on his own. A little woozy, but it passed quickly. He pressed the button that cranked up the bed, then leaned back comfortably.

One of the paramedics bustled into his cubicle, her face set somewhere between pleased and annoyed. "You're not supposed—"

"I'm starving," Doug said. "When do I get something to eat?"

With a swift glance at the monitors, the aide muttered, "I'll get you another tray," and headed out.

Edith snapped her laptop shut and pushed past the departing aide.

After a quick kiss, Doug asked, "Have they found Gordette?"

"No," she said. "He checked out a tractor and went outside just after he tried to kill you."

"A tractor?" Doug's mind raced. "He can't get all the way to Copernicus in a tractor."

"Copernicus?"

"The Yamagata base, Nippon One." Doug reasoned it out. "He knows as much about our situation here as any of us, Edith. He can tell the Peacekeepers exactly how weak we are, what we're expecting from them, how to take us."

"But he can't get that far in a tractor, you said."

"Maybe he's got a pickup arranged with them. He could bounce an emergency signal to them off L-1 and they'll come out and pick him up."

"But L-1 is off the air, isn't it?"

"For us, but they're still working for Yamagata."

The aide brought in a tray heavy with a double portion of dinner. Doug thanked her and began wolfing it down.

"Edith, call Jinny for me. Ask her if there's any way to spot Gordette's tractor. I need to know where he's going."

"Why . . . ?"

"So I can stop him, that's why."

Inoguchi and Zimmerman were sitting at a small corner table in the Cave, sipping fruit juice. The big cavern was nearly empty, yet they hunched together and spoke in low tones like conspirators.

"His throat was cut?" Inoguchi's pretense of impassivity was long gone. There was wonder in his eyes, awe in his voice. "You are certain?"

Zimmerman took a sip of juice, then frowned at the glass. "From the amount of blood in his room, at least one of his carotid arteries must have been opened."

"But he seems hardly hurt at all."

"The machines work on millisecond time scales."

"So do the natural blood-clotting factors, but they could not have stopped arterial bleeding in time."

"I think maybe the machines activated muscles in his neck and used them to clamp down the wound," Zimmerman mused.

"Not possible! Is it?"

With the wave of a pudgy hand, the older man said, "You saw the results."

Inoguchi shook his head ruefully. "I am a child. Compared to your work, what I'm doing in Kyoto is kindergarten level."

"The benefits of censorship and your lovely treaty,"

Zimmerman said acidly. "You work in ignorance of what has already been done years ago."

"Yes, I can see that."

Zimmerman started to take another swig of the fruit juice, then decided against it and put the glass down firmly on their little table.

"That young man is my long-term experiment. He was dying from radiation overdose when I injected the nano-machines into him, eight years ago—"

"Eight years?" Inoguchi seemed startled. "Was he at the south pole with Brennart?"

Zimmerman blinked. "Yes. Brennart died there."

"I was there also. Or close by, actually. I broke my ribs in a landing accident. Yamagata and the Masterson Corporation were racing to claim the ice fields discovered at the south polar region."

"So. That was when I injected Douglas Stavenger with the nanomachines. Some were specialized, others programmed in a more general way."

"And they have been inside him all these years?"

"They will always be inside him. They have formed a symbiotic relationship with him."

"How can inanimate machines create a symbiosis with an organism?" Inoguchi challenged.

"You see what they have done! What else can you call it?"

"But true symbiosis . . ."

They argued for hours, neither of them raising his voice, both of them waxing passionate for his position and against the other's. Zimmerman enjoyed the debate immensely; he hadn't had this kind of intellectual stimulation since he'd left Switzerland.

"It's a shame you must return to Kyoto," the old man said at last.

"Perhaps I won't," said Inoguchi.

"You want to remain here? You want to work with me?"

"Most certainly."

Zimmerman beamed at him. "Very good! You can ask for asylum and—"

"No, I'm afraid you don't understand," Inoguchi said, smiling politely.

"What don't I understand?"

"My work at Kyoto, fumbling and childlike as it is, must be done in great secrecy because Japan has signed the nanotechnology treaty and therefore such research is technically illegal."

"So come here to Moonbase!"

"Once Yamagata Industries has acquired Moonbase, I will certainly come here and engage in nanotechnology research without all the hindrances I experience in Kyoto. I offer you the opportunity of remaining here even after the others have been removed. You may remain here and work with me."

Zimmerman took a moment to digest what he heard, then sputtered, "You would allow me to remain at Moonbase and work *under* you?"

"With me," Inoguchi corrected.

"We would be working for Yamagata, then?"

"Yes, of course."

Zimmerman scowled at the younger man.

"You could continue your research unhindered," Inoguchi promised. "There is no need for you to be sent back to Earth, no need for you to stop your work."

Coldly, Zimmerman said, "You are assuming that Yamagata will conquer Moonbase."

With a wan smile, Inoguchi replied, "That is inevitable, Professor. Regretful, perhaps, but inevitable. There is no way that Moonbase can resist the combined strength of the Peacekeepers and Yamagata's special forces."

"Even if I can make the entire base invisible to you?"

"What?" Inoguchi's brows knit with consternation. "What are you saying?"

"Never mind," Zimmerman replied, shaking his head.

"Invisible? How?"

"I will tell you only this much, young man. Your Peacekeepers and Yamagata forces might be able to destroy Moonbase and kill everyone in it, but they will never take us over. We will not be conquered! I will see

to it that every man and woman in this base dies before
we surrender to you!"

"You can't be serious! I'm offering you an opportunity to continue your work as if nothing happened."

With an angry snort, Zimmerman said, "You think I
am a fool? You think I am an amoral egomaniac like
your Georges Faure? Or like some renaissance tinkerer,
content to work for any prince as long as he gets paid?
I'm not a von Braun, I don't work for any regime that
allows me to pursue my goal. Moonbase is my home and
I will defend it to the end! Freedom or death!"

Inoguchi had never felt so stunningly surprised in his
entire life. *The man thinks like a samurai,* he realized.

DAY FORTY-THREE

"You can't go after him," Edith said. "You can't even
get out of bed!"

Doug smiled at her and hiked a thumb at the monitors
over his head. "Look at the screens, Edith. Everything's
in the normal range, isn't it?"

She glanced upward, then looked back at him. "The
doctor told me—"

"The doctor's playing it by the book. Zimmerman
wants to observe how his nanobugs are working. But
I've got to find Bam and stop him."

"Why you? Why not a security team?"

"He wouldn't give up without a fight. I don't want
anybody hurt."

"After he tried to murder you?"

"It's my job, Edith," said Doug calmly. "My
responsibility."

She started to shake her head. "I'm not going to help you risk your butt all over again."

"I've got to, Edith. Go back to our place and get a fresh set of clothes for me."

"No!"

"You can come with me," he said, struggling to convince her. "You said you wanted to come outside."

"Zimmerman won't allow it."

"He can't stop us if nobody tells him about it."

"Doug, you almost *died*!"

"But I'm okay now, really I am. What do I have to do, jump your bod to show you I'm in good condition?"

Her green eyes turned thoughtful. "Let's see if you can get out of bed, first."

Doug pushed the swivel table with its emptied food tray away from the bed and swung his legs out from under the sheet. He planted his bare feet on the warmed tile floor and stood up. No alarm bells went off. The monitors showed no change in his condition.

"See? No hands."

She broke into a grin. "That gown looks pretty silly on you."

"Go get me some clothes while I peel off these sensor patches."

"You'll really take me with you? Outside?"

He nodded soberly. "I promise."

"And they'll let you out?"

"Hey, I'm the chief administrator of this base. Rank has its privileges."

"Uh-huh."

With a furtive glance at the observation window beside his bed, Doug added, "But you'd better get my clothes before Doc Montana comes back for another check."

"This is absolutely crazy," Edith said. "I love it!"

She was sitting beside Doug in the open cockpit of a massive lunar tractor, encased in a cumbersome spacesuit, waiting inside the big metal womb of the main airlock while the pumps sucked out the air so they could go outside and track down Bam Gordette. The airlock was suffused with a dull red light, like an old-fashioned darkroom.

She had figured that if Doug was strong enough to make it down to the garage and actually get himself into a spacesuit, maybe she'd go along with him instead of blowing the whistle and getting him shipped back to the infirmary. It was she who needed help, though, when they started to pull on their spacesuits.

Edith was surprised when Doug went to the new cermet suit, standing in a locker marked DO NOT TOUCH: EXPERIMENTAL EQUIPMENT.

"You're going to use *that* suit again?"

He grinned at her. "This is the best tested and inspected suit in the whole Earth-Moon system, believe me."

She took one of the regular suits from the row of lockers, muttering, "I never know if I'm a small or a medium." Doug was already in his leggings and boots when he saw Edith struggling with hers and clumped over to help her.

At last they got completely suited up, filled the backpack air tanks, and checked out each other's suits from the safety list Doug called up on their wrist display screens. Then came the interminable wait while Edith eliminated the nitrogen in her blood by pre-breathing the suit's low-pressure air.

Now Edith sat beside him in the tractor's unpressurized cockpit. In the eerie light of the airlock, all she could see of Doug was an anonymous lump of reddish-tinged white, like the Pillsbury Doughboy by firelight, topped with a helmet and a gold-tinted visor that reflected her own red-tinged helmet and visor.

"Are you sure you're strong enough to do this?" Edith asked as the noise of the pump faded down to silence.

Doug's voice said in her earphones, "Listen to me, Edith. My body's building up my blood supply. I'm a lot stronger now than I was an hour ago."

"You're sure?"

He laughed. "Yep, I'm absolutely, positively certain. I might be wrong, but I'm sure."

Doug had talked their way past the technician on duty at the main airlock, who wondered why the Big Boss was going outside in the middle of the lunar night with the flatlander news reporter and an insulated container big enough to hold a dead body.

"Lunch," Doug had explained about the container. It held a dozen quarts of fruit juices and soymilk that they had picked up at the Cave on their way to the garage. They had loaded four spare air cylinders onto the tractor's bed, as well: two at normal room pressure and two at the low pressure Edith's standard suit required.

The display light on the panel set into the scuffed metal wall of the huge airlock next to the outside hatch abruptly switched from amber to green.

"Here we go," Doug said as the outer hatch began to slowly slide open. "Once we're underway I'll show you how to operate the tractor. That'll take less than fifteen minutes."

"Driving lessons?" Edith's eyes were focused on the growing gap as the hatch opened wider. It was dark out there, even with her vision already dark-adapted from the red lighting inside the airlock.

"Yeah," he replied. "That way, in case anything happens to me you can drive back here."

"Oh." Edith realized that beneath his casual demeanor Doug was weighing the risks as carefully as he could.

The airlock hatch opened fully and Doug put the tractor in gear. Edith heard no sound at all in the dead vacuum, but she felt the electric motors' vibrations as they turned each of the tractor's wheels individually.

I'm out on the surface of the Moon! she exulted. Her first time, with Captain Munasinghe and the Peacekeepers, she'd been too busy recording her story to appreciate the scenery. Now she looked about and saw nothing but stark desolation. Dusty flat ground, cracked here and there. Rocks of all sizes, from pebbles to boulders. Craterlets, too, as if children had been digging into the ground with sticks and shovels.

Off to one side was the deep pit that would one day be the grand plaza of the Moonbase that Doug envisioned. Maybe, she thought. If we can keep Yamagata from taking over.

It all looked about as romantic as a slag heap to her, yet Doug loved it.

"It's kind of dark right now," Doug said. "Nothing up there except a crescent Earth. When it's full, or even gibbous, it's a lot brighter."

"I can't even see—what's that?"

A big round *thing* was sitting on the ground off to their right, like a giant beach ball the size of their tractor. Peering at it, Edith saw that it was not solid, but built of some kind of wire mesh. And it seemed to be resting on a curved metal track laid across the ground.

Doug laughed. "That's the laundry."

"Laundry?"

"Sure. Dirt dries almost immediately in vacuum and detaches from fabric while the ultraviolet from the sun kills germs. We pack the dirty laundry in there when the sun's up and roll the sphere back and forth along the track for an hour or so. Clothes come out clean and sanitized."

"My clothes have been cleaned in there?"

"Yep."

"How do you iron them?"

"The old-fashioned way," Doug answered. "With automated ironing machines that use waste heat from the base's living quarters and machinery."

Edith shook her head inside her helmet. Her clothes seemed clean enough when she got them back from the laundry, but rolling them around out here . . . ?

"I'm switching to the base's standard comm frequency," Doug told her. "First keypad on your comm set."

It took Edith a few moments to remember which row of pads on the wrist of her suit was the comm set. In the dim lighting, little more than the glow from the tractor's dashboard instruments, she figured it out after a few moments.

". . . yes, I'm outside with Edith," Doug was saying.

"Are you crazy?" Jinny Anson's voice snapped. "What the blazes are you doing outside?"

"Trying to get to Gordette before he reaches Yamagata's people," said Doug. "Any joy with tracking his tractor?"

"Hell no." Anson sounded thoroughly unhappy. "He was smart enough to turn off its transponder, and now he's so far over the horizon that even if he had it on we couldn't hear it."

"Any idea of which way he went?"

"I checked the automated radar plot," Anson replied immediately. "Shows he was heading on a bearing of three-forty-five degrees, relative to true north."

"Three-forty-five?"

"That's out past the mass driver, heading almost due north."

"So he's not taking Wodjohowitcz Pass, then."

"Not yet. He's probably trying to knock out the mass driver first. The magnets, I betcha."

Doug's voice caught in his throat. "The magnets! So we can't use them to drive Wicksen's particle beam gun."

"Which means we won't have any chance at all of stopping an incoming nuke."

"I've got to stop him."

"Get real! He's got a six-hour lead on you."

"I've still got to try. Does Wix have any people out at the driver?"

"Not for the past ten days. His whole crew's been inside here, working on the new hardware."

"Do we have anything at all that we can use to spot his tractor, Jinny?"

She humphed. "Crystal ball? Tarot cards . . ." Suddenly her voice brightened. "Hey! What about Kadar's survey satellite?"

"Is it still functional?"

"We can power it up and see. Lemme check on when it'll swing over Alphonsus again."

"Good. Call me as soon as you can."

"Will do, boss."

Edith asked, "Aren't we over the horizon from Moonbase?"

"We will be in another fifteen minutes," Doug said.

"Then how will you be able to talk with Jinny? Or anyone at the base?"

"Antennas up on top of Mount Yeager," Doug explained. "We can reach more than half of the area within the ringwall, and a considerable amount of territory out on Mare Nubium."

"Then why can't they find Gordette's tractor?"

"The antennas are for communications, not radar tracking."

"Oh."

"We'll get him."

Edith was worried that he was right.

Doug began to show her how to run the tractor. It wasn't much different from driving a car.

"Not a lot of traffic out here," he said, "but you've got to be on the lookout for craters and rocks that can get you stuck. Stay with the flattest, clearest ground you can find."

"Like you're doing."

"Right."

"Do you know where you're going? I mean, without knowing where his tractor is?"

Doug pointed a gloved finger over the hood of the tractor. "I'm following his trail."

"His trail?"

"Look. The cleat tracks."

She saw a maze of tracks running pretty much in the same direction: out to the mass driver, she supposed.

"His are the brightest," Doug explained. "Nobody's been out here for ten days or so, so Bam's tractor has churned up the newest tracks. Surface dirt is darkened by solar ultraviolet. New bootprints, new tractor marks, they uncover the brighter stuff underneath."

"Shades of the Lone Ranger and his faithful Indian companion," Edith muttered.

"Who?"

He knows so much, Edith thought, and there's so much he doesn't know. She settled back to watching the landscape, trundling by at a frustratingly slow thirty kilometers per hour or so.

"Do you really find this rock pile beautiful?" she asked.

"Don't you?"

"It's so barren! So empty and lifeless. There's not even air to breathe."

It took him a few moments to reply. "It all looks a lot better when there's a full Earth. Fifty times brighter than a full Moon, back Earthside. It's breathtaking. Everything glows like silver out here. And you can watch the Earth, see its clouds and oceans; it never stays the same for very long."

"It's only a sliver now," Edith said, glancing upward at the thin crescent hanging in the starry sky.

"Take a good look," Doug said. "Stare at it for a few minutes."

There's nothing better to do out here, Edith thought. She looked at the bright crescent Earth, a scimitar-slim curve of bright blue with flecks of white.

And saw that there was a blue glow stretching beyond the points of the crescent. The Earth's air was gleaming, catching the Sun's light and warmth.

"Look on the dark side," Doug told her. "Focus your eyes a little to the left of the crescent's bulge."

She did, and saw nothing but darkness. The night side of Earth, she realized. Dark and—

There were lights glittering there! At first Edith wasn't certain she really saw them, but the harder she stared, the more she saw. Cities aglow with light. Thin twinkling threads of highways linking them.

"Holy cow!" she blurted.

"See the cities?"

"It's like a connect-the-dots map," Edith said excitedly. "I can see Florida . . . at least I think it's—no! That's Italy! And over there must be Paris! Wow!"

"And look at—" A sharp buzz interrupted Doug. "Hold it. Incoming message."

It was Anson again. "Gotta hand it to Kadar: his bird chirped right up when we interrogated it. It's at periluna over Alphonsus, of course, so it'll be zipping by at its fastest when it comes over us."

"How soon, Jinny?" Doug asked.

"Five minutes. No, four-fifty. I'll get the data wrung out and pipe it to you in half an hour, max."

"Good."

It took longer. Doug let Edith drive the tractor while he dug into the food box. There was no way to eat solid food in a spacesuit, but he pumped a quart of milk and three containers of juices through the feeding nipple in his helmet.

"Milk and orange juice?" Edith asked, grimacing. "Chugging them down one right after the other?"

"The last one was beet juice," Doug said. "Got to thank Lev for that: he likes to make borscht."

Anson called again. "Got him! He's way past the mass driver, out beyond the central peaks. Still heading north."

Doug thought a moment. "Jinny, if he's that far out he couldn't have stopped for long at the mass driver, could he?"

"Prob'ly not," she answered. "I doubt that he stopped at all. He's been truckin' right along, I betcha."

"Then he hasn't tried to sabotage the magnets."

Anson hesitated, then replied, "Unless he left a bomb there to go off later."

Doug started to ask where Gordette would get explosives, then realized that a man with his smarts could convert rocket propellants into a bomb easily enough.

"The satellite'll swing by this way again in sixty-three minutes," Anson said. "I'll update you then."

"Okay. Thanks, Jinny."

"Just doin' my job, boss."

They drove past the mass driver. It seemed intact to Doug, but he made a mental note to send a team out to look for booby traps, just to be on the safe side.

Edith rode beside him in silence. She picked a container of fortified dietary supplement and sipped at it unhappily. It tasted somewhere between chalk and sweat socks.

"I'm glad it was Bam."

After the long silence, Edith wasn't certain she had heard his muttered words correctly.

"Glad?" she asked.

"Well . . . not glad, exactly. But . . ." His voice faded away.

The damned spacesuits took away all the visual clues, Edith realized. All she had to go on was his voice in her earphones. She couldn't see his face, his eyes.

"You see," Doug said slowly, as the tractor trundled along the bleak landscape, "we didn't have any problems with sabotage or attempted assassination until—well, until you came into Moonbase."

That jolted her. "You thought I was a hit man?"

"No, I didn't. But the possibility was there. And I hated it."

"You never—I mean, we were sleeping together! How could you think . . ."

"I had to consider it," he said, his voice sounding miserable. "I never really thought you were the one who tampered with my suit, but I had to consider the possibility. *And* the possibility that I wasn't thinking straight because I love you."

"You love me?"

"I had to get my throat slit to finally figure it out. My last conscious thought after Bam cut me was that I was glad it wasn't you."

Edith blinked several times inside her helmet. "Douglas Stavenger, that's got to be the *least* romantic announcement a man's ever made to a woman!"

For several moments she heard nothing but her own breathing, magnified inside the helmet. Then Doug burst into laughter.

"You're right, Edith," he said, laughing. "That was about as romantic as reading an inventory list. I'm sorry."

She felt a smile tugging at her lips. "Nothing to be sorry about, I guess."

"I do love you, Edith. I really do."

"And I love you, too," she said, surprising herself.

His laughter only increased. "We picked a great time to bare our souls, sealed up in these suits."

She began to giggle. "Yep, guess so."

Doug reached for her gloved hand and pressed it to the visor of his helmet. "That's the best I can do right now. But we ought to be coming up on a tempo pretty soon."

"Tempo?"

"One of the old temporary shelters. We keep them stocked with emergency supplies. We can go inside and get out of these damned suits for a while."

"Uh-huh. And what about Gordette?"

She heard his sharp intake of breath. "Gordette," Doug said, all the laughter gone. "I had almost forgotten about him."

"Doug, if we're going to have to surrender anyway to the Peacekeepers or Yamagata or whoever, why are we chasing after Gordette?"

It took several moments before he answered, "Because I don't want to surrender to them, Edith. Deep inside me I'm still hoping for a miracle."

"What kind of a miracle?"

"I wish I knew."

DAY FORTY-THREE

Grand Cayman Island had been a haven for tax-weary investors for more than a century, the Switzerland of the Caribbean, a home away from home for money that was to be hidden, laundered, or otherwise kept out of the sight of the tax collectors of the world.

Still a Crown Colony of the British Empire, the tiny

flat island—a few minutes' flight from Cuba, less than an hour from Miami—possessed more banks than hotels, more financial offices than brothels, more citizens in business suits than beach wear.

Yet the beaches were lovely, Joanna thought as she and Lev strolled along the concrete walk from her hotel to the restaurant where she had been told the meeting would take place. It's a shame we won't have the time to go snorkeling or enjoy the sunshine.

The street was lined with restaurants and shops vending beach wear and souvenirs. They were dressed like tourists, as they had been instructed. Joanna was in white shorts and a flowered sleeveless blouse, with a big floppy straw hat; Lev wore comfortable baggy slacks, a loose-fitting mesh shirt hanging over them, and sunglasses.

"I see the string bikini is making a comeback," Lev said, grinning. "I'll have to buy a few for you."

Joanna pretended to grimace. "One woman on the entire beach in a string outfit doesn't make a fashion trend, Lev. And she's very young, probably still in her teens."

Her husband shrugged. "She *is* a bit on the emaciated side, but still she seems quite attractive."

"Honestly."

"You would look much better than she does."

"I couldn't wear a skimpy thing like that on the beach!"

"Who said you'd wear it on the beach?" Lev countered. "We have fourteen rooms in Savannah. I could spread a little sand in the sun porch and chase you through the entire house."

"You would, too, wouldn't you?" Joanna said, laughing. Lev was trying to lighten her mood, she realized. Ease the tension.

Arranging a meeting with Seigo Yamagata had been easier than getting to see Georges Faure. And more difficult. Yamagata was even more inaccessible than the U.N. secretary-general, but his aides had responded with swift politeness to Joanna's call. Very indirectly they suggested that a luncheon might be of interest to both parties. Joanna refused to come to Japan; Yamagata's aides said with deep regret that a meeting elsewhere would probably be impossible.

At Lev's suggestion, Joanna suggested a neutral territory. Within an hour Yamagata's twenty-year-old son Saito called back to propose meeting at Grand Cayman. Quietly. Discreetly.

"Many corporations conduct business on Grand Cayman," the young man said, looking earnest. "It would not be out of the ordinary for a very high officer of this corporation to be present on the island at a certain time and place."

Joanna nodded at his image on her phone screen. "Yes," she agreed. "Masterson Corporation does business with several banking establishments there."

The time and place were set. Now Joanna and Lev walked along the beachfront street in the brilliant late morning sunlight and brisk sea breeze, heading toward the Sunrise Hotel.

"I wonder how many of these Japanese tourists are actually Yamagata security people," Lev murmured.

Joanna had noticed them, too, strolling innocently along the beach walk, window shopping, lolling in the sunshine. "About the same number as our own Masterson troops," she replied.

Lev's brows rose. "Are *any* of these people actually tourists?"

"A few, I suppose."

At last they stood before the Sunrise Hotel, a quiet little modernistic construction of concrete painted pastel blue on the far end of the beach, away from the gaudier shops and restaurants. The arrangements for the meeting included the requirement that they walk to this hotel from their own corporate-owned condo; no taxi whose trip record could be traced, no ostentatious limousine.

Joanna thought that Yamagata was being melodramatic, overly cautious. It's understandable to want to keep your movements private and avoid the media paparazzi, she thought, but the man's acting downright paranoid.

She noticed that Lev walked up the hotel's front steps stiffly, like a man in pain.

"Are you all right?" she asked.

He looked surprised. "Yes, of course."

"You looked . . ." Joanna didn't know how to say it without hurting her husband.

"Like an old man," he finished for her. "My dearest one, I *am* an old man."

"As soon as this mess is over," she said, almost whispering, "we're going back to Moonbase and you are going to start nanotherapy."

Instead of protesting as Joanna expected he would, Brudnoy nodded. That told her worlds about how he truly felt.

Then he said, "Assuming, of course, that there is a Moonbase left standing, and nanotherapy will still be allowed there."

Joanna murmured, "Yes, assuming all that."

Once they stepped into the cool shade of the hotel's lobby they saw that it was completely staffed by Japanese.

"Why do I feel like a fly walking into the spider's web?" Lev whispered to his wife as they followed a smiling young woman in an old-fashioned kimono through the lobby and out into a small but pleasantly decorated restaurant.

It was completely empty. The minimalist decor was decidedly Japanese: polished wood and lacquered low tables with cushions on the floor. No chairs.

They took off their sandals at the door and the young woman led them to a table by a window that looked out onto a garden of raked sand and bare rocks.

"I'm glad I wore shorts instead of a skirt," Joanna said as she sat cross-legged on one of the cushions.

Grunting, Lev slowly lowered himself onto the cushion next to her. Once his long legs were settled properly, he pointed through the window. "We could have gardens like that at Moonbase," he said.

"If Yamagata has his way," Joanna whispered, "probably they'll turn the entire floor of Alphonsus into a rock garden."

"An exercise in esthetics," Lev murmured.

The slightest of noises made Joanna turned her head. A middle-aged man in a deep blue kimono that bore the white symbol of a flying heron had entered the otherwise empty restaurant and was striding toward them.

Lev scrambled to his feet. He towered over the Japanese.

"Please, please, be seated. Make yourselves comfortable," said Seigo Yamagata, in a strong, deep voice. "I am so sorry to be late. A last-minute call from Kyoto."

He was wiry thin, with black hair combed straight back from his receding hairline, face round and flat with deep brown eyes that sparkled with intelligence and what might even have been humor.

As he sat on his heels opposite Joanna, Yamagata shook his head and put on a rueful expression. "No matter how carefully you pick your assistants and how well you train them, they always seem to find some emergency that only you can resolve." He laughed heartily.

"How true," Joanna said. "I trained Ibrahim al-Rashid for many years, and now that he's risen to the top of Masterson Corporation he's trying to undermine everything I stand for."

Yamagata's brows rose a few millimeters.

Three young women in identical kimonos brought each of them individual trays of sake and, kneeling, placed them on the table.

Yamagata used the moment to consider Joanna's words. "Yes," he said slowly, "I can see that you do not agree with the direction Rashid has taken. I hope this little meeting can clear up the difficulty between us."

He looked directly into Joanna's eyes as he spoke, ignoring Lev. At least he's not a male chauvinist, Joanna thought.

"I didn't realize until just a short time ago," Joanna said, "that Faure is actually being controlled by you."

Yamagata's eyes widened momentarily, then he threw

his head back and laughed. "Controlled? By me? Whatever gave you that idea?"

"He's using the nanotech treaty as a pretext for seizing Moonbase, yet he intends to have your people run Moonbase and continue to use nanomachines just as we are doing now."

Instead of answering her, Yamagata lifted his tiny cup of sake. "A toast. To better understanding."

Joanna clicked her cup against his, then Lev's. As if it were an afterthought, Yamagata touched his cup to Lev's also.

"Do I misunderstand the situation?" Joanna asked, after sipping the warm rice wine.

"It's not a question of misunderstanding," Yamagata answered, "so much as comprehending the entire picture."

"Please enlarge my understanding, then," she said.

"Gladly. Moonbase is the leading center of nanotechnology development, that is true. Faure is using the nanotech treaty as a means of establishing U.N. control over the nations of the Earth, that is also true. As long as Moonbase continues to defy the treaty, Faure will bend every effort at his command to stop you."

Joanna nodded. "That much I already know."

"However," Yamagata raised one finger, "once the U.N. has taken control of Moonbase, Faure will turn the operation of the base over to Yamagata Industries."

"I knew that, too," Joanna said.

"Yes, of course. Yamagata will continue to operate Moonbase just as before, but under the direction and supervision of United Nations inspectors."

"How will that be different from the way Moonbase is being run now?"

Yamagata took another sip of sake. "The major difference," he said, after smacking his lips, "is that Yamagata Industries will stop the manufacture of Clipperships and their export to Earth."

"Stop building Clipperships!"

"The market will be saturated within a few years," Yamagata said. "Your diamond craft are *too* good! They are so reliable and durable that the need for new ones will soon decline steeply."

"But how will you maintain Moonbase?" Joanna asked. "Economically, I mean. Clipperships are our main source of income."

Yamagata hesitated a moment, then said in a lower tone, "Moonbase will be maintained at a smaller size and level of activity."

"Downsized?"

"To some extent. Yamagata Industries will support the scientific studies being done there, of course, and the research work in Moonbase's laboratories."

"But not Clippership manufacture."

"Nothing that has touched nanomachines will be exported to Earth," Yamagata said firmly. "Except helium-three, of course."

"Fuel for fusion power generators," Joanna realized.

"Yes."

"So this is nothing but a power grab, after all," she said. "You're using Faure to take Moonbase from us, just as I thought."

"Not at all! I am offering Masterson Corporation a share of the greatest opportunity since the discovery of fire: a share of the fusion power industry."

"That's Rashid's doing," Joanna said.

"He has tried to interest your board of directors in fusion for many years, to no avail. Now Yamagata Industries offers you a partnership in this new industry."

"You want to take over Masterson Corporation."

"A merger makes much sense. Cooperation is much to be preferred over competition."

Lev spoke up. "May I interrupt?"

Yamagata turned his head toward the Russian.

"If you gain control of Moonbase, why do you want to pursue a cooperative partnership with Masterson Corporation? You will have the nanotechnology to produce fusion fuel on the Moon. Yes?"

Yamagata smiled politely. "Just so. But why not be generous to a defeated competitor? Masterson can mar-

ket fusion systems in the western hemisphere while Yamagata markets them in the eastern hemisphere."

Scratching at his beard unconsciously, Lev replied,
"And when the market for Clipperships opens up again,
you can resume manufacturing them despite the nanotech treaty. No?"

Yamagata shook his head vigorously. "No. Not at all.
That point is clear. The forces arrayed against nanotech-
nology will not allow Clipperships to be brought to
Earth. Not for the foreseeable future."

Lev frowned, puzzled.

"You must realize," Yamagata said, shifting his attention to Joanna again, "that not even I can openly flout
Faure and the nanoluddites. Helium-three they will accept, diamond Clipperships are too obvious a symbol of
nanotechnology for them to put up with."

Joanna watched the man's face as he spoke. Even
though Yamagata maintained a bland mask that revealed almost nothing of his inner emotions, there was
something going on inside him, she was certain. He's not
telling us his real motivations.

"You will maintain the nanotechnology laboratories
at Moonbase?" she asked.

Yamagata avoided her eyes. "Yes, I think so. Although we will have to keep their work quiet, so that
the fears of the nanoluddites are not aroused."

"Including the medical research?"

"Of course."

"But what good will the researchers' work be, if their
results can't be used on Earth?"

He shrugged. "It is my belief that scientific research
should always be encouraged."

"Even if its results have no practical uses?"

Yamagata dipped his chin slightly.

"Or even if the results can be used only on the
Moon," Joanna guessed.

He seemed to freeze, like a small animal caught in the
headlights of an onrushing car. Joanna saw something
flicker in his eyes. Fear, perhaps?

At last Yamagata replied, "Yes, even if the results of the research can be used only on the Moon."

Suddenly understanding, Joanna asked, "Mr. Yamagata, do you intend to live at Moonbase someday?"

Yamagata had been sitting ramrod straight. Now he sagged back on his heels noticeably. He eyed Lev carefully, then turned his gaze back to Joanna.

"Perhaps," he said, in a near whisper. "I may retire there, eventually."

"So that you can have the benefits of nanotherapy without worrying about the reactions of the luddites," Joanna said. It was not a question.

Yamagata did not reply.

"What is the problem?" Joanna asked softly. "Cancer?"

Still he did not reply. He sat rigidly on his heels, eyes staring now on infinity, looking stiffly at the wall behind Joanna and Lev.

"It is cancer, then," Joanna said.

Yamagata's earth-brown eyes focused on her at last. He sighed, then said tonelessly, "If you even hint to anyone on Earth—or the Moon—that I am afflicted with cancer, I will have you assassinated."

Joanna stared at him from across the lacquered table.

"Do you understand?" Yamagata said. "I will not tolerate any insinuations or rumors about my health."

Joanna's mind was racing. He's got cancer and he needs nanotherapy. He needs Zimmerman and he can't bring him back to Earth for fear that the nanoluddites will find out and try to assassinate them both. *That's* why he's surrounded himself with all this security! He's already tried nanotherapy. If the fanatics learn of that . . .

"There is no need for threats," Lev said. "If you want Moonbase's nanotherapy expertise and Moonbase's nanotechnology to ferret out helium-three for your fusion reactors, why not simply enter into a cooperative arrangement with us? Why the U.N. and this attempt to take Moonbase away from us?"

"The answer is obvious," Yamagata said, looking

squarely at Joanna instead of Lev. "I must be in control. Cooperation is fine—as long as I am in complete command of our cooperative efforts. That is why I must have Masterson Corporation, including Moonbase."

"But if Moonbase wins its independence—"

With iron in his voice, Yamagata replied, "That is why I am helping Faure to assemble a Peacekeeper force. Before the World Court convenes in November, Moonbase will be operated by Yamagata Industries."

"Or destroyed," Lev said.

"We will try to avoid that," said Yamagata. "No one wants to see Moonbase destroyed."

"Except the fanatics."

"Yes," Yamagata agreed. "They are a danger to all of us."

"Then cooperate with us and stop this military confrontation!" Joanna urged.

Yamagata shook his head. "No. I will take Moonbase. I must take it. I cannot rest easily until Moonbase is in my hands."

"So all your talk of cooperation is a sham," Joanna said.

"Not so! I welcome your cooperation. And you will cooperate with me—once I have Moonbase."

Joanna bit back the reply she wanted to make. Instead, she took a deep breath to calm herself.

Yamagata interpreted her silence exactly. "I know that very little of this pleases you. But I hope you can understand why I must act so."

"I can understand," Joanna replied, "without agreeing."

Yamagata dipped his chin slightly. "Now that you understand, please tell your son that resistance is futile. If Moonbase resists the Peacekeepers again, the results will be very bad for all of us."

"What do you mean?"

With an unhappy sigh, Yamagata answered, "If your son tries to fight the Peacekeepers, forces will be set in motion that not even I can control."

"Forces?" Lev asked. "What forces?"

"You think that I control Faure. I thought so too, once. But he has the backing of fanatics, madmen who send out assassins and terrorists to accomplish their ends. Faure has turned into a monster," Yamagata said bitterly, "a Frankenstein that I helped to create."

"You're talking about the nanoluddites," Joanna said.

"The nanoluddites. Fanatics who are so frightened of nanotechnology that they will destroy Moonbase if you try to resist the Peacekeepers."

"How could they destroy Moonbase?" Joanna challenged.

"If your son tries to fight against the Peacekeepers, Moonbase will be wiped out," Yamagata replied. "All its people will be killed. And there is nothing that any of us can do to stop it. It is too late to stop it. The forces are already in motion. That is why I urgently plead with you to allow us to take control of Moonbase. Cooperate with me, or Moonbase will be utterly annihilated."

DAY FORTY-THREE

Doug's helmet earphones chirped.

"Doug, this is Jinny." Her voice sounded weak, faint. "Latest imagery from Kadar's bird show Gordette's tractor parked outside tempo six."

"Parked?"

"Didn't move all through the satellite's pass overhead," Anson said. "That's only five minutes or so, granted, but it sure looks like he's either inside the tempo or out there on foot."

Pushing the volume control on his wrist keyboard, Doug thought aloud, "Maybe his tractor broke down? Dust. Electrical malfunction."

"Maybe," Anson said. He could barely make out the word.

"Okay, thanks. We're heading that way. Call you when we get there."

"Hell you will. You'll be over the horizon even for the antennas up on Yeager."

They were passing the crater's central peaks, Doug saw, where the astronomical center was located.

"Okay, then," he said into his helmet mike. "I'll call you when we're coming back."

"I'm sending a security team out after you," Anson said, a faint whisper being drowned in crackles and hisses.

"No!" he snapped. "No need for that."

"Can't hear you, boss," Anson said through the growing interference. "You're breaking up too much."

Doug clicked from the long-range frequency to the suit-to-suit freak. "She's pretty smart, Jinny is," he said to Edith. "Knows how to use the systems."

"I feel better knowing there's a security team backing us up."

"By three hours or so," Doug said.

"What makes you think she waited until now to send them out?"

Doug felt his brows rise. "You're pretty smart yourself, you know."

Edith replied, "You're just figuring that out?"

She could see Gordette's tractor trail easily now that there were no other cleat marks chewing up the regolith. No one's been out here in a long time, she thought.

"Tempo six was one of the original shelters my father built," Doug explained. "Before they decided where the permanent base would be sited they dug shelters into a dozen spots on the crater floor and outside the ringwall on Mare Nubium."

"Do you think Gordette has really stopped there?" Edith asked.

She waited for several moments before Doug replied, "I don't know. I can't understand why he headed this far away from the base. There aren't any easy passes

over the ringwall up in this region. If he wanted to get
out of Alphonsus, Wodjo Pass around Yeager would be
the easiest way."

"Maybe he's going to meet somebody or get picked
up, something like that," Edith said.

"Maybe."

She went on, "That'd mean he'll have other people
with him, wouldn't it?"

"If they've been waiting for him at the tempo, yeah,
maybe."

"Then we're steering ourselves right into a trap, Doug.
He's tried to murder you twice. You're giving him another shot at it."

A longer silence this time. Edith stared at Doug's
spacesuited figure, trying to peer through it to see the
man inside. All she saw was the cermet suit, like armor,
and the strange metal pistons of the muscle amplifiers
on the backs of his gloves, like a skeleton's hands.

"Jinny didn't say there are any other vehicles parked
at the tempo," he said at last. "I don't think anybody
else is there."

"Then why did he stop there?"

"That's what we're going to find out," he said.

"Why don't you wait for the security team to catch
up with us?" Edith urged.

"I can't let him get away. He can tell the Peacekeepers exactly how to knock out our electrical power and
take over the base."

"You don't think they know that already?"

"Bam knows what we've been doing, what we've been
thinking. I can't let him tell it all to the Peacekeepers."

"Doug, you're full of bullshit," she said, feeling anger
rising in her. "You're acting like some macho gunslinger
who's got to face down the bad guy all by himself."

"It's not that, Edith."

"The hell it isn't. You're going to get yourself killed,
and me too."

"No! I—" Doug realized there was some truth in
Edith's accusation. He turned to look at her and saw

only the reflection of his own blank visor in the dim Earthlight.

"At least wait for the security team," she repeated.

"Edith . . . I trusted him. I thought I saw a man I could rely on. I don't why he tried to kill me—"

"Because he's an agent from the U.N.," Edith snapped. "Or Yamagata, more likely."

"Or maybe the nanoluddites," Doug heard himself agree. "I never thought of that before, but maybe they were able to infiltrate Moonbase, after all."

"Then why confront him?"

Yes, why? Doug asked himself. The man's a murderer, a hired assassin, maybe a nanoluddite fanatic. So what if he can tell the Peacekeepers about the pitiful defenses we're trying to set up? Big deal. They're going to walk in here and take over the base no matter what you do.

Then he thought of Tamara and how he helplessly watched Killifer rape and kill her. Murderer! his conscience shrieked. You let him murder her while you stood by as impotent as a baby. He saw Killifer's smug, hateful face, the glint in his eyes, the snarl of his voice. I'll find him, Doug told himself. I'll track him down wherever he is and kill him. I'll rip his guts out. I'll tear him apart.

But Killifer's a half-million kilometers away, on a world you'll never return to. Gordette's within reach; you'll be face-to-face with him soon. Are you going to kill Bam? Are you going to make him pay for Killifer? Why not? What difference does it make? They're all killers, all murderers. It's time to start paying them back. Time to even the score.

Yet another voice in his head spoke: I *liked* Bam. We could have become good friends, in time. He seemed so steady, so focused, like a big brother . . .

And then Doug remembered. "Greg tried to kill me, too."

"What?" Edith asked.

"Maybe it's me. Maybe there's something wrong with me."

"What're you talking about, Doug?"

"My older brother, Greg—half-brother, really—he went berserk and tried to wipe out the whole base. He wanted to kill me, just like Bam does."

"What happened to him?"

"I killed him," Doug said, the memories choking his voice. "I didn't want to, but there was no other way . . ."

It was Edith's turn to fall silent. Doug steered the tractor automatically, following the bright cleat marks in the eons-darkened regolith, remembering, remembering.

"So you want to confront Gordette to bring your brother back, is that it?" she asked at last.

Doug shook his head inside his helmet. "No, I don't think so." Then he had to admit, "I don't really know, Edith. It's just something I've got to do."

Yet he could not erase the sight of Killifer's leering, twisted face.

Georges Faure found the three-second lag in communications with the Moon especially aggravating. How can one conduct a proper conversation when there is such a wait between words?

"One week," the Peacekeeper colonel said at last, in reply to Faure's question. "Ten days, at the outside."

"Why so long, Colonel Giap?" Faure inquired. "Why not tomorrow?"

And now we wait again, the secretary-general fumed, staring at the colonel's image on his desktop screen.

Colonel Giap's face was a study in oriental patience: calm, expressionless; his hooded eyes showed no emotion whatsoever.

"You have your full complement of troops," Faure blurted, not waiting for the colonel's reply. "All the weapons have been delivered, have they not?"

Giap might have been a statue of teak, for all the response he showed. Faure fidgeted in his swivel chair, fighting the urge to pick up one of the mementos adorning his desk and fling it into the phone screen.

"The battalion is now at full strength, quite so," the colonel said at last, "and all our logistics are in place.

Also, the special force that Yamagata Industries organized has arrived."

"Then why do you wait? Strike! Strike *now*!"

The colonel had not stopped talking. ". . . necessary to train the combined team in the precise tactics we will use to take Moonbase. Also, all of the troops must become fully acclimatized to the lower gravity here on the Moon and to working in spacesuits. It is crucial that they are able to function as easily and as well as they would on Earth, even in the suits."

Faure sank back in his chair as the colonel painstakingly reviewed every step of his planned conquest of Moonbase: the deployment of the Peacekeeper troops outside Alphonsus' ringwall mountains; the nuclear strike that will knock out Moonbase's solar power farms; the missile with the penetrating warhead to destroy their buried nuclear generator; the routes over the ringwall and across the crater floor to the base itself, the assault on the main airlock and the penetration of the base's corridors, the seizure of Moonbase's key nerve centers.

"By the time we enter their corridors," Giap was reciting from his action plan, "the people in Moonbase will have less than an hour's worth of electrical power available to them. They must either surrender to us or die of asphyxiation."

"What if they decide to blow themselves up?" Faure demanded. "A final grand suicidal gesture of defiance."

When Giap finally heard the question he almost smiled. "That is most unlikely. Psychological profiles of all Moonbase personnel have been made available to us, through the Masterson Corporation. Those people are not fatalists. Suicide, even on an individual basis, would never occur to them."

Faure nodded agreement. He had personally requested the psychological files from Ibrahim al-Rashid. Nominally the files belonged to the Kiribati Corporation, but it was apparently a simple thing for Rashid to appropriate them through Masterson's computers.

Giap continued, "However, the special Yamagata

force is quite ready for its suicide mission, if our frontal assault is not immediately successful."

Faure knew that Yamagata's special force had been recruited from nanoluddite fanatics in Japan and elsewhere.

"We will bring two nuclear power generators in tractors over Wodjohowitcz Pass and offer to provide electrical power," Colonel Giap went on, "in the event that Moonbase surrenders to us."

"And if they refuse?"

Again the infernal wait. "We will walk in and take the base. Failing that, the special Yamagata force will destroy the air and water systems, the control center, farms and nanolabs."

Faure sighed deeply. There will be nothing left of Moonbase after that, he thought. But what of it? Yamagata wants Moonbase taken intact, but it will be better if it is wiped out of existence altogether.

Now, if only the colonel would start his troops moving at once. Why wait? Strike swiftly.

Yet he said nothing. He had ordered the Peacekeepers to strike swiftly the first time and it had turned out to be a fiasco.

But this time will be different, Faure told himself. Looking into Colonel Giap's expressionless eyes, Faure concluded that the colonel's plan would work, and he should not meddle in the tactical decisions. Moonbase would be brought to its knees within a week to ten days.

Or destroyed utterly.

DAY FORTY-FOUR

"Do they have toilets in the tempos?" Edith asked.

Startled out of his inner thoughts, Doug replied, "Yes. Sure."

"Good."

"There's a vacuum toilet behind the seats," he said, jerking a gloved thumb over his shoulder. "Kind of tricky using it, but the toilet hatch connects to the port in your suit."

"How long will it be before we get to the tempo?"

Doug glanced at the electronic map on the tractor's dashboard. "Less than an hour."

"I'll wait, then."

Looking at his wrist displays, Doug saw it was after midnight. Neither of them had slept. For the past few hours Doug had been wrestling with his inner demons, wondering why he was driving himself to confront Gordette. Why not just give up? he kept asking himself. Yet something inside him refused to. He couldn't let Killifer win without at least trying to fight back.

"You want me to drive a while?" Edith asked.

"I'm not tired."

"You certain? Aren't you sleepy? I sure am."

"Crank your seat back and catch a few winks," Doug suggested.

Edith tried; whether she fell asleep or not, Doug could not tell. Steering the tractor was fairly easy; it was built to clamber over rocks and across craterlets, like a tank. Doug followed the bright marks of Gordette's trail,

314

which avoided the boulders and deeper pits scattered across the crater floor.

He saw a rille snaking off to the left, like a narrow riverbed waiting for water. You've been waiting a while, haven't you? Doug asked silently. Four billion years, give or take a week.

In the dark lunar night the stars were like dust strewn across the bowl of the sky. He could see them gleaming at him right down to the chopped-off horizon.

One star in particular seemed to beckon. Red, bright, hovering just over the horizon straight ahead.

Doug realized it was the beacon light atop the radio mast of tempo six.

We'll be there in half an hour, he told himself.

Then what?

Doug took in a deep double lungful of canned air. We'll find out when we get there.

In the airlessness of the Moon Gordette won't hear us coming up, if he's inside the tempo. The first warning he'll get is when I start the airlock cycling. I'll park the tractor and let Edith keep on sleeping. No sense getting her involved in whatever's going to happen inside when I confront Bam. Things could get messy.

All of a sudden they were there. The dark hump of dirt that marked the site of the buried shelter loomed in front of Doug's straining eyes. A single tractor was parked to one side of the airlock.

Doug stopped his tractor and looked over at Edith. Not a stir from her. Good, he thought, she's sound asleep.

He climbed down slowly from the cab and walked over to the other tractor. One set of fresh boot prints in the sandy regolith led straight to the airlock. Bam's in there. Alone.

Okay, Doug told himself. This is it.

A gentle slope led down to the airlock's outer hatch. No wind on the Moon to cover the grade with newly-blown dust; it would remain clear for eons, except for the occasional tracks of boots. Doug slid the hatch open and stepped into the phonebooth-sized airlock. He closed the outer hatch, sealed it, then pressed a thumb against the electronic pad that activated the pumps. The telltale light above the pad immediately went from red to amber.

It seemed to take an eternity. Doug could feel the vibration of the pump working against the soles of his boots, but for several long moments he could hear nothing. Then, as the chamber filled with air, the chugging of the pumps became audible.

He knows he's got a visitor, Doug thought, clenching his fists involuntarily. The tiny whine of the gloves' servomotors surprised him and he unflexed his hands. It took an effort of will.

The light turned green. Doug slid the inner hatch open.

Gordette stood at the far end of the shelter, by the two tiers of bunks. He was apparently putting his spacesuit on again; torso, leggings and boots were in place. His helmet rested on one of the lower bunks. Doug could not see his gloves.

Gordette's brows knit as he recognized the cermet suit that he had once sabotaged.

"Who the fuck are you and what're you doing in that suit?"

Doug slid his visor up. "It's me, Bam."

The man shuddered visibly. He staggered back a step and leaned against the bunks for support.

"You're dead! I killed you!"

"You tried," Doug said, stepping further into the shelter. "Why?"

"Stay away from me!"

"Why did you try to kill me, Bam?"

Gordette's eyes showed white all around the irises. "I cut your fuckin' throat!"

Doug sighed. "The nanomachines inside me. They closed the wound and kept me from bleeding to death."

"That's not possible!"

"Of course it is. There's nothing supernatural here, Bam. No magic. Just those little nanobugs."

With the spacesuit on, it was impossible to see Gordette's chest rising and falling. But his mouth hung open, panting.

"Why'd you want to kill me, Bam? What did I do to you that you wanted to murder me?"

For several heartbeats Gordette said nothing, did not move. Then he sagged down onto the lower bunk.

"It wasn't you," he said, sinking his head into his hands. "Had nothing to do with you."

"It was me you tried to kill."

"You or me, man. Life or death. I had to do it. Had to. One of us had to go. I should've slit my own throat; been better that way."

"Why?" Doug asked again. "Why did you have to do it?"

"I'm a soldier. I follow orders. Or else."

"You were sent here to kill me?"

Gordette looked up at Doug with reddened eyes. "You know that little shit Faure's been planning this for years."

"You work for the U.N.? The Peacekeepers?"

"Naw. I get paid by Washington. Special security forces. They pulled me out of the army. Trained me to be an assassin."

"You've killed other people?"

His face looked awful. "That's my profession, man. That's what they trained me to do. Either that or spend my life in jail."

"Why jail?"

He laughed bitterly. "Why else? I killed somebody. It was an accident, but I did it and the only way to stay out of jail was to go into the army. They always held that over me; do what they want or they send me to jail for life. No parole. No sweetheart minimum-security farm, either. Jail. In with the perverts and the maniacs."

Doug unfastened his helmet, pulled it off over his head, then walked the length of the narrow shelter to sit on the bunk opposite Gordette. He placed the helmet on the bedsheet beside him.

"Okay, Bam. That's all over now. You can live here. You can be free of them."

The black man stared into Doug's eyes. "Live at Moonbase?"

"That's right."

"I tried to kill you and you're offering me asylum?"

"That's what Moonbase is all about, Bam. A place to build a new life."

Gordette said nothing, but his expression showed doubt, suspicion, scorn.

"I'm a fugitive, too," Doug said. "On Earth I'd be a marked man waiting for some nanoluddite fanatic to assassinate me. On the Moon I can live—"

"Until some hired assassin knocks you off."

Doug reached out his gloved hand. "Join us, Bam."

"I don't *deserve* to join you," Gordette said, recoiling. "I'm a murderer! A killer!"

"You were a murderer. Now you have the chance to change, to start a new life."

"Doing what?"

Patiently, Doug said, "Doing whatever you do best. It's up to you."

"I killed my own mother!" he screamed, leaping to his feet. "I killed her!"

Doug looked up at him and saw fear, guilt, and the depths of hell in Gordette's red-rimmed eyes.

Gordette bent over him and yanked Doug to his feet so hard that Doug's helmet rolled off the bunk and bounced on the concrete floor.

"I killed my mother!" he roared into Doug's face. "Don't talk to me about starting a new life."

He pushed Doug down onto the bunk again and went for his own helmet. Doug watched him put it on, seal the neck ring. Then Gordette started to pull on his gloves.

"Where are you going?" Doug asked.

"Out there. Anyplace. I'll keep going until I run out of air. That'll put an end to it."

Doug got up from the bunk. "Bam, you can't do that! I can't let you do it."

Staring grimly at him through his open helmet, Gordette muttered, "How you gonna stop me, man?"

Doug walked toward him. "Don't kill yourself, for god's sake. You can start a whole new life here."

"Yeah? For how long? In a week or so the Peacekeepers are gonna come marching in here and I'll be on my way back Earthside, heading for jail 'cause I didn't nail you."

"We can keep the Peacekeepers out," Doug said, feeling almost desperate. "We can stay free."

"Yeah. Sure."

"Don't kill yourself, Bam!"

Gordette looked at him with eyes suddenly grown calm and cold. "One of us has to die, Doug. I'd rather it be me. Even if I killed you, they'd just set me up for some other piece of shit. Let me end it, man. Let me put an end to the whole fucking mess."

"No!" Doug snapped, and grabbed for Gordette.

Almost by reflex, Gordette backhanded Doug across the jaw, knocking him off balance, staggering in his spacesuit halfway down the length of the shelter.

Gordette slammed his visor down and turned for the airlock hatch. Doug charged after him. Gordette spun to face him, snapped Doug's head back with a straight left, then levelled him with a right. Doug's eyesight blurred as his head hit the concrete flooring, then everything went black.

Edith woke up, stiff and groaning, in the tractor's seat. She went to rub her eyes, but her hands bumped the helmet visor. Pulling herself up to a sitting position, she saw that the tractor was stopped in front of the tempo and Doug was gone.

He must be inside with Gordette, she thought, suddenly alarmed. Quickly she searched around her seat for something that might be useful as a weapon. If there was a tool kit on the tractor, it wasn't in sight.

Empty-handed, she started to climb down to the ground. As she put one boot on the sandy regolith she saw a spacesuited figure march determinedly past her, past the other parked tractor, and away from the tempo. It wasn't Doug's suit, she knew.

Ignoring the distress signals her bladder was sending, Edith went to the open airlock hatch. Doug must be inside, she thought. It took an eternally long moment for her to find the instructions printed on the inner wall of the airlock, alongside the control keypad. Edith had to turn on her helmet light to read them.

It was simple enough. She slid the hatch shut and activated the pump. When the light turned green she opened the inner hatch and stepped into the shelter.

Doug was on the floor, his helmet off, pushing himself up onto his elbows.

"He wants to kill himself," Doug said to her. She barely heard him through her sealed helmet.

Sliding her visor up, she knelt beside Doug. "What happened? Are you all right?"

"He wants to kill himself," Doug repeated.

"Let him," she snapped. "Better him than you."

Slowly, Doug pushed himself to a sitting position, shook his head a few times, then started to clamber to his feet. "Where'd my helmet get to?" he mumbled.

"You're not going out there after him!"

He looked at her. "I can't let him die out there, Edith. He . . . I just can't."

"I'll go with you, then."

"You stay here," Doug said firmly, walking back to pick his helmet off the floor. "You're a lot safer here inside the shelter."

"And you're going out to catch him?"

"To find him. To help him—if he'll let me."

"Not without me!"

"Yes, without you. You stay here. If I'm not back in an hour, get into the tractor and go back to Moonbase."

Edith started to argue, but one look into Doug's determined blue-gray eyes stopped her. It would be pointless, she knew.

As soon as Doug left the shelter she went to the toilet, then waited another ten minutes, by the watch on her spacesuit's wrist. Then she went to the airlock and started after him in the tractor.

From her perch in the driver's seat she could see two pairs of bootprints clearly etched into the dark sandy ground. I won't need an Indian guide to help me follow their trail, Edith told herself.

DAY FORTY-FOUR

Doug followed Gordette's boot prints, gleaming bright and new in the ancient regolith. The only sounds he heard were his own breathing and the comforting soft buzz of the suit's air fans. He had stopped at the tractor to refill his air tank. Hunger gnawed at him, but there was nothing he could do about that.

How much air does Bam have left in his suit? he wondered. How long can he roam around out here before he runs out?

Gordette's trail seemed to meander, with no specific aim or purpose. Doug followed it around a house-sized boulder, never even thinking that Gordette could be lurking behind the rock, waiting to ambush him. He wasn't. His bootprints skirted a worn old crater the size of a baseball diamond, and so deep that its bottom was lost in dense shadow. Meteoroid must have come almost straight down to dig that one, Doug thought.

Soon, though, Gordette's trail started to run alongside a sinuous rille that snaked along the dusty ground like an arroyo in desert country. Doug remembered his first walk out on the Moon's surface, his eighteenth birthday. With Foster Brennart. They had come across a rille that had suddenly spurted a ghostly cloud of gasses from deep within the lunar interior. Methane, ammonia, other volatiles. They had glittered in the sunlight like a billion fireflies.

Brennart thought it was a good omen, my first walk on the surface. Maybe it was, Doug thought. I could use a good omen now.

Suddenly Gordette's bootprints ended. Disappeared. Doug stopped, puzzled. He backtracked a few steps, then saw that Gordette had climbed down into the shallow gully cut into the ground by the rille. Turning on his helmet lamp, Doug spotted faint boot marks heading along the bottom of the rille, some two meters below the surface on which he stood.

The prints still headed in the same general direction that Gordette had been following. Why'd he jump down into the rille? Doug asked himself. Was he afraid I'd follow him and he's trying to hide his trail? The prints down inside the rille were faint, but still visible.

Staying on the surface, Doug followed the rille as it wound across the regolith. It could be dangerous down there, Doug told himself. The rilles are old fissures where gas from below ground had seeped out. The ground down there can be brittle as glass, and who knows what's underneath it?

Edith trundled along in the tractor, trying to keep its speed down to the pace of a walking man. The trail of bootprints was easy to see, and she didn't want Doug to know she was following him. Not yet.

Once she thought she saw the curve of his helmet above the horizon, and she tromped on the tractor's brakes. If I can't see him, he can't see me, she figured. And he sure can't hear me coming after him, not out here in all this vacuum.

The nearness of the horizon bothered her. It didn't look right. She knew, consciously, that the Moon was only a quarter of the Earth's size and the horizon was therefore much closer than it would be on Earth. But still, at a deep, primitive level, it almost frightened her. As if there really was an edge to this barren, desolate world and she might drop off it.

Yeah, she told herself derisively, you're right in there with Columbus' crew. Sail on, babe. Sail on.

*   *   *

Doug didn't realize he still had the suit-to-suit frequency on until he started hearing strange sounds in his earphones. Gasps? Moans? The sounds came through for a moment, then disappeared, like ghosts vanishing into thin air.

Very thin air, around here, he told himself.

The rille had been getting progressively deeper, sinking more than four meters below the crater floor, Doug guessed. It was hard to tell, and almost impossible to see if Gordette's boot prints were still marching along down there, even when he leaned carefully over the worn, rounded smooth edge of the rille to shine his helmet lamp on its bottom.

He came to a spot where a meteoroid had slammed into the ground just next to the rille, collapsing its side into a heap of rubble. Doug spent several minutes searching for bootprints; he found none. As far as he could see there were no prints on the other side of the narrow rille, either.

And the eerie sounds in his earphones had stopped, too.

I've overshot him, Doug told himself. He's back behind me someplace. Down inside the rille. Hiding.

Slowly, bending over the edge of the rille to examine its bottom, Doug started backtracking. He couldn't see the bottom of the arroyo, it was too deep for his helmet lamp to reach.

He stopped and listened. Nothing. Gordette had gone silent. Is he dead? Maybe what I heard was his last gasping for air.

With great reluctance, and more than a little fear, Doug carefully climbed down inside the rille, lowering himself slowly down as far as he could with his arms fully stretched, then letting himself slide the rest of the way down.

He felt the rough side wall grating against the chest of his suit. Couldn't do this in a fabric suit, he thought. The cermet won't tear. But he knew that grinding some dust or larger particles of grit into his suit's joints could immobilize him as thoroughly as the Tin Woodsman caught in a monsoon rain.

Doug had never felt the panic of claustrophobia, but as he stood shakily inside the narrow rille he saw that the sky above him was nothing more now than a constricted slice of stars cut off on both sides by the steep black walls of the arroyo. Like the view from the bottom of a grave, he thought.

He took a step forward and his boot slid on the glass-smooth rock. He had to grab at both sides of the gully to keep himself from falling. Hardly any dust down here, he realized. This rille must be brand-new, maybe still active.

"New" and "active" were relative terms on the Moon, he knew. A new rille might have opened up only a few thousand years ago. Its activity might be a slight sigh of underground gas every century or so.

A cough. In his earphones Doug heard somebody cough. Couldn't be anybody but Bam.

Slowly, moving cautiously along the slippery rock floor of the rille, both hands extended to touch its steep confining walls, Doug made his way forward.

Another cough, followed by a quick, desperate gasping.

"Bam!" he called into his helmet mike. "Bam, where are you?"

No response. Standing stock-still, Doug listened hard. Is he holding his breath? No, it's just so faint I can hardly hear him.

Doug pushed along the slick arroyo and the sound of Gordette's breathing grew louder. It sounded strained, labored, as if the man were in pain.

"I'm coming, Bam," Doug called again. "I'll be with you in a couple of minutes. Hang on."

"Don't . . ." Gordette's voice was weak. It broke into a gasping cough.

"Save your breath. I'll be there."

"Careful . . . the ground . . . gives way . . ."

Doug scanned the ground before him in the light of his helmet lamp. It looked solid enough, glassy and slick,

but solid rock. Yet he knew this volcanic vent might be
no sturdier than a soap bubble.

More coughing from Gordette. He must be almost out
of air, Doug realized. Got to get to him quickly.

The smooth rock floor ended abruptly, like a shattered
pane of glass. Black nothingness yawned in front of
Doug.

And clinging to the edge of the break like a ship-
wrecked sailor desperately clutching a piece of flotsam,
was the spacesuited figure of Leroy Gordette.

He had one forearm hooked on the crumbling edge
of the precipice, and the gloved fingers of his other hand.
Doug could see the top of his helmet.

"Hold on," he said, and immediately felt foolish. What
else was Bam trying to do?

"Don't!" the black man warned. "Fuckin' rock breaks.
It's as thin as tissue paper. Brittle, too."

Doug lowered himself to his knees, then got down on
his belly and wormed his way toward Gordette.

"Got no purchase for my feet," Bam said, panting.
"Every time . . . I try to haul my ass up . . . fuckin' rock
crumbles more."

"How deep is the hole?" Doug asked. "Can you see
bottom?"

Gordette coughed. "Must go . . . all the way down . . .
to Chicago. No bottom . . ."

Inching closer to the man, Doug felt the brittle rock
beneath him crack, like thin ice.

He stretched out his arm as far as he could. "Can you
grab my hand?"

"I'm runnin' out of air," Gordette said, gasping. "Forget it. Get outta here."

"Grab my hand!" Doug insisted.

"Can't."

Doug pushed himself a few centimeters closer. A
chunk of the rock floor just in front of his helmet gave
way and plummeted down into silent darkness.

"Grab it!"

"Leave me alone . . ."

With gritted teeth Doug slid closer and wrapped his

fingers around Gordette's wrist just as the edge collapsed into shards and fell away.

Through his suit Doug could feel the vibrations of the servo motors in his glove as they tightened on Gordette's wrist. The man's whole weight dangled from Doug's hand. It felt as if his arm were being wrenched out of its shoulder socket.

"That's . . . a helluva grip . . . you got," Gordette grunted.

Doug could feel Gordette's body swaying as it hung in the deep black emptiness. Pain burned through his arm and shoulder. The exoskeleton would keep his fingers clamped on Gordette's wrist, he knew. Good thing we're on the Moon, Doug thought. With his spacesuit and all he'd yank my arm right out of my shoulder on Earth.

For moments that stretched like years Doug lay there, flat on his belly, with Gordette hanging in his hand.

"Lemme go . . ." Gordette panted. "Lemme die . . ."

"If you go," Doug said grimly, fiercely, "I go with you. We're in this together, Bam."

"You . . . crazy . . ."

Doug tried to worm his way back, away from the brittle, crumbling edge of the abyss. Gordette could do nothing to help, even if he wanted to.

Got to haul him out of there, Doug told himself. Got to get him on solid ground before he runs out of air.

But it was almost impossible to edge his way backward with Gordette's dead weight dangling from his outstretched arm. Grunting, teeth gritted, eyes stinging with sweat, Doug inched back along the glassy rock. It was painfully, agonizingly slow. He felt woozy, head spinning.

"What're y'all doing down . . . oh my god!" Edith's voice.

Doug couldn't see her, didn't know how she had gotten there. But she sounded like an angel to him.

"Edith! Where's the tractor?"

"Right here," she said, her voice anxious, high. "I rode out on it."

"Great! Get the tow cable. Quick!"

It seemed to take an eternity and a half for Edith to find the tow cable and then clamber down into the rille behind Doug and tie it to one of the attachment rings on his backpack. She used the cable to climb out again, then went up to the tractor.

"Use the winch," Doug called to her. "Controls are on the dashboard."

Edith stared at the dashboard, but couldn't figure out which of the toggles or keypads ran the winch. Instead, she revved up the engines and started backing away, slowly.

"Easy—easy," Doug's voice crackled in her earphones. "He's in a fabric suit."

Edith thought of all the rodeos she had seen, with cowboys guiding their tough little ponies in steer-roping competitions. Just ease on back, she said silently to the tractor. That's it, honey, nice and slow and easy.

"Hold it," Doug commanded. "We're on safe ground but I think Bam's passed out."

Edith clambered down from the tractor and went to the edge of the gulch. Doug was connecting his emergency air hose from his backpack tank to Gordette's, watching the regulator gauge on his wrist to make sure he didn't overpressurize the man's suit. She shook her head inside her helmet. If it'd been me, I'd've let the sumbitch die down there. He tried to kill Doug!

But she heard Gordette cough and sputter and knew he was going to make it. Doug had saved him.

It took the better part of an hour to get them both out of the rille and their air tanks topped off from the tractor's supply. Then Edith started back toward Moonbase with Doug sitting between her and Gordette.

For hours Gordette said nothing. The man just sat on Doug's other side, wrapped in his spacesuit and total silence.

At last Doug said to him, "I've been pretty close to death, Bam. It changes your outlook on life."

"Does it?" Gordette muttered.

"It did for me. I think you're going to find it will for you, too."

Gordette said nothing. Edith thought Doug was wasting his breath.

"When we get back to Moonbase," Doug went on, "you'll have the chance to start a new life. Start all over, with the past gone forever."

"Until they throw you out of Moonbase," Gordette said.

"They're not going to do that, Bam. With your help, we can beat them."

"With my help?"

"I want you with us. I want you to be part of Moonbase."

"Do you?"

"We've gone through a lot together, Bam. We're bound together. Life or death, what affects one of us affects us both."

Gordette was silent for several moments. Then he said grudgingly, "You got some grip, all right. Once you get your hands on a man you don't let go, do you?"

"That's up to you," Doug answered.

"You're crazy, you know that?"

"Maybe," Doug admitted.

"And what about you, lady?" Gordette asked sullenly. "You as crazy as this man here?"

Edith almost snapped out her true feelings. But she realized that Doug had risked his life to save his would-be murderer. And now it all hung on what she had to say.

She swallowed her anger. "If Doug wants you to be with us, that's good enough for me."

"You'd trust me?"

Edith blurted, "Not very far. Not at first, anyway."

For a moment there was silence, then Gordette laughed: a low, ironic chuckle. "Fair enough, I guess. Fair enough."

Edith wished she could see the man's face. Doug's not crazy, she thought. He's wiser than all of us put together. But I wish I could see Gordette's face. I'd feel better about this if I could see his eyes.

PART III
BATTLE

But when the blast of war blows in our ears,
Then imitate the action of the tiger . . .

—SHAKESPEARE
Henry V

THE HAGUE

"Telephone for you, Senator. The White House."

Jill Meyers looked up from her computer screen. Despite the fact that she had not been a member of the U.S. Senate for nearly six years now, her private secretary still called her "Senator."

"Who is it?" she asked warily.

"The president," he replied, in his usual near-whisper.

Jill grinned at her oldest assistant. "I guess I can make time for the president."

Almost instantly the face of an intense young man appeared on her desktop screen. "Justice Meyers? One moment, please, for the president."

His image disappeared and the screen showed the seal of the president of the United States on a royal blue background. The American eagle held a sheaf of arrows in one talon and an olive branch in the other: war or peace.

It took more than a moment for the president to come on, of course. The power trip. The president doesn't get on the horn until she's absolutely certain that the party she wants to talk to is already on the line. No flunkies.

Jill glanced up at her private secretary and realized with a pang that he'd been a fresh-faced kid just out of law school when he'd first come aboard as a senatorial aide. We're all getting old, she thought, catching her own reflection in the phone screen. Her face was as round and ordinary as a pie pan, she thought, with mousey brown hair as straight and limp as overcooked spaghetti.

And still that scattering of freckles across her snub of a nose, like a tomboy version of Huck Finn.

"Jill," said the president, "you're looking very pensive today."

The president looked elegant, as usual. Silver-gray hair swept back stylishly, bright blue eyes sparkling. Her latest facelift had tightened the sagging flesh beneath her chin and made her seem ten years younger.

"What can I do for you, Madam President?" Jill asked, genuinely curious about the reason for this call. It had to be nearly seven AM in Washington, early for her.

"It's this request for extradition—"

"Oh. The Killifer business."

"Yes. I don't understand what you've got to do with it."

"I've been asked to intercede, in my official capacity as a justice of the World Court," Jill said.

"Asked? By whom?"

"Joanna Brudnoy."

"I see." The president's tone went decidedly frosty.

"The Justice Department has apparently refused to extradite the man to Kiribati."

"We have no treaty of extradition with that nation," the president said.

"That's why the World Court has been asked to intercede," said Jill.

"I see."

"Killifer was identified as the man who raped and murdered Tamara Bonai, yet the American government has refused to extradite him to Kiribati to stand trial. The victim was Kiribati's head of state, for god's sake."

"That's a very serious charge," said the president.

"There's an eyewitness."

"Douglas Stavenger, I know. But he's on the Moon and his so-called eyewitnessing was done through a virtual reality link. Any competent defense lawyer will make mincemeat of that."

"I'm not so sure," Jill said. "In any event, I'd think you'd want the sonofabitch to be brought to justice."

The president did not flinch at Jill's deliberate profanity.

"Jill, this is all tied up with the Moonbase business."

"Which means it's all tied up with the New Morality people, right?"

"Those are my supporters, Jill."

"And they're protecting a murderer?"

The president's face was a smooth, blank façade. She gave away nothing. "An *alleged* murderer," she said coolly.

"I may not be a lawyer," Jill countered, "but I do know a few points of law. You're protecting Killifer. Why?"

"Jill, I thought you were one of my supporters, too. I know you don't agree with everything the New Morality does, but you've always been on my side."

"Why are you protecting this man?"

"There's much more here than you're aware of, Jill."

"Wait a minute," Jill said. "I've served time at Moonbase. I was there with Paul Stavenger when it was nothing but a bunch of tin cans stuck in the ground."

"You had an affair with Paul Stavenger," the president murmured.

"Name me one woman who served at Moonbase in those days who didn't," Jill rejoined happily. "He was one helluva guy before he married Joanna."

"Joanna," the president said, with obvious distaste.

"If I were still in the Senate instead of stuck here in the World Court, I'd be fighting you on this Moonbase business. You're making a bad mistake."

With the ghost of a smile, the president said, "That's the thanks I get for nominating you to the International Court of Justice?"

"Come off it, Luce."

"You backed me on the nanotech treaty when you were in the Senate."

"Because I didn't want nanotechnology turned into a new arms race," Jill said. "I never thought the treaty'd be used against Moonbase. They can't exist without nanomachines and you know it."

The president sighed. "So I suppose you'll vote in favor of their independence if the question comes up before the World Court?"

"It's on our docket for November. I've tried to get an emergency session to hear the matter, but I was voted down."

"It doesn't matter, Jill. By November the question will have been settled conclusively. In fact, it should be settled in about a week or so."

"You're going to do it, then? Attack Moonbase?"

"The United Nations is doing it, not me."

"But you're not raising a protest? If you hollered, Faure would *have to* listen."

"I am not going to interfere with a U.N. operation," said the president.

Jill fumed in silence for a moment, then grumbled, "Well, I hope you don't expect to get reelected."

This time the president's smile showed teeth. "The New Morality will reelect me *because* I backed the enforcement of the nanotech treaty."

"You think so?"

"All the polls show it conclusively."

"So you're not going to let Killifer be extradited?"

"Under no circumstances."

"Damn! If I were Doug Stavenger I'd come down there and hang the man myself."

"Vigilante justice? From a judge of the World Court?"

"Justice," Jill snapped. "When your own government won't give you justice, you've got the right to make your own move. Jefferson wrote that into the Declaration of Independence, remember?"

"But Jill dear, Stavenger and the rest of his Lunatics don't regard us as their government anymore. Do they?"

Jill had no answer. Luce always was the better debater; she could score points off the devil himself whenever she chose to.

MOONBASE

Jinny Anson's office was crowded. Doug sat at the foot of the table that butted against her desk, flanked by Zimmerman and Cardenas, the heads of Moonbase's major departments, and the physicist Wicksen. There was no room at the little table for Edith, so she sat slightly behind Doug and to his right.

Bam Gordette sat alone on the couch by the door, separated from all the others by a meter of empty floor-space and an uneasy distrust that was almost palpable. The others are treating Bam as if he's a leper, Doug thought.

"You're certain the Peacekeepers are gonna make their move so soon?" Jinny Anson was asking.

"We've got maybe a week, if we're lucky," Doug replied grimly. "What can we accomplish in that time?"

A gloomy silence filled the office. Even the normally perky Anson looked downcast.

"Wix?" Doug asked. "We need the beam gun up and working in a week."

The physicist shook his head slowly, his big soulful eyes staring straight at Doug. "I told you it would take two lunar days . . . two months."

"You've got seven Earth days," Doug said. "Maybe less."

Wicksen started to shake his head.

"Put every man you've got onto it," urged Doug. "And every woman."

"We're already working flat out."

"How close are you?"

The physicist shrugged uncomfortably, more like a writhing. "The beam collimator is finished. The aiming circuitry is ready to be tested. Then we've got to bring the kloodges out to the mass driver and mate them. Then we need to test the complete system."

"Kloodges?" Edith asked. "What are they?"

"Ramshackle collections of hardware," Harry Clemens answered in his laconic twang before Wicksen could respond. "Clinking, clanking, caliginous collections of junk."

"Oh."

"Makeshift hardware," Wicksen said, grimacing slightly at Clemens. "Slapped together quickly, without worrying about how it looks."

"Kloodges," Edith repeated.

Doug demanded, "Can you put it all together by the end of this week?"

"We have to test—"

"We don't have time for testing!" Doug said sharply. "Get the hardware together, make it functional. You can test it after it's completely assembled, if the Peacekeepers give us enough time."

Wicksen's big eyes widened even further. "You'd hang the survival of this base on untested equipment?"

"If it doesn't work, we're dead anyway," Doug pointed out. "Right?"

The physicist thought it over for a moment, his big tarsier's eyes staring at Doug. At last he admitted, "Right."

"Wait a minute," Anson said, from behind her desk. "Wix, will you have enough time to rig the control system so you can operate the beam gun from inside, here?"

"No. We'll have to run it manually, out there at the mass driver."

"In suits," said Vince Falcone.

Wicksen nodded solemnly.

"With a nuclear warhead coming at you," Falcone added.

Another grave nod.

Anson said, "So if the beam gun doesn't work you and your people get fried by the nuke."

"That's right," Wicksen said slowly. "We'll be operating an untested apparatus, in the open, in surface suits, and if it doesn't work the first time we'll all be toast."

All eyes turned to Doug.

"The alternative is to let the Peacekeepers nuke our solar farms," he said. But he was thinking, *I can't force Wix and his people to go out there under the gun. I can't order him to do it.*

Wicksen smiled a strange, enigmatic smile. "Well . . . I can see that we'll have to make the apparatus work the first time." He pushed his chair back from the table. "I'd better get back to the workshop. We have a lot to do and not much time to do it."

The others watched him walk out of the office and slide the door shut softly behind him.

Anson shook her head. "The Japs aren't the only ones who've got kamikazes."

Falcone, his swarthy face set in a scowl, said to Doug, "You're gonna let him go out on a suicide job?"

"Do you see any alternatives?" Doug returned, forcing himself to sound much firmer than he felt.

Before Falcone could answer, Doug added, "Except surrender?"

"Okay, Wix has made his decision," Anson said. "Let's move on."

Gratefully, Doug turned to Zimmerman. "Professor, what have you cooked up for us?"

"Nothing," said Zimmerman flatly.

"Nothing?"

"Nothing that can be ready in a week."

Doug turned to Cardenas. "Kris?"

"We're ready to inject therapeutic nanomachines into anyone who'll accept them. After your recent experience," she glanced inadvertently at Gordette, "lots of people have come to realize that nanomachines can be *extremely* helpful to them, healthwise."

"Good," said Doug.

"But there's a downside, too," Cardenas added, raising a warning finger. "Most of the people here intend to return Earthside, sooner or later. They're scared of trouble down there if they're carrying nanomachines in them."

Doug slumped back in his squeaking little plastic chair. "So what's the bottom line, Kris?"

"Most of our people refuse to be injected. But we're ready for emergency nanotherapy for people who're hurt or wounded."

The stupid fools, Doug thought. Then he realized his own fears of returning Earthside, where nanoluddite assassins waited. Like Killifer. Like the fanatics who murdered anyone who publicly espoused nanotechnology.

"Okay," he said wearily. "I assume you're working with the medical staff."

Cardenas grinned. "All three of 'em."

Neither Debbie Paine nor Harry Clemens had anything useful for Moonbase's defense. By the time Doug reached Vince Falcone, though, the burly, swarthy engineer had a knowing glint in his eyes.

"I been thinking," Falcone said.

"I thought I smelled wood burning," quipped Clemens.

"They'll be comin' over Wodjo Pass, right?" Falcone asked rhetorically.

Doug looked over at Gordette, who nodded warily.

"Maybe we can block the pass," said Falcone.

"Block it?"

"Sure. You know the foamgel we use for insulation and whatnot? Smart hydrogel is what it is. Expands or shrinks, depending on how you set it up."

Doug remembered that foamgel had been used on his sabotaged spacesuit. He glanced over at Gordette again; Bam was staring at him with unwavering eyes.

Falcone was grinning now with self-satisfaction. "Suppose we spray a ton or so of the glop along Wodjo Pass, see? The Peacekeepers are coming across the pass in tractors, right? When they're in the middle of the pass we radiate the gel with microwaves from the antennas on Mt. Yeager."

"And the gel swells up to a couple hundred times its original size!" Anson said eagerly.

"You got it," said Falcone. "Their tractors are caught in the glop like flies in a spiderweb. Like trucks stuck in deep mud."

"You can stop their tractors?" Doug asked. It was the first piece of good news he'd heard.

Still grinning, Falcone said, "I think so."

"But couldn't the troopers get out and walk across the foam?" Debbie Paine asked. "It hardens like concrete, doesn't it?"

"Yeah, that's right," Falcone admitted.

Doug turned to Gordette. "Bam, what do you think?"

The room fell utterly, uncomfortably silent.

Gordette spoke up, "Even if they can get out and walk to the crater floor, they'd have to leave most of their heavy equipment behind, in the tractors."

"Heavy equipment?" Clemens asked.

"Missile launchers," said Gordette. "Artillery. Ammunition cases. They could only bring what the troopers could carry. That's a big advantage to us."

"Can you produce that much foamgel in a few days?" Doug asked.

Falcone scratched at his stubbly chin. "We got some in inventory already . . . I'll get the chem lab to turn out as much as they can."

"But will it be enough?"

"Dunno," Falcone answered. Then he brightened. "Wait a minute," he said, looking excited. "It could get even better."

"What?"

"If we can divert enough power from the solar farms to the microwave antennas on Yeager—"

"Assuming Wix's beam gun works and the farms aren't nuked," Anson interjected.

"Yeah, yeah," Falcone said impatiently. "Anyway, gimme enough power for the microwave transmitters and we can fry the Peacekeeper troops while they're still up in the pass."

Doug felt his brows knitting. "What're you saying, Vince?"

"The troops'll be in suits, right? Lotsa metal in their suits. A microwave beam of sufficient strength'll heat up the metal, even penetrate the suits and cook the guys inside!"

Anson nearly came up out of her chair. "You can wipe 'em out up there in the pass before they ever get near us!"

"No!" shouted Edith.

Surprised, Doug turned toward her.

"No, you can't do that," Edith said, her face set with determination.

"Whattaya mean we can't?" Falcone snapped. "I haven't gone through the numbers but I'm willing to bet—"

"You mustn't kill any of them," Edith said.

"Mustn't kill . . . ?"

"How can we fight 'em if we can't kill 'em?"

Edith edged forward slightly in her seat. "The worst thing you can do, the absolute worst, is to kill any of the Peacekeepers."

Doug realized what she was driving at. "Captain Munasinghe," he muttered.

"Right. Faure tried to make a martyr out of him, tried to use him to work up public opinion against you."

"But he killed himself," Debbie Paine said. "It wasn't our fault."

"Okay," said Edith. "Now imagine what happens if you cook a hundred Peacekeeper troops. Picture what the media Earthside will do with that."

Silence descended on the office again, gloomier and deeper than before.

"We've been working for weeks now to present Moonbase's side of this story to the media, the weak little guys being bullied by the big, bad U.N. and Peacekeepers," Edith said. "And it's starting to work.

Public relations polls in the States and Europe show that the people are rooting for us and against the U.N."

"With that and five bucks I can buy a cup of coffee," Falcone grumbled.

"Your claim of independence is coming up before the World Court in a few months," Edith went on. "You *need* to have the best possible public image."

"And that means we can't kill the soldiers attacking us?" Anson demanded.

"That's exactly what it means," said Edith heatedly. "Right now a lot of people Earthside are on your side. The underdog always gets sympathy. But you start sending body bags back to Earth and your support will evaporate damned quick."

"So we could win the battle and lose the war," Doug said.

Nodding, Edith answered, "That's what it comes down to. Kill Peacekeeper troops and you'll just convince everybody Earthside that Faure is right. They'll come at you with still more troops. Or missiles, or whatever it takes to wipe you out."

"So we can't kill the Peacekeepers," Falcone muttered unbelievingly.

"Then how do we keep them from taking over?" Anson wondered aloud.

Doug echoed her. "How can we win the battle without killing any of the enemy?"

"Damned good question," Clemens murmured.

For long moments no one said a word. Finally Doug turned to Gordette.

"Bam, how can you stop soldiers without killing them?"

They all turned to Gordette, still sitting by the door. Doug saw the distrust, the outright repugnance on their faces; he wondered what Gordette saw, what he felt.

Gordette looked them over with a gaze that swept the small, crowded office. Then, turning to face Doug squarely, he said, "You'll have to incapacitate them."

"How?"

Gordette cocked his head to one side, thinking.

"They'll all be in spacesuits. They'll be linked by their suit radios. Can you jam their communications?"

Doug said, "We ought to be able to do that."

"If they can't talk back and forth they'll lose their cohesiveness. Instead of a battalion they'll be a handful of individuals."

"Like ants!" Paine exclaimed. "One ant by itself is pretty useless. But a whole nest of them can mount an invasion of another nest."

"Cut off their communications," Doug repeated.

"Not enough," said Falcone. "You'll still have a few hundred soldiers armed with guns and whatnot. They can be directed by hand signals, for chrissakes."

"Not if they are blind," rumbled Zimmerman.

"What?"

"I have been stupid," Zimmerman said, shaking his jowly head. "Invisible I cannot make you . . . but I can make *them* blind!"

"Blind them? How?"

"Simple," said the professor. "Let them come into our tunnels. We fill the air with nanomachines that cling to their visors and darken them so they cannot see."

Doug immediately asked, "Can the bugs cling to their suits, too? Jam up their joints, immobilize them?"

"Like the dust outside!" Anson said.

"Yah! Better than dust," Zimmerman replied. "My nanos will turn them into statues!"

"But only once they're inside the base, in the corridors," Clemens said.

"Yah. The nanos must have air to float in."

"So we can make them deaf, dumb and blind," Falcone said.

"And immobile," Cardenas added.

"Freeze 'em in their tracks," said Anson.

"Can you produce these nanos in a week?" Doug asked.

For the first time since Doug had known the old man, Zimmerman's fleshy face looked uncertain. "One week? Not possible! But I will try."

Doug nodded, but he thought that it was awfully risky

to allow the Peacekeepers into the base in the hopes that Zimmerman's nanobugs could neutralize them. Assuming Zimmerman could make the bugs and they worked as advertised. Even then, everything depended on Wix's beam gun stopping the incoming nuke. And Falcone's foamgel stopping the Peacekeepers' heavy equipment up at Wodjohowitcz Pass.

One untested idea on top of another, Doug realized. And if any of the Peacekeepers gets killed, we've lost everything.

NIPPON ONE

Colonel Giap tried to suppress the distaste he felt for the Yamagata volunteer.

The man was Japanese, short and wiry, quite young. He had an air of superiority about him, an aura of other-worldliness, as if all of Giap's responsibilities and worries did not matter at all.

The slow buildup of three hundred Peacekeeper troops—and these seven special volunteers—had strained Nippon One's facilities to the breaking point. Never a large or comfortable base, its cramped little compartments were now jammed with the extra personnel. Four people were sleeping in cubicles designed for one. Peacekeeper troops even slept in the tunnels on thin foam mattresses or tatami mats.

Giap's "office" was a storage bin that had been half-emptied by the enormous drain on the base's logistics. We had better move on Moonbase within the week, the colonel told himself. There will be no food left for us in eight days.

He looked directly into the dark brown eyes of the

Yamagata volunteer and saw a placidity, an almost amused sense of superiority. This man is actually looking forward to his death, Giap realized. Then he wondered how much of his bravery or fanaticism came from narcotics. The Sacred Seven, as the suicide volunteers called themselves, lived by themselves, crammed into a single cubicle; they had brought their own food and drink. And so-called medicines.

Three Japanese, three Americans, and an Iranian made up the Sacred Seven. One of the Americans was a woman. All of them were either serenely otherworldly, as their leader was, or brittle and wired, with eyes that glittered with the burning intensity of fanaticism. All of them wore a shoulder patch that showed a fist clutching a bolt of lightning.

There was no space for a desk in the compartment. The two men sat on the floor, cross-legged, facing one another barely centimeters apart, Giap in his light blue uniform, the Japanese volunteer in a gym suit—with the shoulder patch. Above them rose stacks of half-empty shelving. Giap's personal computer, hardly bigger than his fist, lay on the bare stone floor at his side.

"My orders," Giap was saying, "are to capture Moonbase intact."

"If possible," the volunteer added.

Giap seethed inwardly at the man's smug attitude. He knows what my orders are. Someone has been leaking the information to him.

"It will not only be possible," Giap hissed, "but inevitable."

"Assuming all goes according to your plan."

"My plan is very thorough."

"Of course," said the volunteer airily. "However, should the assault fail, for any reason, my team will destroy Moonbase for you."

"And destroy yourselves in the doing of it."

"That is nothing. To give our lives in the service of God is the greatest good."

Giap wondered whose god this man thought he was serving. These zealots all professed loyalty to the New

Morality, even though their individual religions must obviously be different from one another.

"I want you to understand that you are not to make any move whatsoever unless and until I order it," Giap said.

The volunteer nodded benignly.

"You and your people are under my command. You will obey my orders."

"Yes, of course. But you *will* assign a squad of your troops to help us open up the old plasma exhaust vents."

It was not a question, Giap knew.

"Yes, as soon as we have secured the main garage area," he replied.

"Good. Then we will climb into the vents and make our way to the key Moonbase facilities: the water factory, the environmental control center, the control center, the farm, and the nanolabs. I myself and one of the Americans will knock out the nanolabs."

"Only if I order it," Giap insisted.

"Of course," said the volunteer, with his maddeningly patient smile. "We will need your troopers' assistance to climb up into the vents, won't we?"

Giap nodded slowly. The volunteers will each be carrying a hundred kilos of high explosive. Not an easy burden to shoulder in a spacesuit, he knew.

Suicide bombers. The idea rankled him. Someone in the Yamagata chain of command did not trust him to capture Moonbase. Someone in the Yamagata chain of command was working for the New Morality in addition to the corporation. Whoever it was has added these insane volunteers to make certain that Moonbase will be eliminated if it can't be taken intact.

SAVANNAH

The two women were taking lunch on the patio, shaded by a pair of ancient oaks and cooled by a breeze generated from hidden fans built into the brick walls that edged the meticulously cultivated garden of show flowers.

Joanna Brudnoy wore a light sundress of rose pink; Jill Meyers a tailored blouse and knee-length skirt. They had known each other since Jill had been a NASA astronaut working with Paul Stavenger in the very earliest lunar shelters that eventually became Moonbase; long enough so that neither felt the need to try to impress the other.

"We're in summer recess now," Jill Meyers said.

"And how long will that last?" Joanna asked, glancing out at the two men working in the garden. One of them actually was a gardener, the other a security guard in disguise.

Jill gave her a freckle-nosed grin. "The International Court of Justice has its own calendar, Jo. Officially, it'll stay summer until November, when we reconvene."

"And that's when you'll hear Moonbase's petition?"
Justice Meyers nodded.

"Isn't there any way of hearing it sooner?" Joanna pleaded. "A special session, perhaps?"

"I tried, Jo," said Jill. "I went all-out, but I got out-voted, ten to five."

Joanna toyed absently with the salad in front of her. "Is that how they'll vote in November, do you think?"

"No, not at all. They just didn't want to go to the trouble of a special session, that's all." Before Joanna could comment, Jill added, "And they're waiting to see if Moonbase can last until November. If Moonbase survives that long, it'll be a strong indication that they really can be independent."

Joanna let go of her fork and it clinked against the glass dish. "Faure's going to attack them again any day now."

Nodding, Jill agreed, "That's what I hear, too."

"Isn't there *anything* you can do?"

"I talked with the president. She's not going to lift a finger."

"We've been putting as much pressure on our senators as we can," Joanna said. "But Moonbase is a private operation, not part of the government."

"There's not much they can do about it," Jill said.

"But there must be something!"

"Wait," Jill said gently. "Wait and pray."

Joanna eyed her. "You sound like a New Morality convert."

Jill took it with a smile. "You don't have to be a New Morality fanatic to believe in the power of prayer, Jo."

Several miles away, in the riverfront headquarters of Masterson Corporation, Jack Killifer sat tensely in one of the tight little stalls that passed for offices among the corporation's personnel department employees.

"I'm taking an awful chance, Mr. Killifer," said the young woman sitting at the desk. She spoke in a near-whisper; the padded partitions that marked off her tiny space did not extend all the way to the ceiling. Soft music purred from the hand-sized radio on her desk next to her computer monitor screen.

"Like I'm not?" Killifer snapped, low enough to avoid eavesdroppers, he hoped. His appearance had changed: his gray ponytail was gone; now his hair was dark and clipped short, military style. He had also grown a bushy moustache that he had darkened to match his hair.

"I found your personnel record," she said, looking worried, "but, Lord's sake, it's almost nine years old!"

"I don't want my old record," he almost snarled. "I want you to generate a new one."

"But that would be a total fabrication."

"So what?"

"What if my supervisor checks on it? What could I say?"

Killifer had thought it all out beforehand. "I won't be around long enough for anybody to notice. A week, maybe less."

"It's an awful risk," she repeated. "For both of us."

"No risk at all for you," Killifer said, getting fed up with her fears. "If anybody complains, you just tell 'em I showed you documentation."

"Documentation?"

Killifer pulled a thin sheaf of papers from his jacket pocket. They were not forged, since they were written by a bona fide personnel executive from the Urban Corps' headquarters in Atlanta. The information in them, however, was completely false.

"Here, scan these into your records before you piss yourself."

"Sir!"

Killifer sighed. These damned New Morality uptights. Can't even spit without them getting wired over it.

"Forgive me," he said.

"Forgiveness is the Lord's work," she chanted. Then she turned to her keyboard and activated the scanner.

Good, Killifer thought as he handed her the falsified personnel documents. By the time I walk out of here I'll be on the payroll as a member of the Masterson security staff. If this uptight little broad doesn't faint on me first.

MASS DRIVER

"Everything takes longer to do in these suits." Wicksen's voice was calm, not complaining, not making excuses; it was as if he were reading a report aloud.

Doug watched the men working at the end of the mass driver. While those who worked on the surface regularly had personalized their spacesuits one way or another, Wicksen's physicists and technicians were in unmarked, anonymous suits straight off the standby racks.

At Doug's insistence, a team of construction engineers was building a makeshift shelter for Wicksen's people a few dozen meters from where they were busily putting together the equipment for the beam gun. Like one of the old tempos, the shelter was dug into the ground and would be covered with loose rubble from the regolith. Wicksen and his assistants could run the beam gun from there. Maybe the shelter would protect them from the radiation of a nuclear explosion, if the gun didn't work.

"How's it going?" Doug asked.

"Slowly," said Wix. "But we're making progress. We connected the beam collimator this morning. By tomorrow the aiming circuitry should be functional. Day after tomorrow, at the latest."

"And then you're ready to shoot?"

Wicksen's flat, unruffled voice came through Doug's helmet earphones, "Then we'll be ready to see if anything really works. After testing the assembly we can power up the magnets and see if the circuitry can handle the load without shorting out."

"But your calculations—"

"Mathematics doesn't necessarily reflect the real world," Wicksen said. "Physics is more than numbers in a computer."

"Oh. I see."

"I remember when I was a kid in high school, we had a volunteer teacher's aide come in and help us in our science class. He was retired, used to be a big-time physicist. His daughter was a famous folk singer."

Doug wondered what this had to do with the defense of Moonbase, but hesitated to interrupt Wicksen.

"He took us out to the gym and attached a bowling ball to one of the climbing ropes. The rope was hanging from a beam way up on the ceiling. Then he carried the bowling ball up to the top tier of the benches where we sat during the basketball games."

"What was he doing?" Doug asked, curious despite himself.

"Teaching us physics. The law of pendulums. He held that big old bowling ball a centimeter in front of his nose, and then let it go."

"And?"

"It swung on that rope all the way across the gym, like a cannonball, then swung right back toward him again. We all started to yell to him to duck, to get out of the way. But he just stood there and grinned at us."

Wicksen paused dramatically. Doug waited for him to finish the story.

"The bowling ball stopped a centimeter in front of his nose, then started swinging back again. And he said, 'See? It works that way every time. That's physics!' And I was hooked for life."

Doug thought he understood. "The demonstration was a lot more convincing than reading the equations about pendulums, right?"

"Right," said Wicksen. "Of course, you've got to know what you're doing. You've got to release the bowling ball without pushing it even the slightest little bit. If you push it, it'll come back and smash your head in."

"Is the gun going to work?" Doug asked.

He could sense Wicksen trying to shrug inside his suit. "We don't know. All the equations check out, but we won't know until we try it."

"And you probably won't get a chance to try it until a nuclear warhead is falling on our heads."

"Probably." If that thought perturbed Wicksen in the slightest, it didn't show in his voice.

He's actually happy about this, Doug realized. He's running an experiment that might get himself and all his people killed, but the whole project excites him. Like a hunter tracking down a lion in thick underbrush: dangerous, but what an adrenaline rush!

Doug took his leave of the physicist, wishing he could be as fatalistic as Wicksen. As he climbed into his tractor and trundled away from the mass driver, heading back toward Moonbase, he tried to see things the way Wicksen did. Either the experiment works or we all get killed. Is that the way he really thinks? Or is it that he's so absorbed in the experiment itself that he's not thinking at all about the consequences?

Doug's first stop after getting out of his spacesuit and cleaning it was the control center. Everything looked normal in the big, dimly lit room. The quiet hum of electronics. Rows of consoles monitored by men and women staring at the screens, pin mikes at their lips and earphones clamped to their heads. A controlled intensity, with the big electronic wall displays that showed schematics of the entire base looming over all of them.

He saw Jinny Anson bending over the shoulder of the chief communications technician.

Walking over to her, he asked, "What's up, Jinny?"

She straightened up and Doug saw that her face was somber. "Lot of activity at L-1," she said, gesturing toward the comm tech's center screen.

Doug saw a radar plot of the space station that hovered nearly sixty thousand kilometers above them. Several additional blips clustered around the red dot marking the station.

"Resupply?" Doug mused.

"Not likely," said Anson. "Their regular resupply run

took place on schedule last week. No, they're delivering something to the station, but it's not life-support supplies or propellant."

Doug took in a deep breath. "The nuclear missile?"

"Maybe more than one."

For a moment Doug was silent, thinking. Then he said, "I'm going to call Harry Clemens. It's time to pop an observation satellite so we can keep an eye on Nippon One."

Anson nodded, then grinned ruefully. "You might not like what you see, boss."

Gordette was sitting in the Cave, nursing a mug of the stuff that passed for coffee at Moonbase. It was midday, and the cafeteria was filling up with the lunchtime crowd. But no one sat at Gordette's table. No one came near it; a ring of empty tables surrounded him.

Pariah, he said to himself. That's the word. For days he'd been trying to recall the term. At last it came swimming up from his subconscious. Pariah. Outcast. Murderer. Assassin. That's me and they all know it.

It would've been better if Doug had let me die, Gordette told himself. He says he trusts me, but none of these others do. They all know about me now, or they think they do. And they all hate me.

Then he saw Paula Liebowitz carrying a tray in both hands, making her way through the crowded tables, heading straight toward him. She walked with a determined stride and an odd, tenacious expression on her face, right up to Gordette's table.

"Do you mind if I sit here?" she asked, almost truculently.

Gordette spread his arms to take in all the empty chairs. "Be my guest."

Liebowitz plopped her laden tray on the table and took the chair next to Gordette.

"Is it true? Did you really try to kill Doug Stavenger?"

Gordette couldn't make out what was in her eyes. It wasn't anger, exactly. But it wasn't tenderness, either.

"It's true," he said flatly.

"You're a hired assassin? A hit man?"

He puffed out a sigh. "When I first met you I was trying to sabotage Doug's suit."

"Son of a bitch," Liebowitz said. She wasn't calling Gordette a name, he realized; merely expressing her emotions.

He tried to shrug. "That's what I was sent here to do."

"And when you invited me to dinner, that was part of it? You were going to try to use me to help you kill Stavenger?"

"No," he answered slowly. "I invited you to dinner because I liked you."

"Yeah. Sure."

"Even trained assassins need some human companionship now and then," Gordette told her.

"Don't try to make a joke out of this!"

"It's no joke, believe me."

"Why should I believe anything you say?"

"Why do you ask me, then?"

"I *liked* you," Liebowitz said. "I was even thinking about going to bed with you."

"Get your kicks with a black man, huh?"

She frowned with puzzlement. "What?"

"I'm black."

"And I'm a Jew. What's that got to do with anything?"

Gordette thought it over for a moment. "Nothing. Nothing's got anything to do with anything."

"What's that supposed to mean?"

"I don't know," he said, getting irritated with her cross-examination. "So I liked you and you liked me. So what?"

"Stavenger's letting you stay here? You're still working with him?"

Gordette nodded.

"He trusts you? After you tried to kill him?"

"I told him the story of my life," Gordette said, acid in each word, "and he decided he's gonna reform me.

Start me a new life here on the Moon, where everybody loves me and trusts me."

"Yeah, you've made it so easy to be loved and accepted."

"The only thing I've made easy is being black, so you can spot me at a distance."

"What the hell's this black business got to do with it?"

"You see any other black people up here?"

Liebowitz almost laughed at him. "My supervisor's black. There's dozens of Afro-Americans and blacks from other countries here." She turned in her chair and pointed. "Look. Black people. And Asians. Hell, they even let Italians up here!"

"Very funny."

"The first American astronaut on Mars was black."

"Big deal."

"Stop feeling sorry for yourself."

"Okay. Good advice. I'll do that," he mumbled.

Liebowitz glared at him like a disappointed mother. "You really tried to kill him?"

"I slit his throat. Alright? Is that what you wanted to hear? My fuckin' confession?"

He said it loudly enough so that people at the nearest tables turned to stare at him.

"What I want to hear," Liebowitz said, her voice low, "is where you're going from here."

"Straight to hell," Gordette said.

"So you're going to isolate yourself, build a wall and not let anybody near you."

He pointed to the ring of empty tables around them. "You see anybody trying to make friends with me?"

"I am," she said.

He blinked, uncomprehending.

"I'm having lunch with you, aren't I?" Liebowitz said. "Maybe you can tell me the story of your life and make me believe that you're something more than just a hired killer."

SPACE STATION *MASTERSON*

Like a growing frontier town, space station *Masterson* had succumbed to urban sprawl. But now it was starting to look like a ghost town.

Orbiting some two hundred fifty miles above the Earth, at first glance *Masterson* looked like a disconnected conglomeration of odds and ends, a junkyard floating in space. The modules where personnel were housed spun lazily on opposite ends of three-kilometer-long carbon filament tethers, like oversized aluminum cans glinting in the sunlight, connected by strings so thin and dark they were for all practical purposes invisible. The modules formed a huge disjointed wheel more than ten kilometers in circumference, with the tethers as spokes.

Outside the circumference of the habitation modules' arc floated the factories, labs, repair shops and transfer center, their angular utilitarian shapes dwarfed by huge wings of solar panels and radiators, massive concave solar mirrors that collected and focused the Sun's heat for smelting and other processing work, and forests of antennas and sensors—all in zero gravity, or the nearest thing to it.

Like most of the major complexes in permanent Earth orbit, *Masterson* was a combination of several purposes: part manufacturing facility, part scientific research laboratory, part observation platform, part maintenance and repair center, and part transfer station for people and

cargo heading onward to Moonbase. There was even a
tourist hotel module, twice the size of all the others.

Since the U.N.-imposed embargo on Moonbase traffic,
however, there were no transfers of people heading out
to the Moon and no arrivals of lunar cargo carriers. The
manufacturing facility had shut down for lack of raw
materials. No lunar transfer vehicles needed maintenance or repair; they were all hanging silent and useless
in weightless geodesic cocoons that protected them from
incoming radiation and the occasional meteoroids that
peppered cislunar space. The tourist hotel was still running, but its business had dropped sharply since the war
against Moonbase had started.

Jill Meyers gazed sadly through an observation port
in the hotel module. She had helped to build *Masterson*,
back in the days when she'd been a government astronaut. She was accustomed to seeing spacesuited figures
bustling from module to module, jetting along in solo
maneuvering units, or riding the bare-bones shuttlecraft
called broomsticks. But now the whole region was quiet,
empty. This war was costing Masterson Corporation millions of dollars per day, and even though the U.N. promised reparations, Meyers knew that nothing could repay
time lost, careers interrupted.

"There you are!"

Jill turned from the circular glassteel observation port
to see Edan McGrath standing in the hatch. His sizable
bulk almost filled the hatchway, the lighting from the
central corridor silhouetting him dramatically.

"You finally got here," Meyers said, taking a step
toward him.

"I've been looking all over this tin can for you," he
replied gruffly. "Come on, let's eat. I haven't had a bite
since breakfast."

The hotel's restaurant was nearly empty—only two
other couples sitting at the elegant tables, and a family
of four off in the farthest corner, where the children
wouldn't annoy other diners. They've got more waiters
than customers, Meyers noticed as she scanned the richly
decorated room. Windowall screens displayed astronom-

ical scenes, glorious interstellar nebulas glowing delicate pink and electric blue. Meyers realized that real windows would have shown the scenery outside spinning lazily; not the most soothing background for flatland tourists to eat and drink by.

McGrath had ordered champagne. They clinked their fluted glasses and toasted each other's health. Meyers had dressed in comfortable tan slacks and a loose blouse embroidered with flowers. McGrath wore a bulky white turtleneck sweater over jeans that looked stiffly new.

With a lopsided grin on his beefy face, McGrath asked, "Do you come here often?"

It was a corny line and they both knew it.

Meyers laughed politely. "I used to, in the old days."

"I understand you were quite a hell-raiser back then," he said.

Her smile turned reminiscent. "Back then," she murmured.

The waiter brought them oversized menus. McGrath ordered three courses and more wine, Meyers only a salad.

"Okay," he said, after the waiter had left, "you asked me to meet you here. What's up?"

Meyers looked into his pale blue eyes. "Edan, you know that if I were still in the Senate I'd be raising all kinds of hell about this war against Moonbase."

"I'd hardly call it a war," he said.

"That's what your network calls it."

McGrath shrugged. "That's show business, Jill. You know how it is."

"I need your help to put pressure on the president," she said.

His brows rose slightly. "I thought you were on her side. You're the same party—"

"Not on this," Meyers snapped. "I've never been a blind supporter of the New Morality and she knows it. She named me to the World Court to get me out of the Senate because she knew I'd raise hell about going after Moonbase."

"Why don't you raise hell now? I'd give you all the air time you want."

"I can't," Meyers said, shaking her head. "As a judge in the International Court of Justice I've got to stay strictly out of politics."

With a laugh, McGrath asked, "What you're doing now isn't politics?"

"This is private, just between you and me."

"And Global News and the White House," he added.

Meyers gave him a disdainful look. "You know what I mean, Edan."

"Okay, okay," he said, raising his hands in mock surrender. "But what more can I do? Global's been airing Edie Elgin's reports from Moonbase. Faure's pissed as hell with me over that."

"You could start by showing what a ghost town this space station has become," Meyers said. "American jobs are down the tubes because of Faure."

"And the New Morality's insistence that the nanotech treaty be enforced even on the Moon."

"Right."

"You want me to take on the New Morality?"

She hesitated, studying the expression on his face. McGrath had been handsome before he'd let himself start going to fat. He still looked pretty good. But is he strong enough? Meyers wondered.

Carefully, she said, "I want you to show the American public—the world public, really—how much this war against Moonbase is really costing."

The waiter brought McGrath's first course. Once he left, McGrath lifted his soup spoon, but instead of digging in he jabbed it in Meyers' direction.

"You know," he said, "there's nothing like a really good controversy to boost ratings."

Meyers grinned at him.

MOONBASE

"What on Earth are you doing?" Claire Rossi blurted.

Nick O'Malley was dragging a bulky container into their one-room quarters. It looked like an oversized piece of soft-sided luggage, and it made their little compartment crowded.

"Emergency procedure," O'Malley said, pushing the container into the corner between the bunk and the desk. Still it took up almost half the floor space.

Rossi watched impatiently as her husband knelt on one knee and began to rip open the Velcro seams of the container. She leaned over his broad shoulder and looked inside.

"A spacesuit!"

"Right," O'Malley said. "I'm going to show you how to get into it, in case you need to while I'm not here."

"Why would I—oh."

As he hauled the torso and leggings of the suit out and spread them on the bunk, O'Malley said, "When the attack comes we might lose air pressure. This gadget here will yowl when the pressure drops below a safe minimum."

He put a small gray box on the shelf carved into the stone wall above the bunk.

"When you hear this go off, you get into the suit as fast as you can. Here, I'll show you how."

"But suppose I'm in the personnel office when it happens?" she asked.

O'Malley shook his head. "When the Peacekeepers

start their attack everybody not on essential duty will go to their quarters. That's orders from management."

She almost started to twit him about her personnel job being considered nonessential, but the dead-serious expression on her husband's face stopped her.

Instead she asked, "Is everybody getting a spacesuit?"

"Not enough to go around," he answered, shaking his head.

"Then why do I get special treatment?"

He smiled bleakly at her. "Because you're a special person. You're married to me. And you're pregnant."

"But that means somebody else will have to go without a suit."

His lips were a grim, pinched line. "Claire, hundreds of people here are going to go without a suit. But you're not. Now let me show you how to put it on properly."

She knew better than to argue with him. He's trying to protect me, she told herself. And the baby. But if the air pressure goes down, lots of people will die here. And how long will the suit keep me?

Aloud, as she struggled into the clumsy leggings, she asked, "Where will you be when the shooting starts? Not operating the tractors, of course."

He scowled. "No. I've been assigned to help Professor Zimmerman, for the sake of St. Ignatius."

"Zimmerman?"

"I think Doug Stavenger wants me to be the old man's bodyguard."

"Is the professor getting a suit?" Rossi asked as she tugged on the boots.

"There isn't one in the base that'd fit him."

"Oh dear."

As he knelt at her feet and helped her zip the boots and leggings together, O'Malley said, "After just half a day with the old bugger, I almost wish somebody would knock him off."

"That's no way to talk, Nick."

"He's impossible."

"He's a genius and geniuses have their quirks."

O'Malley made a sour face. "You know what I've been doing for him all morning? Collecting dust!"

"What?"

"I've been teleoperating a tractor all damned morning, scooping up dust off the regolith for him to experiment with."

"That sounds crazy."

"Tell me about it. He wants to build nanomachines that behave like dust particles, so he tells me he needs samples of dust to work with."

Rossi wormed her arms into the suit's torso, then popped her head through the neck ring.

"Why does he want to make nanomachines that behave like dust particles?" she asked.

"Because he's way beyond quirky, that's why. He's outright daft."

SAVANNAH

"It's easy duty," said the security chief. "Four men outside, two inside. Pretty soft, really."

Jack Killifer sat in the stiff little plastic chair in front of the chief's metal desk, trying hard to keep his face from showing what he was feeling inside. I'm in Joanna Brudnoy's house! he exulted. Okay, it's just the servants' wing of the house, but still—here I am.

The security chief wore a tan summerweight uniform with epaulets and shoulder patches and even a couple of medals pinned above his left breast pocket. Tin soldiers, Killifer thought.

He himself was in a baggy shirt and Levis, the "uniform of the day," as instructed.

The security chief kept glancing at the array of display

screens that made up one whole wall of the bare little office. They showed security camera views of the grounds around the house, the garage, the pool area, and every room inside except the master bedroom.

"The only thing you've got to remember," the chief said, swivelling his attention back and forth between the screens and Killifer, "is that she doesn't like to *see* uniformed guards around the place."

"So we dress like gardeners," Killifer said, putting just a hint of disdain in it.

"Yeah. Both chauffeurs are on the team, of course, and the butler's supposed to be a black belt. He carries a nine-millimeter, too. All the time."

They had issued Killifer a brand-new Browning machine pistol: fifty rounds, either semi- or full-automatic. It still smelled of packing grease.

"But the butler only works the day shift, doesn't he?" Killifer asked.

The chief hiked an eyebrow. "The butler works until they both go to bed. He don't sleep until they do."

"Uh-huh."

"So all you've got to do is patrol outside, make yourself look like a gardener, and keep an eye out for strangers."

"What about people coming up to the house in cars?"

"You don't have to worry about that. The two inside guys take care of that. And the butler."

One of the inside "guys" was a terrific-looking redhead, Killifer had already discovered. Hard as nails, though.

"What's she need all this security for?" he asked, probing for weak spots in the security system. "You don't need six people and machine pistols for burglars."

The chief shrugged carelessly. "I don't ask and they don't bother to let me in on their secrets. It's a cushy job, so don't knock it."

Killifer shrugged back at him. "Yeah, okay, but I'd kinda like to know what I'm supposed to be looking out for."

Eying the display screens, the chief muttered, "Religious fanatics."

"What?"

"She's worried about fanatics from the New Morality trying to kill her."

"No shit?"

The chief's tic of displeasure told Killifer that he was probably a Believer himself.

"If some religious nutcase wanted to kill her, why not just drive a car bomb into the house?"

"Not their style," said the chief. "The fanatics do their killing face-to-face, and they don't believe in taking out innocent people when they hit somebody. Besides, she's in and out so much—travels all the time, really—you can't be sure she's home unless you actually see her."

"Yeah," said Killifer. "I guess that's right."

"Listen," the chief said, suddenly intense, leaning across his desk to stare directly into Killifer's eyes. "Don't judge the New Morality movement by the actions of a few crazies. Most of those assassins are foreigners, not Americans. Fanatics."

Killifer nodded, knowing that the chief was certainly a Believer. Wonder what he'd say if I told him I worked for the Urban Corps. And that General O'Conner his own god-almighty self has sanctioned the assassination of Joanna Brudnoy.

It had been ridiculously easy to get hired onto the Masterson security team that guarded Joanna's house. New Morality adherents had faked his employment record in the corporation's computer files and provided a lucrative transfer to one of the women employed in the house guard detail. Killifer had miraculously popped out of the personnel files and been taken on within two days.

The weakest link in the security system is the system itself, Killifer knew. Manipulate the system and make it work for you.

The next step is to get into the house, on the night detail, when the butler's asleep and Joanna's in her bedroom where there are no cameras watching.

MOONBASE

"Well, how much of the stuff can you make?" Vince Falcone asked, his patience obviously fraying.

"How much time do I have?" asked the head of the chemistry lab.

"I don't know."

"Then I don't know, either."

"Days," said Doug, stepping between them. "Maybe only two days, maybe a few more."

"Two days?" the chemist gasped. She pushed back a strand of dark blond hair from her forehead. "Only two days?"

Doug wondered where she'd been all this time. "We're expecting the Peacekeepers' attack before this week is out," he said.

She looked past Doug to Falcone. "How much do you need?"

"Four tons."

She blinked, swallowed. Then, straightening her back, she said, "We'll have to get the processing plant devoted completely to the job."

Falcone's frowning, swarthy face relaxed slightly. "Maybe three tons'll do."

The chemist shook her head. "Still, that's impossible to produce in two days. We don't have any time to lose."

"Can you come close?" Doug asked.

She was a petite wisp of a woman, her orange coveralls stained and faded from hard use. "We generate the foamgel as part of the process for making the insulation tiles we use for flooring and wall covering and all."

The insulating tiles were a small but consistent export to the space stations in Earth orbit, Doug knew. Moonbase also exported an even smaller but growing trickle of them to building contracting firms on Earth.

"We'll have to shut down the back end of the production line," the chemist was musing, "and rev up the foamgel production end."

She looked up at Falcone again. To Doug they seemed like a dark lumpy storm cloud and a light graceful swirl of cirrus.

"I can put all the raw stock we have on hand into producing foamgel, but I'll need more raw materials. Every tractor you can get scooping regolith."

"You got it!" Falcone promised.

Doug left them huddled together over her phone console and hurried down the corridor to Zimmerman's nanolab. One of the base's best tractor teleoperators, Nick O'Malley, had been assigned to work with the professor. But if we need every tractor scooping outside, I'll have to shift Nick back to his regular job.

He could hear their arguing voices from fifty meters down the corridor: Zimmerman's heavy rumbling and O'Malley's higher-pitched yells. Nick's not taking any guff from the professor, Doug thought as he pushed through the door marked NANOTECHNOLOGY LABORATORY—PROF. ZIMMERMAN—AUTHORIZED PERSONNEL *ONLY*.

"So you are the expert here and not me?" Zimmerman was bellowing angrily.

"I know more about it than you do, damned right I do!" shouted O'Malley, red-faced.

"Stop it!" Doug commanded. "Shut up, both of you!"

Zimmerman whirled on Doug, his loose jacket and vest flapping like sails with the wind taken out of them.

"An assistant you gave me? A *führer* you gave me! A dictator!"

"What's the problem?" Doug asked as calmly as he could.

"He thinks *he* is the professor and I am *his* student!" Zimmerman complained loudly.

"I only said—"

"You are not to *say*!" Zimmerman roared. "You are to *do*. You are my assistant, not my colleague!"

"Professor, please!" Doug insisted. "What is the problem?"

Gesturing with both hands, Zimmerman grumbled, "He thinks to tell me what I should do. He thinks he is the expert here."

"All right, all right," Doug said, trying to be soothing. He turned toward O'Malley. "Nick?"

"I just said that if he needs nanobugs to act like dust, why doesn't he just use the flaming dust itself?"

"You see!" Zimmerman snapped.

"Wait a minute," said Doug. "Nick, what do you mean?"

O'Malley sucked in a deep, deep breath. Doug realized he was trying to hold onto his own temper. He was a big man, and if he got truly angry there could be real trouble.

"What I mean," he said slowly, "is that we don't need to invent nanomachines that behave like dust particles. We can pump the corridor sections full of regular lunar dust. Run 'em through an electrostatic grid so they'll stick to the Peacekeepers' suits and visors just like you want 'em to."

"An electrostatic grid?"

"We can rig that up easy; just need to connect some electricity to the air filter screens in the corridors."

"*We*, he keeps saying," Zimmerman muttered.

Doug put a hand on the old man's shoulder. "Professor, I think he's right."

"And I am wrong?"

Forcing a smile, Doug said, "No, but we don't have time to produce your specialized nanomachines. Nick's worked out on the surface; he knows how the dust clings to suits."

"So I must sit back and retire like a useless old man?"

"No, not at all," Doug said. "You can work with Kris

Cardenas on the medical side. We're going to need your nanomachines to take care of the injured and wounded."

Zimmerman huffed out an enormous sigh. "You expect injured and wounded? How many?"

"I have no idea," Doug answered truthfully.

The professor turned away and walked a few steps deeper into his lab. Then he spun around and pointed a trembling finger at O'Malley. "Very well! Go play with your *verdammt* dust! I will stay here and do *important* work!"

O'Malley started to reply, but one glance at Doug and he shut his mouth with an audible click of teeth.

"We need you, Professor," Doug said softly. "You know that. I need you. Moonbase needs you."

"Yah. While you and this young lummox here go out to fight, I sit here like a dreamer."

"It's your dreams that we're fighting for," said Doug. Then he took O'Malley by the arm and led him out of the nanotechnology laboratory.

Harry Clemens seldom showed tension. Word around Moonbase was that he didn't have any bones, that's why he always looked so relaxed.

But he was sitting rigidly in one of the little swivel chairs in front of a console in the control center, eyes riveted on the screen that showed the little tubular rocket vehicle, as the launch computer counted aloud: " . . . four . . . three . . . two . . . one . . . zero."

Clemens saw a flash of smoke and dust. The rocket was gone when it cleared.

"Radar track on the line," said the technician sitting to his right. He saw the radar display on the screen just above his view of the now-empty launch pad.

"Looks good."

He swivelled slightly to see Jinny Anson standing behind him.

"Now we'll see if they try to shoot it down," Anson said tightly.

"L-1's painting it," the radar tech called out.

"I launched it retrograde," Clemens said to Anson,

"so L-1 won't have more than a few minutes to calculate its trajectory."

The Moon rotates on its axis so slowly that very little momentum was lost by launching a rocket in the direction opposite to its spin. On Earth, a launch westward could cost four kilometers per second of precious velocity, or more, depending on the launch site's latitude.

"They won't need more than a few seconds to nail your orbit," Anson said flatly. "Besides, they know goddamned well it's gonna pass over Copernicus. They got lots of time to focus a laser on it."

Clemens' high forehead wrinkled. "You think they'll zap it?"

"If the Peacekeepers've put a big enough laser at L-1, yeah, they will."

"Do you think they've put weapons-strength lasers in Nippon One?"

Anson gripped Clemens' shoulders and grinned down at him. "We'll find out pretty soon, won't we?"

Edith was reviewing her day's shooting in the video editing booth at Lunar University's studio facility. The studio itself was dark and empty; no lectures or demonstrations, no interactions with Earthside students had taken place since the U.N. had cut off regular communications. The editing booth felt almost like home to Edith, though. Even though she was alone in it, she enjoyed working the big control console. When she had first started in television news, sitting at the console with all its switches and keypads made her feel like the captain of a starship in some futuristic drama. Now it just felt like a familiar, comfortable place where she could edit her work until it was a finished, polished piece of TV journalism. The fact that she was doing the work on the Moon no longer impressed her.

She was splicing together scenes from three separate shoots, trying to put together a coherent report on the preparations that Moonbase was undertaking to face the impending Peacekeeper attack—without betraying any of the steps that might tip off the U.N. about what to

expect. Her footage dealt almost entirely with the human
side of the coming battle: the tiny medical staff getting
ready to handle wounded men and women; the highly-
trained technicians and engineers and scientists moping
in the Cave, their work, their careers, their lives in limbo
until this war was settled one way or the other; the silent
emptiness of the construction pit where the grand plaza
was going to be built. Nothing was moving there now,
not even a teleoperated tractor. All work on Moonbase's
future had been stopped.

She had scrupulously avoided the nanotech labs and
the plastics processing center, where Falcone was driving
the chemists to produce tons of foamgel. She had done
a long interview with Claire Rossi, already known to TV
viewers Earthside as Moonbase's first bride. Now Edith
revealed that Claire was pregnant, but could not return
Earthside because of the impending battle.

Good human interest stuff, Edith thought as she ed-
ited Claire's interview. It's a shame I couldn't get her to
cry, though.

The phone's chime startled her out of her concentra-
tion. She swivelled her chair from the editing screens to
the phone screen and tapped the ANSWER keypad.

A young male comm tech's face appeared on the
screen. "A call for you, Ms. Elgin. From Earthside."

"Earthside? I thought all links were shut down."

"This is coming in on a special laser-tight beam, from
Atlanta: a Mr. Edan McGrath."

Edith felt her eyes go wide. "McGrath? Put him on!"

Someone had once called McGrath the sexiest bald-
headed man on Earth. Looking at his image in the
phone screen, Edith thought he wasn't really sexy, but
he sure radiated energy and power.

"Mr. McGrath," she said, surprised at how humble
she sounded.

Three seconds later he said, "Edie, I wanted to tell
you that I think you're doing a fine job up there. An
excellent job! I'm proud of you."

She blinked with surprise. The top boss doesn't break
a U.N. blackout just to praise one of his reporters, Edith

told herself, even if I am his number one on-screen personality.

"Thank you," she said. Again, timidly.

McGrath hadn't waited for her response. He kept on talking. "After this is all over and you get back here, I'm going to *personally* see that you get a regular prime-time slot for yourself. No cohost, all yours. And a full-length documentary on your experiences up there. And a book deal, too. The only reporter at Moonbase. I've got to hand it to you, kid. You're the greatest."

It was the "kid" that broke Edith's spell. He wants something, she realized. Of course he does! He wouldn't go to the trouble of establishing a clandestine laser link unless he wanted something from me.

"I'm glad that you like what I'm doing," she said. "Now what's the reason for your call?"

When her words reached him, McGrath's brows hiked. Then he broke into a big, boyish grin.

"Can't fool you, can I?" he said, brushing at his mustache. Edith thought it had been considerably grayer the last time she'd seen him. He must be coloring it.

"The Peacekeepers' attack is imminent," he went on. "From what I've been able to find out, they'll come at you in another few days. A week, at most."

He stopped, waiting for her reply. Edith nodded and said, "That's the way it looks here."

"Okay," he said after the delay. "Here's my question. Can you cover the battle for us?"

"Cover the battle?"

He hadn't stopped for her reply. He was saying, "I know you're only one person, Edie, but I've been thinking maybe you could get some of the Moonbase people to handle cameras, give us a blow-by-blow, minute-by-minute eyewitness account of the fight. Like Ed Murrow did in London during the Blitz."

Edith knew who Edward R. Murrow was, but she wasn't certain of what the Blitz might be. She didn't fret over it. McGrath wants real-time coverage of the battle! I've got to tell Doug. This could be the biggest publicity break of all for Moonbase, showing the brave unarmed

Lunatics desperately trying to hold off an army of U.N. Peacekeepers with their missiles and guns and all. Wow!

"Can you do it?" McGrath asked, almost plaintively.

"Mr. McGrath," Edith said slowly, feeling the strength welling up inside her, "do you realize that if we show the battle in real-time, it's going to give Faure and the U.N. a terrible black eye? I mean, they'll look like monsters, attacking these unarmed people."

The three seconds were agony now. At last McGrath nodded grimly. "That's right. I'm fully aware of it. I was wrong to back Faure against Moonbase. It may be too late to save the base, but I want the Global's viewers to see what the little shit is doing to you. I want the *world* to see it!"

"Okay!" Edith said happily. "You've got it!"

He broke into a fleshy grin when her acceptance reached him. "Can you do it? How much of the battle can you actually show?"

Grinning back at him, Edith replied, "Moonbase has security cameras in every corridor, in every lab and workshop. And outside, too. I can show you the crater floor outside the base and even a view of the Mare Nubium, on the other side of the ringwall mountains. We'll get it all, don't worry."

Three seconds ticked by, then McGrath said, "Great! Do it. Don't worry about expenses."

She signed off, almost delirious with joy. But as she hurried down the corridors to find Doug and tell him that Global News was now on his side, she realized that what she would really be showing the world was how the Peacekeepers marched into Moonbase and either accepted a surrender or blew the place apart.

BASE DIRECTOR'S OFFICE

"Take a look," said Jinny Anson.

She touched the keyboard on her desk and the wall-screen lit up to show a satellite view of the beautiful crater Copernicus.

Doug paid no attention to the crater's symmetry, however. He stared at the array of tractors and other vehicles parked on the plain of Mare Imbrium, just outside Yamagata's base, Nippon One.

"No wonder they're not flying here on lobbers," Anson muttered. "There aren't enough rockets on the whole Moon to lift that much equipment."

Doug felt almost breathless. "There must be enough transport there for a thousand troops."

Bam Gordette, sitting on the other side of the table that butted Anson's desk, said quietly, "Not that many. More than half those vehicles'll be carrying food, water, air, ammo, missiles—logistics."

Doug sank back in his chair. "How many troops do you estimate, then?"

Gordette waggled a hand. "Three hundred, three-fifty, tops."

"That's enough to do the job," Anson said. To Doug. She pointedly kept from looking at Gordette.

Staring at the mass of vehicles parked out on the open mare, Doug muttered, "What we need is a good solar flare to knock them out."

"That would only postpone the inevitable," Anson said.

Doug looked at her, sitting behind her desk. "Jinny, you used to be a lot of fun to talk to. You're getting morose."

"Yeah, I've noticed that, too," she answered, straight-faced. "Wonder why?"

"How old is this information?" Doug asked, pointing at the wallscreen.

"This is real-time," she said. "The bird's made four passes over the region, so far."

"And they haven't tried to blind it or knock it off the air?"

"Why bother?" Gordette said. "If I was running their operation, I'd *want* you to see how much stuff we got."

"It is kinda depressing," Anson agreed—again, without looking Gordette's way.

"Who else has seen this?" Doug asked.

"Nobody," she replied sharply. "The bits are transmitted from the satellite to our computer and straight to my office. That's why I asked you to come here and see it. Not even Harry Clemens is getting this data."

"Good," Doug said. "It certainly is depressing."

"Three hundred troopers," Anson mused. "With missiles and all the other goodies."

"Well," Doug said, trying to brighten the mood, "at least we know they're still at Copernicus. They're not on their way here yet."

"Take 'em about two days to cover the distance?" Gordette asked.

"Just about," Doug replied.

"Two Earth days," Anson said. "Forty-eight hours. Maybe a little less if they push it."

Steepling his fingers almost as if in prayer, Gordette said, "Well, if they're gonna knock out your satellite, it'll be just before they haul ass and start on their way here."

"Why bother?"

"Standard operating procedure. No commander wants the enemy watching his route of march, if he can help it."

Anson looked from Gordette to the wallscreen and back again. "So if our bird goes off the air . . ."

"That means they're starting on their way here," Doug finished for her.

As if on cue, the wallscreen display broke into wild jagged streaks and then went blank.

The three of them rushed down to the control center, once they were certain that the reconnaissance satellite had actually been knocked out, and the dead wallscreen wasn't merely a malfunction somewhere in the communications system.

"You want to launch another recce bird?" Anson asked as they dashed along the corridor, hurrying past startled people.

"Not much sense to that," Doug said over his shoulder.

"Yeah," Gordette agreed. "Just be target practice for them."

The control center was calm, with its usual air of controlled intensity, the quiet hum of consoles, the flickering of display screens in the dimly lit chamber. Doug automatically glanced at the big wallscreen that displayed a schematic of the entire base. The usual scattering of red and yellow lights, but otherwise everything was operating normally.

Doug knew from hours of studying the ballistics that a nuclear-tipped missile could be launched from the L-1 station and reach Moonbase in less than an hour. Even faster if the Peacekeepers wanted to goose it, but Doug thought that they would want to take at least an hour so that they would have time to make pinpoint mid-course corrections. If his reasoning was correct, they would want the nuke to go off over the solar farms inside Alphonsus' ringwall after the Peacekeeper assault force had arrived on the other side of the mountains, shielded from the nuke's radiation pulse, and ready to cross Wodjohowitcz Pass as soon as the explosion had knocked out Moonbase's main electrical power supply.

The radar view of L-1 showed the same cluster of spacecraft hovering around the space station that Doug had seen the last time he'd looked.

"Can we get a visual?" he asked Jinny. "Turn one of the astronomical 'scopes on it?"

She nodded and walked off toward the technician who was monitoring the automated astronomical equipment sitting out by the central peak in the middle of Alphonsus.

Edith came tearing into the control center, breathless.

"Doug," she said, puffing as she skidded to a stop next to him, "McGrath wants me to pipe the battle Earthside in real time!"

"Who's McGrath?"

"The top boss! He owns Global News!"

Doug shifted mental gears as fast as he could; still, it took a few moments for him to realize what Edith was telling him.

"You'll show what's happening here when the Peacekeepers attack?"

"To the whole blazin' world!" Edith said, exultant.

For the first time in what seemed like years, Doug felt a genuine smile curving his lips. "Faure's not going to like that . . . not at all."

Through her sitting room window, Joanna could see a soft twilight descending on the garden and the woods beyond it. The trees had been planted there to cover up the view of Savannah's skyline and give the occupants of her house the feeling that they were truly out in the countryside rather than half a mile from the interstate.

"Global's going to broadcast the confrontation?" she asked Doug's image, grinning at her from the Windowall screen above the fireplace. She could not bear to use the word *battle* or *attack*. She knew that Moonbase could not win a battle or survive an attack.

"Edan McGrath himself called Edith and asked her to do it," Doug said after the three-second lag. "Real-time coverage; blow by blow."

"I've already got a pocketful of senators demanding an investigation of the president's handling of the Moonbase crisis," Joanna mused. "Coverage of the confrontation will show the voting public how you're being attacked by the U.N.'s Peacekeepers."

"This has got to stay confidential," Doug was saying, not waiting for her response. "We don't want Faure to know about it beforehand."

Joanna's brows knit. "But, Doug, maybe if we leaked the information Faure would call off the attack."

She watched her son's image in the display screen. Once he heard her words he shook his head. "The Peacekeepers are already on their way here, Mom. No one's going to call off the attack. Not now."

Alarm tingled through Joanna like an electric current. "You're certain?"

"In forty-eight hours or less we'll be able to see them coming across Mare Nubium."

Joanna suddenly felt as if someone had ripped out her insides. All these weeks she had known it would come to this, yet she realized now that she had desperately clung to an unconscious hope that it could all be averted.

"You'll have to surrender to them, then," she said dully.

Three seconds passed. Doug replied, "Maybe."

"You can't fight them! You don't have any weapons."

Again the agonizing wait. Doug said, "We don't have any guns, that's true enough. But we're not beaten yet."

"Doug, what are you thinking of? You can't fight an armed battalion of trained Peacekeeper troops! You'll get yourself killed! You'll destroy Moonbase!"

He hadn't waited for her response. He was saying, in a calm, carefully measured tone, "I can't tell you what we're planning, Mom, because even a tight-laser link spreads enough for some snooper to eavesdrop. But we're not going to obediently open our hatches and let the Peacekeepers take over Moonbase."

"Doug, they'll kill you!"

He smiled at her words. "If we surrender and have to return Earthside, I'm a dead man anyway."

Joanna started to reply, then realized that her son was right. He had nothing to lose by fighting for Moonbase.

*   *   *

"Naw, I don't mind working the night shift," Killifer was saying. "At least I'll be indoors, under the roof, if it rains."

The security chief looked slightly uneasy. "I don't usually put newcomers inside the house," he said, "but Jonesie's come down with some virus and we need a replacement for him right away."

"It's okay," Killifer repeated, trying hard not to sound eager. "I'll take his shift."

"You already did your regular shift; I don't like asking you to double up."

Killifer shrugged as carelessly as he could. "Four to midnight is easy. I wouldn't go to sleep until after midnight, anyway."

The chief swivelled back and forth slowly in his desk chair, making it squeak slightly, eying Killifer as if he weren't certain he was doing the right thing. Killifer sat in front of the little desk, doing his best to appear nonchalant.

Then he got an inspiration. "I get overtime pay for this, don't I?"

The chief visibly relaxed. "Yeah, sure. Time and a half."

Killifer nodded as if the money was his reason for agreeing to the extra shift so readily. "Double shift isn't so bad," he said. "It's only for a few days, right?"

"Yeah," said the chief. "Until Jonesie comes back."

"I'd just be spending my pay in some bar or someplace," Killifer said. "This way I make plastic instead of spending it."

"All right," the chief said, still uneasy. "Go downstairs and change into a regular uniform. You work with Rodriguez. He monitors the screens, in here, and you sit in the kitchen until she and her husband go to bed. Then you patrol the rooms once every half hour. Check all the windows and doors. Except the master bedroom; just make sure their door's shut tight. Pay particular attention to the sliders that go out to the pool deck."

"Right." Killifer nodded.

"Remember, she doesn't like to see us. Stay in the kitchen until they go up to the master bedroom."

"What about the butler?"

"He'll go to bed after they do," said the chief.

"Okay. Good."

Again the chief hesitated. Killifer could feel his pulse throbbing in his ears as he sat facing the man across the pathetic little metal desk.

At last the chief said, "All right. Go downstairs and get into your uniform."

Killifer got up from his chair slowly, turned and went to the office door.

"And thanks for filling in," the chief said. Reluctantly.

"Nothing to it," Killifer replied over his shoulder. He pulled the door open, then added, "I can use the extra plastic."

The bastard suspects something, Killifer said to himself as he stepped out into the hallway. Not enough to turn me down, but this doesn't sit right with him.

Then he grinned as he clattered down the metal spiral staircase. What the hell! Let him worry all he wants to. I'm in the house for two–three nights and she's home with her creaky old man. Once the butler goes to bed, I'll scope out the house and figure out the best way to get to her and then get away. Shit, they'll be *paying* me to do it. Overtime.

NANOLAB

Keiji Inoguchi was surprised by Professor Zimmerman's call. He hurried to the nanolab, eager to accept Zimmerman's invitation before the crusty old man changed his mind.

"I am most honored that you have asked me to visit your laboratory once again," he said, after he had bowed to the professor.

Zimmerman dipped his chin in acknowledgment. "I am asking for more than a visit, my friend. I need your help."

Inoguchi sucked in his breath. "My help? In what way can I help you?"

Zimmerman led the Japanese scientist back into the bowels of his lab. They walked past rows of computer screens and gray, bulky cryogenic tanks beaded with moisture, Zimmerman in his usual gray suit, grossly overweight, dishevelled, looking distracted and unhappy; Inoguchi in an immaculate white turtleneck shirt and sharply creased slacks, lean and eager, his eyes snapping at every piece of equipment as if they were cameras.

Hands jammed in his trouser pockets, Zimmerman said heavily, "I am relegated to assisting my former student, Professor Cardenas."

"Yes?"

"She has asked me to prepare nanomachines capable of repairing wounds inflicted by gunshot or shrapnel— flying metal from explosions."

"And you want me to assist you in this?" Inoguchi asked.

"I realize you represent the United Nations and are not to take part in the fighting," Zimmerman said. "But for medical work perhaps you are allowed to use your skills, yah? For humanitarian reasons."

"Of course," Inoguchi said without an instant's hesitation. "Humanitarian purposes come before politics and other considerations."

Zimmerman stopped in front of a lab bench that supported a massive metal sphere connected to a desktop computer by hair-thin fiberoptic cables.

"My staff." Zimmerman gestured to the sphere.

Inoguchi understood immediately. "Your processors."

"Yah," said Zimmerman, lowering his bulk onto a spindly looking stool. "Now we must teach them to build other nanos that will seal wounds quick, before the patient bleeds to death."

"Can you do this?"

The old man nodded slowly. "Yah. I have already done it once. Now I must do it again—in a day or so."

Inoguchi grinned at the professor. "We have much work to accomplish, then."

Colonel Giap did not relish being under Faure's direct supervision. The man is a politician, what does he know of military tactics? Giap asked himself. I should report to General Uhlenbeck, through the normal chain of command. Instead I must bear with this politician questioning every breath I draw.

He tried to reassure himself with Clausewitz's dictum that war is merely an extension of politics. It was scant consolation. Yes, politicians such as Ho Chi Minh successfully directed the liberation of Vietnam from the imperialists, he knew. But that was generations ago, and besides, Ho and his comrades had military experience of their own. Faure had probably never even fired a pistol at a target range.

"Was it wise to incapacitate their satellite?" the U.N. secretary-general was asking.

Giap, sitting on the bare floor of his closet-turned-office, replied to the image on his laptop's screen with all the patience he could muster, "It was necessary. Their satellite could observe our time of departure and our route of march. That would be giving the enemy more information than we want them to have."

He waited the three seconds, watching Faure twiddle his mustache. Then the secretary-general replied, "But by disabling their satellite, you have told them that you are ready to march."

"Yes. What of it? Don't you think they have cameras atop their ringwall mountains looking for us to appear over their horizon?"

Faure's face creased deeply once he heard Giap's comment. "Then of what good was it to cripple their satellite? I do not understand your reasoning."

They went around the subject twice more, Giap resolute and implacable, Faure irritable and demanding.

At last Giap said, "Sir, you may consider my action premature or even mistaken, but it has been done and argument will not undo it."

Faure flushed angrily once he heard the colonel's words.

Before he could say anything, Giap added, "If you wish to remove me from command, I understand entirely."

The secretary-general's eyes widened momentarily, then he quickly asserted his self-control. Forcing a smile that narrowed his eyes to slits, Faure made a soothing gesture with both hands.

"No, no, of course not, Colonel. I have every confidence in you."

Of course you do, Giap said to himself, now that our jump-off for the attack is only hours away.

"What you're looking at," said Edith into her pin mike, "is almost certainly a nuclear-armed missile."

The monitor screen in the little editing booth showed what Moonbase's astronomical telescope was focused upon: the clutch of spacecraft hovering around the big space station at the L-1 libration point some 58,000 kilometers above the Moon's surface. The picture, with Edith's commentary, was being broadcast live over Global News Network.

"Despite international agreements that date all the way back to 1967 banning nuclear weapons in space, the United Nations has brought a nuclear-armed missile here to use against Moonbase. Although Moonbase's residents . . ."

Doug watched Edith's performance as he suited up for another surface excursion. It's one thing to reveal to the world that Faure's going to nuke our solar energy farms, he told himself, it's something else to try to knock out the missile once they launch it against us.

Doug hitched a ride on one of the tractors carrying a team of construction workers out to the mass driver. It took the better part of half an hour to trundle the few kilometers in one of the electrically driven tractors. Doug thought that once this war was over, one of his immediate priorities was going to be developing faster ground vehicles. *This is assinine, creaking along at a top speed of thirty klicks per hour.*

Then he realized that the Peacekeeper battalion was chugging along at pretty much the same low speed, and he didn't feel so bad about it. *Besides,* he added silently, *by the time this war is over there might not be a Moonbase and you just might be dead.*

The Sun was up over the ringwall mountains, bathing the crater floor in harsh, brilliant light that cast long slanting shadows. It would remain daylight for another twelve days. The Peacekeepers remembered that the nanobugs Moonbase had used against them the first time were deactivated by solar ultraviolet.

The mass driver was crawling with spacesuited figures. Laser welding torches flashed against the dark bulk of the long metal machines. Doug clambered down from the tractor, leaving the construction team to drive a few hundred meters on, to where their cohorts were digging a trench for the prefab shelter for Wicksen's people.

The suit-to-suit radio frequency was alive with chatter, but Doug found Wicksen visually, from his slight form and the bright blue WIX stenciled on his backpack. There was so much crosstalk on the regular suit-to-suit frequency that Doug walked up to the physicist and tapped him lightly on the shoulder.

Wicksen seemed to recognize Doug's suit and held up three gloved fingers. Doug tapped frequency three on his wrist panel.

"I've saved this freak for private conversations," Wicksen's voice said in his earphones.

"How's it going?" Doug asked.

"Have they launched yet?"

"Not as of half an hour ago." Then he added, "I would've gotten a call if they'd launched while I was riding out here."

"We should have this kloodge put together in another ten or twelve hours."

"Good."

"But there won't be any time to test it."

"Then it better work right the first time," Doug said.

He could sense Wicksen shaking his head inside his helmet. "Nothing works right the first time. Haven't you ever heard of Murphy's Law?"

Ignoring that, Doug asked, "How soon will you have the extra electrical power connected?"

Pointing past the mass driver's long metal track, Wicksen answered, "The extra men you assigned me are doing that now. You're going to have a temporary brownout when we fire the gun."

"Better than having a nuclear explosion inside the crater," Doug said grimly.

Wicksen was silent for a long moment. Then he said, "Thanks for putting the construction crew to work for us."

"The numbers that the safety people ran on their computer said that four meters of regolith rubble should protect you from the radiation blast—if they got the yield from the bomb right."

"Whether it works or not, we all feel a lot better knowing we can sit in the shelter while we're running the gun. Thanks a lot."

"Nothing to it. The construction people have nothing else to do."

Turning back toward the mass driver, Wicksen made a wistful little sigh. "I sure wish we had time to test this beast."

"So do I," Doug said fervently. "So do I."

SAVANNAH

"But I must speak to *Seigo* Yamagata," said Ibrahim al-Rashid. "It is most urgent."

Rashid's office had once belonged to Joanna Brudnoy, when she had been chairman of Masterson Corporation's board of directors. Many was the time that she had summoned him into her sanctum and he had dutifully scurried to her in response. Once he had acceded to the chairmanship, however, Rashid had completely refurnished and redecorated the office. His desk was a sweeping, curving modernistic work of glass, his high-backed black leather chair custom-built to his measurements. The walls were adorned with tapestries from Persia and India, the windows were actually wallscreens that could display any of thousands of scenes stored in his personal computer's memory.

One of those screens now showed the image of a young Japanese man in an open-neck white shirt and tastefully checkered sports jacket, sitting at a desk in an office panelled in what appeared to be teak.

"Seigo Yamagata is not available at present," he said in the homogenized American English of a television announcer. "I am Saito Yamagata, his eldest son. May I be of assistance to you?"

"I must speak to your father," Rashid demanded.

The younger Yamagata smiled gently and said, "I regret to tell you once again that he is not available."

Rashid felt as if he were talking to a brick wall. Or

worse, a large soft pillow that absorbed his words without being moved by them in the slightest.

"This is important!"

"Of course it is," Yamagata agreed readily. "That is why the staff has routed your call to me, rather than some underling."

Rashid blinked with surprise. "You mean that you are in charge?"

His face going serious, the young man replied, "My father left instructions that you are to be received by his personal representative and no one else. That personal representative is me."

Sinking back in his cushioned leather chair, Rashid recognized the oriental manner of stonewalling: polite, gracious, accommodating, but stonewalling just the same.

"How may I help you?" Saito Yamagata asked solicitously.

Bowing to the inevitable, Rashid said, through gritted teeth, "I have received information that among the Peacekeeper troops marching on Moonbase there is a special contingent of Yamagata suicide bombers who intend to blow up Moonbase."

Yamagata's brows rose a couple of millimeters.

"Destroying Moonbase is idiotic!" Rashid snapped, unable to contain his temper any longer. "Our entire operation, my whole understanding with your father, depends on Moonbase providing helium-three for your fusion generators. How can they provide anything if the base is blown to bits?" He fairly shouted the question.

Saito Yamagata's expression had gone from polite interest to mild surprise to the absolute blank face of a man who has much to hide.

"Is your information trustworthy?" he asked softly.

"I have my sources both in United Nations headquarters and the Peacekeepers' chain of command."

"I see."

"This is a betrayal of our understanding," Rashid said harshly. "It also destroys the very thing that your father wants so badly—Moonbase."

The young man nodded. "The suicide bombers are

not Yamagata employees. They are volunteers from the Bright New Sun, an organization of fanatics that is allied with your own New Morality movement."

"Then how are they allowed to be with the Peacekeepers? Who permitted them to come to Nippon One?"

"My father accepted their . . ." Yamagata searched for the right word, " . . . their help, most reluctantly. You must understand that even in Japan, religious zealotry is a very powerful force."

"But you're going to allow them to destroy Moonbase!"

Yamagata smiled thinly. "Not at all. My father is not stupid. He bowed to the pressures of the Bright New Sun and allowed them to add a squad of kamikazes to the Peacekeeper force. But they will not be permitted to damage Moonbase. The Peacekeepers will take the base and there will be no need for suicide bombers."

Rashid closed his eyes for a few moments, trying hard to think it all through.

"Suppose," he said at last, "that the Peacekeepers fail to take Moonbase."

"Impossible," said Yamagata.

"They drove off the first attack, didn't they?"

Yamagata smiled again. "This time there are three hundred troops, armed with missiles and heavy weapons. A nuclear bomb will knock out Moonbase's electrical supply. This time they will not fail."

"But those people at Moonbase are very clever," Rashid insisted. "Suppose they stop the Peacekeepers?"

With a slight shrug, Yamagata said, "Then there will be no option except allowing the kamikazes to blow up as much of Moonbase as they can."

"But that is lunacy!"

"A clever play on words," the young man said, although his expression showed no humor.

"You can't let them blow up Moonbase!" Rashid yelled.

"The forces are in motion," said Yamagata. "How

they will play out remains to be seen. Even if Moonbase is entirely destroyed, it can be rebuilt."

"But . . . but—"

"Patience is a virtue, Mr. Rashid. Yamagata Industries will receive the U.N.'s mandate to operate Moonbase, no matter what condition the base may be in when the fighting is finished. If necessary, we will rebuild it. The important thing is that Moonbase will be in *our* hands."

It was not until that instant that Rashid realized he had put his future into the hands of ruthless men.

Only a few miles away, Joanna paced restlessly through the living room of her home.

"A new exercise regime?" Lev asked, stretched out on the big sofa across from the unused fireplace.

"How can you just sit there?" she blurted. "The Peacekeepers have already started their march to Alphonsus."

Her husband made a wry face. "What can we do about it? The decisions are in Doug's hands. Working ourselves into heart seizures won't help."

"If only we could get there . . . "

"And give Doug two more useless people to worry about?"

She whirled and rushed toward him. "Lev, call him. Talk to him. Make him understand that he's got to surrender! He can't fight the Peacekeepers! They'll kill everyone in Moonbase."

Slowly, like a weary old man, Lev swung his legs off the sofa and sat up. He grasped Joanna's wrist and pulled her down onto the cushion beside him.

"Listen to me, dear one. Doug understands the situation as well as we do, or better. He knows what he can do to defend the base—"

"Against missiles and nuclear bombs? You saw the news broadcast!"

Lev put a finger on her lips, silencing her for the moment.

"It isn't our decision to make," he said softly. "If I called him, not only would it distract him from the thousands of vital things he must think about, but I would end up agreeing with him—victory or death!"

Joanna stared at him as if he had gone mad. "Victory or . . . what are you saying?"

"Doug believes in Moonbase with all his soul," Lev replied. "To him, it is his world, his life. He won't want to live in a world without Moonbase."

"No," Joanna said, feeling weak with shock. "That can't be. Doug can come back here. He can live with us. I'll protect him, guard him . . ." Her voice faded into silence.

Lev shook his head. "Not all the fanatics belong to the New Morality, my darling. In his own very rational way, your son is a fanatic, too. That's what it takes to fight hopeless odds."

Joanna sank back into the sofa, stunned with the realization that Lev understood Doug better than she did.

And in the security office in the servants' wing of the house, Jack Killifer leaned over his partner's shoulder, grinning at the camera display of the Brudnoys in their living room.

Rodriguez glanced up at Killifer. "You ought to be in the kitchen. That's your post, not here."

Killifer grinned at him. "The entertainment's better in here."

MOONBASE

"There they are."

Doug stared at the smart wall display in Jinny Anson's office. Three columns of tracked vehicles had come up over the horizon and were moving majestically across the barren plain of Mare Nubium, churning up plumes

of dust from the regolith. He realized that the dust had
lain there undisturbed for billions of years. No, not really
undisturbed, he reminded himself. Meteoroids fell into
the regolith constantly, adding to it, grinding it up, creat-
ing the dust that the cleated tracks of the Peacekeeper
force were now violating.

The cameras atop Mt. Yeager and two other peaks in
the Alphonsus ringwall showed the approaching attack-
ers clearly. Ahead of the middle column rode a smaller
tractor, clean white except for a blue patch on its side.

"Can we get a close-up of that lead vehicle?" he
asked quietly.

Anson worked her keyboard and the view zoomed in
on the first tractor. The blue square was the U.N. em-
blem: a polar projection map of Earth on a sky-blue
background, surrounded by a pair of olive branches.

Doug snorted with disdain. Olive branches. The symbol of peace. Leading three columns of soldiers and
weaponry devoted to conquering Moonbase.

"We'd better get down to the control center," Anson
said. Her voice was hushed, strained, just as Doug's was.

"Right," he said tightly.

Robert T. Wicksen got the news in his helmet earphones. Automatically he looked across the crater floor
toward Wodjohowitcz Pass. From where the mass driver
stood, the pass appeared as little more than a dimple in
the ring of rounded smooth mountains.

"What about the missile at L-1?" he asked, his voice
shaking just slightly.

"Still sitting there," came the voice from the control
center.

Wicksen puffed out a relieved breath. "Keep me informed, please."

"Will do."

Clicking to the suit-to-suit frequency, Wicksen called
out, "Listen up, people. The Peacekeeper troops are
coming across Mare Nubium. The balloon will be going
up very soon now."

A dead silence greeted his warning. None of his exhausted team had a word to say.

Vince Falcone was swearing under his breath, but his mutterings were loud enough for one of his technicians to ask, "Repeat, please. I didn't get it."

"You don't want it," Falcone said into his helmet microphone.

He and six picked assistants were trying to spread the smart foamgel across the narrowest portion of Wodjohowitcz Pass from storage canisters on the backs of the tractors they were driving. The work was slow, tedious, and made exasperatingly difficult by the fact that the gel tended to clot in the hoses instead of flowing smoothly, as the chemists had promised.

When the clotting problem had first surfaced, hours earlier, Falcone had told his people merely to increase the pressure on the nitrogen gas they were using to force the gel out of the storage tanks. But nitrogen was rare and precious on the Moon, and Falcone quickly saw that they weren't going to have enough to do the job. He had originally wanted to use oxygen for the pressure gas, it was plentiful and cheap, but the chemists had worried that oxygen would react with the gel and change its chemical properties too much.

"Helium would be best," the chief chemist had mused. "If only we had enough helium . . ."

So they had settled on nitrogen, raiding the life support backup supplies for two dozen tanks of it. And now it wasn't doing the job.

Time and again, Falcone and his cohorts had to stop their tractors and physically clean out the jammed hoses with wire brushes that the chemists had provided them.

"Everything in chemistry comes down to plumbing," Falcone muttered to himself. "Might as well be cleaning a goddamned latrine."

A voice crackled in his earphones. "What I don't understand is why nobody's hardening the microwave antennas against radiation."

Falcone looked up from his work and tried to identify

the questioner as his voice continued, "I mean, like what good is this goop gonna do if the antennas are knocked out by the nuke's radiation pulse?"

Newman, Falcone decided. He never could see past his friggin' nose. "What happens if Wix's smart guys don't stop the nuke?" he demanded.

For a moment no one replied, then Newman said, "The warhead goes off above the crater floor, right?"

"And what happens then?"

"Uh . . . it knocks out the solar farms."

"And where do the antennas get their electricity?"

"From the . . . oh, yeah, I get it. If the nuke goes off the antennas are dead anyway, right?"

"So there's no sense sending anybody up to the top of Yeager to harden the antennas. *Capisce*?"

No response, although Falcone thought he heard stifled giggling from somebody.

A few minutes later his earphones chimed, so he dropped his brush and let the kinked hose fall gently to the ground as he tapped the keypad on his wrist.

A comm tech's voice announced, "Peacekeeper vehicles are in sight, crossing Mare Nubium."

"How long before they reach the pass?" he asked.

"Unknown. The thinking here is that they'll stop and camp at the foot of the ringwall until the nuke from L-1 hits."

Grunting an inarticulate reply, Falcone arched his back slightly and looked through his visor up to the top of Mt. Yeager, where the microwave transmitters stood. For the first time he realized that this entire "blue goo" business was totally untested.

Christ, I hope it works, he said to himself. If that nuke isn't stopped by Wicksen's zap gun, the microwave transmitters'll be knocked out and all our work will have gone for nothing.

And, he added as he bent stiffly to pick up the jammed hose again, we got a damned good chance of still being out here and getting fried to a crisp by the mother-humpin' nuke.

*   *   *

The control center was changed. The same hushed intensity, the same low-key lighting, the same hum of murmuring voices and purring electronic machines. Yet the air crackled now; the very smell of the control center was different: nervous, sweaty. It wasn't fear that Doug sensed from the technicians monitoring their consoles, so much as a focused motivation, anxiety masked by the duties of the moment.

Jinny Anson slipped into an unoccupied chair next to the U-shaped set of communications consoles, while Doug paced slowly through the big chamber, walking behind the seated technicians, glancing at each individual display screen. On one side of the room glowed the huge schematic display of Moonbase's systems. The opposite wall showed camera views of the approaching Peacekeeper armada and the spacecraft hovering around the L-1 space station.

Doug completed his circuit of the center and returned to Anson's chair.

"Everything we can do, we're doing," he said.

Anson looked up at him. "It's sweaty palms time now."

Looking at the view of the approaching Peacekeeper vehicles, Doug said, "The longer they take, the better it is for us. Time's on our side."

"For now," said Anson.

He nodded. "Better put out an announcement that all personnel without specific tasks for the defense of the base should meet in the Cave."

Anson hiked her brows. "Not stay in their quarters?"

"No, get them into the Cave. Food's there, and it'll be easier to deal with them if they're all together instead of strung out in their individual quarters. There might be fighting in the corridors; I don't want anybody hurt unnecessarily."

"Collateral damage," Anson muttered, turning to the console keyboard.

The editing booth felt hot and stuffy. Edith sat at the big board, watching the array of display screens half surrounding her, showing views of the approaching Peacekeepers and the spacecraft at L-1.

"The first shot in this battle has already been fired," she was saying into the microphone that sent her words Earthside. "The U.N. Peacekeepers knocked out a reconnaissance satellite that Moonbase had placed in orbit to observe the Peacekeepers' movements."

She pressed the stud that sent the view from Mt. Yeager's camera Earthward. "Now the Peacekeeper assault force is moving across Mare Nubium, approaching Moonbase. What you are seeing now . . . "

Georges Faure was far from composed as he sat in his office, watching the broadcast of Global News. He fidgeted in his big chair, seething with anger. To think that this woman, this slut of a reporter who had seduced him into allowing her to accompany the original Peacekeeper force to the Moon, to think that she was such a traitor, such a propagandist for the rebels—it exasperated him.

Yet a part of him was thrilled at the sight of the Peacekeeper armada crossing Mare Nubium. These are *my* troops, Faure told himself, marching under *my* orders. Let the news media say what they will, in a matter of hours Moonbase will be under *my* control, as it should be.

And if those rebellious fools attempt the resistance, they will be crushed. As they should be.

Colonel Giap compared the electronic map on the display screen of his tractor's cab with the view of Alphonsus' ringwall mountains looming before him. His tractor cab was pressurized and armored, so he could ride with the visor of his spacesuit helmet open. He could have made this journey in shirtsleeves, had he chosen to, but that would have meant that he would have to don his spacesuit once they arrived at their designated campsite. He had decided to endure the discomfort of forty-three hours in the spacesuit, instead.

Most of the trip he had spent worrying about nanomachines. Moonbase had no weapons to speak of, he knew, but what kind of devilish weaponry could their nanoscientists devise? Nanomachines had driven off the first Peacekeeper attack. Giap had chosen broad daylight to make his assault, but inside the tunnels of Moonbase the purifying effect of solar ultraviolet did not penetrate. That was why Giap had included special teams of civilians with powerful UV lamps to accompany his troops. He did not intend to be run off by invisible, insidious nanoweapons.

Their base camp location had been carefully chosen to position them close to the two easiest passes over the ringwall mountains, while still placing them within the sheltering lee of the mountains themselves. Those solid piles of rock would protect them from the radiation pulse of the nuclear explosion. There was no need to worry about blast effects in the lunar vacuum, but even if there were the mountains would shelter them, just as it will protect us from the radiation and heat pulse, Giap assured himself.

Still, a tendril of worry gnawed at him. The missile must be accurately aimed. And its warhead must be fuzed at precisely the correct altitude. If it goes off too soon, or its aim is a fraction of a degree off-target, we could be hit by the heat and radiation.

He reached out a gloved hand to touch the armored roof of the tractor's cab. Enough protection against a slightly misaimed nuclear warhead? he wondered. More likely the metal would serve as an efficient oven, to roast us all to death.

Shaking his head inside the helmet, he tried to push such fears away by attending to his duties. He established communications contact with L-1, although the link was weak and strained with harsh bursts of static. The tractor comm sets were far from satisfactory and sunspots or some other esoteric phenomenon could hash up communications quite maddeningly.

The image of a Peacekeeper junior officer appeared on the little screen, wavering slightly and streaked with electronic snow.

"We are on schedule," Giap informed the junior officer. "All my vehicles will be at their assigned base camp positions within two hours."

"Very well," came the woman's voice, through hissing static. "Missile launch will proceed on schedule unless you order otherwise."

"Yes, launch on schedule," said Giap, wondering how firm a comm link they would have once his vehicle was parked up close to the ringwall mountains.

THE WHITE HOUSE

"Madam President, you've got real troubles with this Moonbase business."

The president gave her staff chief a chilling look, the kind that had been known to cause lesser men to write out their resignations.

The chief of the White House staff was an old hand at this kind of thing, though; he had been with the president since she had first run for the Senate, many elections earlier.

"I mean," he said, hunching forward in the Kennedy rocker in front of her broad, modern desk, "the poll numbers are changing so fast we can't keep up with them."

"The trend?" she snapped.

"Swinging steadily in favor of Moonbase. Those news broadcasts Global's airing are turning the public's opinion around a hundred eighty degrees."

The president turned her chair away from this man she knew so well, away from his earnest, worried face and the problems that slumped his shoulders. She looked out through the long windows to the flower garden that had soothed both Roosevelts and everyone else who had sat at this apex of power in the Oval Office.

"I mean it, Luce," her staff chief said, "this has turned into real trouble."

"What about the New Morality?" she asked, still without looking at him.

He did the unthinkable. He got up from the rocking chair and walked around her desk, forcing her to face him.

Bending his knees slightly and leaning his liver-spotted hands on them so his eyes were on the same level as his, he said gently, "They're not going to be enough, Luce. The public's demanding that you do something."

She glared at him and swung back to the desk. He returned to the rocking chair.

"Are you telling me that O'Conner and Previs and all the other New Morality leaders are abandoning me on this?"

"No, not at all," he said, raising his hands. "The hard core of the Faithful are with you as much as they've ever been. They see this fight on the Moon as the battle between the forces of good and the evils of nanotechnology."

"So where's my problem?"

"It's the peripherals," he said with a sigh. "You've got the hard core, they're solidly with you. But the hard core isn't that many votes, Luce! The New Morality's real strength has been in its numbers, yeah, but most of those numbers aren't fanatics. They're ordinary folks who think the New Morality's ideas about cleaning up crime and vice are pretty good."

"And now?"

"Now they're looking at their television screens and seeing the big, bad U.N. attacking poor little Moonbase. And most of those people at Moonbase are Americans."

"Who use nanomachines."

The staff chief shook his head. "The voters don't care that much about the nanomachines. What's getting them worked up is the sight of a bunch of Americans getting attacked by the Peacekeepers—who are mostly foreigners."

"But they elected me because I pushed the nanotech treaty."

"That's not important to them now. As long as the Moon people keep their nanomachines on the Moon, the average American voter doesn't care a gnat's fart about it."

The president glared at her staff chief for long icy moments.

He gave her a weak grin. "Don't blame the messenger for the message," he said.

She huffed at him, then reached out and flicked on her desktop computer. "I want to see these numbers for myself."

The staff chief leaned back in the rocker and watched her face as the data from the constantly ongoing public-opinion poll flickered across her screen.

When she finally looked up at him she asked, "What should I do?"

"Call Faure and tell him to back off, maybe?"

"Don't be ridiculous! It's much too late for that."

"At least tell him that you're concerned about the safety of the American citizens at Moonbase."

"But they've declared their independence! They don't want American citizenship!"

"We don't know if that's just a ploy or not. Either way, there're probably a lot of men and women up there who want to keep their citizenship and come back to the States as soon as they can."

The president shook her head. "I can't weasel on Faure. I've been one of his strongest supporters! If I turn on him now, the word of this Administration will be worthless all around the world. Nobody would trust us again."

"I'm thinking about your reelection campaign."

She waved a hand in the air. "That's next year, for god's sake. By that time Moonbase will be under U.N. control and this whole flap will be forgotten."

Her staff chief still looked worried.

"All right," the president said, "so Yamagata will be running Moonbase and taking over the spacecraft market. If Masterson Corporation goes for it, what am I going to do about it?"

"Once the opposition starts gnawing on that bone . . . "

She shook her head stubbornly.

"They're already starting to make noises in the Senate," he insisted. "Joanna Brudnoy's been talking with half the committee chairmen on the Hill."

"It's a fait accompli," the president said curtly. "In another forty-eight hours or so the Peacekeepers will have taken over Moonbase and this whole problem will resolve itself."

"Maybe," the staff chief said softly. "But what happens if Moonbase drives the Peacekeepers off? They did it once, you know."

She scoffed at him. "That's impossible and you know it."

"Yeah. But still . . . "

"Don't you intend to sleep?" Lev Brudnoy asked his wife.

Joanna sat in the exact center of the largest sofa in their living room, her eyes riveted to the big Windowall screen above the dark fireplace.

"I couldn't sleep if I tried, Lev," she replied. "Not with this going on."

The screen showed the view from the cameras atop Mt. Yeager. The Peacekeepers' vehicles were slowing to a halt at the base of Alphonsus' ringwall mountains. They were arranging themselves in a single thin, undulating line that snaked along the flank of the mountains, each newly arriving tractor taking its position at the end of the constantly growing line. The cameras' resolution was fine enough to spot individual soldiers, if any appeared, but the vehicles stayed tightly buttoned up. Joanna could see the spokes of their springy wheels and the cleats on the tractors' treads, but no person got out of the vehicles.

They're waiting, Joanna thought. Waiting for the missile that will be launched from L-1. Then they'll attack. They'll storm Moonbase, and Doug will try to stop them and they'll kill my son and destroy everything.

Brudnoy sank his lanky frame onto the sofa next to her, murmuring, "At least we could go upstairs and watch from bed. Nothing is going to happen for another nine or ten hours, at least."

"You go if you're getting sleepy," Joanna said, not moving her eyes from the screen. Edie Elgin had been speaking for nearly an hour, but now her voice had stopped and the screen was silent.

He shrugged and sat beside her for several minutes. "This is like watching ice melt," he grumbled. "It's hypnotic. Don't you feel your eyes growing heavy? Sleepy? Drowsy?"

Joanna poked at him with her elbow. "Stop it, Lev!"

"At least come up to bed," he urged. "The screen up there will show the same picture, I assure you."

"No."

Brudnoy got slowly to his feet, then bent down to put his bearded face in front of Joanna's, noses almost touching.

"My darling wife," he said, blocking her view of the screen. "I have seldom insisted on my rights as your lord and master—"

"My what?"

"But there comes a time when a man must do what a man must do. Either you come up to the bedroom with me, or I will be forced to carry you."

"We're not on the Moon, Lev," Joanna said, smiling at him despite herself. "You'll give yourself a hernia."

"That will be entirely your fault, not mine," he said, very seriously. With that, he reached one arm around her shoulders and the other beneath her legs.

"All right!" Joanna yelped. "All right! I'll go upstairs. I'll go with you."

Brudnoy straightened up. "Good," he said, offering her his hand.

And as she allowed her husband to help her up from

the sofa and started for the bedroom, Jack Killifer—
watching from the dining room door that he had opened
a crack—also said, "Good," in a whisper that only he
could hear.

Doug was nervously munching a sandwich, sitting on
one of the spindly chairs in front of a console in the
control center. Like his mother, like the millions of people Earthside watching Global News, like the men and
women who had gathered in the Cave to wait out the
battle, Doug was watching the camera views from Mt.
Yeager.

"They're not doing anything," he murmured.

Bam Gordette, standing slightly behind Doug like a
bodyguard, said, "That's the army: hurry up and wait."

Doug thought that the thirty-klicks-per-hour pace of
the Peacekeepers' vehicles hardly qualified as hurrying
up, but they were definitely waiting now.

The control center had settled into a waiting mode
also. Everything that could be done to prepare Moonbase's defenses had been done. Nick O'Malley paced
nervously a few consoles away, hoping that his dust
would work as he had promised. Vince Falcone and his
crew had finally come back from Wodjo Pass, grumbling
and griping about the foamgel's intractability, but satisfied that they had covered as much of the pass as they
could.

Wix and his people are still working on the particle
gun, Doug knew. They're the key to our defense, the
crucial link in the chain. If they can't stop that nuclear
missile, we might as well surrender. We'll *have to*
surrender.

Nothing had moved out on the Mare Nubium for at
least an hour.

"They're waiting for the missile strike," Doug said to
no one in particular.

As if in response, one of the comm techs sang out,
"They've launched! Rocket flare from L-1. Their missile's heading our way."

MASS DRIVER

Robert T. Wicksen was still outside, checking the wiring connections from the main magnets to the hastily installed switching panel, when the word came from the control center:

"L-1's launched their bird."

By reflex, he looked up. Instead of the sky he saw the inside of his helmet, dark and confining.

"How much time do we have?" he asked calmly.

"Wait one," the comm tech's voice said in his earphones. Then he heard her muttering, "Doppler plot . . . burn rate . . . acceleration—looks like . . . one hundred thirty-six minutes, according to the computer."

"Two and a quarter hours."

"If they don't light a second stage."

"Keep me informed."

"Will do."

Switching to the suit-to-suit frequency, Wix told the four volunteers still working with him, "We have two and a quarter hours. Double-check everything."

The spacesuited figures bent to their work.

"That's the nuke," Doug muttered.

"Must be," said Jinny Anson. Like Doug, she was staring at the screen showing the blunt-nosed missile. It seemed to be hanging in space now that its rocket engine had shut down; the stars in the background did not move.

Two and a quarter hours, Doug thought. What have

we forgotten to do? Looking up, he traced the glowing lines on the electronic map of the base that covered one entire wall of the control center. Water factory, environmental control center, electrical power—they're as protected as they'll ever be. Turning to the insect-eye array of screens at the console he had commandeered, Doug saw displays of Wodjohowitcz Pass and the crater floor. Off near the brutally short horizon he could barely make out the antlike forms of Wix and his volunteers still tinkering at the mass driver.

Another screen showed the crowd in the Cave. They seemed calm enough. They're safe, he told himself. Even if Wix's gun fails and the nuke blasts out the solar farms, they'll be unharmed. We'll have to surrender, I guess, but they'll be safe.

Then a new fear assailed him. If they knock out our electrical power, we'll only have a few hours worth of juice from the backup fuel cells. The Peacekeepers must have emergency power generators with them. They've got to! Otherwise everybody here will die in a couple of hours, asphyxiated from lack of air to breathe.

The Peacekeepers won't want to kill us all, he told himself. They'll have emergency power supplies with them. Otherwise this'll be a slaughter.

"Why aren't you in the Cave?" Kris Cardenas asked.

Zimmerman looked up from the scanning probe electron microscope's image-intensifier screen at his unexpected visitor. Keiji Inoguchi, on the other side of the room at the processor control board, stared at the sandy-haired, trim-figured Cardenas as if she were a video star.

"And why should I be at the Cave? Am I expected at a party?"

"Everyone who's not assigned to a defense task is supposed to go to the Cave."

"Pah!" Zimmerman snapped his fingers.

"Doug Stavenger's orders," Cardenas said.

"So why are you not in the Cave?" Zimmerman demanded.

She grinned as if she enjoyed fencing with him. "I'm

on duty at the infirmary. I just ran up here to see how much of a supply of therapeutic nanobugs you had left for us."

"We are still working on them," Zimmerman said.

Turning her cornflower blue eyes to Inoguchi, Cardenas asked, "And you're helping him?"

Inoguchi bowed deeply, then replied, "It is my privilege to assist Professor Zimmerman, yes."

"But you're one of the U.N. inspectors, aren't you?"

"Yes, that is true. But the medical work we are doing here is beyond the scope of politics."

Zimmerman scowled. "He's learning everything he can in preparation for running the nanolab once Yamagata takes over the base."

Inoguchi looked stricken. "I am assisting you for humanitarian reasons!"

"You are spying on me," Zimmerman grumbled.

"Now Willi," Cardenas intervened, "you can't attack Professor Inoguchi like that! It's not polite and it isn't fair."

"Yah. Of course. Only it is true."

"It's not Professor Inoguchi's fault that we're being attacked," Cardenas said. "I think it's very generous of him to assist us."

Inoguchi said, "I am most honored to work with you both."

"And looking forward to running this lab once the Peacekeepers have driven us out," Zimmerman insisted.

Squaring his shoulders visibly, Inoguchi said, "Yes, that is true. What would you expect me to do, go back to Japan and allow someone else to take over this laboratory?"

Cardenas laughed. "He's right, Willi. Why shouldn't he want to run this facility? It's the most advanced in the world."

"In the solar system!" Zimmerman corrected.

To Cardenas, Inoguchi said, "I have offered a position here to Professor Zimmerman. I would be most honored if you, a Nobel Laureate, would remain here to continue your work."

Cardenas replied, "Assuming that the Peacekeepers actually do take over the base."

"And hand it over to Yamagata Industries," Zimmerman groused.

Inoguchi snapped his chin down in a nod that almost became a little bow.

Her smile fading, Cardenas said, "Would you offer a position to my husband, as well? He's a neurosurgeon. I won't stay here if he can't."

Inoguchi immediately answered, "Yes, of course."

"Most of the work Pete's done has been by virtual reality link Earthside, since we've come up to Moonbase," Cardenas mused, thinking out loud. "If he can continue doing that he'll stay. Otherwise we'll have a problem."

"Perhaps I can obtain an appointment with Tokyo University for him," Inoguchi said. "Or Osaka. He could remain at Moonbase indefinitely and work with his colleagues through electronic links."

"Is your husband at the Cave?" Zimmerman asked sourly.

"No," Cardenas said, turning her attention to the old man. "He's at the infirmary, ready to help the medics with any surgery that might be needed."

"I sincerely hope that it will not come to that," Inoguchi said.

"So do we all," said Cardenas.

Claire Rossi felt as if she were in a nightmare. She moved through the crowd milling around in the Cave with nothing to do, nowhere to go, and the vision of that missile hanging over her head in the big wallscreens.

"Can I buy you lunch?"

Whirling, she saw Nick O'Malley, big, lumbering redhead, grinning down at her.

"Nick! Why aren't you in the control center?"

"They let me out to eat now and then," he said, sliding an arm around her waist. "Come on, I'll buy you the best soyburger in town."

He kept up a cheerful patter as they picked up trays

and made their selections from the stainless steel dispensers. Once they were seated at a table for two off in a far corner of the Cave, O'Malley dug into his burger.

But Claire found she had no appetite. "I can't eat anything," she said, sliding her plate away from her.

O'Malley pushed it back. "Hey, you're eating for two, you know. Got to keep up your strength."

She looked up at the wallscreen, with the missile hanging there like the finger of death pointed at them.

"They're going to kill us all, aren't they?" she said, her voice choking in her throat.

O'Malley clutched her hand. "Nobody's going to get killed. We're safe and snug in here."

"Don't try to kid me, Nick. Without electrical power we're done."

"If they nuke the solar farms—and that's an *if*, mind you—Doug will surrender and the Peacekeepers will come in without firing a shot. Nobody's going to die in defense of Moonbase, don't you worry."

"You're certain?"

O'Malley's florid face turned solemn. "Listen, Claire darling. I'm stationed in the control center, running the dust. I'll be right beside Stavenger. If he doesn't surrender I'll clout him on the head and take over. I'll surrender for him, if I have to."

Claire tried to smile for him, but she wondered if her husband really had the strength to do what he promised.

"We've got a second-stage burn!" the comm tech yelped.

Wicksen jerked with surprise. "What?"

"Second-stage burn," she repeated. "They held off on it until they made their midcourse correction. Accelerated by a factor of two, at least. Computer's chewing on the numbers."

"How much time do we have?" Wicksen asked, feeling frightened for the first time.

"Looks like . . . forty-two minutes."

"By all the saints in heaven," Wicksen muttered. "All right, thanks for the bad news."

Banging the suit-to-suit key on his wrist pad, Wix called out, "New data. We've got forty minutes, max."

The four spacesuited figures all turned toward him.

"I know it's not enough time," Wicksen said. "Power up the magnets. Check out all the connections. I'll slave the pointing system to the control center's radar plot."

"Better warn the base they're gonna get browned out," one of his assistants said.

"Right," said Wicksen, running as fast as he could in the cumbersome spacesuit to the jury-rigged set of pointing magnets.

This has got to work the first time, he said to himself. It's got to! If there's a saint in heaven who can cancel Murphy's Law for a few minutes, now's the time to do it.

It was as close to prayer as Wicksen had ever come.

Jack Killifer fidgeted nervously in the kitchen of Jo-anna Brudnoy's house. The closer he got to his goal, the more jittery he felt.

Stop it! he commanded himself. Calm yourself down.

He wasn't afraid to kill Joanna Brudnoy, nor her Russian feeb of a husband. It was getting away with it that worried him. Sure, his ID in the Masterson files had been artfully faked. Anybody looking for his picture or prints in the computer would get a totally artificial set of pixels. Nobody was going to trace him that way.

It was the other security personnel that worried him. They knew his face. Even with the mustache and change in his hair color, they'd be able to identify him.

General O'Conner'll take care of me, he tried to assure himself. The Urban Corps had plenty of resources. They could provide him with a complete alibi, show the police that Killifer had been on assignment in Tacoma or Timbuktu, all neatly filed in their computer records.

They had outfaced Interpol, for god's sake, when the international investigators had come asking about Tamara Bonai's death. Thanks to O'Conner's people, Killifer had an iron-clad alibi and Doug Stavenger's identification had been tossed aside. The cops didn't trust virtual reality evidence, anyway: too easy to fake or spoof.

But why did O'Conner insist on me doing this alone? Killifer asked himself again and again.

"God's work has to be done by God's people, Jack," the general had told him. *"It would be wrong to bring in an outsider. Wrong, and dangerous. The fewer people know about this, the better off we are."*

He wouldn't have to bring in outside people, for crap's sake, Killifer growled to himself. He could get a dozen Urban Corps volunteers or people from one of the other New Morality groups. Shit, they've knocked off hundreds of people over the past few years. Why do I have to take on Joanna Brudnoy alone?

Because you're the one who wants to do her, the answer came to him. O'Conner doesn't give a fuck about Joanna; this is *your* vendetta, not his. That's why he won't give you any support, any backup.

Okay, he told himself, trying to steady his trembling hands. She's in the bedroom with her old man. You're the only security guard inside the house, except for Rodriguez monitoring the security cameras down in the servants' quarters. You just go upstairs and pop her. The husband, too. Maybe they're screwing and you can get them both with one shot. He almost laughed at the thought.

But what then? Killifer had rehearsed his moves a thousand times in his mind, but it still didn't come out right. Rodriguez won't hear the shots, he's too far away, too many walls between him and the bedroom.

Okay. Once you leave the bedroom Rodriguez can see you on the security cameras. So you go back to the kitchen and out to the garage, just like you're doing your regular rounds. Only, you get into your car and get the fuck out of here before he figures out that they're dead up in the bedroom.

And then what? Drive straight to Atlanta, he told himself. Straight to Urban Corps headquarters and General O'Conner. Let them hide your car. Stick close to the general, make sure he'll protect you if the cops or Masterson's security people come after you.

That'll work, he tried to assure himself. It'll be okay. O'Conner'll have this killing on me, but I'll have something on him, too: his helping me to get away with it.

Grimacing, he slid the heavy machine pistol out of the oiled holster at his hip and popped its magazine. Fully loaded, ready to go. He slid the magazine back into place, then worked the action with a metallic *click-click*, jacking a round into the firing chamber.

Making certain the safety was off, Killifer carefully slipped the pistol back into its holster, then pushed himself up from the kitchen table and started off toward Joanna Brudnoy's bedroom.

CONTROL CENTER

The astronomical telescope's view showed the incoming missile pointing at them, more and more of a nose-on view as it sped to its target in the crater Alphonsus. Doug watched the display screen almost as if hypnotized.

"For what it's worth," came a man's voice from beside him, "the dust containers are all in place."

Turning, Doug saw Nick O'Malley's muscular form sitting beside him. The man seemed much too heavy for the little wheeled chair; it looked as if the chair would collapse under him at any moment.

"Back from the Cave so soon?" Doug asked.

O'Malley nodded. "Nobody's got much of an appetite just now."

Doug saw Gordette standing a few paces away. "Bam, when's the last time you took a break?"

"I'm okay," Gordette said, folding his arms over his chest.

"Go grab a bite to eat," Doug ordered. "While there's still time."

"I'm okay," Gordette repeated stolidly.

"That's the nuke?" O'Malley asked, pointing to the screen on Doug's console.

"That's it."

"How soon?"

"Should hit in twenty-five minutes or less."

"What's Wicksen waiting for?"

"He knows what he's doing," said Doug, wishing he felt as confident as he was trying to sound.

Then the overhead lights, always dim inside the control center, went off altogether. The display screens wavered and faded, hundreds of electronic eyes blinking, then steadied. A low moaning gasp echoed through the rock-walled chamber.

"It's okay!" Doug yelled. "Wicksen's powering up the beam gun. We expected this. The auxiliary power system's cut in."

Still he felt the cold hand of fear clutching his innards.

"Power's up to ninety percent," said the physicist.

Wicksen, bending over the makeshift control board inside the buried emergency shelter, saw a swath of green lights interspersed with a handful of yellows. No reds, he told himself. So far, so good.

"Power to max," he said quietly.

There was no whine of generators spinning up, no vibration from powerful machinery. Just the low background hum of electrical gadgetry in the cramped, round-ceilinged little shelter. The five of them had taken off their helmets; there'd been no time to get out of the suits entirely. Nor any inclination to do so.

Two red lights suddenly glowered at Wicksen. "Main buss has cut out," he said, tension edging into his voice.

"On it," said the only woman among his assistants. "I'll have to run a diagnostic."

"No time. Go to the backup."

"Right."

The red lights remained, but a new pair of greens lit

up. Wicksen glanced at the countdown clock: fourteen minutes remaining until impact.

"How's the pointing system?" he asked.

"It's tracking okay. Hardly any movement, the bird's coming right down our throats."

"Makes life simpler," Wicksen murmured.

"Magnets are at full power."

He nodded, blew out a breath through puffed cheeks, then leaned his right index finger on the firing button.

A multitude of red lights sprang up on the board.

"What the hell?"

"Main buss shorted out!" the woman shouted. "Back-up's malfunctioned!"

Wicksen swore under his breath. Murphy's Law. Turning toward her, he saw that her face look agonized.

"What's the problem?" he asked calmly. Twelve minutes to impact.

"I don't know," she said, voice jittery, as she stared at the instruments in front of her.

Three minutes later Wicksen had satisfied himself that the main buss itself was functioning properly.

"It's the wiring," he said, reaching for his helmet. "The connections must have come loose."

"That can't be!" said the man who had done the wiring job.

"Can't be anything else," said Wicksen simply, as he pulled his helmet over his head.

"You're not going out there! With the nuke less than ten minutes from detonation!"

"Somebody's got to."

"Let me," said the man who had done the wiring. "It's my responsibility."

"We'll both go," said Wicksen.

Colonel Giap had taken the precaution of having the seven suicide volunteers placed in the same tractor with him. He wanted them under his eye; he was not willing to take chances that such fanatics might strike off on their own once the action started.

The American woman especially intrigued him. She

was not young, and she certainly did not seem fanatical. Giap wondered what could have happened in her life to make her want to embrace death.

So he asked her. There was scarcely any privacy in the tractor, crowded with troops and the seven volunteers, all in spacesuits, but once they were safely parked in the lee of Alphonsus' ringwall mountains, Giap clambered down onto the dusty regolith soil for a quick inspection of his vehicles.

Once satisfied that all the vehicles were properly positioned and there were no problems with the troops— except the usual complaints of soldiers everywhere—he returned to his own tractor. Instead of re-entering it, however, he ordered the American woman outside.

She came without a murmur and stood before him, an anonymous, sexless figure in a white spacesuit. Giap connected their two helmets with a communications wire, so they could speak without using their suit radios.

"I want to know," he said without preamble, "how reliable you and your comrades are going to be."

Without hesitation she replied, "Faithful unto death. That is our motto."

"A motto is one thing. Soon we will be in action."

This time her response took a few moments. At last she said, "We are pledged to give our lives to the cause of eliminating the scourge of nanotechnology. When the time comes, we will not hesitate to act."

"I'm certain," Giap said. "What concerns me is—what if the time does not come?"

"Does not . . . I don't understand."

"Soon a pair of missiles will knock out Moonbase's entire electrical generation capability. They will be forced to surrender, or die within a few hours from lack of air to breathe. There will be no need for you to sacrifice yourselves."

"Oh, I see. You want to know if we will obey your orders."

"There will be no need to blow up Moonbase—and yourselves."

"If all goes as you have planned."

"Well?"

"You have nothing to fear," she said easily enough. "Our pledge includes that promise to obey the authority over us. For the time being, that authority is you, Colonel."

All well and good, Giap thought. But still he had no inkling of why this woman—or any of her comrades—was willing to throw away her life.

As if she could read his mind, she said, "You are wondering why I am not married and mothering children, or building a career for myself."

"Yes," he confessed. "Why have you volunteered to kill yourself?"

"Because I want to die."

"But why?"

Without hesitation she began to tell him: of her abused childhood, of her disastrous first marriage, of her slowly evolving awareness that she was homosexual, of her second husband's violence, of the years she spent in mental hospitals, of the casual rapes by hospital staff and the even more casual applications of mind-altering drugs in an effort to "rehabilitate" her.

Giap wanted to vomit long before she was anywhere near finished. He realized why she thought quick death preferable to continued life.

To interrupt her, he looked at the watch on his wrist-pad. Stopping her unbroken flow of misery, he said, "We must return to the tractor now. The missiles will be reaching their targets soon."

"It's the wiring, all right," said Wicksen's assistant. "My fault, Wix. I did a damned sloppy job. I was so rushed—"

"No time for that now," Wicksen said. Pointing to the equipment still strewn on the ground around the mass driver, he said, "We've only got a few minutes to get it fixed."

The man seemed to freeze for several heartbeats, standing immobile in his spacesuit. Then he said only, "Right." And started for the equipment.

It's not going to do any good, Wicksen thought. We can't get this wiring repaired and then power up the magnets again and get everything running in ten minutes. It's just not enough time. But he bent to his task, forcing all other thoughts out of his mind.

Until his earphones screeched, "Here it comes!"

He jerked up, saw nothing but the looming dark hulk of the mass driver. Then something jarred him off his feet. He sailed like a feather, floating, floating, until he slammed painfully into the ground.

He saw stars flashing, then nothing but darkness.

I'm dead, Wicksen thought. The nuclear warhead went off and it killed me. But why does my head hurt?

Doug and the others in the control center had been sitting tensely, waiting for Wicksen's beam gun to disable the nuclear warhead.

The main overhead lights came on.

"What the hell?" Anson muttered loudly enough for Doug to hear.

"They've powered down the beam gun," a technician's voice said.

"Did they hit the warhead?" Doug wondered aloud.

"How could they know whether they've knocked it out or not?" Anson demanded. "They oughtta be shooting at it until it hits the frickin' ground."

Getting up from his chair, Doug called to the chief communications technician, several seats way from his own, "Can you get Wicksen for me?"

She nodded and worked her keyboard. All eyes in the control center focused on her—or on the screens showing the missile warhead streaking toward them.

"No joy," said the comm tech.

The whole chamber shuddered. Doug felt the solid rock floor beneath his feet vibrate as if a major moonquake had struck.

"The missile hit!" a technician's voice rang out. "Dove straight into the friggin' ground."

"But there wasn't any flash," someone said.

"Radiation counters are quiet."

"Our nuclear reactor just went off-line," said another technician, his voice high and quavering. "Backup power system is down."

Doug looked from one screen to another in the insect-eye array on the console before him. It took him a few moments to realize what had happened.

"It wasn't the nuke!" Jinny Anson's voice sounded exultant. "They sent the conventional bomb first!"

"To check their guidance accuracy," Doug said, his breath shuddering. He half-collapsed back onto the wheeled chair.

"And to see what we had to throw against it," Gordette added.

Doug looked across to O'Malley. Sweat was trickling down his beefy cheeks.

"It wasn't the nuke," O'Malley echoed, sounding relieved, grateful.

"Yeah, okay, but they got our backup generator," Anson said. "Now if they knock out the solar farms we're out of it."

"Another launch from L-1," a comm tech announced.

"*That's* the nuke," said almost everyone in the control center simultaneously.

MASS DRIVER

Slowly, Wicksen pulled himself up to a sitting position. If I'm not dead yet I soon will be, he thought. Radiation poisoning.

Except for the throbbing pain in the back of his head, though, he felt all right. He tried to rub his eyes, but his gloved hands bumped into the visor of his helmet. Feeling sheepish, he looked around. His assistant was on his knees, getting slowly to his feet.

"You okay?" Wicksen asked.

Before the man could answer, Wicksen's helmet earphones buzzed with an incoming message. He punched the proper key on his wristpad, noting with a bit of a shock that his radiation dose patch was still a pale chartreuse.

"Wicksen here," he said, surprised that his voice sounded so calm.

"This is Doug Stavenger," he heard in his earphones. "What happened?"

"We didn't have time to fix—wait a minute! Are you running on auxiliary power or not?"

"The missile took out our nuclear generator. It was a conventional warhead. Their nuke is on its way, launched four minutes ago."

"You mean we've still got two hours to get this kloodge working?" Wicksen felt elated.

"Can you do it?"

Despite his cumbersome spacesuit Wicksen jumped to his feet, not so difficult a trick in the low lunar gravity. "We'll do our best," he cried, overjoyed at still being alive.

Killifer checked his wristwatch before starting out on his regular rounds through the house. With Rodriguez watching everything through the security cameras, Killifer wanted to make it all seem normal, dull routine. Don't give the dumb spic any reason to think anything's out of the ordinary.

It was a big house, and Killifer didn't want to look hurried. He made his way from the kitchen through the dining room and living room, then into the foyer, where he carefully checked the front door to see that it was properly locked. Across the front hall and into the library, then the entertainment room, checking each of the French windows that opened onto the patio.

Unconsciously licking his lips, he started up the back stairs, past the monstrosity of a grandfather's clock

where the security team kept a pair of submachine guns
stashed away. Maybe I should take one of them, he
mused. But he decided against it. His pistol held fifty
rounds, plenty to do the job. Besides, taking one of the
stutter guns from the clock would alert Rodriguez—if he
was watching the screens instead of his favorite video
show. Be just my luck to have him spot me.

So Killifer passed the loudly ticking clock on the landing and went on up to the second floor. All the bed-
rooms up there were unoccupied, he knew, except the
master bedroom, but his job was to enter each one and
check each window.

His palms felt slippery with sweat as he neared the
master bedroom. Rodriguez can see me go in there, if
he's watching the screens like he's supposed to. I'll have
to do it fast and then duck out before he figures out
what's going down. Quite deliberately, Killifer switched
off the palm-sized two-way radio he kept in his shirt
pocket.

At last he stood before the master bedroom's double
doors. He had memorized the electronic lock's combination from the list kept in the security office.

Okay, he told himself, licking his lips once again.
Don't just stand around. Do it!

Swiftly he tapped on the miniature keyboard and saw
its light turn green. He pushed the door open.

It was a spacious room. Lev Brudnoy lay sprawled on
the oversized bed, stark naked. Nothing but gray mottled
skin and bones, Killifer saw, and that ratty little beard.
The wallscreen on the other side of the room showed a
view from the Moon, the crater floor of Alphonsus, it
looked like. No sound; either it was muted or nobody
was saying anything from Moonbase.

"What is it?" Brudnoy said, sitting up, frowning,
reaching for the bedsheet to cover himself.

Joanna was nowhere in sight. Killifer looked across
the room: chaise longue, little desk and chair, a couple
of upholstered chairs, bookcases, bureaus, mirrors—but
no Joanna Brudnoy.

"Where is she?" Killifer hissed, sliding the pistol from his holster.

Brudnoy's eyes widened. Killifer saw several doors: closets, all closed. And one other door, half ajar. The bathroom.

"Get out of here!" Brudnoy shouted, reaching for the phone console on the night table.

"Where is she?" Killifer yelled back, heading for the half-open bathroom door.

Brudnoy banged the red emergency button on the phone console as Killifer strode swiftly across the bedroom carpeting.

"Joanna!" Brudnoy hollered. "Look out!"

And Killifer felt something thump against his shoulder. Whirling, he saw Brudnoy reaching for another book to throw at him, a skinny naked old man trying to stop him by throwing books.

With a wild laugh, Killifer fired twice. Brudnoy's chest erupted in blood and he jerked back against the bed's headboard, arms and legs flailing like a rag doll. Killifer pumped another two shots into him for good measure.

Joanna screamed. Killifer turned and saw her standing naked, frozen, in the bathroom doorway.

"Remember me?" Killifer taunted, levelling his gun at her. For a moment he thought how much fun it would be to rape her, to make her kneel to him, turn herself inside out for him, before he blew her head off. But there wasn't time.

In that moment Joanna slammed the bathroom door. Killifer heard its lock click.

Laughing even louder, he fired three shots into the lock, then kicked the door open. He stepped into the bathroom—

And Joanna, standing beside the door, drove the point of her hair-styling scissors into his wrist with every molecule of strength in her. Killifer's hand went numb and he nearly dropped the gun. Her face white with fury, Joanna snatched a hairbrush and whacked it as hard as she could against his bleeding wrist.

Killifer felt pain flaming up his arm. The gun fell from

his fingers. He staggered back, but not before Joanna grabbed the end of the scissors still sticking in his wrist.

"Bastard," she snarled, working the scissors back and forth. "Murdering bastard!"

Pain searing his whole arm, Killifer cuffed her with his free hand, driving her back against the marble sink. But she held firmly onto the scissors, yanking it from his bleeding wrist.

The gun was on the tiled floor. Killifer bent to reach for it but Joanna kicked it away.

"That's not going to help you, bitch," he growled at her. "I'm not leaving here until you're dead."

He lunged at her, but Joanna raked the point of the scissors up his chest and throat and lodged the blades in the underside of his jaw.

Yowling with pain, Killifer staggered back into the bedroom.

Rodriguez was at the hallway door, submachine gun levelled at Killifer's waist.

"You killed them!" Rodriguez shouted, eyes wide.

"No . . ." Killifer choked. "No, wait . . ."

"General's orders," Rodriguez said. He fired half a dozen rounds into Killifer's midsection.

Killifer felt nothing. The bedroom tilted and he was staring at the ceiling. It faded, though, slowly turning dark. He thought of General O'Conner telling him, *"The fewer people know about this, the better off we are."*

Rodriguez is one of them, Killifer realized. That sonofabitch O'Conner planted him here to get rid of me once the job's done.

It was his last thought.

CONTROL CENTER

"When we power up," Wicksen was telling Doug, "you're going to be totally blacked out."

There was no video from the mass driver; Doug spoke to a blank screen.

"We're plugging in the fuel cells," he said. "They can keep us going for the few minutes your gun will be running."

He sensed Wicksen nodding. "Well, we're doing everything we can here. That missile blast shook half our connections loose and the other half aren't all that sound, either."

Doug grimaced, then recalled, "I remember a professor of mine saying that if something scratches or bites, it's biology; if it stinks or pops, it's chemistry; and if—"

"If it doesn't work," Wicksen finished with him, "it's physics."

Neither of them laughed.

"We're going to power up in fifteen minutes," Wicksen said. "Will you have the fuel cells on-line by then?"

"If we don't I'll call you."

"That only leaves us six minutes to fire at the nuke," the physicist said, "assuming they hold off detonation until the warhead's only three hundred meters above the crater floor."

"If they detonate higher they'll shower the Peacekeeper troops with radiation."

"They're not digging in?"

Doug shook his head. "No, they're staying buttoned up tight inside their vehicles, as far as we can see."

"I'll bet they're praying for a low-altitude detonation even more than we are."

"Probably so," Doug agreed.

"All right," said Wicksen. "I've got work to do. Call me if you can't get the fuel cells patched in."

"Will do."

Jinny Anson leaned over Doug's shoulder. "The fuel cells are up and ready, no sweat."

"Good," he said, wondering if Wicksen heard her before he clicked off.

For the thousandth time Doug checked out every corner of Moonbase through the screens on the console before him. It felt as if the wheeled typist's chair on which he sat had welded itself to his butt and spine. The level of tension in the control center was palpable, but it had been so electrically high for so long that it seemed almost normal. People went about their duties mechanically, studying their screens or fingering their keyboards. Hardly a word was spoken now, and no voice rose above an edgy, tightly controlled murmur.

Doug saw that the Cave was almost filled with men and women milling about aimlessly, sitting huddled in small groups, staring up at the wallscreens. Must be really tough on them, Doug thought, waiting with nothing to do. Then he looked at the camera view from Mt. Yeager; the Peacekeeper troops were also waiting, and the nuclear missile that would end everyone's suspense was hurtling toward Alphonsus now.

They've won the first round, Doug realized. They aimed at our nuclear generator and hit it. Our backup power system is gone. There must be a considerable amount of radioactive debris splattered across the far side of the crater floor.

But they don't suspect we've got a beam gun to knock out their nuke, he told himself. Almost bitterly, Doug admitted that their big success so far had been that Wicksen's beam gun hadn't worked. Our ace in the hole, he thought wryly. They don't know we might be able to prevent their nuclear warhead from going off.

He leaned back in the squeaking little chair, trying to ease the stress that was knotting the muscles of his neck and shoulders. Nanomachines can't relieve anxiety, he thought.

Staring up at the dimly lit rock of the ceiling, Doug asked himself, Who am I trying to kid? There are at least three hundred armed and trained troops on the other side of the ringwall. A nuclear bomb is heading toward us. Not a nation in the world has lifted a finger to help us. How on earth can I pretend that we can stand up to the Peacekeepers? We don't have a chance, not a prayer, against the force of the United Nations.

Why not just let them walk in here and take over? Why risk the lives of two thousand people? Over what? My own ego? My own fear that once they ship me Earthside some New Morality fanatic's going to murder me? So what? I'm dead either way. They can kill me here, trying to defend Moonbase, or kill me back on Earth. At least if I surrender to them the rest of the people here will live.

And Moonbase dies. Yamagata takes over and turns it into his private clinic instead of using it as a springboard to push the frontier outward.

He shook his head. You're debating philosophy when a couple of thousand lives are hanging in the balance. That's not fair. It's stupid.

The phone light at the bottom right corner of his set of screens began winking yellow. Shaking himself from his inner misgivings, Doug reached for his headset and slipped it on.

"Incoming call from Savannah," a comm tech's voice said. "Urgent top priority."

"Put it through."

Doug saw his mother's face on the lower right screen: hair dishevelled, eyes red and swollen, skin ashen, a silk robe pulled tight around her.

"What's wrong?" he blurted.

But Joanna was already telling him, "Lev's been

killed. Murdered. He was trying to kill me, but I'm all right. But your stepfather's dead."

"Killed? Who did it? Why? Are you really all right?"

The three seconds it took for her reply stretched like hours.

"We don't know who it was. The security guard got him. We're checking it out. It all happened just a few minutes ago . . ." Joanna seemed to be gasping, her words barely getting out of her mouth.

"Are you hurt? Do you have a doctor there?"

She's holding back tears, Doug realized, watching his mother's agonized face. She won't let herself cry.

"Paramedics are here and my personal physician's on his way," she said, seeming to pull herself up straighter. "I'm not hurt. But Lev . . ."

Joanna turned away from the screen. A man's face slid into view, square jaw unshaved, narrow eyes hard and bitter. "This is Captain Ingersoll, I'm with Masterson security. Your mother's physically unharmed, sir, although she's had a tremendous psychological shock. I'll see to it that she calls you back as soon as her doctor's looked her over and we've had a chance to sort things out a bit. Thank you."

The screen went blank.

Doug sat there in stunned silence. If anyone overheard his phone conversation, if anyone tried to talk to him or question him, he didn't know it. He merely sat staring blankly at the array of screens, his thoughts spinning.

They tried to kill her. Who was it? Part of Faure's scheme? Or maybe Yamagata, trying to get her out of their way so they can take control of Masterson Corporation more easily. No, not even Yamagata would go that far. Would they? New Morality zealots, more likely. Fanatics who knew that Mom was backing Moonbase and nanotechnology. Maybe they even knew she'd had a few nanotech treatments herself, over the years.

She's all right, though. Lev's dead, but she's all right. They murdered Lev. Killed him.

Jinny Anson was shaking his shoulder. "Wix is ready to power up."

He looked up at her. "Okay," he said dully. "Okay."

Anson peered at him. "Are you all right, Doug?"

He nodded. "Yeah. I'm okay. Don't worry about me. Tell Wicksen to shoot the hell out of that missile."

Anson looked surprised, but she said merely, "Right."

Claire Rossi looked up as the overhead loudpseakers blared through the Cave:

"WE'RE GOING TO AUXILIARY POWER IN SIXTY SECONDS. LIGHTS WILL GO DOWN TO EMERGENCY LEVELS. ALL UNNECESSARY EQUIPMENT WILL BE POWERED DOWN. THIS SHOULD LAST APPROXIMATELY TEN TO FIF- TEEN MINUTES."

The Cave buzzed with conversations. When the lights suddenly turned down, a chorus of "ooohs" surged through the crowded cafeteria.

Then somebody called out, "The lights are low! Time for an orgy!"

Claire didn't laugh. Neither did anyone else.

The lights flickered briefly in the nanolaboratory, then steadied and returned to their normal brightness.

"See?" Zimmerman said to Inoguchi. "We are essen- tial. We stay at full power."

Inoguchi looked up from his work. "I am afraid that the power surge has knocked out the timing circuitry in the assembly feeder," he said apologetically.

"What?" Zimmerman bellowed, rushing across the lab to the Japanese scientist's side.

"The timing circuitry must be reset," Inoguchi said. "This batch of nanomachines—"

"Ruined!" Zimmerman roared, pounding a fist on the lab bench so hard that Inoguchi nearly jumped off his stool. "A microsecond pulse of electricity! Ruined!" He lapsed into German.

Inoguchi could not understand his words, but the tone was painfully clear.

*			*			*

"Power at ninety-two percent."

Wicksen was inside the cramped shelter again. This time he had not bothered to take off his helmet, he merely slid the visor up.

"Can you goose it higher?" he asked, eyes on the makeshift control board.

"When I do," the woman replied, "the needle starts wobbling. I think ninety-two's the best we can do without risking another shorting out."

"Okay," Wicksen said softly. "Hold it at ninety-two."

"Holding and stable."

"How's the radar plot?"

The man standing to his left was bent over a screen that displayed a single lurid red spot against a spiderweb of concentric circles.

"Coming straight at us, practically zero deflection," he said tightly. "Pointing system's holding good, slaved to the radar."

Wicksen scanned the board full of gauges and telltale lights: mostly green, a handful of ambers, two reds, but they had been cut out of the circuitry.

"Anybody see a reason why we shouldn't shoot the cannon?"

Dead silence. No sound in the low-ceilinged little shelter except the hum of the electrical equipment.

"Okay. Here goes." Wicksen leaned on the red firing button.

Nothing in the shelter changed. No new noise, no vibration, no sense of having accomplished anything.

"Power holding steady."

"Beam collimation looks good."

"Just hold together, baby," Wicksen pleaded, almost cooed, like a father urging a baby's first tottering steps. "Just stay together for another five, six minutes. You can do it, baby, you can last that long. You're a good little pile of junk, you are, you're working just fine. Keep it up, baby, keep those protons moving."

His assistants had never heard Wicksen speak like that, never heard anything remotely like this cooing, coaxing, imploring tone that he was half-whispering, half-singing to the impassive electronics and machinery they had slapped together. They stood in shock for fully five minutes as Wicksen kept up his impromptu lullaby, his supplication, his prayer that the beam gun would work right and do the job they intended it to do.

As the clock on their control board showed five minutes and nine seconds, Wicksen's female assistant called out, "Starting to get arcing on the main buss."

Wicksen raised one hand in a gesture of patience.

"It's going to short out again!"

"Hold it as long as you can," he said calmly.

Half the needles on the board's gauges suddenly spun down toward zero.

"It's gone," said the man to Wicksen's right.

"Main buss shorted."

"Power down," Wicksen said with a sigh. "If we haven't knocked out the nuke's fuzing circuitry by now we never will."

A small tremor shook the shelter, like the passing of a train nearby.

"Ground impact."

"Yeah, but did the nuke go off?"

ASSAULT FORCE

Colonel Giap studied the watch built into the keypad on his spacesuit's wrist. The nuclear bomb should have exploded almost a full minute earlier.

His command center inside the tractor was little more than a windowless metal box shoehorned between the tractor's cab and its rear bed, where a dozen Peacekeeper troops and the seven suicide volunteers sat wedged together like sardines in a tin.

"Where is the confirmation from L-1?" Giap demanded of the tech sergeant in charge of communications.

The sergeant said through the upraised visor of his spacesuit, "L-1 wants to speak to you, sir."

With an impatient huff, Giap took the laptop comm rig from the sergeant. "We are scheduled to push off in three minutes," he said sharply. "Where is the confirmation of the nuclear blast?"

The officer's image in the small, snow-streaked screen looked strained, worried. "There is no confirmation of the blast, sir," she said, her voice scratchy with static.

"No confirmation!"

"Diagnostics are negative," the officer said dolefully, "and there is no visual confirmation of the detonation."

Giap demanded, "Did the bomb go off or not?"

"As far as we can tell, sir, it failed."

"Failed! Then Moonbase's electrical power system is still intact."

"As far as we can tell, sir."

Giap angrily slammed the laptop shut and shoved it back into the sergeant's gloved hands. It doesn't matter, he told himself. It would be better if their electrical power was cut off, but it really doesn't matter. We will march across the mountains and blast open their airlocks if they refuse to surrender to me.

He held up his wrist again. At precisely the second called for in his schedule, he commanded, "Start engines. All vehicles are to move to their assigned locations on the crater floor. *Go!*"

Grins and thumbs-up gestures filled the control center; the overhead lights were back to full brightness.

"It didn't go off!" Jinny Anson crowed, exultant, almost jumping up and down.

"Wicksen did it," said Doug, still only half believing it.

O'Malley got up from the chair beside him. "I'm going to check out the dust dispersal systems one more time.

Looks like we'll need 'em now." He was grinning broadly as he strode out of the control center.

"Put through a call to Wicksen," Anson said. "We ought to congratulate him."

Doug nodded, but asked, "How much damage did the warhead do when it hit the ground?"

A technician's voice answered, "The bird bull's-eyed on the central solar farm. Knocked out eleven panels and a main feeder line. Our power capacity is down by two percent."

"We can live with that," Anson said quickly.

Yes, Doug thought. We can live with that. We can even fight with that.

In the tight confines of the editing booth, Edith had followed the telescope view of the incoming missile warhead, holding her breath, not daring to speak. But when she saw no flash of an explosion and the warhead clunked into the middle of one of the arrays of solar panels spread across the ground, she whooped an involuntary Texas victory yell.

"It didn't go off!" she said into her headset microphone, hovering a centimeter from her lips. "Moonbase's missile defense system worked!"

She reached out across the control board and activated a chip that held a prerecorded interview with Wicksen, explaining how the particle beam accelerator at the mass driver could be turned into a beam gun. While the canned interview played out, Edith checked with Doug at the control center.

"He's on another call," said the comm tech. From the radiant smile on the technician's face Edith knew that she'd been right; the nuclear warhead hadn't exploded.

"I just want confirmation from him that the nuke didn't go off," Edith explained.

"It didn't."

"Yeah, right. But I need to get his handsome face on Global Network for the whole world to see him saying it didn't go off."

"I'll give him your message."

"Do that," Edith snapped, feeling nettled. But then she thought, Doug must be up to his scalp in snakes. He won't have time for the news media.

She put through a call to Wicksen, out at the mass driver, instead.

"I swear to you, Joanna, I knew nothing of this," said Ibrahim al-Rashid.

He was perched nervously on one of the upholstered chairs in Joanna's living room. It was two in the morning. Rashid looked baggy-eyed, his clothes hurriedly thrown on. The house was still swarming with police and Masterson Corporation security people. Lev's body had been taken away, zippered into a black body bag. His murderer's body, cut almost in half by the submachine gun bullets that had killed him, remained up in her bedroom while the police and security team took fingerprints and photographs.

"He was a Masterson security guard," Joanna said, her voice venomously low. "He was trying to kill me."

"Joanna," Rashid said, almost pleading, "you can't believe that I had anything to do with this!"

"I don't know what to believe," she replied, staring hard at him. She was sitting tensely on the sofa, still wearing nothing more than the silk robe she had pulled on upstairs.

"He must have been a New Morality fanatic," Rashid said.

"Or an assassin from Yamagata."

"No! Why would Yamagata want you assassinated?"

"I don't know," Joanna said tightly. "I intend to find out."

"I'm so sorry about Lev," Rashid said, his head drooping. "I liked him."

"He looked familiar to me," Joanna murmured.

"Familiar?"

"The security guard, the assassin. He'd been around the house for several days and I thought that somehow he looked familiar, but I couldn't place where I'd seen him before."

"Are you sure . . . ?"

"I should have told the security chief then and there," Joanna said in a choked whisper, speaking more to herself than to Rashid. "I should have realized something wasn't right."

"It isn't your fault," Rashid said.

She focused her gray-green eyes on him, like a pair of guns. "Then whose fault is it?"

"Not mine!" Rashid fairly yelped. "Joanna, I know we've had our differences over corporate policy, but I would *never*—I mean, something like this . . ."

Joanna leaned back against the sofa's soft pillows. "I want to believe you, Omar. I hope you're telling me the truth."

Rashid swallowed visibly. There was nothing he could say to erase the suspicion in her eyes.

"Mrs. Brudnoy?" Captain Ingersoll called from the dining room doorway.

She looked up at him. "Yes? What is it?"

Stepping slowly, hesitantly into the living room, Ingersoll held up a hand-sized computer. "I think we've made a positive ID on the killer."

"Who is it?"

Aiming his handset at the Windowall screen above the fireplace, Ingersoll said, "We ran a computer check on his fingerprints . . ."

The big screen atop the mantle showed two sets of inky whorls.

"He used to work for the corporation years ago, mostly up at Moonbase."

The fingerprints were replaced by two photographs: both ID pictures, taken twenty-five years apart.

"Jack Killifer!" Joanna gasped.

"That's his name," Ingersoll agreed, nodding. "The photo on the right was taken when he joined our security department, a few weeks ago. You can see he trimmed down his hair, darkened it, and grew a mustache."

"Jack Killifer," she repeated. "He's hated me all these years . . . hated me enough to kill me."

"You think his motivation was personal, then?" Ingersoll asked.

She glanced at Rashid before answering. The man looked puzzled. Of course, Joanna realized; Omar doesn't know anything about Killifer or his history.

"Yes," she said to Ingersoll. "Personal."

"Can you tell me something about it?" the captain asked.

"Tomorrow," Joanna said. "Call me tomorrow, around noon."

"Because we still got a problem here," Ingersoll went on, slow, measured, not easily deterred.

"A problem?"

"The other security guard, Rodriguez."

"The one who shot Killifer."

"Yes'm. He's nowhere to be found. Apparently took off for parts unknown. We found the stutter gun he used; he left it on the kitchen table, nice and neat. But his car's gone and him with it."

Rashid's brows knit. "Why would he run away?"

"That's what I'd like to know," said Ingersoll.

"Tomorrow," Joanna said firmly.

Ingersoll seemed to think it over for a heartbeat or two, then nodded and walked back into the dining room.

"Omar, thanks for coming over," Joanna said to Rashid. "I'm sorry if it looked as if I suspected you. It's been . . . it's been a terrible few hours."

Rashid knew he was being dismissed and he felt grateful for it. Getting to his feet, he asked, "Will you be all right? Do you need anything?"

"My doctor's here," she said, remaining seated on the sofa. "He's already dosed me with tranquilizers and god knows what else. He'll stay here in the house and there are the servants, of course."

"Of course," Rashid murmured, eager to get away, glad that the burning fury of her suspicion had passed over him.

Joanna summoned the butler, who accompanied Rashid to his car, then returned to the living room.

"What else can I do for you?" he asked.

"Nothing," she said. "That's all for now. Go get yourself some sleep."

"And you . . . ?"

"I'll sleep here," Joanna said.

"I've had the guest suite prepared for you," the butler suggested.

She shook her head. "No, I don't want to go upstairs. Not just yet. I'll sleep here on the sofa. I'll be fine."

The butler left, silent as a shadow, then returned a moment later with a downy white blanket and a flowered pillow. Joanna watched him place them on the end of the sofa, then leave the room again.

I should cry, she told herself. I should let it come out. Lev didn't deserve this. It was me he was after. Lev died trying to save my life.

Instead of crying, she reached over to the phone console and told its voice-recognition system, "Get Seigo Yamagata for me. No intermediaries. This is an emergency call for him and no one else."

It's time to end this war, Joanna told herself.

EDITING BOOTH

"Moonbase has survived the Peacekeepers' missile attack," Edith was saying into her microphone. "But not unscathed. The first missile destroyed Moonbase's backup power generator. That was a conventional explosive warhead and it hit the buried generator precisely."

The display screens running across the top of the control board showed the quiet frenzy of Moonbase's control center, the crowd milling around in the Cave, a view of the crater floor where Wicksen and his crew were riding back to the main airlock in a jouncing tractor, and the scene from Mt. Yeager showing the Peacekeeper assault force's vehicles trundling up toward Wodjoho-witcz Pass.

Selecting the view of Wicksen's tractor, Edith continued without missing a beat, "The U.N.'s second missile was a nuclear weapon, aimed to wipe out Moonbase's main electrical power solar panels, which are spread across the floor of the crater. The people here call them solar farms. Thanks to the brilliant work of a handful of scientists and technicians . . . "

She praised Wicksen and his people, explained how the beam gun had deactivated the nuclear warhead and turned it into a dud.

But her eyes were pinned on the screen showing the Peacekeepers' vehicles creeping up the outer slope of the ringwall mountains.

Vince Falcone was watching the same view, sitting at a console in the control center. He was sweating, perspiration beading his upper lip and forehead, trickling down his swarthy cheeks.

This has gotta work, he kept telling himself. It's gotta work. Otherwise they'll be able to bring their missile launchers right up to our front door and blast it open.

For the twentieth time in the past half hour he checked the circuitry to the microwave antennas atop Mt. Yeager. One of the bright young short-timers had done a computer simulation that showed the microwaves would be reflected by the rock walls of Wodjo Pass and effectively reach all the foamgel goo they had spread there. The rock absorbed some of the microwave energy, of course, but reflected enough to get the job done.

Falcone hoped.

He looked across the row of consoles to where Doug Stavenger was sitting, deep in conversation with somebody on his screens. The kid's got all this responsibility on his shoulders, Falcone told himself. Least I can do is get this mother-lovin' foamgel to work.

He returned his attention to the screen showing the

approaching Peacekeeper force. And felt a shock race through him.

They're splitting up! Falcone saw. The vehicles were dividing into two columns, one of them coming up toward Wodjo Pass, but the other snaking around the base of the ringwall mountains toward the steeper notch some two dozen kilometers farther away.

And it looked like a small party was starting out on foot to climb Mt. Yeager, where the microwave antennas were.

Stupid shitfaced bastards, Falcone raged, offering the assessment both to the Peacekeepers and his own short-sightedness. They're only sending part of their forces across Wodjo. The rest of 'em will get through without being stopped by the goo. And if they knock out the antennas up on Yeager, the goo won't do us any fucking good at all.

The earphone of the headpiece clamped over his thickly curling hair suddenly crackled. "Vince, this is Doug Stavenger. They've divided their force."

"Yeah, I can see it."

"It looks like that second group's heading for the northwest notch."

"And they're sending a team up Yeager."

"They're going to get through with no trouble, aren't they?"

Falcone nodded bitterly. "Even if we could spray some goo over that pass, the microwaves from Yeager couldn't reach it. Assuming they don't disable the antennas before we want to use 'em."

"Well, what can we do?" Doug asked.

Falcone wished he had an answer.

We should have known they'd split their forces, Doug raged at himself. I should've figured that the Peacekeepers wouldn't send their whole force through Wodjo. That was wishful thinking, nothing but wishful thinking.

"It's not so bad," Gordette said, pulling up a chair to sit beside him.

"Bad enough," said Doug.

"Their main force is coming across Wodjo Pass," Gordette said, pointing to the screen. "The second force is a lot smaller, looks like."

"But if they disable the antennas . . ."

"It'll take them an hour to get to the top of Yeager, at least."

"But still . . ."

Gordette said, "Count the missile launchers. That's their heavy artillery. Looks to me like almost all of 'em are coming through Wodjo."

Doug studied the screens for a few moments. "Maybe the secondary force is going to head for the mass driver?"

Gordette shrugged, then said, "Whoever's in charge of the Peacekeepers probably wants to keep the secondary force as a reserve."

Doug wished he could believe Gordette's assessment. He's just trying to cheer me up, Doug thought. Trying to lighten the load. It doesn't matter what the secondary force's mission is, once their main group gets in trouble in Wodjo Pass, they'll still have these other troops to attack us. With all their weapons.

Maybe Falcone was right and we ought to fry them as they come through Wodjo Pass. Get them before they knock out the antennas. Kill as many of them as we can while we've got the chance. They're here to kill us. They killed Lev, they tried to kill Mom. Why shouldn't we kill them?

The blinking message light on the console told him that people were waiting to talk with him. He pulled up the list on the comm screen. Wicksen, Edith, Kris Cardenas down in the infirmary, four others.

Edith. Doug recalled her urging against killing any of the Peacekeepers. She's right, he knew. Kill some of their troops and the whole world will turn against us. They'll keep sending armies here until they beat us. Faure won't stop until he wins, not if he has the world's public opinion behind him. And once we start sending coffins Earthside, world public opinion will swing totally against us, no matter how much people may be rooting for us now.

Beat them without killing them. Even though they're trying to kill us.

He had put through a call to Savannah earlier, but it had not been answered so far. Is Mom all right? What happened down there? Who killed Lev? Is Mom safe?

They should've stayed here, Doug told himself. Then he realized the absurdity of it. Yes, stay here where all we have to worry about is being attacked by a small army of Peacekeeper troops.

Looking at his top left screen he saw that the first of the Peacekeeper vehicles was already entering Wodjo-howitcz Pass. Doug glanced over at Falcone, staring grimly at the same view on his console.

Gordette was right; those troopers climbing Yeager won't get to the antennas for another hour, at least.

He got up from his chair, spine creaking after being seated for so long, and walked stiffly to Falcone's post.

"Wait until you've got as many in the trap as possible. Then spring it."

Falcone nodded without taking his eyes from his screens. They had been over this a hundred times, at least.

"It's your show, now, Vince," he said, gripping Falcone's burly shoulder.

"Right, boss," said Falcone, his eyes still fixed on his screens.

Colonel Giap had learned long ago not to be the first in line of march through enemy territory. His tractor was the third in line as they threaded up the flank of the mountains and into the narrow defile of the pass.

"Force B, report," he said into his helmet microphone.

All his communications were relayed through the L-1 station, hovering nearly forty thousand kilometers above. There was a noticeable, annoying little lag as the electronic signals bounced back and forth.

"Force B reporting," crackled in his earphones. "No opposition. Proceeding on schedule."

"Good. Report any problems immediately," said Giap.

"Yes, sir."

The colonel nodded inside his helmet. Keeping to schedule was important. He had planned the conquest of Moonbase down to the minutest details, and included every contingency he could imagine in his plans. The nuclear bomb did not go off; Moonbase still enjoyed its full capacity of electrical power. Giap had included that possibility in his planning. It made no difference. His primary force would batter down their main airlock and enter the garage area precisely on schedule, while Force B deployed on the crater floor as a strategic reserve, after sending a small contingent to take the mass driver—which Giap expected to be undefended.

His special team of mountain climbers would disable all of Moonbase's communications antennas, cutting off the rebels' reports to the news media back on Earth. Faure had insisted on that, and for once Giap agreed with the secretary-general. Cut out their tongues.

The first wave of assault troops would include the decontamination squads with their powerful ultraviolet lights, to deactivate any nanomachines that the Moonbase rebels might try to use. Giap smiled thinly at the memory of how the rebels had used nanomachines to panic the first Peacekeeper force sent against Moonbase. That trick won't work a second time, he assured himself.

His earphones buzzed. Switching to the tractor's intercom, Giap asked testily, "What is it?"

"Sensors are picking up an unusual level of microwave radiation, sir," his surveillance officer reported.

In the cramped confines of his windowless command center, Giap barely had room to turn and face the woman. Even so, sealed inside her spacesuit, he could not see her face, merely the reflection of his own helmet in her closed visor.

"A dangerous level?" Did the rebels have exotic weapons, after all?

"No, sir, nothing dangerous. It's more like a radar scan, but it's coming at us from all directions, as if the microwaves are reflecting off the mountain walls around us."

Giap felt his brow wrinkle. Microwaves? What are they trying to accomplish?

"Lead tractor calling, sir," said his communications sergeant. "Emergency."

Giap switched to the proper frequency. "Sir! Our tractor is stuck. We can't move!"

"Can't move?"

The voice in his earphones sounded more puzzled than worried. "It's as if we hit some deep mud . . ."

"There is no mud on the Moon!" Giap snapped.

"Yessir, I know. But we're mired in *something*. We can't move forward or back. My engineer is afraid of burning out the drive motors."

Giap's own tractor lurched and slowed noticeably.

"What's going on?" he yelled to his comm sergeant.

"I don't know!"

Within minutes the first twenty-two tractors in the assault force reported being stuck fast. Several burned out their drive motors trying to force themselves through whatever it was that had mired them down.

"Get out and see what it is!" Giap screamed at his own driver as he motioned his sergeant to open the overhead hatch.

In his anxiety, Giap forgot the gentle lunar gravity and pulled himself up so hard he nearly soared completely out of the tractor. He sprawled across the roof of the cab, legs dangling inside his shoebox-sized command center.

Pulling himself up to a sitting position, Giap looked around. His first sensation was relief at being out of the metal coffin of the command center. He saw smooth-walled gray rock mountains and a dark, star-strewn sky.

Then he looked down and saw that his tractor, and every other one up and down the line that he could see, were engulfed halfway up their drive wheels in a weird, bright blue sea of spongy-looking *stuff*.

"Sergeant!" he yelled into his helmet mike. "Get up here."

The sergeant popped the hatch to his cab and scrambled up to sit on the roof next to him.

Pointing at the sea of blue, Giap commanded, "Climb down the side of the tractor and test the consistency of that material."

"What is it?" the sergeant asked. Then he added, "Sir."

"If I knew what it was I wouldn't need you to test it!"

"Maybe it's some sort of Moon creature," the sergeant said, his voice hollow.

"Don't be stupid!" Giap barked. "It's man-made. It's something the rebels have cooked up to slow us down."

The sergeant climbed down the ladder built into the tractor's side, slow and awkward in his cumbersome spacesuit. Very gingerly, he touched the blue surface with a booted toe.

"It feels soft, sir," he reported.

"How soft? Can you walk on it?"

The sergeant pushed his boot in deeper, then—still grasping the ladder rungs with both hands—he tried standing on it. His boots sank in until their tops were covered in blue.

"Well?" Giap demanded.

He heard his sergeant puffing and grunting. "I'm stuck in it, sir. I can't pull my feet out."

In the half hour it took for Seigo Yamagata to answer Joanna's call, she paced the living room, trying to burn up some of the fear and anger and grief that the tranquilizers had dulled but not removed.

While she paced, she watched the Global News channel that was devoting full time to live coverage of the battle for Moonbase. Edie Elgin's voice sounded strained, slightly hoarse from long hours of nonstop talking, but she was still going strong.

Joanna learned that the Peacekeepers' nuclear missile attack had failed and Moonbase's electrical power supply was still intact. Now she watched the view from atop

Mt. Yeager as the main Peacekeeper assault force came to a halt in Wodjohowitcz Pass.

"The smart foamgel will set to the consistency of concrete," Edie Elgin was saying. "Wodjohowitcz Pass is effectively blocked, as far as the Peacekeepers' vehicles are concerned."

As she paced and watched, Joanna thought about getting dressed in something more substantial than her thin white robe, but that would have meant going upstairs. Even though the police were finished now with the bedroom, Joanna found she could not willingly go in there, not yet, not with Lev's blood still staining the bedclothes. Tomorrow, maybe. After they've cleaned everything up.

The phone chimed at last and she went to the sofa where the camera could focus on her. Seigo Yamagata's lean, lined face appeared on the screen above the fireplace, replacing Edie Elgin's report from the Moon. It was impossible to tell what time it might be in Tokyo from the wide window behind Yamagata's desk; the downtown city towers were drenched in driving rain.

"I'm sorry if I disturbed you," Joanna began.

Yamagata raised a hand. "It is of no consequence. I have just been informed of the attempt on your life. Please accept my deepest condolence for the loss of your husband."

Rashid must've phoned him, Joanna thought swiftly. Or maybe not. He's got his own sources of information, certainly.

"I've decided that Moonbase isn't worth the loss of more lives," Joanna said, holding herself together with a conscious effort of will. "This war must end before more people are killed."

Yamagata drew in a breath. "I sincerely regret what has happened. This was not of my doing."

"I understand that," Joanna replied, a slim tendril of doubt still in the back of her mind. But she pushed it away. "What kind of an agreement can we reach?"

Rubbing his chin in apparent perplexity, Yamagata said slowly, "The Peacekeepers are already attacking Moonbase. The battle has started."

"I know that."

"Within a few hours," Yamagata said, "Moonbase will be under U.N. control."

"I *don't* know that," Joanna replied coldly. "And neither do you."

"Surely you do not believe that your people can hold out against several hundred trained Peacekeeper troops."

Joanna allowed a ghost of a smile to curve the corners of her lips. "The Peacekeepers' nuclear missile failed. And now their assault force is bogged down in the ringwall mountains. I'd say there is a fair chance that Moonbase will hold out quite well."

Yamagata shook his head. "No. It is not possible. Despite their temporary successes, Moonbase will fall within a few hours."

WODJOHOWITCZ PASS

Colonel Giap was in a frenzy of frustrated anger. Not only was his main assault force mired in this devilish blue muck that had hardened to the consistency of concrete, trapping his main assault force in the narrow defile of the mountain pass, but now Georges Faure was demanding that he get on with the conquest of Moonbase.

"It is unacceptable," Faure was saying, his mustache bristling. "Entirely unacceptable."

Giap glowered at the secretary-general's pale image in the small screen of the laptop. The colonel was sitting atop his tractor, buttoned up in his spacesuit. A meter or so from him, where his sergeant still stood hopelessly imbedded, six Peacekeeper troops were chipping away at the hellish blue slime with makeshift implements from the tractor's tool kit. Two of the troopers were even using the butts of their rifles to bash the sludge in their attempts to release the boots of their sergeant.

"I agree," Giap said to Faure, tightly reining his anger. "It is unacceptable. But in battle the unacceptable is commonplace."

Faure sat behind his desk, trembling with rage as he stared at the faceless image of the Peacekeeper colonel in his blank-visored spacesuit. How can a handful of rebels stop a fully armed column of Peacekeeper troops? It is unthinkable, a farce, a disaster. Everyone will be laughing at me, unable to quash a tiny group of scientists and technicians, powerless to bring them under the rule of the law, impotent.

"I tell you this, *mon colonel*," Faure said, seething. "If you cannot take Moonbase, then you are to release the volunteers. Do you understand what I am saying?"

In three seconds, Giap replied harshly, "You would rather destroy Moonbase than see it repulse us."

"Exactly!" Faure snapped.

While he waited for Faure's reply to reach him, Colonel Giap turned slightly to watch the activity he had ordered. Troopers were placing metal panels scavenged from the marooned tractors' flooring from the roof of one cab to the tail of the next tractor, forming a bridge across which they could march to the front of the column of stalled vehicles. From the leading tractor they slid more panels across the treacherous blue slime, to where the dusty gray regolith lay bare—and safe.

"Exactly!" Giap heard Faure's reply.

Taking in a deep breath and then releasing it slowly, to calm himself, Giap said, "There is no need to call on the suicide volunteers as yet. I am extricating most of my troops from the pass. We will march down into the crater floor on foot."

Faure's image was a red-faced thundercloud with a quivering mustache.

Before the secretary-general could speak again, Giap went on, "We will meet our secondary force on the crater floor and march on Moonbase. Our numbers will be diminished by less than five percent."

There, he thought, let the pompous little politician chew on that for three seconds. I am the military commander here. I will counter the enemy's moves. It was I who insisted on splitting the force. Only a fool of a politician would send his entire force through a single mountain pass that could be guarded or blocked by the enemy so easily.

When Faure's response came it was a little more restrained. But only a little. "And your equipment? Your missile launchers and other heavy weapons? Your men carry them on their backs, I presume."

"No," Giap said, bristling at Faure's sarcasm. "We will not need them. If the rebels do not open their airlocks to us, we have enough firepower to blast them apart."

Three seconds later, Faure asked, "Without the heavy missiles?"

"We have the shoulder-launched anti-tank rockets. They will knock down an airlock hatch, I assure you."

The secretary-general seemed to fidget unhappily in his chair. He fiddled with his mustache, smoothed his slicked-back hair, adjusted the collar of his shirt. Giap sat motionless atop the tractor cab, waiting.

"Well . . ." Faure said at last. "Perhaps you can carry it off, after all. I hope so, for your sake."

Giap restrained a bitter reply.

Faure went on, "Remember the volunteers. If all else fails, use them! Moonbase must not survive this day!"

"They're assembling on the crater floor." Jinny Anson stated the obvious.

Anson, Gordette, O'Malley and several others were clustered around Doug's console now, watching the screens over his shoulders. Command central, Doug thought. Wherever I am is the nerve center.

He punched up the imagery that Edith was sending out to Global News and saw the same view: a couple of dozen white Peacekeeper vehicles inching across the floor of the crater, each of them piled high with Peacekeeper troops who had marched down from Wodjo Pass.

"The invaders are moving cautiously," Edith's voice was saying. She sounded tense, edgy, her voice raw and strained. She ought to take a break, Doug thought. But I can't spare anybody to spell her.

Then his eye caught the screen still showing the crowd in the Cave. Maybe there's somebody there who could take over for her for a while. But Doug immediately put that thought aside. He didn't have time to go recruiting. And, knowing Edith, she'd sooner burn her vocal cords out entirely than surrender this once-in-a-lifetime chance to narrate a battle on the Moon.

"They'll deploy around the main airlock," Gordette said. "Ought to be knocking on our door in less than an hour."

Doug nodded. "Okay, we're ready for them. Right?"

Everyone nodded and murmured assent. Doug focused on O'Malley. His dust was going to be crucial.

"Remember," Doug said, "all we have to do to win is survive. We don't have to kill any of the Peacekeepers. We don't have to drive them off the Moon. All we have to do is survive. Like the Confederacy in the American Civil War; they didn't have to conquer the North, all they had to do was prevent the North from conquering them."

With a grunt, Gordette shot back, "Which they failed to accomplish."

The others stared at him. O'Malley looked downright hostile. Anson turned and walked away a few steps. Doug thought, Bam's not winning any popularity contests.

But he admitted Gordette's point with a shrug. Moonbase against the United Nations, he thought. That's what it boils down to. Moonbase against the world.

So far, so good, he told himself. We've still got our electricity and we've forced the Peacekeepers to abandon their heavy weapons.

But as he watched the implacable approach of the

Peacekeeper troops, Doug realized that what had happened so far was just the preliminary phase of this battle. The real fighting was about to begin.

Then the screen showing Edith's broadcast Earthside winked off.

CRATER FLOOR

Colonel Giap held the electro-optical binoculars to his visor and carefully studied the main airlock to Moonbase. The massive hatch had been slid wide open; the garage inside was brightly lit, clearly visible.

They could be hiding behind the tractors parked in the garage, Giap reasoned, waiting to pick us off as we enter the garage.

Pick us off with what? he asked himself. They have no guns. A few industrial lasers, of course, but those make awkward weapons. Trained troops could silence them in a few minutes.

"The men are deployed and waiting for your orders, sir," said his sergeant. Not his original aide; that poor devil was still back at the mountain pass, freed at last from the blue slime but in no emotional condition to be relied upon.

"Men and women, sergeant," Giap reminded him. "It is better to use the word 'troops.'"

"Yessir," the sergeant's apologetic voice hissed in Giap's helmet earphones. "The troops are waiting for your orders, sir."

Giap's timetable was a shambles, but that no longer mattered. They were about to penetrate Moonbase's perimeter defense.

Putting down his binoculars and letting them dangle

from the cord around his neck ring, Giap turned to face
his team of officers. Three captains, six lieutenants. His
second-in-command, a South African major, had been
left with the stalled vehicles up in the mountain pass.
We have too many officers anyway, Giap thought. The
Peacekeepers are topheavy with brass.

His nine officers straightened to a semblance of attention, a posture difficult to accomplish in their spacesuits
and virtually impossible to maintain.

"Stand easy," Giap said mildly. "We will attack in two
waves. First platoon will advance through the airlock
and into the garage area on tractors. Second platoon
will follow on foot. Third platoon will remain in reserve.
Any questions?"

A tenth figure had joined the little group, uninvited.
"What are we volunteers to do?"

Giap turned on the questioner. In his spacesuit it was
difficult to determine which of the suicide fanatics it
might be; the voice sounded American.

"You are to return to the command tractor and remain there, all of you, until I summon you," Giap said
firmly.

"How will we know what to expect?"

Giap allowed himself a sneering smile, knowing that
no one could see it behind his tinted visor. "You can
follow the progress of the battle on Global News, just
like everyone else on Earth."

Just at that moment his earphones buzzed, signalling
an incoming message. Tapping the keypad on his wrist,
Giap asked his replacement communications sergeant,
"What is it?"

"Report from the mountain-climbing team, sir. They
have reached the summit and cut the power lines to all
the antennas up there. Moonbase has been silenced."

For the first time in hours Giap smiled with genuine
pleasure. "Good," he said. "Send them my congratulations and tell them to report back to me on the crater
floor as soon as they can."

"Yes, sir."

Nodding inside his helmet, Giap told himself that

Moonbase was now entirely cut off from the Earth. At
last.

The president looked bleary-eyed as she sipped at her
first cup of coffee of the morning and stared at the
muted wallscreen that showed Global News' coverage of
the Moonbase battle.

"You're up early," said her chief of staff, taking his
customary place in the Kennedy rocker.

"So're you," said the president.

"I haven't been to sleep all night," he said, running a
hand over his bald pate. From behind her desk, the president could see that he was perspiring.

"It'll all be over in a few hours," she said, gesturing
toward the wallscreen with the hand that held her coffee mug.

"No it won't," said the staff chief gloomily.

"What's that supposed to mean?"

"Luce, we've got a shitstorm of public opinion coming
down on us. I spent the whole damned night trying to
calm down committee chairmen, media reporters, ump-
teen different governors and state party officials, even
some goddamned *church* leaders are yelling that we
ought to pressure the U.N. into letting Moonbase go!"

The president knew that her loyal assistant never used
profanity in her presence unless he was truly upset—or
trying to make a crucial point.

But she shook her head. "Harry, it's just too late to do
anything. The Peacekeepers are already there. Look."

She pointed to the wallscreen again. Turning in the
rocker, her staff chief saw dozens of tracked vehicles
advancing slowly toward the main airlock hatch of
Moonbase.

Suddenly the picture winked off.

"What the hell . . . ?"

Before the president could reach the remote control
unit on her desk, the screen flicked a few times, then
showed a harried-looking announcer in a suit and tie.

"We regret to report that technical difficulties have

cut off Edie Elgin's report from Moonbase. We are trying to reestablish contact."

As the scene switched to a news anchorwoman, who
began to summarize what they had been watching live,
the president eased back in her desk chair and cast a
knowing look at her staff chief.

"It's all over but the shouting, Harry. Moonbase is
finished and all those jerks who were yelling at you will
forget about it by this time tomorrow."

Doug wished he could talk with Edith, now that her
marathon performance had been cut short, but he had
no time for that. He watched the advancing Peacekeeper
troops. So did everyone in Moonbase. In the control
center, in the Cave, in the infirmary and labs that were
still working, every resident of Moonbase looked at the
screens and held his or her breath. Doug had never
heard the control center so absolutely silent. Even the
hum of the machinery seemed muted.

The white Peacekeeper tractors edged cautiously
through the airlock. Big as it was, the airlock could only
accommodate two vehicles at a time, so the invading
tractors came in pairs, then deployed around the edges
of the garage.

"They're expecting us to fire at them," Gordette said,
almost whispering. Still, his voice broke the silence
jarringly.

"With what?" Anson muttered acidly.

Doug looked past Vince Falcone to Nick O'Malley.
"Ready with the dust?" he asked, also in a near-reverent
whisper.

"Ready and waiting," O'Malley replied firmly.

Doug nodded as he thought: Waiting. We've been
waiting a long time. But we won't have to wait much
longer.

"The garage is clear," Giap heard in his earphones.
"No enemy troops."

The colonel had established his command post just

outside the main airlock, where he could see easily into the broad, brightly lit garage.

Four teams of specialists were sweeping the garage floor with powerful ultraviolet lamps. So far there was no sign of nanomachines, but Giap did not want to take any chances. His teams would sterilize the hatches on the other end of the garage, as well, the hatches that led into Moonbase's corridors.

No opposition so far, Giap mused. Either they intend to surrender once we enter the corridors and occupy their critical centers, or they have a trap waiting for us inside.

He played his plan through his mind once again. The first wave of troops was to open the corridor hatches. They were airlocks, of course, double hatches that protected the corridors from the vacuum outside. They had been built as a secondary level of protection, since usually the garage was pressurized and vehicles and personnel left it for the lunar surface through the oversized main airlock.

If the rebels have sealed the hatches, Giap's men were under orders to blast them open. If they had been able to bring their missile launchers with them they could have blown the hatches apart from where he was standing, outside the main airlock. As it was, the lighter, shoulder-fired missiles would have to do the job. The troops also had grenades. The hatches would pose no problem, Giap told himself.

Once inside the base proper, his troops would quickly move to the water factory, the control center, the electrical distribution station and the EVC—their environmental control center. Hold those, and you command Moonbase. For good measure, Giap had assigned squads to the underground farming area and the nano-laboratories.

"Sir, the airlocks seem to be operating normally," one of his captains reported. "The outer hatches are not sealed. Repeat, not sealed."

Giap suppressed a thrill of elation. So the rebels were going to surrender, after all.

"Have the outer hatches been UV sterilized?" he asked, still worrying about nanoweapons.

"Yes, sir."

"Very well. Open all the outer hatches," he commanded, "and check the inner hatches—after they've been UV treated."

"Yes, sir."

Don't congratulate yourself too soon, Giap warned himself. There could still be ambushes, traps, inside those corridors.

But he doubted it. What could the rebels do against armed troops in their midst?

CORRIDOR ONE

Ulf Jansen's only distinguishing feature was that he was the tallest trooper in the Peacekeeper battalion. At one hundred ninety-three centimeters, he towered over the Asians and Africans and Latinos who made up the bulk of the force. He dwarfed his commanding officer, Colonel Giap, and was a full head taller than Sergeant Slavodic, who headed his squad with an even-handed ferocity.

An easygoing, likeable Norwegian, Jansen had joined the Peacekeepers mainly to earn a U.N. scholarship to engineering college. In the four years of his enlistment he had been to Cyprus, Sri Lanka, the Malvinas Islands (which the British still insisted on calling the Falklands) and now he was on the Moon. Another three months and his enlistment would be over; he could start college in the winter semester.

He had been wounded slightly by an antipersonnel mine in Cyprus; otherwise his duties with the Peacekeepers had not been truly dangerous. He had to wear a germproof bio suit most of the time in Sri Lanka, a real misery in all that heat, but it had been better than coming down with the man-made plagues that both sides had used in the last round of their civil war.

Now he clumped into a smooth, metal-walled airlock, wearing a spacesuit that was much more comfortable than the biological protection gear from the Sri Lankan expedition. And everything was so light on the Moon! Jansen hefted his assault rifle as easily as he'd carry a toothpick.

"Move it up, move it up," his sergeant growled in the English that was the Peacekeepers' basic language. The whole squad was filing through the airlock, one man at a time. So far there'd been not the slightest sign of enemy opposition. As far as Jansen could tell, Moonbase might have been abandoned and left empty.

Both airlock hatches were fully open. The Moonbase rebels had pumped all the air out of the corridor on the other side of the hatches, so the troopers were filing through the airlock as quickly as they could.

The corridor on the other side of the hatch was dimly lit. Jansen could see another airlock about a hundred meters down the tunnel.

The sergeant brought up the rear. Once he stepped through the airlock he hustled up to where the officers—two lieutenants and a captain—were standing, poring over a book-sized computer.

"The water factory is on the other side of this hatch here," Jansen heard the captain saying as he tapped a gloved finger on the computer's tiny screen. "Down this corridor and through the cross—"

Jansen's earphones erupted with a brain-piercing screech, like electronic fingernails on an electronic blackboard. Jagged bursts of noise blasted at him. He put his hands to his ears, banged them into his helmet instead. The noise was painful, cutting through his skull like a surgeon's bone saw.

He saw the other troopers clutching at their helmets,

reeling, staggering under the agonizing assault of noise. Even the officers were flailing around helplessly.

His eyes streaming tears from the pain, Jansen fumbled for the control stud on his wrist and shut off his suit radio.

The noise cut off immediately. Blessed quiet.

"What is it?" Giap screamed. "What's going on?"

The noise assaulted his brain like a thousand rock concerts, all out of tune. Like a million jet planes taking off. He couldn't hear anything else. He couldn't speak to anyone. He couldn't think.

All around him, the troops of his third wave were pawing at their helmets, tottering across the dusty regolith in obvious agony, some of them falling to their knees.

Giap did the only thing he could think of. He switched off his suit radio. The silence was like a soothing balm, even though his ears continued to ring.

"Turn off your radios!" he commanded, then felt immediately foolish. His own radio was off; his words never got farther than the padding inside his helmet.

But he saw, one by one, his troopers were stopping their gyrations, standing still. Giap knew he himself was panting from the unexpected onslaught. He suspected the other troopers were, too.

He waved the captain of the third wave over to him as he yanked a communications wire from the thigh pouch of his suit. Plugging the wire into his helmet port, he handed it to the captain, who connected it to his own helmet.

"Now we can talk without need of the radios," Giap said.

"Yes, sir," replied the captain. Giap could hear his breathing, still heavy.

"The rebels think they can stall our attack by jamming our suit radio frequencies," the colonel said, with a hint of contempt.

"Yes, sir," the captain said.

"They didn't think that we can communicate directly by wire, without using the radios."

"Yes, sir. But sir, if I may ask: We can speak to each other through the wire, but how will you communicate with the rest of the troops? Especially the first and second waves?"

Giap blinked behind his gold-tinted visor. The first and second waves were inside Moonbase, out of reach, even out of sight.

Jansen stood patiently as the sergeant went down the line, plugging his comm line into a trooper's helmet, speaking a few words, then unplugging and going to the next trooper.

When his turn came at last, the sergeant said gruffly, "No radio. Follow the original plan. Watch my hand signals."

"Right, Sarge," Jansen had time to say before the sergeant popped the comm line out of his helmet and went to the next man in line.

Once the sergeant had relayed his message to every trooper in the squad he hustled back up to the front with the officers. He looked funny in the spacesuit, a short thickset figure in the heavy white suit, like a snowman with an assault rifle and a bandolier of grenades flapping lazily against his sides with every stride he took.

Jansen realized that no one could hear anything he said. Grinning delightedly, he called out, "You look stupid, Sarge!"

No reaction from anyone.

"You look like a fat white grub! You and the idiot officers, too!" he said in Norwegian.

The sergeant turned his way and for an instant Jansen's heart froze in his chest. But then the sergeant pointed to the hatch up ahead and motioned for the squad to follow him.

"Seal the hatches," Doug commanded quietly.

"We got 'em in the cages," said Anson, leaning over his shoulder. "Now we lock 'em in."

"Airlock hatches sealed," came the voice of one of the control technicians.

Doug turned to O'Malley. "Start your dust."

"Right," said O'Malley, tight-lipped.

Something made Jansen turn around as he started marching toward the next hatch. To his surprise, he saw the airlock they had already passed through sliding shut.

"Hey!" he yelped. "It's closing!"

No one heard him.

He stopped, and the trooper behind him bumped into him, jostling them both.

Jansen pointed and hollered louder, "They shut the hatch behind us!"

The whole line, from Jansen to the rear, came to a stop. Jansen turned toward the officers up front and waved his arms. "They shut the hatch behind us!" he screamed.

They paid not the slightest attention until they stopped at the closed hatch up front. Then, turning, they seemed to jerk with surprise—whether from seeing the hatch to their rear closed off, or from seeing half the squad loitering down the corridor, it was impossible for Jansen to tell.

He pointed at the closed hatch, jabbing his gloved hand in its direction several times. The sergeant came clomping down the corridor toward him, radiating anger even though his spacesuit.

"It's closed," Jansen said to the unhearing sergeant.

The lights seemed to be going dimmer. Jansen blinked and reflexively wiped at his visor. His glove left a dark smear across the tinted plastiglass.

"What's happening?" he asked, feeling the edge of panic. He was going blind. The world outside his helmet was nothing more than a misty blur. And it was getting darker by the second.

"What is happening in there?" Giap demanded.

The captain, the only person who could hear him,

pointed across the expanse of the garage. "It looks as if the inner hatches have closed."

"Closed?" Giap fumbled with his binoculars, got them to his visor, and swept his field of view across the four airlocks. The inner hatches of each of them were sealed tight.

"Get teams to each of those hatches. If they can't be opened manually, blast them open!"

The captain unplugged the communications line from his helmet, leaving it dangling across Giap's shoulder, and trotted off, fumbling in his thigh pouch for his own comm line.

This is absurd, Giap fumed. We are reduced to speaking to each other like children with a couple of paper cups connected by a length of string.

Everything took so damnably long! Commands had to be relayed from one officer to the next, down the chain of command, one person at a time. Fuming inside his spacesuit, Giap summoned a sergeant from the squad waiting as reserves.

Not bothering with the comm line, Giap pressed his helmet against the sergeant's, like embracing a loved one.

"Sergeant, pick six troopers and bring them to me. I will use them as runners."

"Runners, sir?"

"To carry messages, fool!"

"Ah! Runners! Yes, sir. Right away, sir." The sergeant was still babbling as he headed back to his squad.

Everything slowed down to the pace of a nightmare. Giap ordered a runner to find out what the captain was doing at the airlock hatches. It took long minutes before the woman came back, puffing, picked up the colonel's comm line and plugged it into her own helmet.

"The captain says the inner airlock hatches are closed, but they don't appear to be locked or sealed. He thinks he can open them manually."

"Why hasn't he already opened them?" Giap demanded.

"He's waiting for your orders, sir."

"Tell him to open those hatches and get the second wave into the base! And I want a report on what the first wave has accomplished."

"Yessir."

The trooper hustled off across the garage floor, looking to Giap more like a white humpbacked alien cyclops than a human being.

Edging closer to the wide-open hatch of the main airlock, Giap once again put his binoculars to his visor. It took agonizingly long, but at last the sergeant seemed to have gotten his order across to the captain. Gesticulating severely, the captain motioned one of his troopers to work the controls of the inner airlock hatch.

Giap saw the trooper step into the metal chamber and tap a button. At last! he thought, as the inner hatch started to slide open.

A ghostly gray mist seemed to waft out of the darkness from beyond the hatch. The trooper inside the airlock, the captain standing just outside it, the runner and several other troopers nearby began to paw at their visors. Giap watched as they staggered backward, gloved hands swiping at their visors like people trying to knuckle dust from their eyes.

Then they stretched their arms out, tottering uncertainly like blind men. The captain bumped into the runner and fell backwards in a dreamy, lunar slow motion until his rump bounced on the smooth rock floor of the garage.

Horrified, Giap shouted inside his helmet, "What's happened to them? They act as if they're blind!"

CONTROL CENTER

"It's working!" Anson said excitedly.

Doug nodded without taking his eyes off the console screens. The Peacekeepers inside the tunnels were truly deaf, dumb and blind now. Helpless. Even a few out in the garage had been blinded by the dust when they'd opened one of the inner airlock hatches.

"You did it!" Doug called over to O'Malley. He grinned boyishly and his cheeks reddened slightly.

"Are your people suited up?" Doug asked Anson.

"Ready to go," she replied.

He felt a touch on his shoulder and, turning in the little wheeled chair, saw Edith smiling wearily down at him.

"They cut me off," she said tiredly, her voice raw and cracking.

"You did a great job, Edith," Doug said, clutching her hand. "A wonderful job."

"You'll get an Emmy," Anson said, patting her shoulder.

"A Cronkite," Edith croaked. "It's more prestigious."

"Whatever." Anson pulled up a chair at the next console and slipped a headset over her blond curls.

Gordette slid a chair to Edith, who half-collapsed into it. "I forgot to time myself," she complained hoarsely. "I don't have the exact number for how long I was on the air nonstop."

"We'll dig it out of the computer," Doug said.

"Might be a record."

456

"You ought to get some rest. Go back to our quarters and take a nap. You've earned it."

"No," she murmured. "I want to stay here and see it all. I need a couple of cameras . . ."

"The security cameras are logging everything that's going on in here. Grab a bite at the Cave and then get some rest."

"I've got to go back to the studio. Get a camera. You guys ought to be immortalized for future generations and good ol' Global News."

Before Doug could stop her, Edith got to her feet and stumbled toward the door.

He watched her briefly, feeling a sudden urge to get up and put his arm around her, help her, share the comfort of closeness. But he fought it down and turned back to his screens. He had more important things to do.

Jansen fought down the urge to unseal his visor. He could see nothing, hear nothing, and no one could see or hear him, he was certain. It was scary. *If only I could see!* On Earth, he would have night vision goggles and infrared systems attached to his battle helmet. But they wouldn't fit inside a spacesuit, so the battle helmets had been left aside.

Something inside him was starting to shake. Lost. Alone. No one to give him orders. No one to tell him what to do. *Maybe the others are all dead! Or maybe they all got out okay; you might be the only one left in the tunnel.*

An enticing voice in his head urged, *Just open up the visor and see what's happening out there.*

But he knew the tunnel he was in had no air in it. *Open your visor and you kill yourself.*

But I've got to do something! his mind screamed. *I can't just stand here, blind and deaf. Maybe I can feel my way out, back to the garage . . .*

He tried a few steps, holding his arms out stiffly in front of him like a blind man. His gloved hands touched something solid and smooth. A wall. *Which way to the outside?* he asked himself. He started walking along the wall, keeping one hand on its reassuring solidity, taking small, frightened, hesitant steps.

And bumped into another figure. He stepped back and tripped over something: someone's legs, a body on the floor, he had no idea what it was. He lost his balance and began to fall in the slow, nightmarish languid gravity of the Moon.

He sprawled on the tunnel floor, yelling and cursing, tangled in somebody's limbs, hollering all the louder because nobody could hear him. His shouts became panicky; inside the total isolation of his helmet he heard his own voice screaming wildly, swearing, pleading for light and help and mercy. He wanted to cry; he wanted to beat his head against the wall that he could no longer find.

Something tapped at his helmet. He fell silent, trembling inside. Then he felt the poke of a communications line being inserted into the port on the right side of the helmet.

"Just relax, trooper. Everything will be fine." It was a woman's voice, but Jansen had never heard this woman before. A stranger.

"We're going to take care of you," she was saying, soothingly. "But first you have to let us take your rifle and other weapons."

"What's happening to me?" he asked, shocked at how high and weak his voice sounded. Like a frightened little boy's.

"Your officers have surrendered to us," said the woman. "Once we get these weapons off you, we'll bring you out to the crater floor and return you to your own people."

Jansen felt his rifle being lifted from his shoulder. Other hands took his bandolier of grenades and ammunition. Then they helped him to his feet.

"Okay, just walk this way . . . easy now."

Jansen let the strangers lead him blindly down the corridor. There was nothing else he could do. His spacesuit felt oddly stiff, the way an arthritic old man must feel. He thought he heard a grinding, rasping noise whenever he flexed his left knee.

Colonel Giap watched helplessly as, one by one, his troopers were led out of the tunnels by spacesuited rebels. The troopers had been disarmed, their weapons were nowhere in sight. They had not raised their hands above their helmeted heads, but it was clear that they had surrendered. They were prisoners. Defeated.

One of his runners trotted up to him and held up the communications line from his helmet. Impatiently, Giap gestured for him to plug it into his comm port.

"Sir! The Moonbase commander wishes to speak with you. On the radio, sir."

Giap felt his brows rise. "They have stopped the jamming?"

"The Moonbase officer that I spoke with said they will stop the jamming once you agree to speak to their commander."

Giap nodded inside his helmet. "Tell them I will speak to their commander." What else could he do?

The runner headed back into the garage. Giap turned and walked to a small rock, then sank down carefully onto it. He had been standing for hours, and even in the low gravity of the Moon, his legs were aching.

He watched as, one by one, his troopers were led out of the tunnels and into the garage like a collection of blind beggars, helpless and disarmed. He had to turn his entire body to see his reserve troops, loitering around their tractors out on the crater floor, some of them sitting on the cab roofs, watching and waiting.

His runner came back at last and told him, "The jamming will stop at precisely thirteen hundred hours, sir."

Giap peered at his wrist. Seven minutes from now.

"We've got all of 'em out," said Anson, from the console next to Doug's. "And we've got all their weapons."

"Those are shoulder-fired anti-tank rockets," Gordette said, pointing to one of the screens. "We could hit their tractors with 'em."

Not that we'll use them, Doug said to himself. But their commander doesn't know that. I hope.

His eye on the console's digital clock, Doug gestured to Anson to cut off the jamming signal at precisely fifty-nine minutes and fifty seconds after noon. Ten seconds later, he opened his radio channel to the Peacekeepers' suit-to-suit frequency.

"This is Douglas Stavenger, chief administrator of Moonbase," he said. "Am I on the proper frequency to speak with the commander of the Peacekeeper forces?"

"I am Colonel Ngo Duong Giap," came the reply. "This frequency is good."

There was no video; Doug's comm screen remained blank.

"Colonel Giap," he said, "I believe it is time we discussed an armistice."

"Armistice?" The colonel's surprised reply came immediately. The radio link between the Peacekeepers in the crater floor and the control center did not need to be relayed through L-1; the antennas built into the face of the mountain, just above Moonbase's main airlock, handled the link directly.

"Truce, armistice, whatever you want to call it," Doug said, feeling the tension and hope in the people clustering about him.

This time the Peacekeeper commander hesitated before replying.

Doug added, "Your attack has failed. Your troops had to surrender to us. We've let them return to you, but as you'll see, their spacesuits are heavily contaminated with dust. They can't see, and the joints of their suits will soon fail."

"That was merely my first wave," Colonel Giap snapped.

"The same thing will happen to your second wave," Doug replied. "And your third and fourth and fifth. We can blind your soldiers and jam your radio communications. We can gum up the joints of their spacesuits to the point where they'll quickly become immobilized. There is no way you can get through our tunnels."

"Nonsense!" spat the colonel. "We have enough weaponry to blast through your tunnels whenever we choose to."

Glancing at Anson and the others crowding around him, Doug said darkly, "And we have the weapons of your first wave soldiers now. We can shoot back. And men in spacesuits are extremely vulnerable. We won't need sharpshooters."

Giap sputtered something unintelligible.

"We have no desire to harm anyone," Doug said. "All we want is for you to withdraw and leave us alone."

After several heartbeats, Giap said, "This situation is beyond my authority. I will have to discuss this with my superiors."

"Fine," Doug replied. "I'll call again in exactly one hour. Until then, your suit-to-suit frequencies will be jammed again."

The nerve-shattering screech of the jamming pierced Giap's skull like a pair of icepicks driven into his eardrums. He banged on his wrist keypad to shut off his suit radio. As he got to his feet he saw that the other officers were doing the same.

Stomping angrily to the tractor that he had commandeered to be his command center, Giap clambered up into its cab. His communications sergeant was nowhere in sight; he would have to work the laptop himself. Worse still, he would have to face Faure.

No, he realized. There was something even worse. The insufferable Sacred Seven. Their young Japanese leader was waiting for him in the tractor's cab, sitting in the rear seat. Giap recognized the shoulder patch symbol on his spacesuit: a fist holding a lightning bolt.

And the volunteer was holding the end of a communications wire that was already plugged into his own helmet.

Reluctantly, Giap took the proffered wire and inserted it into his own helmet's comm port.

"Your attack failed," said the young Japanese. He sounded almost pleased.

"That was merely the first wave—"

"It failed," the volunteer said. "And I heard what the Stavenger person said to you. Now they have your first wave's weapons to repel your second wave."

Giap pulled the laptop communicator from the shelf under the tractor's dashboard. "I must contact the secretary-general."

"No need," said the volunteer. "Let *us* go in. We will destroy Moonbase and turn your defeat into a victory."

"I am not defeated!" Giap snarled. "Not yet!"

The volunteer leaned forward and rested his arms on the back of Giap's seat. The colonel could sense the young man's tolerant, insufferable smile.

"Why wait?" he said calmly, softly. "You have the means to destroy Moonbase at hand. Why not use it now, without asking permission from your superiors?"

Giap took several long breaths before replying, trying to calm himself. At last he answered, "I am a soldier, sir, not a savage or a madman. I fight to achieve a political goal, not merely to destroy."

"But you cannot fight without killing, without destruction, can you?"

"Death and destruction are the constant companions of soldiers, that is true," Giap admitted. "But they are not our *purpose*! They are not our *goal*! We fight because the politicians have failed to keep the peace. We do not fight for the love of killing, for the delight of destruction!"

"Admirable," said the young volunteer. "I am almost convinced that you truly believe that."

Giap's hands clenched into fists. For a burning moment he was ready, anxious, to give this young fanatic the death he was seeking. But the moment passed and he flipped his laptop open.

"I must speak with the secretary-general," he muttered, yanking the comm wire out of his helmet before he could hear the volunteer's sneering reply.

UNITED NATIONS HEADQUARTERS

It had been a hot, humid, hazy summer day in New York City. The kind of day when, in earlier times, before the Urban Corps, children would have turned fire hydrants into neighborhood sprinklers.

Now an early evening thunderstorm was booming across Manhattan, sending people scurrying indoors, slowing traffic on the streets and throughways, washing the city better than its maintenance workers ever did.

In his climate-controlled office George Faure was not bothered by the weather. Indeed, he had not even glanced out the dramatic ceiling-high windows since the Peacekeeper assault force had started its trek across Alphonsus' ringwall mountains.

The assault had not started well and Faure had been spitting with helpless rage as the Peacekeeper colonel reported being stalled in the pass across the mountains. But events had progressed better as the hours wore on.

The frustrating thing was that Faure had to watch the progress of the battle on Global News television, narrated by that turncoat slut Edie Elgin. But then her broadcast had been abruptly cut off, and Faure celebrated with a little dance across his office carpeting from his desk to the built-in bar, where he poured himself a stiff Pernod and water.

Now, slumped in his desk chair, he realized that his celebration had been premature. Colonel Giap was on his wallscreen, reporting in morose detail the defeat of his attack on Moonbase.

"In the tunnels my troops were blind and cut off from all radio communications. They ceased to be a cohesive military unit and were reduced to helpless individuals."

Faure stared at the faceless image of the spacesuited colonel, his chin sinking to his collar. He could hear his pulse thundering in his ears; burning fury seethed inside him like lava bubbling up from the depths of hell.

But he kept his silence. Mustache twitching, face glowering red, eyes narrowed to slits, he stared at the wallscreen until Colonel Giap finished his report.

"And what are your options?" Faure asked once he realized the colonel was waiting for him to say something.

For three long seconds the secretary-general stared at the image of the Peacekeeper officer.

At last Giap replied, "I can send in the second and third waves, but I believe the results would be the same. Once in Moonbase's tunnels, my troops are at the mercy of the rebels."

"And you did not foresee this?" Faure snapped.

Again the interminable wait. Then, "I did not foresee that the enemy would be able to blind my troops. I had considered the possibility that they might jam our suit radios, but the blinding was a surprise."

"So what do you recommend, *mon colonel*?"

The gold-tinted visor of Giap's spacesuit might as well have been a blank piece of modernistic sculpture, Faure thought. He would get no brilliance from this man, no military genius.

Giap said, "I recommend that we sever the electrical lines from their solar cell arrays into the base itself. That will cut off their electrical power and force them to surrender."

"No." Faure was surprised to hear his own response.

He realized that he had made his decision before he consciously recognized it. Yamagata wants Moonbase intact, so he can take it over and use it for his own purposes. I want Moonbase destroyed, Faure finally understood. Utterly destroyed. Its inhabitants killed. I want it levelled the way the Romans razed Carthage.

And then salt strewn across the ruins to assure that nothing will grow there again.

Moonbase has defied me, and for that they must be punished. Why should I allow Yamagata to have it as a gift? He will continue to use nanotechnology and show all the world that I am merely his puppet. But that is not the case, no, not at all. Georges Henri Faure is no one's puppet! I am secretary-general of the United Nations and Moonbase must bow to my will or be destroyed. And Yamagata must understand that I do not serve him; he serves me.

Giap was asking, "You don't want me to cut off their electrical power?"

"No," Faure repeated, realizing that it was all playing into his hands. Everything was going to be exactly as he wanted it. "Use the volunteers."

It was all falling perfectly into place, after all, Faure thought. Instead of accepting Moonbase's surrender, I will annihilate them. The nanotechnology treaty will be enforced; Yamagata will not be allowed to make a mockery of it. Or of me.

"Sir, I want to be certain that I have understood you correctly," Giap said. "Are you ordering me to use the volunteers?"

"Yes, *mon colonel,* that is an order."

The delay from Giap seemed to take longer than three seconds this time. "They will destroy Moonbase," he said, his voice hushed. "There will be many casualties."

"So be it," Faure replied. Better to destroy Moonbase than to allow Yamagata or anyone else to make a farce of my power, he told himself.

"Their hour's almost up," Anson pointed out.

Doug had been pacing around the control center, getting some circulation back in his legs, working out the stiffness of his back and shoulders.

The center had been in a state of suspended animation since Doug's discussion with Colonel Giap. Is it over? Have we won? Or will there be another attack, something new, something we haven't thought of, something we're not prepared to meet?

Why haven't they tried to cut the lines from the solar farms? Doug asked himself. Is it because they thought their nuke would do that job for them? We're still vulnerable, still hanging by a thread.

Unbidden, a line from a literature class came to him: *The ides of March are come,* Caesar says to the soothsayer, as he goes into the Senate, deriding the old man's warning. *Ay, Caesar,* says the soothsayer; *but not gone.*

We've stopped them, Doug told himself. But for how long?

They were all watching him: Jinny, Falcone, even Gordette, standing alone off by the wall. Every technician and specialist in the control center had his eyes on Doug. I wonder where Edith is? he asked himself. Did she go to our quarters for a nap? Bet not.

Edith was napping, but not in the quarters she shared with Doug.

She had tottered back to the university's studio, dog tired now that the adrenaline of being on the air had drained out of her, but intent on getting a camera and recording the doings in the control center.

She looked into the editing booth, still hot and sweaty from her hours in it, feeling slightly nettled that she didn't know for certain how many hours she'd spent broadcasting to Global News and, through Global, to the world.

She started for one of the hand-sized cameras resting in its rack, but Zimmerman's big plush couch looked too inviting to resist. Just a few minutes' snooze, she told herself. Stretching out on it, she was asleep within seconds.

"You heard the secretary-general's orders," said the volunteer. "*We* will bring you victory."

Giap turned to the leader of the self-styled Sacred Seven, sitting beside him on the tractor's bench.

"Not victory," he snarled. "Annihilation."

The young Japanese must have smiled behind his helmet visor. "As the secretary-general said, so be it."

The colonel had no reply. Yet he was thinking, I could still cut their electrical power lines. How long could they hold out then? A few hours, at most. They would have to surrender to me. That would be better than allowing these insane suicide bombers to kill everyone.

"I suggest," the volunteer said, "that you reestablish negotiations with the Moonbase commander, while your troopers help us to break into the plasma vent tunnels, as per our plan."

Giap noticed a slight but definite stress on the word *our*.

Precisely one hour after his conversation with the Peacekeeper commander ended, Doug sat at his console again and reopened the communications link.

"Have you spoken with your superiors, Colonel?" he asked.

"Yes. They are reluctant to admit that we have reached a stalemate here," came the colonel's voice.

Doug wished he could see the man's face. He sensed a tone he hadn't heard in their first discussion.

"What are you trying to say?" he asked.

"I am responsible directly to the secretary-general of the United Nations," Giap said. "My orders come directly from him."

Doug leaned forward anxiously in his chair. "And what are those orders?"

"He expects me to accept your surrender."

Doug heard Anson mutter behind him, "When he can breathe vacuum, that's when we'll surrender."

He said mildly to the blank screen, "Your first wave had to surrender to us, colonel."

Giap seemed to hesitate. Then he replied, "It would be quite easy for us to cut off your electrical power supply."

There it was, at last. Doug almost felt relieved. "Not as easy as you may think, Colonel," he replied. "We've buried secondary lines to take over if the primaries are cut."

"We have sensors that will find all the lines."

"And we have your first wave's weapons," said Doug, putting some steel into his voice. "Don't force us to use them."

"So we will have a firefight? I believe my troops have more guns—and more ammunition for them."

"How much oxygen do they have?" Doug asked.

"What do you mean?"

"How long can you remain out on the crater floor, colonel? Remember, we have some of your shoulder-fired missiles now. We can hit your tractors."

"We have all the logistics we need. You should surrender to me and avoid useless bloodshed."

Before Doug could reply, Gordette leaned over his shoulder and pointed to the screen showing the floor of the crater. "There's some activity out there."

Doug glanced at the screen. "Wait a moment, Colonel," he said. "I'll be back with you in a few minutes."

Cutting the connection to the Peacekeepers, Doug punched up a request to rerun the outside camera view.

"Look," Gordette pointed. "Over there."

A dozen spacesuited figures marched purposefully toward the main airlock. As they approached they walked out of the camera's field of view.

"What do the cameras inside the garage show?"

Checking on them, Doug and Gordette saw that the view from inside the garage did not show the dozen troopers at all.

"They stopped outside, off to one side of the main airlock," Doug said.

"Why?" asked Gordette.

"I'll try to find out," said Doug.

Colonel Giap was alone in the tractor's cab now. Through his binoculars he could see a squad of his troopers helping the Sacred Seven up an aluminum ladder they had placed against the face of the mountain, just to the side of Moonbase's main airlock. They were struggling to open the square hatch that led into the old plasma vents.

Giap had studied Moonbase's layout until he knew it as well as the face of his beloved mother. The plasma vents were from Moonbase's earliest days, when the builders were excavating tunnels by boiling away the rock with high-temperature plasma torches. The vents let the ultrahot vapors blow out into the vacuum outside. The vents had not been used, as far as Giap knew, in years. Yet they threaded through the rock above the main corridors of Moonbase. Crawling through them, a man could reach every critical part of the base.

The volunteers will penetrate the base before the rebels know they are being infiltrated. Their first warning will be when the fanatics begin to blow themselves up. Themselves, and every crucial part of Moonbase.

"Colonel Giap?" Stavenger's voice sounded in his earphones.

"I am still here," he answered.

"We saw a dozen or so of your troops move off to one side of the main airlock. Now they're out of our camera's view. What's going on?"

Giap was prepared for the question. "They are setting up a maintenance station to repair the spacesuits your dust has fouled. They are trying to remove the dust from their faceplates and joints."

Stavenger did not reply immediately. *Does he believe my lie?* Giap wondered.

"Let's get back to the main point," the Moonbase commander said at last. "Are you willing to withdraw and leave us in peace?"

"I am not allowed to do so," Giap stalled. "My orders do not permit it."

"If you try to cut off our electricity, we'll be forced to fire on you."

Giap thought the man's voice sounded very reluctant.

"Then I suggest you surrender, *now*. While you have the chance."

*   *   *

"... While you have the chance." Giap's voice had an urgency to it that made alarm bells ring in Doug's head.

"What do you mean?" he asked. "You won't accept a surrender if you're able to cut off our electricity?"

No answer for several long moments. Then the colonel replied, "If you fire upon my troopers, if a firefight is started, who knows what will happen next? A battle is not a predictable thing. There will be many deaths."

Doug got the distinct feeling that there was a hidden subtext in the colonel's words. He wants me to read between the lines, Doug thought. What's he trying to say?

"Colonel, I wonder what—"

The control center shook so abruptly that Doug nearly toppled off his chair. A low rumble echoed through the rock chamber. The lights flickered.

"What was that?"

"A quake?"

"An explosion!"

Doug scanned his screens with newfound intensity. The solar farms seemed intact; no was even near them.

"The water factory!" a technician yelped. "We've lost contact with the water factory."

"The bastards have blown up the water factory!"

CONTROL CENTER

"Give me a view of the water factory!" Doug yelled.

"Cameras are out," a technician hollered back.

Doug saw a blank screen where the view of the factory should have been.

"Jinny, get a repair team in there!"

"Already on their way," Anson yelled over her shoulder, halfway to the door.

"How did it happen?"

"Rerun the security camera."

With Gordette grasping both his shoulders from behind him, Doug saw the camera's view of the automated water factory. A blur of a figure dropped out of the top of the picture; a flash and then the camera went dead.

"What was that?" Doug asked.

"A man," said Gordette. "A person, anyway."

"In a spacesuit," someone else said.

"Spacesuit . . . ?" Doug's heart clutched in his chest. "The plasma vents! He came in through the old plasma vents!"

"What the hell are plasma vents?" Gordette asked.

The explosion staggered Zimmerman in his nanolab. A metal cylinder rolled of the bench and crashed to the tiled floor. Inoguchi grabbed the edge of the lab bench where he was standing to steady himself.

"A bomb?" Inoguchi asked.

"Or an accident of some sort," said Zimmerman. The two scientists had been working flat out on producing therapeutic nanomachines for Cardenas and the medical team in the infirmary. They had not followed the course of the battle. Zimmerman had insisted that he didn't want to know, not until it was over and decided, one way or the other.

"Should you try to find out?" Inoguchi said, looking worried. "Perhaps we should evacuate this laboratory?"

"Leave?" Zimmerman's shaggy brows shot up. "Before we have finished this batch? Abandon our work? Never!"

Inoguchi edged toward the nearest phone console. "Perhaps we should at least attempt to determine what has happened."

"Good. You call. I want to check the progress—"

An overhead panel ripped open with a blood-freezing screech of metal upon metal and two spacesuited figures dropped down in dreamy lunar slow-motion into the middle of the lab.

"*Gott in Himmel!*" Zimmerman roared. "What is this? How can I work with such interruptions?"

The two figures walked slowly among the lab benches, turning every which way, like children wandering through a toy store, as they approached the two scientists. Their spacesuits were bundled around their middles with bulky packages wrapped in plastic, with a simple small black box taped to them.

Inoguchi saw a red pushbutton on the black box of the intruder nearest him. Detonators! he realized.

The person nearest Zimmerman raised the visor of his helmet, revealing the face of a handsome young man with a neatly clipped dark beard.

"This is the nanotechnology laboratory?" he asked, in Oxford-accented English.

"Who are you?" Zimmerman demanded. "What are you doing in here?"

"Bombs," Inoguchi gasped, backing away toward the door to the corridor. "Suicide bombers!"

"Do not move!" the bearded young man commanded. Inoguchi froze in his tracks.

The other intruder raised her visor. "You are Professor Zimmerman, aren't you?" she asked in a sweet, lilting voice.

"Yes, and you are interrupting work of the utmost importance," Zimmerman blustered.

The young woman smiled. "God is great," she said, and pushed her detonator button.

Zimmerman saw a flash and then nothing.

The second explosion rattled the control center even harder than the first.

"They got the nanolab!"

"We're under attack!"

The plasma vents, Doug thought, remembering how he himself had crawled through the old vents, years ago, to get to the environmental control center before his insane half-brother could destroy it.

There's a double hatch in the face of the mountain, he recalled, a sort of primitive airlock. The vents are filled with air, but they can be opened to vacuum from here in the control center. Then he recalled that the intruder who dropped in on the water factory was in a spacesuit.

Someone was replaying the security camera view of the nanolab. Two spacesuited figures dropped in from the overhead vent.

Zimmerman! Doug suddenly realized.

"You've killed Professor Zimmerman!" he bellowed into his microphone. "You've killed Professor Zimmerman!"

Sitting alone in the cab of his tractor, Colonel Giap heard Stavenger's agonized wail.

"What are you doing to us?" the Moonbase leader howled. "Why? Why kill that old man?"

Why, indeed? Giap asked himself. Because a politician in New York ordered me to do it and I obey my orders. A soldier must obey orders, no matter how distasteful they may be. Without iron discipline no army can endure.

"This isn't war," Stavenger was shouting in his earphones. "It's butchery. It's indiscriminate slaughter."

"Yes," Giap said, so softly that he wasn't certain he said it at all. "Their intention is to wipe out Moonbase and everyone in it."

"You're going to kill us all."

"Not I," Giap said. "This is not my doing, not my wish. I am only following orders."

"So were Himmler and Borman and all the other Nazis." Stavenger's voice was acid.

Giap was silent for a moment, thinking, I have no orders that forbid me from telling him what he is facing. Faure did not command me to silence. Perhaps . . .

The colonel heard himself say, "You are being attacked by suicide bombers. Fanatics. Not Peacekeeper troops. Volunteers from the New Morality." His words came in a rush, as if he were afraid that if he stopped for an instant, took a breath or even a thought, he would close his mouth and say no more. "There are seven of them: one each for your water factory, environmental control center, electrical distribution station, control center and farm. Two for the nanotechnology laboratories."

Stavenger's voice was instantly calm, hard. "They're coming in through the old plasma vents?"

Giap nodded inside his helmet as he said, "Yes."

"And even if we surrender, they're going to blow up so much of Moonbase that we'll all be killed."

Again Giap nodded, but this time he couldn't force even the one syllable past his lips.

He turned off his radio connection with Moonbase. Further discussion would be fruitless, purposeless, ridiculous, he told himself. Now it is up to the people of Moonbase to defend themselves, if they can. I have told them more than I should. Now we will see what they can do with my information. If anything.

A screech of metal on metal startled Edith from her nap. She jerked up to a sitting position, blood running cold. Again! Like fingernails across a chalkboard.

As she blinked and looked around the darkened studio, a man in a spacesuit floated down from the shadowy ceiling and landed with a thump that buckled his knees.

Edith got up from Zimmerman's wide couch and went to the man, helped him to his feet.

"What're you doing here?" she asked. "What's going on?"

His reply was muffled by his helmet. Something about the control center, she thought.

"Can't hear you. Lift up your visor, you don't need to be sealed up inside your suit."

He lifted his visor. He was young, oriental.

"This is the control center?" he asked.

Edith shook her head. "You're way off base. The control center's almost half a—"

She stopped. She realized that this stranger was wrapped in what looked like explosives.

The main door to the water factory was warped by the explosion. Jinny Anson had to get two of the biggest

men she could find among the maintenance crew to push
the damned door open.

Inside was nothing but carnage, a smoking wreckage
of pipes and pumps, water gushing out into a crater
ripped into the rock floor. Water! Being wasted, sloshing
around across the floor, running out of pipes blasted
loose and dangling from shattered supports.

Coughing as she advanced into the smoky ruins,
Anson saw that the blast had dug a crater into the rock
floor and water from the broken pipes was rushing
into it.

"Get those pipes shut off," she said to the maintenance team. "Turn off that water flow."

"Water could leak into the tunnel below," one of the
men said.

Anson shook her head. "Doesn't look like the crater's
deep enough. The blast didn't penetrate into the lower
level."

A woman engineer pointed out, "Maybe so, but the
water's flowing into the piping and conduits between levels. Could short out the electrical lines."

"Jesus on jet skis!" Anson growled. "If water seeps
into the main distribution station . . ."

"Blackout," said the engineer.

"First thing is to stop the incoming flow," she said,
pointing to the maintenance crew already working on
the ends of the shattered pipes.

This water's come all the way from the south pole,
Anson told herself. And some brain-dead geek has to
blast the factory apart and splash it all over the base. It
was sacrilegious to her, to any of the old-time Lunatics,
to waste precious water.

"How can we remove the water that's already pooling
in the crater?" the engineer asked. "It must be seeping
along the conduits already."

Anson's answer was immediate. "We vacuum it out!"

"Huh?"

Doug sat frozen in front of his console, his mind spinning. Suicide bombers. Religious fanatics. How do we

stop them? They've already knocked out the water factory and Zimmerman's lab. The EVC and the electrical center and the farm are farther inside the base; the kamikazes haven't had time to reach that far yet. But the colonel said one of them is supposed to hit the control center. Why isn't he here yet?

"Bam," he said, turning to Gordette. "Get teams of people to guard the EVC—"

"And the other points, I know," Gordette replied. "We can use the guns we captured. Shoot the bastards soon's they open the ceiling vents."

"If you can do that without setting off their explosives."

Gordette shrugged. "Don't make that much nevermind, one way or the other, does it?"

Reluctantly, Doug admitted, "No, I guess not. But we've got to try *something*."

"True enough," Gordette agreed.

A comm tech's voice in his earphone called, "Urgent call from Anson at the water factory."

"What is it, Jinny?" Doug asked.

There was no video from the water factory, only Anson's tight, excited voice.

"You've got to open the plasma vents to vacuum," she said without preamble. "That's the only way to suck the loose water out of here. Otherwise it's going to seep down to the electrical distribution station and short out the whole goddamned base, I betcha."

"Open the vents to vacuum?"

"Right."

"But you've got people in the water factory."

"We'll be outta here in five minutes, tops. The place is a complete wreck. Got a team turning off the incoming stream, but there's a crater filling up with water and it's seeping into the pipes and conduits between levels."

Doug glanced at the big electronic schematic of the entire base on the wall above him. The water factory was dark, and he saw that one section of living quarters on the lower level had already blacked out.

"We're getting shorts in residential tunnel two," he said.

"Open the vents!" Anson urged. "Before the whole damned base shorts out!"

"Will do," he said, adding silently, If the controls still work.

"Give me five minutes to get my people out of here," Anson added.

"Will do," Doug repeated.

It took almost that long to call up the ancient program that operated the plasma vent baffles. There were two out at the mountain face, and single baffles spaced almost haphazardly along the old vents, hinged to flap open in one direction only—outward—like the valves in a human body's arteries.

He remembered that many of those partitions had been very tough to open when he'd crawled through the vents, seven years earlier. Hinges caked with lunar dust, almost welded shut. Will their motors work? Will they respond to the program commands?

A shadow fell across him and he looked up. Gordette was standing over him with an assault rifle held across his chest.

Before Doug could ask, Gordette smiled grimly and said, "I'm guarding the control center. Security's sent teams out to the other areas to guard them. They told me to stay here with you; they didn't want me with them."

Doug didn't have time to worry about Gordette's feelings. Blinking with a sudden idea, he said, as much to himself as to Gordette, "If we open *all* the plasma vents, we might flush out any of the kamikazes crawling through them."

Gordette's brows rose a half-centimeter, but he said nothing.

"Especially if we start pumping high-pressure air into the far end of each of the vents," Doug muttered. "We'll turn those old vents into wind tunnels!"

He called Vince Falcone over to him, hurriedly explained what he wanted, and then hunched over his keypad and began banging away at it.

PLASMA VENT TUNNEL

It was easy to become disoriented in the dark, empty plasma vent tunnels. Crawling along inside a spacesuit with a hundred kilos of explosive strapped to your waist did not make the job any simpler.

But I'll get there, Amos Yerkes told himself. I have the most difficult assignment, but I'll carry it out. They gave me the farthest target, the hardest one to reach, because they know I'm the best of the batch. The others needed drugs to buck up their courage, but I've never touched them. I'm better than they are and they know it. That's why they've entrusted me with the most demanding task: blowing up their environmental control center.

Yerkes was twenty-two and considered himself a failure as a son and as a man. But this is one thing I will not fail at. Nothing in my life, he slightly misquoted Shakespeare, will so become me as my leaving of it.

In the light of his helmet lamp he saw another of those dreadful partitions. It had taken him far longer to open the last few than he had thought it would. Hours, it seemed. They were all stuck fast, and he had been sweating inside his spacesuit before he could pull them down on their creaking hinges. Then, once he had crawled over them, they had each snapped shut again with a startling clang that could probably be heard over the length and breadth of the base.

This partition was no different: a thin baffle of metal, hinged on the bottom. Stuck fast with caked dust.

Yerkes brushed doggedly at the dust with his gloved fingers, wishing he could open his visor and blow the stuff out of his way. But he had been ordered to keep his spacesuit sealed, just in case the vent tunnels did not hold air as they believed.

As he worked, sweat stinging his eyes, he pictured the services that would be held in his honor back in Atlanta. General O'Conner himself will give the eulogy, he thought. My parents will cry and wish they had treated me better.

Vince Falcone was grateful for the Moon's low gravity as he and six other men trundled heavy cylinders of oxygen down the corridor toward the environmental control center.

Doug's idea was wild, Falcone thought, but he couldn't think of anything better.

This had better work, he told himself. Otherwise we'll all be dead in another half hour or so.

"You will take me to the control center," the space-suited Japanese said.

"I can't," Edith blurted.

He grabbed her wrist hard. "Why not?"

Thinking as swiftly as she ever had, Edith lied, "The corridors are guarded. We'd both be shot the minute we stepped outside."

He glared at her.

"And we're so far away from the control center," Edith quickly added, "that your bomb wouldn't touch it if you set it off in here."

Still glaring, he looked around at the studio's cameras and fake-bookcase sets. Not a worthy target.

"You're hurting my wrist," Edith said.

He let go. "You are my hostage," he said.

"Okay," she said, looking around the empty, sparsely lit studio. Nowhere to hide, nothing here but video and VR equipment. Even if I grabbed a camera or tripod or something and tried to bonk him, he's protected by his helmet. And he might set off his bomb.

"You will call the control center and tell them to surrender to me," the young man said, his voice harsh, guttural. "If you refuse I will kill us both."

"Oh, I'll call them, don't worry about that."

Doug fidgeted on his chair, waiting for Falcone to report he was ready to pump high-pressure oxygen into the plasma vents.

"We're clear of the factory," Jinny Anson reported from a corridor wall phone. "Had to seal the whole section of corridor, 'cause the door to the factory's been damaged by the blast."

"Okay, fine," Doug said. "We ought to open the vents to vacuum in a few minutes." Silently he added, Come on, Vince!

"Call from the university studio," a comm tech's voice said in his earphone.

Edith, he knew. Doug nodded and touched the proper keypad.

Edith's face appeared on his central screen. She looked strained, worried. Then Doug saw, behind her, the face of an oriental in a spacesuit helmet.

"Doug, I'm a hostage—"

The intruder pushed her aside. "You must surrender to me immediately! If you don't, I will blow up this chamber with this woman in it!"

Doug felt as if someone had pushed him off a cliff. His mouth went dry. It took him two swallows to work up enough moisture to reply, "Hold on. I'll surrender. Just don't do anything foolish."

"I must speak to the commander of Moonbase!" the suicide bomber insisted. "No underlings!"

"I'm Douglas Stavenger, the chief administrator of Moonbase."

The Japanese's eyes widened momentarily. "Douglas Stavenger? The one whose body is filled with nanomachines?"

"Yes, that's me." Doug felt Bam Gordette's presence behind him, strong, protective.

"You must come here and surrender to me personally!"

"I understand."

"Now! Quickly! Otherwise I kill her!"

"Okay, I'm on my way," Doug said. He cut the connection and jumped up from his chair.

Gordette stood in his way. "You go in there, he's gonna set off his explosives."

"If I don't go, he's going to kill Edith."

ENVIRONMENTAL CONTROL CENTER

Falcone and his team threaded their way through the maze of piping and pumps that recycled and circulated air through Moonbase, dragging the cylinders of high-pressure oxygen clunking loudly along the narrow metal mesh walkways that twined through the throbbing equipment.

"There it is!" one of his men shouted, pointing to a metal hatch set into the rock ceiling.

Falcone squinted up to where the man was pointing. The ceiling was shadowy, criss-crossed with pipes.

"Naw," he said. "Farther back. We want the last one of the hatches. The very last one."

The man grumbled but moved on, deeper into the EVC.

"Is this really gonna work?" asked the guy just behind Falcone, gasping with exertion as he dragged a bulky oxygen cylinder.

"High-pressure gas on this end, vacuum on the other end. Oughtta blow out anything in the vents that ain't fastened down."

"Oughtta," the man puffed.

Oughtta, Falcone said to himself. If the team with the friggin' hoses shows up in time.

Doug spoke into his handheld phone as he ran along the corridor toward the university studio.

"How soon?" he demanded.

"Got the hoses, finally," Falcone's voice crackled. "Gimme five minutes."

"We've got to open the vents to vacuum, Vince! Water's shorting out half the sections on level two."

"Three minutes."

"Call the control center when you're ready. Jinny's back and she'll handle it."

"What about you?"

Glancing at Gordette, loping along beside him with his assault rifle gripped tightly in his hands, Doug replied, "I've got other problems."

As far as Amos Yerkes could tell, this was the last partition between him and the environmental control center. Blinking at the sweat trickling into his eyes, telling himself he should have thought to wear a headband, he pulled out the schematic map of Moonbase and tried to check out where he actually was.

Yes, that should be the end of the tunnel, on the other side of this partition. One more to go and he'd be directly over Moonbase's environmental control center.

When I blow *that* up, he thought happily, they won't have any air to breathe. I won't go alone; I'll take *all* of them with me!

He started working on the partition with newfound energy.

Face streaked with grease, Jinny Anson sat at the same console Doug had been using, finger hovering over the keypad that would open all the plasma vent baffles.

Come on, Vince, she grumbled to herself. Move it, you big ape.

As if he'd heard her, Falcone's swarthy face appeared on the screen showing the environmental control center.

Grinning broadly, he said, "All connected. We're ready anytime you are."

Anson let out a grateful sigh, then said, "Ten seconds?"

"Ten seconds," Falcone said, teeth flashing.

"On my mark . . ." She glanced at the console's digital clock. "Mark!"

"Ten seconds and counting," Falcone said.

As they approached the double doors of the studio, Doug said to Gordette, "Are you a good enough shot to get him without hitting the explosives?"

Gordette grunted. "Which eye do you want me to hit?"

Doug almost stopped running. We're going to kill a man, he realized. Deliberately kill him. Or try to.

"Besides," Gordette added, "they're most likely carrying plastic explosives. Bullets won't set 'em off."

"You're sure?"

"Yep," said Gordette, without missing a stride.

As he worked on the final partition, Yerkes wondered how the other volunteers had done. He had felt the rumble of two explosions, it seemed like hours ago. Since then nothing. The others must be having the same troubles I've had, he thought. But they don't have as far to travel as I do. I'll blow up my target before they even get to theirs.

The thought pleased him.

The partition was loosening, he could feel it as he dug the accumulated dust away from its hinges. Not merely loosening, it was shaking, flapping—

It sprang open, banging on his helmet, half stunning Yerkes. He heard a rushing sound, like wind, like a roaring hurricane.

He was sliding along the vent, skidding backwards on his belly, being pushed by some giant hand faster and faster. The dim circle of light thrown by his helmet lamp showed the vent walls speeding past.

Desperately he tried to stop himself, dig his gloved fingers into the vent floor, but there was nothing to grab onto. He reached out sideways toward the tunnel walls, but the force of the wind tore at his hands, his arms, and he skidded along backwards, screaming now in fear as he slid down the vent like a feather caught in a tornado.

Colonel Giap had climbed up onto the roof of his tractor's cab. There had been no word from Moonbase since he'd told Stavenger about the suicide bombers. His troops loitered around their vehicles, waiting for the inevitable. The ground had trembled twice, almost an hour earlier. Then nothing but silence and stillness.

Giap looked at the watch on the wrist of his spacesuit. They're all dead in there by now, he thought. Dead or dying. I should send the troops in, perhaps we can save a few.

Something caught his eye. He blinked, not sure of what he was seeing. A cloud of glittering sparkles was erupting slowly from the hatch that opened into the plasma vents. The ladder that his troops had placed there toppled slowly, like a stiff, arthritic old man, and fell flat on the crater floor in complete silence, sending up a puff of dust.

It was like a geyser, Giap thought, but a geyser of scintillating little jewels that flashed and twinkled in the harsh sunlight. On and on it went, spewing slowly out from the plasma vent hatch across the dark lunar sky, a thousand million fireflies flickering in all the colors of the rainbow.

Then something solid and heavy came shooting out of the hatch. Giap saw arms and legs flailing. A spacesuit! A man! One of the suicide volunteers, he realized. The body soared across the crater floor and landed with a thump that raised a lazy cloud of dust. It did not move once it hit.

Giap stared, not knowing what to think, what to do. Another body came flying out, tumbling like a pinwheel, landing helmet-first on the regolith. And then a third, limbs hanging loosely, already unconscious or dead. It fell near the other two.

THE STUDIO

Doug stopped in front of the double doors marked lunar university video center: DO NOT ENTER WHEN RED LIGHT IS FLASHING.

As he reached for the door pull, Gordette grabbed at his hand.

"Hold it," Gordette said. "Look before you leap."

Doug nodded and went to the wall phone next to the doors. Calling the control center, he asked for the security camera view of the studio.

The wall phone's screen was tiny. It showed the panoramic view of the studio from the ceiling.

"Maximum zoom," Doug ordered, "and pan across the room."

The picture tracked across the studio, shadowy and dim in its spotty lighting. Cameras, monitors, racks of electronic equipment, the editing booth—empty—the sets where Zimmerman and Cardenas and others had given their lectures and demonstrations, also empty.

The thought of Zimmerman sent a pang through Doug, but he swiftly suppressed it. Edith is in there with a crazy man, he reminded himself. That's what's important now.

"Hold it there," Gordette snapped.

The camera stopped. Doug could see Zimmerman's extra-wide couch had been pulled from the wall; Edith and the spacesuited suicide bomber were crouched behind it.

"Well, he's no fool," Gordette muttered. "Dug himself in as far from the door as he could. Long as he stays behind the couch I won't be able to snipe him. Have to spray the whole couch."

"And kill Edith?"

"Maybe you can talk him into letting her—oh, oh!"

"What?"

"Is that the best magnification we can get?"

"Yes," Doug said. "What is it?"

Squinting hard at the little screen, Gordette said, "Looks like he's already got his thumb on the detonator button."

"So?"

"That arms the detonator. When he takes his thumb off the button the bomb goes off."

Doug felt his insides sink. "So if you shoot him it explodes?"

"Yeah."

"What can we do?"

"Talk him into disarming the detonator."

Doug knew how futile that was. "Or into letting Edith go."

Gordette inclined his head slightly in what might have been a nod. "There is that."

Anson peered at the screen showing the camera's view of the crater floor just outside the main airlock. Spacesuited Peacekeeper troops were gathering around the three unmoving bodies sprawled on the ground.

"Two hit the nanolabs," she said, ticking off on her fingers, "one did the water factory. That's three. One's in the studio, that's four. And those three make seven. That's all of 'em."

"The water's out of the factory," said the technician next to her. "Maintenance crews are reestablishing electrical power in the areas that were shorted out."

Vince Falcone trudged into the control center, a bright grin slashing across his dark stubbly face.

Anson got up from her chair, yanked off her headset, and threw her arms around Falcone's neck. "We did it!" she said, then kissed him soundly.

Despite his swarthy complexion, Falcone blushed visibly. "Yeah, okay, we flushed out the garbage," he said. "But there's still one of the bastards in the studio, isn't there?"

Colonel Giap was almost glad when he told Faure, "They have defeated us. There is nothing more we can do."

Faure's image on the colonel's laptop screen was nearly purple with rage. "But there must be something! Your second wave of troops! The solar farms! Something!"

Resignedly, Giap said, "If I send more troops into those tunnels, they will be blinded and neutralized just as the first wave was. If I try to destroy their solar energy farms, they will engage us in a firefight that will cause unacceptable casualties."

Then he waited three seconds, watching Faure's helpless frustration. Perhaps the little man will give himself a stroke, Giap thought.

Faure's reply was explosive. "Who are you to decide how many casualties are unacceptable! I am your superior! I make such decisions!"

"Throwing away lives will be pointless," Giap said. "I will not do it."

As he waited for Faure's reply, Giap reflected that battles are won or lost on the moral level. One side loses the will to fight, and that's what has happened to me. Why should I throw away my troopers' lives for that pompous little politician in New York? To destroy Moonbase? To kill two thousand civilians?

"Are you saying to me," Faure replied at last, voice barely under control, "that you would refuse my direct order?"

"I am saying that I will resign my commission before carrying out such an order," Giap said, almost surprised to hear his own words.

We could tear up their radiators, he thought. Or simply cut the pipes that connect the radiators to the inside of the base, and then leave. That would take only a few minutes and it would leave them to cook in their own waste heat. There would be no firefight, not if we left immediately afterward. But what good would that do? They would come out and repair the damage.

No, he said to himself, best to leave now while the entire force is alive and unhurt. The Sacred Seven have killed themselves, that's enough. No sense killing more.

"It's me he wants," Doug said, reaching for the studio door again. "He'll trade Edith for me."

"Maybe," Gordette replied.

"It's the only chance we've got."

"What's this 'we,' white man? He wants to blow *you* away!"

"I can't stand out here and let him kill Edith."

Gazing at him with red-rimmed eyes, Gordette said softly, "I know."

Gordette seemed to relax. He let go of the assault rifle with one of his hands, holding it only by its barrel, letting its butt touch the floor.

"You stay out here, Bam," said Doug. "If he sees you with the gun, he might touch himself off."

"Yeah," Gordette said with a resigned sigh. "Go ahead."

He watched Doug open the door and step inside the dimly lit studio, thinking to himself, Doug wants to die. He's ready for it. They've worn him down to the point where he's willing to give them his life in exchange for hers. Then Gordette realized that it wasn't merely in exchange for Edith. It's for Moonbase, he understood at last. He's willing to give his life for ours. All of us. For chrissakes, he's willing to die for *me*.

And what am I willing to do for him? Gordette asked himself. Then a new thought touched him: If he dies, what happens to me? The rest of the people around here don't trust me. They hate me. They'll even blame me for not protecting Doug. But what can I do? What do I want to do? Am I willing to get myself killed for him?

Doug, meanwhile, had taken a few steps inside the studio. He called out, "Edith, are you all right?"

She rose to her feet slowly. "I'm okay." Her voice was shaky.

The suicide bomber poked the top of his head above the couch's back. Doug saw that he had taken off his spacesuit helmet, but couldn't see where his hands were.

"You are Douglas Stavenger?"

"I am Douglas Stavenger."

The man hissed with satisfaction. "*Kami wa subarashi!* You will come here, to me. Now!"

"First you've got to let her go," Doug said.

"When you are here beside me I will allow her to leave."

"No," Doug said. "You release her first. Once she's safely out of this room, I'll come and stand beside you."

"You do not trust me?"

Doug almost smiled. "I want to make sure that she's safe. That there aren't any . . . accidents."

"Why should I trust you? You are filled with the devil machines!"

And you are filled with hate, Doug thought. Or is it fear? Can I work on his fear, or will that just make things worse?

"My nanomachines can't harm you or anyone else," he said.

"It makes no difference," the young man said. "Soon we will both be dead."

"Yes, that's true. But let the woman go. She has nothing to do with what must happen between you and me. She's a visitor here, trapped by the war. Let her go."

"When you come to me, she can go."

Stalemate. Then Doug thought, "At least allow her to get a camera and make a video record of our last moments together. So the whole world can see what you did."

Even from across the half-lit studio Doug could see the young man's eyes brighten. He started to respond, then hesitated.

Doug felt his pulse thundering in his ears.

At last the suicide bomber said gruffly, "Very well, she can video our last moments."

If Edith minded that both the men were talking about her in the third person, she didn't show it. Without another word being said, she walked purposefully from behind the couch to the rack of electronic equipment near the door.

The suicide bomber remained almost totally hidden behind the couch. Is there enough of him showing for Bam to get a shot off? Doug wondered.

"Now you come here!" the young man commanded.

"No!" Gordette roared.

Wheeling, Doug had just a split-second to see Gordette's fist coming at his jaw. Then everything went blurry and he felt himself sagging to the floor.

"Get out of here!" Gordette yelled to Edith. "Take him with you!"

"No! Stop!" the suicide bomber screamed. "I will kill us all!"

Doug felt Edith's arms clutch him, dragging him toward the door. It was only a few steps away, but it seemed like miles.

"Wha . . ." he heard himself mumble, still dazed, legs stumbling awkwardly. "Wait, don't . . ."

"Stop! Who are you?" the suicide bomber yelled, ducking behind the couch again.

Walking deliberately toward the couch, assault rifle levelled at his hip, Gordette said, "I'm the angel of death, man. You want to die? Well, so do I."

Gordette smiled as he realized the beautiful, inevitable truth to it. I'm the one who's been rushing toward death, he knew at last. I'm the one who needs to die. At least now my death will mean something, accomplish something.

"I'll kill us all!" the bomber screamed.

"You go right ahead," Gordette answered calmly.

Doug was struggling to his feet out in the corridor while Edith was sliding the door shut. He heard the chatter of the assault rifle and then an explosion ripped the doors off their slides and flung Edith across the corridor.

*   *   *

It took fully half an hour for Georges Faure to calm himself to the point where he could touch his intercom keypad with a trembling finger and say, his voice hardly shaking at all:

"I see that several calls have accumulated while I was speaking with the Peacekeepers on the Moon. Tell them all that I am unavailable."

His aide replied from the outer office, "Mr. Yamagata is most insistent, sir."

Faure saw that Yamagata's name was at the top of the list on his desktop screen.

"I am unavailable," he repeated sternly.

"Yes, sir."

For long moments Faure sat there in his desk chair, feeling cold sweat soaking him. I must look terrible, he thought. He pushed himself to his feet and tottered across the thick carpeting to his lavatory.

In the mirror over the sink he saw the face of a defeated man. The Moonbase rebels have won the victory, he told himself.

He splashed water on his face, mopped it dry, then carefully combed his hair. I must change the clothes, he thought. This suit is wrinkled and damp.

As he reached for the cologne, the phone beside the sink chimed. He ignored it.

Moonbase has won the battle, he said to himself, patting the musk-scented cologne on his cheeks, but not the war. Straightening his slumped spine, squaring his shoulders, he repeated to his image in the mirror, No, not the war.

The phone chimed again. And again.

Banging its keypad, Faure snarled, "I told you that I am unavailable!"

His aide's awed voice said, "But it's the president of the United States, sir."

Faure's shoulders sagged. Perhaps the war is lost after all, he thought.

THE INFIRMARY

Edith swam up out of the black depths and tried to open her eyes. They were gummy, as if she'd been asleep a long, long time. A figure was standing over her, its face a blur. Blinking, she brought it into focus.

"Doug," she croaked. Her voice sounded strange to her, as if she hadn't really spoken at all but merely mouthed the word.

He smiled down at her, and she noticed that he had a jagged red line running across one side of his forehead. He leaned down and kissed her lightly on the lips. His mouth moved, but no sound came out of it.

Still smiling, he reached toward her. She felt him pushing something into her ear.

"Can you hear me now?" he asked. His voice sounded tinny, as if it were coming through a bad radio. And there was an annoying ringing sound in the background.

She nodded.

"The explosion deafened both of us," he said, as if his voice were coming through a tunnel from Mars. "My nanomachines fixed me up in a couple of hours, but you'll have to wear an earplug for a few days."

Edith realized that her vision was partially blocked by a large white lump, a bandage. She put her hands to her face; they were both heavily bandaged.

"You got pretty badly banged up, saving my life," Doug said. "You got me out into the corridor, but when the doors blew they knocked you into the opposite wall."

"My face?" she asked.

"The best plastic surgeon in the States is on his way here. You'll be good as new in a few weeks. Faster, if you'll accept nanotherapy."

"Nano—" Suddenly what he was saying clicked in her mind. "A surgeon from the States? The blockade's over?"

"The war's over," Doug said. "We've won. Sort of."

Edith tried to push herself up to a sitting position, but a jagged bolt of pain made her sink back onto the pillows. Doug reached for her.

"Take it easy," he said. "You're not ready to go dancing yet."

"You are."

"I get a little help from my friends," Doug said.

"You can put nanos in me? Help me recover?"

"Yes," he said. "Kris Cardenas will talk to you in a little while about it."

"What about the war? We won?"

"The Peacekeepers have gone back to Nippon One, with the bodies of three of the suicide bombers. Japan and the United States have both demanded a Security Council review of Faure's actions against Moonbase. The World Court has agreed to hear our petition for independence in November. They've ordered Faure to leave us alone until they make their decision."

"We've won," Edith said. It seemed to take what little strength she had. "You've won, Doug."

"It's cost us a lot. Zimmerman, the water factory, Bam Gordette."

She remembered those last moments in the studio. "When he hit you, I thought he'd turned traitor again. I thought he was on their side."

"He saved the two of us," Doug said. "He gave his life for us."

"He wanted to die," Edith remembered. "He said so. Just like the suicide bomber."

Doug shook his head sorrowfully. "Bam. Zimmerman. My stepfather, Lev, too. And Tamara."

"You've lost a lot."

"We can rebuild the water factory," he said, his voice low, mournful. "But the people can't be replaced."

"All because of Faure."

"No, it's not just him. He couldn't have gotten anywhere if he didn't have the backing of so many people. You're the real hero of this war, Edith. You turned public opinion onto our side and against Faure."

"All I did was blabber."

A faint smile tweaked his lips. "Damned good blabber."

She pretended shock. "Profanity? Out of you?"

Doug's smile widened a bit. "It's been a long, hard day. And then some."

"That's all right," Edith said. "It's been worth it. Despite everything, it's been worth it."

He nodded. "Maybe you're right. I hope so."

CHRISTMAS EVE

Doug checked his wristwatch against the digital wall clock as he paced the empty lounge of the rocket port.

It's going to be close, he said to himself. Razor close.

As he waited impatiently, he thought back to the days when he'd sneak out to the old rocket port just to watch the lunar transfer vehicles land or take off. It was not even eight years ago, but it seemed lost back in the hazy mists of ancient history.

Now he watched a wall-sized screen in the underground lounge of the rocket port as the LTV carrying his mother gracefully descended on invisible jets of rocket exhaust, kicking up a small storm of dust and pebbles around the concrete landing pad. The big ungainly spacecraft settled slowly on its strut-thin legs. With its bulbous glassteel pods for the crew and passengers, it looked to Doug like a giant metallic insect squatting on the lunar surface.

Okay, they're down. Now get the access tube connected. We don't have a minute to spare.

The newly decorated lounge was empty, except for him. His mother and the medical team were the only passengers on this LTV, except for the body of Lev Brudnoy.

Doug had expected his life to simplify once the war was over, but it had become more hectic. While Joanna and Seigo Yamagata personally negotiated a merger between Masterson Aerospace Corporation and Yamagata Industries, Ltd., Doug was drawn into the whirl of establishing a government for the independent Moonbase and handling the delicate personnel problems of men and women who wanted to remain on the Moon without giving up their Earthside citizenships.

Tomorrow Toshiro Takai was scheduled to arrive from Nippon One, his first visit to Moonbase in the flesh after years of virtual reality contacts. Doug was going to broach the extremely sensitive subject of inviting Nippon One to join Moonbase and declare its independence from Japan. He doubted that Takai would be able to carry that off, but he knew his VR friend would feel slighted if he didn't at least ask.

And there was so much to do before Takai arrived. Again Doug looked at the wall clock. Its digital numbers seemed to be leaping ahead.

At last one of the port technicians entered the lounge, ambling too slowly to please Doug, and tapped at the wall pad by the access tunnel hatch. The gleaming metal door popped open a few centimeters, with a sigh of air blowing in from the slightly overpressurized tunnel.

Feeling nervous, anxious, Doug watched as the LTV's two pilots pushed the hatch fully open from the other side. The medical team was right behind them, four doctors, two men and two women. They looked self-assured, competent in their Earthside business clothes as the port technician led them to the tractor that was waiting to whisk them to the infirmary.

At last Joanna stepped through, looking years older than the last time Doug had seen her, but still regally splendid in a Yuletide green dress that glittered in the light from the ceiling panels.

"Welcome to Moonbase," Doug said ritually, then embraced his mother.

She was tired, he could see, dark rings circled her eyes. But he urged her, "Come on, we don't have a minute to lose."

"My things . . ."

"The ground crew will take care of them. I briefed them myself. They know what to do."

She nodded, just a trifle hesitant, but let Doug take her by the wrist and lead her out to the tunnel that ran back to the main section of the base. He helped her up into the old standby tractor, then climbed into the driver's seat and started its electric motors.

"I hope we're not too late," Joanna said.

"We're shaving it close."

As they drove through the long, straight, featureless tunnel, the wide-spaced overhead lights casting shadows across their faces like the phases of the Moon, Joanna told her son about the negotiations with Yamagata.

"We've got to be able to continue manufacturing Clipperships," Doug said. "That's the important thing. That's Moonbase's economic lifeblood."

"Seigo's agreed to that," Joanna said. "He's all in favor of it, now that Faure's stepping down from the U.N. We're even talking about manufacturing automobiles."

"With nanomachines?"

"In Japan."

"Wow! Things really have changed!"

"In fact," Joanna continued, "it turns out that one of the major reasons why he wanted control of Moonbase was your nanotechnology capability."

Doug shot her a puzzled frown. "But I thought—"

Joanna silenced him with an upraised hand. "Seigo

has a genetic predisposition to cancer. He wants to be able to come up here and have nanotherapy to remove any tumors he may develop."

"That's why he wanted Moonbase?"

She nodded. "That's his real reason. He was willing to go along with Faure to gain control of Moonbase, as long as he could have nanotherapy in secret."

"And he killed Zimmerman in the process."

"Kris Cardenas is still here."

Anger simmering in his guts, Doug grumbled, "Why should we let Kris help him? He killed Zimmerman! He might even have been involved in Lev's murder."

Joanna seemed strangely unperturbed. "Don't leap to conclusions, Doug. Seigo's not the devil incarnate. Have some Christmas charity."

He stared at her as the lights flashed by. "What's going on between you two?"

"Nothing," she said quickly. "Except—I think we've learned to respect each other. And he had nothing to do with Lev's death. That was strictly the New Morality's doing."

"You're sure?"

"My security people found that the corporation is honeycombed with New Morality zealots. That's why I've decided to live up here permanently."

"Can't you do anything about them? Back Earthside, I mean."

Joanna said matter-of-factly, "There are too many of them, Doug. As long as we can operate here on the Moon and use nanotechnology, let them stew in their own juices for a generation or two. They'll get what they deserve."

"You sound like Jinny Anson," he said. "If she had her way, we wouldn't have any contact with Earth at all."

"That wouldn't be so bad, at that."

Doug suddenly saw the full Earth in his mind's eye, hanging in the dark lunar sky, shining bright and beautiful.

"We can't let them strangle themselves," he murmured.

"Doug, there's more than ten billion people on Earth," Joanna said. "We can't save them."

"Yes we can," he insisted. "We can try, at least."

She shook her head. "I thought you wanted to look outward and push the frontier."

"That's the best way to help them. Create new knowledge, new wealth. Keep the safety valve open for anyone who wants to use it."

Joanna took a deep breath. "You almost sound religious."

He broke into grin. "Well, it is Christmas—almost."

She had no reply and they rode to the end of the tunnel in silence. As they got down from the tractor, Doug said, "I hope the medical team got there in time."

He had to slow his pace to accommodate his mother, a little wobbly in the low gravity despite the weighted boots she wore. As they approached the infirmary Doug saw that a small crowd had gathered outside: Anson, Falcone, even Janos Kadar was out there, waiting.

Doug pushed through them and into the infirmary's observation room, Joanna right behind him.

Nick O'Malley was just stepping through the door from inside the infirmary, stripping off a surgical mask. His face was sweaty, pale.

"I hope I never have to go through that again," he said, his voice shaking.

Kris Cardenas and her husband Pete, the neurosurgeon, came out right behind O'Malley.

"Your Earthside team was too late," Kris said, smiling broadly.

As O'Malley sank into one of the chairs along the far wall, Pete Cardenas announced, "It's a six-pound, five-ounce baby girl."

"Mother and daughter are both fine," Kris added. "Natural childbirth without the obstetrics team you brought in from Earthside."

"The first baby born on the Moon," Joanna said, sitting in the chair next to O'Malley.

"Congratulations, Daddy," Kris said to him.

Doug held out his hand and O'Malley took it in a limp, weary grip. "Never again," he muttered.

"Look!"

Turning to the observation window, Doug saw Edith holding a conglomeration of blankets in her arms with a tiny, red, squirming bald baby in the middle of it.

"I got the whole thing on camera," Edith said through the window. "She'll be on Global News in a few hours."

O'Malley brightened a bit and pushed himself to his feet. "She's kinda beautiful, isn't she?"

"Even in the midst of life, we are in the midst of death," intoned Robert Wicksen. Doug had been surprised when Wix had volunteered to preside at Lev Brudnoy's burial service. The physicist was also a lay minister, he had revealed.

Now they put Lev's remains into the soil of the farm he had lovingly tended over the years.

"Ashes to ashes," Wicksen murmured. "Dust to dust."

Doug stood at his mother's side. Joanna sobbed quietly as Lev was lowered into the ground where he had planted the Moon's first flowers.

Hours later, after dinner, Edith and Doug joined practically everyone else in Moonbase in decorating the three-meter-tall aluminum tree that had been erected in the middle of the Cave. There was plenty of rocket juice going around, and god knows what else. The party went from festive to raucous as the hours wore on.

Long after midnight, Doug walked beside Edith as they headed for their quarters. The alcohol he had consumed was quickly and efficiently broken down by the nanomachines inside him. Doug regretted that he couldn't get drunk even when he wanted to.

Edith seemed quite sober, as well. The gashes on her face were completely healed, not even the slightest trace of a scar, thanks to the nanotherapy Kris Cardenas had supervised.

"You're pretty quiet," Edith said.

"Yes, I guess so."

"Postpartum blues?" she kidded.

He looked at her: smiling blond Texas cheerleader. "Prepartum blues," he replied.

"Pre . . . I don't get it."

"Claire's had her baby. You've got your Christmas story. The nanomachines have been cleaned out of you. There's not much reason for you to stay here now, is there?"

Edith's face went serious. "You know about the offer Global made me."

"Jinny told me about it. Managing editor of the entire news department and your own prime-time show every week."

"I don't want to be managing editor," Edith said. "That's more headache than anything else."

"But prime time . . ."

"Yep. That's the real plum."

Doug knew that the LTV sitting at the rocket port would have space for her to return Earthside.

"I've talked it over with Jinny and Kris," Edith went on. "We'll have to haul in some new equipment from Earthside, but the studio oughtta be able to handle it."

He stopped in the middle of the corridor. "You mean you'll do your show from here? From Moonbase?"

"Sure," Edith answered. "You didn't think you're going to get rid of me, did you?"

He grabbed her and kissed her mightily. Two Lunatics passing by muttered something about mistletoe.

As they lay in bed in the darkness, warm and pleasantly tired, Doug whispered to Edith, "By the way, Merry Christmas."

"And to you, sweetheart."

"We've got a new year coming in a week. A new era, really."

"Hey, now that you're an independent nation, what're y'all gonna call yourselves? You can't call a whole nation Moonbase."

"No," Doug said. "We're going to call ourselves Selene."

"Selene?"

"A Greek moon goddess, from ancient times."

"Selene," Edith repeated. "Sounds neat. Where'd you find it?"

"I read it in a book, when I was a kid."

"I like it."

"Good. Now get some sleep. Big day tomorrow."

"Lots of big days coming up," said Edith.

"Yes," Doug agreed. "Lots of really big days."